STOLEN
GOODS

STOLEN GOODS

Susan Dworkin

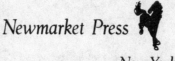

Newmarket Press

New York

Manufactured in the United States of America

For Moish

The author wishes to gratefully acknowledge the invaluable criticism and advice of Esther Margolis, Kathy Heintzelman, and Suzanne Levine. My thanks as well to Elliot Sagor, Haig Messerlian, Majorie Dobkin, the management of Admiral Photo Offset, and Susanne Goldstein. A tremendous debt of inspiration is owed to Lucille Megerdichian Bills, as well as to her parents.

Chapter 1

VARTAN GAVE THE FORD DEALER A CHECK FOR A LITTLE OVER THREE thousand. Then he and Hank loaded up the trunk with everything Vartan still owned in California, and they set out in the shiny new car for New York and the wedding and Anna. The weather in Fresno had been perfect all week. All week, Vartan's mother had begged him to cut his hair, just a little, he could leave the sideburns, she said, but she begged him to trim some of his thick black rather frizzy hair. He refused, saying that Anna loved his hair.

His mother modeled her dress for him. He said she looked beautiful. She fed him as though he had not eaten since he had left home for college and work more than a dozen years before and would never eat again, but he was excited, thinking of his bride-to-be and the honeymoon he had planned at a Caribbean hotel with Emerald in its name, and he couldn't really eat much.

His mother was looking for things to be irritated about.

Rose was *her* color, she said, yet Mrs. Karavajian had announced on the phone that she and her other daughters would be wearing rose-colored gowns; therefore, Vartan's mother would probably prefer to wear blue. So now, Vartan's mother felt that she had been trapped into this blue dress, gorgeous though it was, all lacy and very expensive. She felt oppressed by Mrs. Karavajian's reports on what the food would be like and what the church and their priest were like and most of all she felt oppressed by the fact that she had never met Anna, never once. The whole courtship had taken place in New York City and the New Jersey suburbs where Anna's family lived. Vartan's mother had not been consulted—Mom, do you like this girl? Instead, she had been told—Mom, this is the girl I want, we're getting married, you'll love her, she's Armenian.

Some friends in Fresno had met the Karavajians socially during trips to the East and reported that Vartan was quite right, Anna was indeed a lovely girl and her family prominent in the Armenian community. Her father, a prosperous printer, did all the brochures and announcements for the Armenian General Benevolent Union at far less than his own cost. The family stayed well out of stormy political feuds (although Mrs. Karavajian had cousins in Erevan, soft core communists who had moved slightly to the East while others were fleeing to the far West). The Karavajians are just like us, said the friends of Vartan's mother, just like you. There will be shared history, a common language, instant understanding, complete communication. Vartan could not have made a more suitable choice. But Vartan's mother suggested that when she and her late husband married off *their* daughter, they had hired a six-piece orchestra and would never have depended on the homemade music of some brother-in-law and his hippie fiddler friends.

They aren't hippie fiddlers, Mom, said Vartan. Anna's brother-in-law is George Margosian, he plays cello at the Philharmonic and is considered one of the foremost classical oud players in the entire Western world!

His mother clucked and pouted, lifted Vartan's hair off his neck and flopped it down again with great distaste, as though she had found dust and crumbs swept underneath. She was, she said, terrified of flying, and the least he could do would be to make the trip with her, so she would be properly escorted when they landed in New York and she finally set eyes on this strange woman for the very first time.

Vartan's sister reminded her that six members of their family would be on the same plane, so that was enough of an escort for anybody.

But Vartan's mother wanted her baby boy, her only son, on the plane, on her arm, at her table, if she could, she would have stuffed him back in her belly. She wanted him more than ever before—now that he was leaving her. She longed for her dead husband, longed for her old life. She did not *want* to love the wonderful, suitable Anna Karavajian. She was frightened that her blue dress did not flatter her. She was frightened that Mrs. Karavajian would turn out to be a better cook than she. When her own daughter had married, the wedding had been the work of her hands, and now the work belonged to someone else, she had nothing to do.

She shopped for a wedding present.

She decided to buy Anna very fancy table silver. The word from New Jersey was that Anna had already picked out some other pattern and her own family was giving it to her. So now Vartan's mother couldn't even buy the present she wanted!

A sense of helpless spectatorship engulfed her at night. She needed to take sleeping pills.

Seeing her anxiety, Vartan hugged his mother constantly. He kissed her constantly and squeezed her plump hands. When she woke him in the morning, she found herself astounded by how much hair he had on his thick body, how strong his arms and legs looked, flung like logs on the bedding. In this room she had awakened him with kisses and tickles, rubbing her face against his silky cheek. But now she only called to him from the doorway of his room, afraid to touch him. She wondered if he had made love to Anna Karavajian; if he was a considerate lover. She worried that Anna was somewhat taller than Vartan. A woman should always be smaller than a man, she told her daughter, but her daughter laughed at her, and embarrassed by her obsessions, she tried to laugh at herself.

While Vartan and his best friend, soon to be best man, were loading up the new car that would be the first car of Vartan's wedded life, his mother sat down on his rumpled bed, transported by the smell of the slept-on sheets. The room had not been changed essentially since Vartan had gone off to college. His degrees were on the wall; a BS in biology from UCLA, a diploma with honors from the school of physical therapy, the new book he was reading with a title incomprehensible to his mother—*The Peter Principle*—and a little television set he had brought from his last VA hospital. But otherwise, it was his old room. High school paperbacks, pictures on the mirror of girls she had thought he might marry and boys she had thought he would know forever and she would feed forever from a refrigerator packed with spicy leftovers and cheeses and honeyed cakes that boys love to eat after concerts and plays and wrestling matches.

His wrestling trophies were all there. When he won them, her husband had been alive, grumbling that his only son should excel at a Turkish sport, but really they were so proud of him, their stocky champion, borne high on the shoulders of cheering Americans.

She sat on the bed and knew that in fact Vartan was probably stronger now than he had ever been; that came from lifting the dead weight of the maimed. He had worked for three years at VA hospitals, had risen in rank (his mother felt sure) because of his patience and steadfast faith in the recovery of men who would never really recover. After his discharge from the Army, he had brought home, with the television set and the book and the uniforms, a box of letters. You take care of these, Mom, he said. If I leave them with you, I know they'll be saved.

The letters came from men all over America, who had passed through the jungle fires and into her son's strong arms. They reported on how their artificial limbs were working; they related obscene jokes—and something she would never understand, jokes about Polish people—so that he would have new material to amuse the wards; they told of their marriages to wonderful women who refused to leave them; they told of new jobs they had and reported the suicides of addicted buddies.

To Vartan's mother, the proliferating tales of addiction that poisoned so many conversations in the spring of 1970 seemed like a curse brought over from the other side. More than any other single thing, these stories evoked the nightmare landscape of her childhood. With lovely, innocent-looking fields of poppies, a nation of crazed butchers had sickened a nation of fair and easygoing liberals—that was how Vartan's mother viewed the drug problem.

Her daughter reminded her that the guys who got hooked in Vietnam surely used East Asian not Turkish hash, but the facts did not shake her belief in a satanic Ankaran plot to destroy America, the best, the very best and greatest of countries, savior country. She thought of her fine, righteous boy, carrying other women's helpless children, the poor black kids who would never own the city streets again, the pale-eyed sons of snow-colored farmers who would never ride the seas of grain again, she felt the press of their unstrung bodies on Vartan's back as he walked the night away with them, holding them when they shivered and coughed, wiping their vomit off his shoes, and she said to her daughter: Wars never end. We thought we had saved our children and look, there's your brother still cleaning up the sickness of the Old Country, still burdened with the sickness exported beyond time and unto generations. The drugs have been sent to remind us that wars never end.

Praying for peace, praying that Anna Karavajian would be blessed with healthy children, she made Vartan's bed and sealed the smell of him inside.

VARTAN'S MOTHER WOULD HAVE BEEN ASTOUNDED TO KNOW HOW thoroughly he had hated his work at the VA hospitals to which he had been sent after his induction into the Army. It was not that he ever doubted his calling; on the contrary, he had always loved his job when he worked with kids. He crouched like a patient wolf watching them in the orthopedic wing of a sunny California hospital, as they slowly tested their weight on mending bones. If they were lazy or scared or self-pitying, he would growl at them, guilt tripping them without mercy like his wrestling coach and (she would have been outraged to hear this said of her) his mother. Sometimes they cried. Sometimes they hated him. Sometimes they demanded another physical therapist. Sometimes they got better and thought of him fondly in years to come, if they thought of him at all.

He was impervious to their pain.

Impossible, his mother would have said, my sweet boy, my loving, caring angel from God could not be impervious to anybody's pain.

But Vartan was tough as a leather strap, smacking at the kids with his scorn.

What are you, a fucking pansy?! he hollered at the thin boy with the broken hip who said he couldn't, he just *couldn't.*

Smack! went Vartan, you want your mother to pull you off the can for the rest of your life?

Smack! you want to ride up the stairs in an elevator like an old fart?

Now put your weight on that leg, don't give yourself any breaks, you had your hip replaced, asshole, just your hip, let's see if you've still got your balls! . . . and the boy would take two steps, maybe three, and scream with pain and cry like he hadn't done since he was a little baby, humiliating himself before all the other kids in the hospital gym.

Nor was Vartan kinder to the girls, and this was an important principle to him. The atrophied legs of a juvenile arthritis patient he pulled and lifted. Please no more! she cried.

Twenty-five times each leg, that's what the book says, Vartan answered.

Fuck the book! she screamed.

Fuck you, little princess, he answered, stop whining and put some effort into this, you think I got all day to sit here and pump your skinny legs?

The girl's father complained about him to the hospital administrator. The hospital administrator said that Vartan's record with the kids was so embellished with success that obviously his peculiar bedside manner was paying off and the irate father should please butt out.

Eventually the girl walked out of the hospital, leaning on her father.

Vartan waved goodbye.

She pushed her father away and made it to the car on her own.

On the weekends, Vartan didn't think about the kids. He cruised Los Angeles with handsome Hank Ingersoll, who had become a stockbroker, and they got tan and wore gold chains. They showed up at the pads of hungry actresses, tooting their horn and waving steaks. If you can cook it, you can eat it! they crooned, and were welcomed like kings.

They had wild parties in the beautiful apartment they shared in Marina del Rey. Man by man, they built a Sunday football game, out of lonely screenwriters from New York and plastic surgeons entering the market for perfect flesh, computer geeks astonished by their recent success with women and tech-heads from the movie industry whose magic eyes and ears would one day serve as substitute for the blunted senses of millions of Americans.

These drop-in friends, skilled young men on the rise, on the make, provided Vartan with wonderful material to regale the kids with, for numbers of them actually made their living from *writing* jokes. When they got some extra money, they threw it toward Hank, who would invest it for them. So they felt secure. They felt secure enough to play football on the beach, clambering over each other like happy bear cubs. The flower children sold them sand-dipped candles on the sidewalk and the sun would not stop shining, and if they were sad they could always count on a liberated neighbor to throw open her door and turn on the Stones and shake off her clothes.

Eventually the spreading war took Hank and Vartan from their happy bachelor pad.

Hank became an ordnance officer and returned home from Asia safe and rich and better connected than ever before.

Vartan was stationed first in Virginia, then in Boston, finally, for most of his service, in Queens, in a faceless building which stacked up the veterans of America's wars like an immense archive. There were guys in that building who had not left for forty years. There were guys who had been wounded in battles nobody remembered. The young soldiers were brought in from Vietnam and unloaded like TV sets being delivered: fragile, don't drop; and all of Vartan's brilliant and challenging technique, long practiced, flew out the barred windows and sank in the dirty bays of the strange city.

He had no patter for these guys. He could not browbeat them into hope. Their sawed off legs had decomposed in the jungle by now; their eyes had been pecked out by indifference. They cried and screamed and defecated helplessly and in every single bed, he saw himself.

On his time off, he would journey into Manhattan. He found it an unbearable place. Even when the weather was good, the weather seemed to be bad in New York; and the great challenge of the city, he felt, was like the challenge of a foxhole—how much screaming and roaring, filth and dread can you take and still survive?

However, he was a fair-minded, liberal guy and assumed that what seven million people professed to love must have some charm somewhere so he looked for it.

He went to the movies. That year, they were all political.

He went to the Knicks games. At moments of maximum excitement when the transported crowd rose and exploded, he found himself staring at the scattered popcorn squashed under the boots of the fans, wondering how much longer Willis Reed would have the use of his knees.

He went to the opera, just to see it one time in his life, and wore his uniform. He had to pass through an anti-war demonstration. Some strangers shook his hand; others glared at him as though he had personally burned little children with napalm.

You don't know the half of it, he wanted to say.

He thought about his patients all the time, as he had never done before. Women found him uninteresting.

Lines which he and Hank had used successfully for years offended these women; they would not cook for him.

The despair of his patients seemed to spin itself into a tight white rope, like the twisted cheese his mother always used, which locked around his lower gut. His stomach always hurt. He stank of Tums. He couldn't sleep. He was very tired. He had no friends.

One day on a twenty-four-hour pass, he went to the Armenian cathedral. The choir was practicing. He sat down toward the back and listened to the singing. Soon he fell asleep.

"Are you okay?" she asked. He opened his eyes and saw Anna.

Trying to explain to Hank in the bright new Ford on a Pennsylvania highway why he felt he actually wanted to marry Anna was harder than anything Vartan had had to say in all the years of their friendship, because it was so amazing to Hank, silly-sounding, and seemed also to upset him.

Anna had come to the cathedral with her father in order to pick up some revisions for a concert program they were printing. Mr. Karavajian and the old priest fell to gossiping. Waiting for them to be done, Anna listened to the choir rehearse. She saw Vartan walk in; slip into a back pew; he was holding his belly, she told him later, like a man who had been knifed.

When I woke up and saw her, Vartan said, she looked a little gold to me, must have been the light. She was wearing overalls like a hippie. Her hands were very big, strong-looking, and she had ink under her fingernails. She had long dark hair, kind of messy, and dark eyes but they also looked goldish, and big black eyebrows and a big nose. Her voice was deep and scratchy, I thought she had a cold, but that turns out to be her voice. I noticed her earrings, silver, with little blue stones, like earrings my mother has from the Old Country.

The priest and Mr. Karavajian helped Vartan to a sofa at the back of the church where he slept for the rest of the afternoon. When he woke, Karavajian and his daughter were gone. The priest gave him some food and found out all about Vartan, placing his family in the web of ancestral acquaintance, discovering friends they had in common, and Vartan found out as much as he could about the girl with the silver earrings.

The next day he called her from a pay booth in the hall of the hospital, stepping out of the way of a swishing mop as it cleaned beneath his feet. He could hear the clatter and hammer of presses in the background; he could hear the yelling of men at work. She sounded breathless, as though she had run to the phone. She agreed to go out with him.

He borrowed a car and went to collect her in New Jersey at a big Tudor house with a forest of rhododendrons in the front yard. This time she was all dolled up. Her fingernails were white and clean, her hair swept northward and orderly. She wore makeup and a white dress with blue flowers. Her father seemed glad to see him and poured him a drink. Her mother clearly reserved judgment.

In the car sitting next to him, Anna huddled in her light gray coat. She smiled but without abandon and spoke little. Everything about her was dark and calm, like twilight, yet Vartan had the feeling that if he were to touch her, she would be hot as a coal smoldering under its ashy camouflage.

He began to be so obsessed by this idea that he had to pull the car over and kiss her.

Yes; true; right; she was burning.

Vartan began to tell Anna everything that had ever happened to him in his whole life. He told her elementary school teachers by name and described specific wrestling matches. He told her the arthritic girl and the boy with the mending hip, he told her his mother, his father, even his sister and his sister's husband and his sister's kids, people to whom he had paid almost no attention in the last ten years. (He could not remember having ever described his nephews to anyone ever.)

Anna listened. She listens, he told Hank, with her mouth slightly open, she is so intent on what you're saying that you can stop in the middle of a story and go to a whole movie with her and afterwards she will tell you exactly where you left off so you can finish your story. She was a math major at college, and now she's getting her teaching degree, working part time for her father. She loves her father better than she loves her mother, but she looks like her mother, who prefers the other sisters, there are two other sisters, both older, they are Anna's best friends and worry about her.

She is stronger than all of them, stronger than me. But Anna doesn't know that.

She thinks I'm a success. I tell her how I fail with my patients, how I am unable to comfort them or reconcile them to their fate, how my jokes don't go over, and how often they hit me and tell me to go fuck myself. But when she tells it to her sisters and her father, and the guys at the printing plant, it comes out like I'm a heroic farmer struggling with bad weather or some other temporary obstacle and for sure absolutely I will prevail. She is an inch taller than I am, and she wants to wear flat shoes, but I like her to wear those high heels, I push her in front of me all the time so I can watch her ass when she's wearing the high heels. She's very wholesome. She drinks vodka straight but only in public, if we go to a party; when we're alone, she never drinks and the one time she says she did some grass she fell asleep so she doesn't know whether she liked it. Once the family went off to some aunt's house, and Anna and I stayed back and I watched while she fixed her brother-in-law's car. She actually *retuned* the car. She was all greasy and sweaty and went inside to clean up and I followed her into the bathroom and showed her a few things. She's not a virgin but she's an amateur. She loves me, he said, and Hank grew sad on the highway, in the fast traffic, among the trucks and the glorious spring trees. I love her father; I love her sisters and her brother-in-law George the musician. I love New York City now too, and I'm gonna live with her in a big apartment on the Upper West Side and take the subway to work at the Rehab Center, she's gonna teach eighth grade math in a public school down in the Village.

I think if I marry her, said Vartan, I can stay doing what I'm doing and not go crazy. I guess I'm tired. I wouldn't want to go back to the life we had. I guess I just want to make sure that every day I can feel like I felt when I opened my eyes in that church and Anna was leaning over me and she said, "Are you okay?" I felt safe at that moment. I felt saved.

Hank was blinded for an instant by memories of good old times, irretrievable times.

Vartan looked out at the shore of the lush highway and saw the face of his bride-to-be in the sturdy branches of oaks.

Thus they were neither of them aware of death when it came, mindless accident, killing several others as well that fine day before Anna's wedding; and they slept in their graves in Fresno forever on the verge of a new life.

Chapter 2

A PRIVILEGED KID, SHE HAD LIVED IN COMFORT AND IDLENESS AND had never known a moment's grief.

Now it swallowed her.

Of the smoldering coals, nothing remained for a long while but ashes. They made her grayish. They clouded down her bold features to shadows and imprecision.

She had prepared herself for marriage, the only fate she had ever imagined. She had assumed that motherhood would occupy her third decade. So now, she did not know what to do. She remained in the bedroom on the top floor of her father's house like one of her own old dolls, a relic of herself. The flowered wallpaper and the matching bedspread sickened her, then lulled her, then put her to sleep. She woke up astonished to be still breathing, for she had dreamed herself lying under the flowers of the grave.

In the deep of her nights, she prepared weak tea with milk and huddled in the little study off the living room where her father worked, his sanctuary, a room she had rarely been allowed to enter as a child; she glanced through the Armenian books and magazines, the galley proofs of works their company would soon print, regretting that she had lost so much of the language, and sometimes she slept there, in her father's chair.

Anna saw that when she remained in the house all day, her mother fretted and muttered and worried, never daring to let a silence last too long, dropping pots if necessary. So she realized she would have to go to work. The job in the Village was no longer open to her; she found another teaching position, also eighth grade math, but in the Bronx.

The school was located in a reasonably safe neighborhood, adjacent to a terrible neighborhood. One day driving to school, Anna forgot who she was and became lost. She entered a hideous slum which she felt she had seen before, in war movies. The rubble in the streets gnawed at the under-belly of her car. The wasted buildings stared.

A junkie sauntered up to Anna's car window.

She was young, emaciated, she wore ragged brown panty hose, and although she was black, she was gray.

Anna rolled down the car window. "Help me," she said, "I got lost."

The junkie smacked Anna's face very hard. Anna didn't cry out. She wasn't afraid. She gave the tattered junkie all of her money, scrounging in her pockets for the last dime. She pressed everything into the gray cobweb hands of the sick old girl, out of respect, she realized later, the respect for death that elderly people have and also those who have been critically injured.

The bruise on her face created concern at home, so Anna made up some story to explain it, she didn't dare tell the truth, that would have upset her father too much.

Her sisters counseled each other: So. Our Anna has come back to life, but as an old lady; and we must strive to help her reach middle age.

Maybe later she'll be young again. Maybe later on.

TWO YEARS AFTER VARTAN DIED, ANNA'S SISTER MARY, THE HIPPIE vagabond of their family, manager of rock groups and concerts, suddenly decided to marry a quiet guy named Spike Russo and settle in an old New York farmhouse and take a job as a librarian and have children. Even though Mary had rarely been seen in their father's house in recent years, her change of lifestyle made Anna feel bad; made Anna more spinsterish in her mother's eyes (the one remaining single daughter . . . twenty-four years old and still grieving like a widow and not one date . . . *"Am-man . . ."* sighed Mrs. Karavajian in Armenian). Anna couldn't stand that. She felt it would be better to live alone without people than to live alone among them. So she moved out of the big house in Tenafly and took a one-bedroom garden apartment only two towns away.

The azaleas outside Anna's apartment window—shocking pink, brand new, very small—grew their garish blossoms sparsely and all on the top where they had not been pruned. It was best to look down on them from the window, where Anna often sat for hours at a time, not reading. Out-side, black men in white uniforms rolled out the new grass in strips, like plastic wrap. They raked it with machines and sprayed it from tankers.

It had taken all of Anna's strength to make the move into this apartment.

"All right, you're alone!" her mother cried. "But do you have to *make yourself* alone?!" Endless ramifications on that theme wasted a whole weekend.

Mrs. Karavajian called Lucia, her oldest and most sensible daughter. Lucia was in the middle of preparing a vitally important dinner for six friends and two music critics.

"Get over here right away!" the distraught mother cried. "Anna is leaving."

"I can't do anything about that now, Mom," said Lucia, beating the egg whites for the mousse.

"Make her listen to reason!"

"Okay, put her on the phone."

Anna took the phone.

"First tell Mom that you will think seriously about continuing to live at home with her and Daddy," Lucia said. "Then go rent an apartment, buy a bed, a dresser, two chairs and a table, and move in."

"Oh, please," Anna said. "Just talk to Mom, will you? She'll listen to you."

"Okay, put her on the phone."

Mrs. Karavajian took the phone.

"Mom, listen . . ." Lucia said.

"She has turned you against me!" the mother cried, and hung up.

She then called her middle daughter, Mary, who lived far up 9W over the rustic New York border. "Could you come, please? When you have a minute?" Mrs. Karavajian asked, speaking more politely to Mary because she trusted her less than Lucia.

Mary slipped through the back door, and into the hall outside the living room, not making a sound. She always moved with extraordinary silence. Her husband, Spike, said it was because she had inherited a trait for sneaking-around-unnoticed, selected for by the dangers of her ancestors' lives.

At five-foot-ten, Mary stood taller than anyone in their family. She alone among her sisters had straight heavy chocolate brown hair and solid black Asian eyes. Lucia and Anna possessed eyes of intricate gold-green amber and curly black hair that looked best on the short side. Mary had not cut her hair since the civil-rights movement, nor had she changed her style of clothing since Woodstock.

Mary overlistened a while to the fighting.

Kid sister Anna, five years younger than Mary, eight years younger than

Lucia, trying at twenty-four to leave home; Mrs. Karavajian sure that such a move would mark the beginning of terminal spinsterdom; Mr. Karavajian locked in his study, hiding, waiting for Lucia or Mary to come and bring peace.

Mary listened while Anna lost ground. Anna was not a good fighter. Neither she nor Mrs. Karavajian yet knew that Mary had entered the house.

"Hi, Mom," Mary said.

Mrs. Karavajian screamed.

"How long have you been standing there?!"

"You must let Anna move out, Mom," Mary said. "If events had not intervened, she would have been gone two years ago."

"You know what happens to girls who move into their own apartments?" Mrs. Karavajian wept. "They become eccentric. They indulge all their own little peculiarities. They become very interested in their work. *And they never get married!*"

"I got married, Mom," Mary said.

"But you never moved into your own apartment! You floated around from place to place, you did this and that, Anna isn't like you; she's strong and solid, she will make a nest whether there's a man in it or not!

"And don't think I forgive you for the way you came in here, Mary, like a ghost or a cat, it is the worst thing you do, you have the footsteps of a *traitor!*"

She ran up the long staircase crying. She knew she had lost the first round. Anna would move out. It wasn't the thought of losing Anna that upset her, because of the three girls she liked Anna the least, a humorless person, she felt, disinterested in literature or music or beautiful things. It was that she couldn't stand being voted down in her own home. She preferred the old deal, in which a woman who scraped the floor with her eyes all her life possessed absolute power over her daughters.

To console her for her loss, Anna let Mrs. Karavajian choose the apartment and the furniture.

"Oh great. Terrific," Mary muttered. "I come all the way down from Rockland to make a settlement between you and Mom which is advantageous to you, and the first thing you do is blow your advantage. Have you no *resolve?* What is this well of wimpiness which drowns you from within?! I want you to know, I am deeply disappointed in you, Anna."

And with that, Mary washed her hands of the whole matter.

So Lucia had to come along when Anna's furniture was being purchased to make sure that no real horrors were perpetrated.

Lucia Margosian had already completed her family—two daughters, no more. With relentless ambition, she cultivated the social connections that would propel her gifted husband forward in his career. She cleaned her chic apartment near Lincoln Center every day. She baked divine cakes which opera singers loved to eat. She went shopping in pert suits and big jewelry and high heels that clicked away the midtown stores like metronomes. Anna had never been able to keep up with her, and the furniture buying trips were no different.

Anna watched Mrs. Karavajian and Lucia feel fabrics. She heard their views on rugs. She learned that blue fades, that big soft deep sofa pillows capture men. Since Anna had no idea what she liked, she bought what *they* liked, and if what they liked was too expensive for her math teacher's purse, they called her father at the plant, and he said yes, sure, enjoy yourselves, my beauties, and paid the difference, with the result that Anna's new apartment sparkled, her mother reported proudly to relatives everywhere, "like a little jewel box," with splashy flower prints and enormous cushions.

Anna stayed in the garden apartment for seven years. Every day she commuted to the Bronx, where she taught math to eighth graders. She drove an aging Volare and shared the carpooling costs with two other women teachers, both married. They did not actually need to work, they explained, it was the pension, not the income. But as times hardened, Anna saw clearly that it was the income as well.

Things got lost in the garden apartment. At least, Anna always had trouble finding things there. She put her forks and knives in the flat drawer all kitchens have for that purpose, but when they were used and washed, she somehow never put them away in their drawer again; they turned up in the refrigerator, on the living room carpet. Whenever she cleaned her apartment, Anna tried hard to establish its contents firmly in her mind once and for all. Inevitably the blither of dust invited by all those enormous sofa cushions fuzzed up her thinking. By evening she could not remember where she had put her razor.

Sometimes when she woke in the morning, she found that she had forgotten her own whereabouts in her sleep. If there was a man sleeping with her—the lawyer she dated for six months, the English teacher who gave up after a year—she wondered if she was not actually married to him and what the wedding had been like and whether he got along with her father.

In her bedroom she had a gray metal folding chair, left behind by her brother-in-law Spike who had brought it to stand on while installing the traverse rods that carried her curtains. (The rods did not work. Spike possessed no talent for installing things. Anna could have done a much better job herself, but Mrs. Karavajian had ordered the curtains and the rods and enlisted Spike without consulting her. In addition, Anna would really have preferred straw blinds on all the windows. She did not *know* that, however, until she had been living with the awful curtains for years.) Now this gray metal chair which Spike brought was more to her liking. It was plain and straightforward. She could always find it. She could make it immaculate with a damp cloth in seconds.

She placed it at the foot of her bed.

Under it she kept her comfortable foam-soled walking shoes. On its seat she kept her soft jeans and, draped over the back, her favorite cotton flannel shirt, a blue-white-gray Alaskan plaid. When she came home from school, her feet aching in the arch, burning in the heel, she would kick off her shoes, peel down her panty hose and her slip together, carefully hang up her smoky brown suit or her blue tweed suit, throw her blouse in the hamper, replace her bra with a T-shirt, and slip into the wonderful gray chair clothes.

She turned on the heavy metal music she preferred and went searching through the apartment for things she had lost. Dishes. Papers to grade. *Natural History.* Then she walked to the small shopping center half a mile away and did a few errands.

Her errands always took Anna a long time, not because she was a careful shopper but because she was an uncontrollable listener. She did not read newspapers and generally watched science shows and bits of sitcoms on television and so she had only her encounters with merchants and neighbors to fill out what her political sister Mary had told her about the world and its concerns.

The bitter-looking woman at the grocery checkout counter discussed the slow progress of her retarded child, only leaving off the fascinating tale if another customer got on line. The fat man at the bakery store delivered a lecture on how the best liberals were always southern liberals, which was why he, the fat man, had decided to vote for Jimmy Carter; what did Anna think?

Anna said that her sister Mary preferred Betty Ford.

This reminded the fat man of his wife's mastectomy, so he began to describe it in detail, but then the bakery had to close.

Anna had one more stop—at the cleaners. There, the small Korean woman in charge told her that America was entering a great decline, would surely become the overweight cripple of the twenty-first century just like the Ottomans of yesteryear and had most to fear not from the Russians, who were all drunks, but from the Japanese, who were still just a bunch of unreformed samurai looking for a war to die with honor in; you couldn't trust them to stay peaceful for more than a generation because they really *believe,* said the Korean woman of the Japanese, that they are the world's most superior race.

Such notions as these—good liberals, the decline of the country, dying with honor—meant as little to Anna as they would have meant to any old lady who has washed her hands of the mad world. She listened well, being in no rush; however, if any thought registered, it did so in silence and secret while she slept, maybe while she walked slowly home at twilight.

An old man, one of her neighbors in the garden apartment complex, fell into step with Anna and offered to carry her groceries. His hands shook. His teeth clacked. He had shrunk to a scant four and a half feet. Anna removed the heavy juice and milk from the brown paper bag and gave the old man the cottage cheese and the napkins to carry, thanking him for his gallantry.

He told her about his wife in the nursing home, about the ingratitude of his evil son and the brilliance of his dog, Daniel.

In time, the old man's wife died and he was moved out of his apartment by his extremely solicitous and pleasant son (but all along Anna had known the son would be nice).

"This is my son Bernie," said the old man. "Bernie, this is Miss K. Often I helped her out by carrying her groceries from the market. Give her Daniel."

The son hesitated.

"Give her Daniel, this is my last wish!" roared the old man.

With an apologetic look at Anna, Bernie went to flush out Daniel from where he hid, broken hearted, bereft of his toys, among the packing crates.

The old man pressed her hand and whispered: "You should have a brilliant dog like Daniel, my dear, now that you're gonna be all alone here without me to watch over you."

He kissed her hand and went off to his fate.

Daniel, a small dog, short brown hair, pointed ears, thick legs, climbed amiably onto Anna's sofa and immediately sank between the fat cushions, howling and gulping piteously as the down filled flowers closed over him. Anna plucked him from the deep and hugged him close, patting and cooing and crooning until Daniel's hysteria passed. She cooked him a hamburger and made him a soft bed near hers, pleased to find next morning that he had abandoned it to sleep on her feet.

"THIS IS A SICK SITUATION," LUCIA TOLD HER HUSBAND, GEORGE. "If she gives all her maternal attention to the dog, she'll have none left for her own children."

"But she has no children," George commented.

"We've got to get her out of the suburbs and into New York where we can introduce her to men."

George Margosian envisioned his dead-serious sister-in-law with the lumberjack shirts and the preference for electronic bass being systematically fixed up with every unattached male in the New York Philharmonic.

He began to perspire. He gripped the warm brown shoulders of his cello. The black hairs on the backs of his brawny hands bestirred themselves with fear.

"She teaches in the Bronx," George said, "she should move to the Bronx."

Canceling a rehearsal, missing an audition, he invested an entire day driving Anna, Lucia, and his two incessantly babbling little girls through Riverdale.

He took them to the Bronx Botanical Gardens.

"Look at all these beautiful flowers and trees," he said.

"But this is *nowhere!*" Lucia insisted. "Anna should move to the Upper East Side of Manhattan where the swinging singles live."

George could have choked her.

Mary disagreed with George and Lucia both. "Move to the Upper *West* Side, where the intelligentsia lives," she advised Anna.

For some reason, Anna didn't want to. "Those old apartments aren't comfortable," she explained.

"Great, terrific, so much for the liberal tradition, now mere math teachers think of comfort first."

"*You* live in comfort," Anna protested. "Does that mean you're no longer a liberal?"

"Don't be snide," Mary said. "I was once ready to die for the cause."

"And now?"

"Now I'm dying for a cigarette and a baby."

Anna laughed and kissed Mary, murmuring, *"Seerelee kuyreegus,* my wonderful sister . . ."

Mary was her idol: smart, droll, political, musical, beautiful, and completely greed free. She was as content to work in the countrified public library as her husband, Spike, seemed content with his job directing the county wildlife center. Anna envied them their sense of sufficiency. She herself had begun to suffer, as the years went by, from desires for things. Not clothes and jewels, but machines like tape decks and speakers and electronic typewriters and excellent cameras. She did not admire this materialist ambition in herself. She wished she could be more like Spike and Mary, who felt that whatever they had was enough and who primarily wanted a better deal for suffering humanity.

Mary and Spike went to plays all the time. They read a book a week. They kept the radio of their old Volvo station wagon tuned to country. On Wednesday nights, other sensitive, well-educated women came to Mary's ramshackle ex-farmhouse to meet and take counsel together. Sometimes their group participated in marches and demonstrations. At the very least they seemed to have a lot of laughs.

No one had more friends than Mary.

Real friends, who told her the truth of their hearts.

Lucia seemed less able to trust other women. She suspected them of desiring George (a notion which made Anna and Mary giggle). She wondered incessantly how, despite the fact that other women appeared to live on their husbands' salaries, they managed to develop alternative sources of income guaranteeing independence *while* married and *if* divorced.

Anna had no women friends. Sufficed by her sisters, she sought none.

Anna felt that Mary was much stronger and more idealistic than she, that Mary would never have let herself be upset, as Anna was, by Middle School Number 18 in the Bronx or the kids or their labyrinthine graffiti.

Every day Anna pulled into the parking lot of the elaborately defaced school. She said hello to the security guard, unloaded her passengers, checked the lock on every aperture in her car including the gas tank, said hello to the next security guard, passed beyond the heavy metal doors into corridors faced with tan ceramic tile, and not until the school day had ended and she was back in New Jersey did she cease being frightened.

She feared that the kids would kill her, even though her escape routes had been well planned ("Leave the classroom; call the guards. If things get really rough, quit teaching and go to work for Daddy").

And she feared that the kids would be killed.

They stashed drugs behind loose tiles in the halls and sold each other into oblivion. Grown-ups beat them up during the night. They joined gangs of thieves; often Anna noted the lump of a weapon inside their shiny satin basketball jackets. The police waited for them at the school gates. They did not go quietly, but ran and cursed and never escaped. Even those with working parents, from peaceful homes, sometimes broke into lockers, stealing things they certainly did not need.

The boys backed their girlfriends against the cold walls talking softly. They clustered around huge radios in the school yard like lumberjacks around a stove in the Yukon, warming up, just trying to get warm. The smartest of them considered making a career in the military.

Anna limited her smiles, staying aloof because she did not know what would become of them, and imagined the worst, and didn't want to care too much, desperately did not want to love the kids.

She noticed that her early morning classes behaved fiendishly by contrast to the classes after lunch, which consistently paid best attention and made good grades.

She began bringing half bushels of apples, a dozen oranges, a couple of pounds of raisins to her morning classes, just leaving them in a plastic bowl on her desk.

At first those who were hungry were shy to eat.

She said: "My uncle the fruit king sent us a bushel of apples; did you know that many Armenians are farmers and specialize in fruit? I cannot possibly make that many pies, so do me a favor, finish the apples or they will rot, I have no objection to you eating in class."

Soon the apples and the raisins and the oranges were all gone. The bad classes quieted down considerably and even did some math. Anna found that, having started her free fruit program, she could not now stop it, so since she could afford to, she continued.

The other teachers were furious. They called her "Miss Kiss Ass Lady Bountiful" and spread nasty rumors about her father's wealth. Her car pool mates made no secret of their disapproval and found another way to get to school.

"You can't blame them," said her sister Mary.

"I don't," answered Anna. "I don't blame them, but I still don't care what they think."

TWO GIRLS IN THE MID-MORNING CLASS GOT INTO A FIGHT (CELESTE, the toughest girl in school and one of the poorest; Shanti, head of the cheerleading squad, strong as a ballerina). They rolled and screamed and slapped, overturning chairs and desks. All the kids gathered around to enjoy the spectacle. Celeste spat in Shanti's face and called her "pussymouth." Shanti kicked Celeste in the knee and said she looked like "a cockeroach."

Anna couldn't help herself, she began to laugh. (Call the guards.) The whole class began to laugh. (Call the guards and leave the classroom.) Shanti and Celeste punched and tore and rolled over and over on the floor.

Celeste pulled out a screwdriver.

"Arthur!" Anna yelled. "Take that screwdriver away from her!"

Arthur was only fourteen and six-foot-two and still growing and rooting for Shanti. Anna belted him in the arm to get his attention. He didn't even feel it. (Never touch a student; never.) So she began to tickle him.

"Oh no, Miss K., not that! Please!"

He waded giggling into the fight, picked up Celeste, and confiscated her screwdriver. Celeste was bleeding from three holes on the crest of her cheekbone, which Shanti had dug with her fingernails. Shanti was bleeding from her nose, which was broken.

"All right, Arthur, now take these two assholes into the hall," Anna commanded, "and let them fight out there. When they are through fighting, take them to the nurse."

Of course, Arthur took the whimpering girls straight to the nurse, carrying them like groceries, one under each arm.

When he returned to the class, he took a couple of bows and everybody laughed and cheered and did math again, invigorated.

"What the hell was that?!" Anna's supervisor hissed. "Fights are meant to be stopped, not continued elsewhere, are you crazy?"

"How could I stop it?" Anna said. "They were hysterical and much stronger than me. Besides, the fight did not continue."

"You *told* them to go in the hall and continue fighting!"

"Once Arthur got the screwdriver away from Celeste, you should have called the guards."

"But they didn't, they went straight to the nurse."

"You *laughed!*"

"That was fear."

"You should have called the guards."

"By the time the guards came, Shanti would have had a screwdriver in her lung."

"Once Arthur got the screwdriver away from Celeste, you should have called the guards."

"But by then half the period would have been over, and we're not even through reviewing fractions!"

"Goddammit, Anna, you can't just revise the rules every time you get an inspiration. The rules say no food in the classrooms but you bring apples. The rules say don't talk dirty to the kids and you call Celeste and

Shanti a couple of assholes in front of the entire class. The rules say don't touch a student and you grab the school giant by the armpits. The rules say in case of a fight, call the guards and you call Arthur. What if Shanti had a switchblade that escaped your omniscience and Arthur got it in the lung?! *You* are the asshole, Anna, you're a dangerous woman to have in the public schools."

Anna saw that he was right; she apologized. The next time there was a fight in her classroom (Mark versus Jesus, no weapons, but a tremendous amount of blood), she rushed into the hall to call the guards. However, before they arrived, Big Arthur (now renowned as the in-house bouncer of eighth grade math) had thrown the two murderous boys into the hallway and invited Anna to return to the class, where the kids had already resumed taking their quiz in fractions.

The best nights at school were dance nights. Unlike any other teacher, Anna loved to chaperone. She loved how successful the kids looked when they were all dressed up, like Motown recording stars who had beaten the odds and conquered America. She also loved the basketball games and never missed one. The coach concluded she was infatuated with him. He remarked on all the things they had in common—they were both white; they both owned blue Volares—and groped her in the parking lot.

To set things straight, Anna began bringing dates to the games. Very often, her dates would have preferred to spend the evening elsewhere.

"He's third chair violin with the Philadelphia Orchestra, and Anna took him to an eighth grade basketball game in the toughest neighborhood in the city!" George Margosian raged.

Lucia patted George and refilled his wineglass.

Anna explained to Lucia that she was really sorry the violinist didn't like the basketball game, but she couldn't help it, she just felt it was really important to be there when her kids played ball.

"But they're not your kids," Lucia said.

"No, they are not your kids," Mary said, regretfully.

My big sisters are quite right, Anna thought, I'm getting too attached. She decided to miss a game.

Unaccustomed to being home on a Saturday night in the season, she made tuna fish for Daniel, urging the reluctant mutt to eat. Daniel had not been feeling well. Anna had fed him so much *luleh kebab* in the last few years that now he was overweight and tended toward high blood pressure, and the vet had placed him on a low cholesterol diet.

A nice man she sometimes dated called her. He took her to dinner. She told him she was looking for an apartment in New York. He told her to stay in New Jersey where it was safe. On Monday morning, Big Arthur ducked through the doorway of her math room and hung on the lintel, saying, "Why didn't you come to the game Saturday? Were you sick? Shanti and me and my mother was worried you was sick or somethin'."

Anna never missed another game thereafter.

The worst nights at school were parents' visiting nights. "Oh it's awful," she told Mary. "Confrontation without resolution, over and over, at fifteen minute intervals."

"Sounds like my sex life," Mary said.

One particular parents' visiting night, when it was so cold the parking lot buckled and gray ice coated the window bars, Anna was chastised by an outraged mother. "Now why did you go and send her to the principal, Miss K.? When she talks back to you, you got to belt her in the mouth, and if you don't want to do that, you call me. I will have her father beat some sense into her, and then she comes to class, she sits quiet and behave herself. But you send her to the principal, all she does is get out of going to math!"

Then a father yelled at her. He called her "a stupid cunt." The small, neat D's and F's on his boy's homework papers infuriated him. "You gotta help him after school!" he shouted at Anna. "You can't just let him fail! He has to get through this year, he has got to get into high school, you understand me, bitch?!"

A small fat Hispanic woman with a small fat purse sat quietly while Anna told her what a fine student her daughter was, how bright and hard working, destined for success in life, and not until the woman rose to leave did Anna realize that she had not understood one word.

For all their failings in math, Anna felt that the kids were a lot sharper than she in many ways. They had finite ambitions—for clothes, cars, specific jobs, particular big nights out at certain hot spots. They got absolutely no pleasure out of intellectual play; their struggle centered intensely on the practical, the do-able. The kids saw the wall and painted it, every single inch of it, with their names and the colors at hand, just that, until the wall disappeared. She, Anna, with more money than they had ever dreamed of, with education, love, security, she could make nothing disappear. Not even one death.

In her deepest heart, Anna believed that her kids were civilized, industrious, and kind-hearted, and would one day achieve degrees from universities, homes in green suburbs, honored places on the boards of charities. But the world expected trouble from the kids, expected them to be always marginal, poor, violent, always stupid. And so Anna, not trusting her instincts, reasoned the world must be right and waited grimly for the conventional wisdom to prove itself true.

And so it did.

During a basketball game they slashed her tires and urinated in her front seat. The sight of her beached Volare, collapsed in the parking lot, made Anna cry.

"Don't cry in front of them," said the basketball coach. "They'll slash your tires every week if they think it's gonna make you cry."

Anna took subways and buses home. She glared at all prospective muggers, her generous face scrunched up like a raisin. She crawled into bed without getting undressed and sobbed into her fluffy pillows.

Mary arrived, silently.

"Jesus Christ!" screamed Anna. "You scared the shit out of me! Haven't I had enough violence done to my psyche for one night without you appearing without warning like the goddamned Holy Ghost?! It's impossible for a rich white teacher to get along with poor black kids in this day and age, do you hear that, Miss New Frontier Miss Freedom Rider Miss Brotherhood Sisterhood asshole?! My tires were cut to shreds and somebody went to the bathroom on my front seat and you are the last person I wish to see, go away! Why did you come?!" Anna stopped hollering and thought a moment. She had not in fact called Mary, did not actually know why Mary had come. "Why did you come?"

"I have lost another baby," Mary said. "They fall out of me like old postage stamps, no glue. No glue. I don't want to sleep with Spike tonight. Can I stay with you?"

When Anna returned to school the next morning with a tow truck, she found all her tires replaced, her front seat shampooed, and a quite literate note of apology (albeit anonymous) tucked under the windshield wipers. It turned out that the slasher had made an error, attacking Miss Karavajian's car instead of the Volare of the basketball coach, who had not allowed a certain person to start all year.

"Sorry for this mistake," said the note. "Can't tell these damn Volares apart in the dark."

THERE CAME A DAY WHEN MOST OF ANNA'S STUDENTS ACQUIRED access to a pocket calculator, which meant that they had now been sprung by technology from even the remotest connection to the process of figuring, and Anna felt that if she could not ameliorate the catastrophe, she had better quit her job.

At lunchtime, she observed her very worst student, a tall Haitian girl with gorgeous legs and big red beads on her sweatshirt, sitting on a bench in the school yard with the math homework laid out before her. Transistor phones girded her head. Her feet danced intricate rhythms on the concrete. Yet she was doing her homework with the help of a calculator, and Anna knew she was thinking nothing at all. The music came into her eyes and her fingers. Her brain remained at rest.

"Oh this is terrible," Anna said to a colleague in the faculty lounge. "This calculator thing, this is like the end. I'm a dinosaur and the ice has arrived."

"What difference does it make?" her colleague said. "All of the answers on her homework paper were correct."

For the first time in her teaching career, Anna made a speech to her class. She wrote it out and read it word for word. The kids had never seen her so nervous. They doodled and squinted and shifted, tried to understand what she was saying.

"I feel very strongly about this calculator thing," Anna said, "so I would like to propose a deal.

"Those of you who do not do your homework at all will get D's and those of you who do your homework sometimes will get C's, that stays the same as it always was. Those of you who do your homework all the time with the help of a calculator and bring in the correct answers will get B's. Those of you who do your homework all the time without the help of a calculator will get A's even if you bring in the wrong answers.

"Because I believe it is more important to reward you for thinking than for just doing math."

The kids asked her to repeat the deal.

She did, three times more.

Now everybody understood.

"Do you agree to this arrangement?" Anna asked.

They all agreed. Anna taught on that basis for the rest of the year.

Anna's supervisor noticed something very strange about the year end report cards, and made inquiries. When he found out about the deal, he was outraged.

"Did it ever occur to you that by making up your own rules, you were skewing the results so that a whole lot of dumb kids would wind up tracked into advanced math classes in high school?! Did that ever occur to you, Anna?!"

"Yessir it did, but I felt it was worth the risk."

"Well, the New York school system is not especially interested in taking unprecedented risks with other people's children! And until you have some of your own kids to experiment with, I would suggest that you restrain your creativity. The deal is off, Anna. Understand? *The deal is off!*"

Anna said okay, but she lied; she did not keep her promise. Incoming eighth graders had already been apprised of The Karavajian Deal and had long since mentally accepted the ground rules. Counting on the laziness of her supervisor, Anna continued to grade papers on exactly the same basis as before.

The supervisor, not a lazy man at all, summoned her. He did not hiss or yell. A welling of sweat fringed his upper lip. He seemed black to Anna for the first time in all the years.

"You got to stop," he said. "There's parents ready to file complaints against you, teachers who hate you because they say you're trying to make them look bad. One year it's free fruit, then it escalates to class bouncers, now it's calculator deals . . . Maybe because you don't need this job you don't realize how serious this is . . ."

"How dare you say that to me?" Anna said. "I contribute one hundred dollars worth of food to my kids in a semester and you think that means I'm rich enough not to work."

"Well, everyone knows that most Armeni . . ."

"Don't say it," Anna warned. "It's against the rules."

"I'm trying to save your job, dammit . . ."

"I knew a girl like you in high school in New Jersey. She said: Whatever happened to the starving Armenians? They sure don't look like they're starving to me . . ."

"Don't change the subject," her supervisor said.

"You changed the subject, you bigoted shit."

He caught her hand and held it until she stopped trembling, for she was one of the few teachers in his school who could actually control her classes and he knew he had made her terribly angry.

"I love my kids," she said. "I do what's best for them."

ON HER LUNCH HOUR, ANNA ALWAYS TRIED TO GET SOME AIR, EVEN in the coldest weather. She would trudge the outside perimeter of the school yard, bundled up in her gray coat and white hat and mittens, enjoying half an hour of solitude. An intrigued English teacher tried to walk along with her but found the cold unbearable.

"I like you," Anna said. "I really do, and if you want to, you can call me and we shall see each other on weekends. But this is my time, okay?"

"You look like an inmate exercising in a prison yard," he said.

"No, that's not right. Think of me as a rancher surveying the outer limits of my property," she answered, laughing and pressing his hand inside his pocket.

Such men as this, more sympatico than George's musician friends, partly encouraged, took Anna out to poetry readings at the Y, to movies featuring spacecraft and fathomless starfields. To the pressured men with degrees and ambitions, as to the tough Afro-Hispanic teenagers, Anna's husky voice and self-contained demeanor made her appear peaceful and becalming like a nice old black-and-white TV show, a documentary maybe.

The nicest single thing about the ardent English teacher was that, like Anna, he religiously attended school basketball games, never fearing to become involved with the hopes and affections of his students. ("Well, he's a man," said Lucia. "It's not so sick for him.") He had transferred to a high school in upper Manhattan and tried to get her to come live with him. Anna hesitated. All right, he said, if you won't live with me, at least live near me. She agreed to locate her apartment hunt on the Upper West Side, appalled at the prices, but loving the atmosphere of Columbus Avenue at brunchtime on Sunday and happy to please her sister Mary. The day they found the studio apartment on West Ninety-fourth Street, he took her to a basketball game to celebrate. Several of Anna's ex-students were playing, among them Arthur the giggling bouncer who had grown to over six and a half feet and dominated every play, the hero of his school, already spotted by college scouts. At fifteen he traversed the long court in seconds. His sweat splashed into the bleachers. He needed to tie the lace on his gigantic sneaker, so he called time out, glanced at the crowd, and noticed Anna.

"Heyyyy Mis Kayyyy . . ." he called. "How's it goin'? You actually dating this dumb fool?" (The English teacher knew Arthur liked him and did not take the crack as an insult.)

Anna's grave face opened up suddenly into laughter, and she squeezed the English teacher's arm, clasping and unclasping his fingers in her strong hands. Well, now we're cookin', he thought to himself, and went out the next day and bought season tickets to the Knicks.

"Oh please, Harry," Anna said laughing, after many weeks, "another basketball game?"

"In case you hadn't noticed, I try to play to your weaknesses," he said. "You were so happy when we went to see Arthur play, you looked so alive . . ."

"But that was because . . ." She stopped. She bit her nail.

"What?" he asked. *"What what what?!"*

"I was going to say that it was because he had not forgotten me, I had made an impression on him, that was what I was going to say but then it struck me as such a sad thing, to be so overjoyed just because some kid you once had in a class recalls your face . . ."

"Lots of people don't forget you," said the wonderful English teacher. "I don't forget you, not for one minute of the day."

"But you will," she said, because she was not going to be able to bear it if he begged her to marry him and settle down like her mother and her sister Lucia and now even her sister Mary wanted her to do.

He shook her until her hair flew. He kissed her so hard her teeth cut into the inside of her mouth. But she seemed to float down and down and down beneath him and he just couldn't catch up with her, she escaped him like ashes on a fast wind, and although her body was pressed against his, stuck wetly to his, soon he could not even feel her body.

Harry had lost Anna after a yearlong courtship.

She told him she would not move into the Ninety-fourth Street studio they had found together, that still, in January of her thirty-first year, nine years after Vartan's death, still she could not bear to move into an Upper West Side apartment so similar to the one she and Vartan had rented (painted the typical ecru, with ceiling moldings and parquet floors and rectangular bathroom tiles). Still after nine years, she could not imagine tying herself to any other man.

Harry later heard from friends that she had quit her teaching job, maybe under some pressure, amid some controversy, and that she had ultimately settled in a loft south of Houston. She faded out of his life like an old television show from the days of black and white, and her prediction proved correct: In time, in a remarkably short time, he forgot her.

THE MONDAY MORNING AFTER HARRY LEFT, ANNA CALLED IN SICK and went downtown to Karavajian Press to discuss the state of her life with her father.

At seventy, Gabe Karavajian still bustled with undimmed energy. Never mind that his hair had turned steely gray-white, the hair in his ears and nose remained black, and his green eyes still glittered with big plans and ambitions. (Florida; condos; the endowment of scholarships in his father's name; all projects to be embarked upon after Anna married Henry . . . uh, Harry . . . right. Harry.) Gabe still barreled through the plant like a small, tough tank, crunching discarded papers beneath his feet, his broad shoulders hunched forward. He still laughed like a winner, a steady low rolling laugh, ha ha haha ha ha haha. (Then he would take a breath and think again how delightful it was to have the last word or the cleverest wife or the best seats in the house and he would laugh again, ha ha haha ha ha haha ha ha.)

Physically an unruly man, with all that hair, that dark gray-brown easily blackened complexion, the long nose and big black brows he had bequeathed to his daughter Anna, Gabe expended a good deal of effort reining in his physical persona. He oiled his hair. He oiled his mustache. He acceded to manicures, although these looked a little ridiculous given the blackness of his fingertips, stained forever with printer's ink. He wore his collars secured with buttons and pins and his suits fitted and his shoes shined. He wanted to give the impression of power leashed.

However, when he started telling jokes to his comptroller, Mildred (how she loved a good Polish joke, the bony old spinster), and when he started yelling at his foreman, Tom Sarkissian, about the mismanagement of paper and presses and most of all, TIME! then Gabe's well-prepared image went to hell, his clothes and his hair and his face amalgamated into one inky expressive mess.

For this among other reasons, the fear that he had hoped to inspire in his employees and vendors always eluded him. He was laughed at instead, or loved.

Gabe Karavajian was feeling himself at one of his life's great crossroads on the particularly bitter cold day in early 1979 when Anna journeyed downtown to lunch with him, for he had almost resolved to give up his business and retire. A small but terrifying heart attack six months earlier had convinced him that this was probably a smart thing to do; his wife and physician did not cease reminding him that although he had lived for his business, there was really no necessity for him to die for his business. But Gabe feared he really might die *without* his business. And so he had almost resolved . . . almost . . .

Anna would surely comfort him (didn't she always? . . . his beauty, his baby girl) and help him make up his mind.

The printing business, which Gabe had founded and named for his once-enormous family, nestled under the West Side Highway, just at the mouth of the Brooklyn Battery Tunnel, only a few blocks west from Wall Street. A sheetfed printing operation, Karavajian Press specialized in annual reports and quarterly financial newsletters and snazzy advertising brochures for the nearby brokerage houses. However, Gabe still kept the accounts which had launched him, those low-paying, late-paying communal and charitable organizations requiring their printer to serve as editor and banker too. The Archdiocese, the AGBU, the Union of Soviet Emigres in America, the Tenafly Youth Chamber Orchestra in which Mary had once played the flute, and the Bergen Blue Wave swim team on which Anna had once clinched a relay, all these and many more counted on Gabe Karavajian to print their brochures and schedules, and rewarded him not with riches but with honor, for which he had a vain man's weakness.

The walls of his small, neat office were covered with framed awards of every kind, for generosity, citizenship, caring, unflinching support. "If collecting this kind of art is going to be your life's hobby, Gabriel," his wise wife had once commented, "then you must take steps to pay for it." Wall Street paid for it. When Gabe moved the plant into Manhattan from Long Island City twenty years before, he invested in the finest color separating and plate making equipment, the better to accommodate an apparently unremitting vogue for elaborate graphics and dramatic industrial photography to gild and glorify the financial news.

The twenty or so skilled workers who manned Karavajian's two shifts loved to watch these pictures roll off the press. Look how great corporations represent the lives of their employees! they laughed, strutting and posing and making faces in imitation of rugged miners poised purposefully on the brink of their coal pit and white coated nuclear power plant workers consulting printouts on clipboards and sexy telephone operators, wrapped like Erté cover girls, in a color riot of glamorous wires.

Bullshit! howled the inky men of Karavajian Press.

"Don't look, don't read, don't judge, just print," Gabe said, dispersing the wisecracking crew.

The idea of giving up the genial camaraderie of his shop, and the benign but exhilarating boss power he had so enjoyed in his lifetime, made Gabe feel lonely and old. He had hoped to have a son-in-law or a nephew who might want the business; instead, he had his competitor, Vita Press, with their standing offer to buy him out cheap; and he had his foreman, Tom Sarkissian.

Tom had come to work during the expansion attendant upon the plant's location in Manhattan. He had given two decades of his life to Karavajian Press. Already sixty-two, he was counting on acquiring the business when Gabe retired, for he would not have another chance to be his own boss in his lifetime.

Although Gabe liked Tom and sympathized with his situation, he could not rid himself of the nagging fear that Tom would go broke very fast.

These days, small printing companies were like small farms, not worth it except for the lifestyle, and you had to survive on an increasingly narrow margin of profit, consented to only by those who felt sentimental about your company ("I deal with Karavajian," said the Bishop, "that's it"), or who required special services only a small company cared to give ("I print with Karavajian because he carries Armenian, he carries Arabic and Hebrew, he carries Turkish and Russian, and he's got people over there who can proofread and edit and make sure all those languages are written right, so what if he's a little more expensive?" said the president of the Union of Soviet Emigres in America).

Tom Sarkissian had long urged Gabe to drop these clients, citing the huge ratio of nonsense to profit, trouble for money. Gabe figured Tom would not long put up with the way they called at all hours and changed their minds when the ink had already dried and argued over credits and expected their printer to produce the fund-raising volumes for their charitable affairs at cost, at less than cost, and charge his other customers enough to make up the difference. No, Tom would drop the sentimental accounts right away, and then he would go broke, because what he had never realized was that sentiment was the medium in which the reputation of a small business flourished, providing a passionate sales force and public relations support which larger companies could buy and for which Gabe Karavajian had never directly paid one nickel. Tom understood dollars and cents well enough but he didn't understand the value of a good name.

Gabe's wife would pat him and pour him a glass of wine and say "Stop worrying. Sarkissian will do fine, he'll do just fine."

Gabe didn't believe it. He paced around his little study, worrying and worrying, trying to figure how he could save his business from ruin after he left it, how he could somehow *guard* it against the limitations of Tom's talent, and he couldn't think of any way at all, and that made him so nervous that he thought he was having another heart attack, he gulped for air, tore at his tie, threw open the windows. "My life's work!" he whispered to the rhododendrons outside. "What will become of my life's work?!"

At this moment, when he was contemplating the loss of everything he had built in America, Gabe Karavajian's great comfort was his daughter Anna.

First of all, Anna was beautiful, without a doubt his most beautiful daughter. ("Mary is your most beautiful daughter," said his wife. "Every boy at the Hye in Asbury Park wanted to dance with Mary.") Secondly, Anna was by far his most practical daughter; she did what was necessary and she made up her mind quickly. ("Lucia is your most practical daughter," said his wife. "On a musician's salary, her daughters live like queens.") And Anna loved him the way he wanted to be loved, lavishly. She never tired of his stories about the Old Country, never admitted that she had heard them a hundred times before. She never patted him, like Lucia the living clone of his beloved wife, and she never participated in an anti-American demonstration, something for which he bore a lasting grudge against Mary.

However, when she sat down next to him in the busy restaurant, he was disturbed to see that dark rings were established around Anna's eyes and her long wavy black hair had begun to sprout gray.

She ordered flounder. She said: "Daddy, I have reached an impasse at work. My supervisor and many of the parents and the other teachers object to the way I do my job."

"Can you change?"

"No."

"Are you right?"

"Yes."

"You are right and they are wrong?"

"Yes."

"You are absolutely sure of this?"

"Yes."

"So why don't you quit your job and settle down with this English teacher Henry?"

"I'm not seeing Harry anymore."

Mr. Karavajian sighed and sighed and sighed.

"You wouldn't have been happy with him, Daddy, he's an *odar.*"

"I don't care about those things."

"Really? Do you really not care?"

"Don't try to tell me that you broke with this man because he is an *odar,* I don't believe that."

"Well, you're right," she said. "The reason was that I couldn't love him enough, I didn't love him at all really. I still think I should be able to fall in love the way Lucia did and the way Mary did . . ."

"Mary didn't fall in love with that fool. She fell in love with the antiwar movement, and Spike Russo happened to be around while she was burning the American flag. What good is he to her? He takes the wool off sheep and the syrup out of maple trees and gives lectures to schoolchildren about squirrels and chipmunks, and he cannot even give her a baby."

"Don't blame Spike for that, Daddy. It takes two not to have a baby.

Anyway, maybe this time it'll work, she's never gone this long before, I mean . . . three months . . ."

Karavajian sighed and sighed and sighed. The fish came. A man from a brokerage house which did some printing with Karavajian Press stopped by the table to say hello. Anna immediately regretted that she had not dressed more suitably; she was glad her foam-soled walking shoes were hidden under the table and sorry her hair looked a mess.

"Do you work with your father?" the broker asked. His name was Bite, Clemson Bite. (Real American names, thought Anna, often sounded the craziest of all.)

"Starting this summer, I'll be working for him full time," she answered.

Gabe Karavajian choked on his crab meat.

"Well, I look forward to doing business with you," said Clemson Bite flirtatiously. Anna turned on her smile.

When he was gone, Gabe said, "Women do not belong in the printing business."

"I'm very good at it. I love it."

"Yes, but when I am retired you will have to work for Tom Sarkissian and you won't like that. I won't like that."

"Have you committed the business to Tom?" Anna asked.

"He expects it."

"Maybe he'd like to share."

"He deserves it, Anna."

"Not really. Just by default."

"Don't be clever; he's been waiting twenty years."

"Have you given him your word?"

"A man doesn't have to give his word to have an obligation."

Anna sighed. She picked at her flounder.

She did not have much respect for Tom Sarkissian, and vividly recalled an incident from her youth which made her feel quite sure that he would not run the business the way her father wanted it run.

She was twelve. Mary was seventeen. It was a Saturday during the late fall, always a busy time at the plant, and the girls had been brought in to help with a big mailing.

A new customer whom Tom Sarkissian had met socially stopped by with a job. It was the kind of job Karavajian usually loved—a calendar, four colors, large quantities. The customer specifically wanted a union bug and was willing to pay the somewhat higher prices which accompanied it. He had no objection to Gabe placing the name of Karavajian Press prominently on every page.

So Anna thought it was very strange that her father did not wish to meet with this customer.

Tom Sarkissian prevailed on him, arguing forcefully in Armenian, then jokingly in English. "Don't look!" he cried, imitating Gabe's litanies. "Don't read, don't judge, just print!" Tom knew full well that the way to get Gabe Karavajian to relent was to make him appear laughable in his own eyes. And so Gabe relented and said he would see the man.

He spent half an hour with Tom's customer. As soon as the customer left, Gabe asked his secretary to take a letter. Lurking outside the door to his office, just at the edge of the marbleized glass window, Mary overheard him dictating. "Thank you for considering Karavajian Press," she quoted to Anna. "However, we are not in a position to bid on this job."

Tom then had his own brand of tantrum. His small mouth gathered into a mighty pout. He stomped around and shoved some papers on the floor. He neglected to pull Anna's ponytail as he passed the desk where she and Mary were sealing envelopes.

In the stairwell, Tom complained to Jimmy the head pressman and Vincent the art director that Gabe was "an old lady at heart" and they laughed, the three of them, not dreaming that Mary lurked out of sight on a step above, listening to what they said, or that she would tell her kid sister, and that the Karavajian girls would now grow wild with curiosity about the subject matter of the rejected calendar.

Gabe's secretary taped the letter to the customer's brown paper wrapped artwork, left it on her desk in the "To Be Delivered" pile, and went off to the ladies' room. Jimmy went back to work at the clacketing press. Vincent went back to work at his layouts. Tom stomped home for the weekend. Gabe went to have a drink with Harry Gottlieb of Tacoma Paper, who was in town with samples of his newest number one quality high gloss specialty stock.

"It's now or never, kid," said Mary to Anna.

And with the swiftness and silence of a cat, she abandoned her sponges and envelopes, traversed the plant to the secretary's desk, swiped the mysterious artwork, and sped to the loading dock, where Anna met her by prior arrangement. It was freezing out there, but it was the only place the girls could be alone. Anna hugged her hands in her armpits. She undid her ponytail and pulled her hair forward in two bunches, one bunch to warm each ear, and held the bunches in place with her teeth.

Mary removed a barrette from her hair and slipped the thin silver metal clasp under the tape that sealed the package. It opened.

Mary drew out the twelve pictures that had been suggested for the calendar; they featured laughing women with their legs widely parted and their sleek behinds raised, exposing the scarlet flesh inside their bodies.

Anna gasped.

Mary looked very closely at all the pictures.

Anna said, "Ich! Yuch! Let's go!"

Mary would not move until she was finished looking.

"Please, I'm freezing!" Anna begged.

"Do you realize," Mary mused, "that a person could live her whole entire life and never get such a good look at herself?"

Then Mary replaced the contents of the package and resealed it imperceptibly with fresh tape she had been provident enough to bring along for that purpose. She grabbed the stunned, goggle-eyed Anna firmly and hauled her off the loading dock and settled her back among the envelopes. Then just as Gabe's secretary was flushing the toilet in the ladies' room, Mary placed the calendar art back in its original place on her desk. She rejoined Anna in a twinkling.

The sisters sealed and packed one thousand additional envelopes before they dared look directly at each other and only then did they begin to giggle.

In later years, Mary Russo would recall this incident with waves of sympathy for the women in the pictures, wondering what horrible circumstances of poverty rape incest drunkenness addiction had driven them to such self-hatred and complicity in their own degradation.

Anna tried to care about the women too, but really, she didn't give a damn.

Like most Americans, she had long since grown immune to the shock of similar calendars, glaring casually from the walls of gas stations and parking lots and machine shops.

All she knew was that her father had refused to print the awful thing. She still felt proud of him for that.

Although Mary and Lucia stopped working at Karavajian Press (Mary thought the business dull; for Lucia, it was just too dirty), Anna had continued to help out, on weekends, during vacations, whenever she was needed. As far as she was concerned, the business was her dear father's life, his life's work, and he loved it, so she loved it.

"All right," she said to him in The Fish Place. "How's this? I will come to work for you at the end of the school year. I will do whatever you need me to do. I think that what you need is for me to get all dressed up and have lunch with customers and sell, I will do that gladly. If someone is sick or out, I can as you know substitute on the compositor, the folding machine, the presses, and the prep equipment. If you feel obligated to sell the business to Tom, then sell him half only, obligate him to accept me as his partner . . ."

"That will never work . . . please," Gabe pleaded . . .

". . . and I will guard the family interest, your interests, and make sure that when Mildred quits he doesn't hire some hotshot new comptroller with an MBA who wants to dump all our little customers. And you will be able to retire as you must with an easy heart."

"You are putting me in a terrible position, Anna."

"No, Daddy, I'm not. I will be a great help to the business, I promise, I will not create conflict or hassle."

"But you did at school, right? By your own admission, you broke all the rules at school and now you want to quit before they fire you."

"To tell the truth, Daddy, I don't know how I became such a controversial figure at school, I mean, I didn't *mean* to do anything so outrageous, it just appeared that way. A couple of years ago, I tickled this kid and it's down on my record that I grabbed him by the armpits. Maybe I'm losing my mind. Sometimes when I'm grading papers, I talk to Daniel. I mean I really talk to him . . ."

"Who is Daniel?"

"My dog. My poor sick dog."

"What's he got?"

"High blood pressure. High serum cholesterol. Hardening arteries."

"Ah," said her father. "Like me."

THAT AFTERNOON, ANNA ROAMED LOWER MANHATTAN, LOOKING FOR a place to live not far from the plant. It astonished her, how much money was currently being fetched by caves and dungeons, although she knew full well that she was the one who had been hibernating in the dark, letting fashions and seasons and the nitty-gritty of the pricey world outside pass her by. She interviewed prospective landlords and supers as though she were Rip Van Winkle emerging. They wondered where she had been.

She checked out four apartments and then found the loft.

The loft was on the fourth floor of an eight-story building, now rezoned for residential but still smelling of illegal aliens and their sweatshops. A filthy floor stretched fifty feet long and forty feet wide. There were holes in it at regular intervals where the sewing machines had been bolted. Large sooty windows covered two of the gray cement block walls. Had they ever been cleaned, they would have admitted floods of sunlight, for on the long wall, the loft beat by one story the rooftops of adjacent buildings.

Anna did not especially love sunlight.

However, the owner said she would have to pay plenty for it and so she knew it must be valuable to New Yorkers and she was trying to get in touch with their values this afternoon.

The loft had two hellish bathrooms but no other partitioned spaces.

Big as a gym, it bewildered her.

She thought maybe one ought to treat it like a clearing in the woods. Scrub enough floor in the center to fit a bed on, scrub some more floor and add a night table, scrub some more floor and add a stereo, then a dresser, and when all the things one needed in a bedroom had been added, build a wall and a door and add the kitchen.

Clearly, even a remedial kitchen would cost a fortune to install.

But maybe she would make a lot of money in the printing business.

The advent of this thought—in broad daylight and she was wide awake —made Anna blush. She told the owner she had seen enough.

He took her down the elevator which had no walls at all. It was essentially just a moving platform that creaked along the spinal cord of the old building, passing electrical wires and plumbing pipes and bouncing three times at every landing. He was installing a new elevator very soon, said the owner, but meanwhile most of the coop members—they were all brand new—used the stairway, which was littered with paint cans and plastering tools while the ingenious New Yorkers refurbished.

Anna told him she would think about it although she didn't know whether she really needed such a big space, and even as she said that, she imagined having dinner parties with jingling drinks available at the bar and salads arranged like paintings on the buffet so Clemson Bite of Bite, Charper, and Pollaner could come with his wife and his partners and their wives, and she would have room for live musicians if it was a special occasion . . . assuming of course that Tom Sarkissian was out of the picture by then and she owned the business.

Anna staggered. She almost fell in the dingy street. Ambition was a monster she had never met before (at least not during her waking hours), and its sudden appearance took her breath away. Like a computer attacked by a power surge, she experienced a mental shutdown.

She didn't know where she was.

She didn't know what she was doing in this place.

She didn't know who she was and had to sit on the curb and beat her forehead on her knees.

She walked quickly away from the loft. In the next block, a new restaurant had opened.

It contained only men. However, they seemed replete in their world and not dangerous, and the restaurant itself served fresh looking salads and little cakes and had been paneled like a mountain den. Anna walked around the corner and found a small theater offering original one-acts next to a dry cleaning establishment and then three industrial doorways sheltering drunks and a muttering bag lady. ("God forgive us," Mary always whispered when she passed such unfortunates.) Then, among the sooty stoops, a sparkling new florist appeared, with orchids and gloxinias in its stylish window. Clearly, the neighborhood was changing.

One block down Anna found an Indian restaurant, a laundromat, and a health food store run by two middle-aged women with huge crowns of hair and long earrings. Anna bought some granola. The women—Sarah and Bernice—shared a loft across the street from the building Anna had seen and declared that things were improving every day.

"Is it safe?" Anna asked.

"Well, it's safer than New Jersey," Bernice answered.

Both divorced, they had spent the best years of their lives in the suburbs and became friends during the course of their synagogue's Chinese auction. Their ex-husbands paid for the children to attend private school in the Village, further uptown. Bernice and Sarah had been so successful with their health food store that now they were considering starting a catering service. They showed Anna the flyer they had been working on. She quickly corrected its obvious errors and said she would have her people reset it and run off a thousand copies, to stuff in every mailbox in the neighborhood.

"We can only spend fifty dollars," said Sarah. "That's what we budgeted."

"Save it," Anna said. "I'll do the flyer for free and deliver it day after tomorrow in the evening. You bring me your next job, the brochure and the menu and the price list that you'll need in a couple of months when you start having lots of customers, because that will have to look very nice and be more expensive."

Bernice said, "Done!" before Sarah could have a second thought and immediately served herbal tea, zucchini bread, and dried apple slices. The two women told stories of their ex–mothers-in-law, the "bitches-witches." They recalled days when they went to the beauty parlor every week without fail, and played tennis because they thought their thighs were too fat, and did not know one, not even one homosexual, and now look, they were all around, they were neighbors and customers.

"I could not balance my checkbook," Sarah said. "I let that doctor take out my ovaries when my ovaries were in perfectly good condition, because I didn't know the difference between an ovary and a uterus. No wonder my husband treated me like I was an idiot; I *was* an idiot."

Something about their good nature, their freedom in the pungent store, inspired Anna with more resolve than she had been able to muster in almost a decade. She walked back to the building and gave the owner, who had expected never to see her again, a deposit on the loft. Two evenings later, she delivered the pretty pink flyer to Bernice and Sarah, and took her father to dinner at the Indian restaurant. Her father said, yes, all right, he would introduce her to his banker and guarantee the loan and help her buy the loft (a rather formidable financial undertaking) and let her work at the plant, how could he refuse his baby whatever her heart desired?

"You are making a terrible mistake, Gabriel," his wife said.

"Please . . . who will take care of her if I do not? She is like a widow . . ."

"She is not like a widow. She is like a man. You make her strong and free like a man, and you ruin her life."

"Oh please . . ."

Anna hired a contractor and instructed him to treat the loft not like a clearing in the woods but like a gray metal folding chair; everything was to be dust free and easily cleaned, she said, as though she were a middle-aged woman with grown children who had spent the better part of a lifetime dusting and scrubbing floors, even though of course she had never done anything of the sort. She hated housekeeping, she told the contractor, and expected to have no time to do it, so what did he suggest?

The contractor, who had concluded she was one of these new-type fifty-year-old broads who looked young because they had their faces lifted and went to the gym all the time, suggested paneling.

Nice light colored paneling, Anna said.

The cinder block walls he covered first with insulation and then wallboard and then pale tan paneling. The ceiling he lowered and then padded to protect Anna from the noise of small sneakers bounding on the fifth floor (since she stressed that her life had already been invaded quite enough by other people's kids).

Revising his opinion of her—clearly, she was childless, which had probably caused her dislike for children and her low tolerance for ordinary human mess—the contractor painted Anna's ceiling a low-gloss white enamel and installed track lighting. The floor he covered with tan tiles which had a built-in sheen. Mop and leave.

Anna wanted her bathroom white tile top to bottom, no wallpaper. She ordered Lucite soap dishes and towel rods. For the kitchen, she decided on chrome fixtures and cabinets which gleamed dully under recessed eyeball lights. (The effect was too cold and clean even for Anna. She put four red geraniums on the kitchen window ledge.) She ordered two bedrooms, one for herself and one for her guests.

As good weather approached and the loft became a home, the contractor and his men concluded that Anna Karavajian was not a lesbian—an idea which they had toyed with for many weeks—but a real nice broad who had probably been fucked over by some son-of-a-bitch and deserved better.

The head carpenter on the job waited until it was over and, not telling his co-workers just in case he struck out, called Anna and asked her to go out with him.

Sure, she said, and she went out with him. A couple of times even. She made love with him too, always at his apartment. He never did see how she furnished her loft in the end. He thought she was a very nice woman.

Eschewing upholstery, Anna bought wicker furniture and a hammock. She invested in a large pine dining table with eight caned chairs. For herself, she purchased a queen sized platform bed and made it up with white sheets and a white chenille bedspread, and in the second bedroom, she put two beds which had no spreads at all. She installed her own stereo. On the windows, she hung rattan shades.

She moved into the loft in April.

Although a coffee table was needed, Anna could not immediately find one that suited her so she lived without. Then toward the end of the school year, she passed an inlet of benches in the Bronx where old men often played checkers on decent days and saw that two of them had created an ersatz table by resting a warped piece of plywood on an abandoned truck tire.

This struck Anna as an excellent idea. She improved on it by covering *her* truck tire with a large sheet of green edged glass, and underlying it with a crunchy straw rug.

Lucia and George bought her a television.

Spike and Mary bought her dark red towels.

Sarah and Bernice sent her a beautiful earthenware casserole pot when she moved in. Because she was not yet cooking, she planted dark red spreading coleus in it and set it on the low metal bookcase under her windows. The coleus grew rampantly, requiring baby plants to be propagated. These soon formed a coleus hedge, the only touch of color in Anna's living area.

Mrs. Karavajian went out to buy her some pillows to humanize the wicker furniture, but suddenly in mid-store experienced a change of heart and purchased for her youngest daughter a fully equipped gray metal toolbox.

Was this an expression of rage or an act of surrender? Lucia wanted to know.

Anna decided to take it as a late sign of love.

At school, Anna told her supervisor that she would be leaving for good in June. He was nonplussed.

"But I didn't want you to quit, Anna," he said. "I just wanted you to change."

In July of 1979, just when Anna was starting work full time at Karavajian Press, her sister Mary Russo had a baby. She was thirty-six years old. She had been trying to have a baby for seven years.

The advent of Little John occasioned delirious joy in the family.

The Karavajians had a huge party inside and outside their house, inviting the neighbors, the relatives, everybody they knew from church, the guys from the plant and their wives and children, and the entire staff of the wildlife center. These folksy bird-watchers, squirrel-taggers, and tree freaks constituted the main group of people who loved Spike Russo. In fact, it startled Gabe Karavajian how much they loved Spike—he had thought only Mary found anything interesting in the tall balding man who had no relatives and no past he ever spoke of and not much to contribute to any conversation.

What a beautiful day it was in the spacious yards of Tenafly! The forest of rhododendrons outside the living room window frothed with huge pinkish white blossoms and the fresh-trimmed grass sprang back happily beneath the feet of all the running children. Having an attack of youthfulness, Daniel scampered and leaped among them, and when he got the football he wouldn't give it up without a scratch and a wrestle. Lucia and Anna and Lucia's daughters, Lillian and Delia, coursed back and forth to the kitchen with great platters of steaming *kufte* and *shish kebab* and *pilaf.* Upstairs in his grandmother's fancy bedroom, Johnny gurgled in his crib, unbothered by the endless attention of relatives all of whom swore that it was *their* prayers which had brought him safely into the world.

Mary stopped socializing once to nurse him, throwing all the relatives out of the room except Anna who wanted to be with the baby a little too. Mary had stayed in bed for almost four months to have this child. She had consumed large quantities of hormones to strengthen the wall of her womb that he might live, wondering all the while if they would eventually give her cancer or give him cancer. The strain of the endless miscarriages and fertility workups had robbed her of her beauty for a long while, but in the last months, when she knew the baby was growing and safe, when she knew he would be *born*, she had blossomed again and grown sweet again.

Spike Russo slipped into his in-laws' bedroom and watched for a minute as the black haired baby sucked hungrily at Mary's breast. Spike was a slender man, for the most part quiet; he wore rimless spectacles. He had grown bald but kept a thick brown mustache, now becoming gray, reminding Anna of Bartolomeo Vanzetti in Ben Shahn's pictures. He had acquired the nickname Spike because that was the one thing he had done well on the high school basketball team. His real name was John. Gently he pulled Mary's crucifix around so it fell on her upper back, out of the way of Little John's eyes. Mary hummed an old Melanie song. With one long finger, she tapped the tiny pink soles of her baby's feet. She smiled at Spike.

"Well," he said, "you are the most beautiful woman in the whole world I think."

He left the room but did not rejoin the party. Anna found him sitting at the top of the high stairs, rubbing his mustache, lost in pleasant thoughts. "I was sitting on these stairs where you are sitting one night," Anna told him, "when I was fourteen. I had a furry pink bathrobe and big furry pink slippers with bears sort of implanted in the toes. Mary was having a party. She was nineteen and I thought she was a goddess."

Lucia came up the stairs. "Are you telling him about the night of the party?"

"It was some night," Anna said.

"I was going out with a guy my mother had fixed me up with," Lucia said, settling on the stairs below Spike, "whose mother was her friend or a friend of a friend, I can't remember how I got fixed up with him, but I was twenty-two and Mom was desperate for me to get married, I had met and dated and discarded every boy in the Armenian Student Club at Queens and graduated college and I was working as a bookkeeper under Mildred at the plant, and as far as Mom was concerned, if I didn't get married before I was twenty-three, I would be a spinster and she would die, she would just go into her baroque bedroom up there and pull the covers over her head and die. So I was a good daughter, right, Anna?"

"Yeah, right," Anna said.

"So I went out with this guy, he was a lawyer and his name was Arnold."

Lucia and Anna rolled their amber eyes upward, recalling Arnold.

"So Mary was having this party," Anna said, "to raise money for the civil-rights movement. And she had found a guest speaker: what was his name . . . ?"

"Gizmo," Lucia said. "Gonzo. Gonzago. Jumbo, something like that."

"He was from the West Indies," Anna said, "and gorgeous, absolutely gorgeous. He came up the stairs and asked me where the bathroom was and I thought he was so gorgeous, I could barely speak. He said, 'Don't you *know* where the bathroom is, young lady?' and I finally sort of mumbled 'around to the left,' oh what the hell was his name?"

"Orlando," Mary said. She sat down on the top step and put her long arms down around Spike, he leaned back on her. "He fell asleep," she said of the baby.

"Orlando!" exclaimed Anna, "yes yes yes. So Mary had invited all these musicians from the music department at Douglass where she was studying; she had managed to invite not only the students and their boyfriends, but the professors and their wives and some of their friends too."

"But Daddy didn't want me to have the party," Mary said.

"Oh please, Daddy was in Tacoma buying paper!" Anna insisted.

"Daddy was in Tacoma buying paper and that was why Mary had the party because if he was home she wouldn't have had the party because he never allowed his home to be used for political purposes," Lucia corrected.

"Daddy thinks politics has destroyed the unity of our people," Mary said to Spike. "Tashnags, Ramghavars, blowing up Turkish diplomats seventy years later, nonsense and fanaticism, he says."

"But Mom said okay because Mary told her it would be a party of all musicians and Mom thinks that musicians and artists are good to have around, she thinks they bring culture and beauty with them," Anna said. "Besides, Mom could never refuse Mary anything, she's afraid of Mary."

Mary gasped and pushed her husband slightly aside, bending down over Anna like a shocked eagle. "Is that what you think?!"

"That's what I think too," said Lucia. "So, I'm out with Arnold the lawyer, and he is supposed to be a wonderful guy, right?"

"Great, terrific, how long have you guys been harboring that little hang-up?" Mary persisted to her sisters.

"Smart, eligible, doing well well well," Lucia continued, "but he is a cr-eep. Ugly as a rat. He takes me to the theater and grabs my legs in the dark. We walk down the street, he's got his hand on my behind. I say, Arnold, take me home."

"Meanwhile Orlando was making this great speech about personal conscience and the honor of all humanity. I sat on this staircase in my pink slippers and fell in love," said Anna.

"And Arnold the Rat said I don't want to take you home, Lucy, I want to fuck you."

"Oh please, he did not say that!" said Anna.

"He said that exactly, on West Forty-fourth Street, as we were walking toward the parking lot to get his car."

"Jesus, I thought I knew this whole story," said Anna. "So what did you say?"

"I said, well, I do not want to fuck you, Ratface," said Lucia.

"You were much too young to know the whole story before now," Mary commented, pulling Anna's hair.

"So what did Arnold say?" asked Spike.

"He said, 'Nice girls like you don't know what they want until they've had it.' "

"What year was this?" asked Spike.

"Nineteen sixty-three," Mary said.

"Nineteen sixty-two," Lucia said.

"I guess that's what he would have said in nineteen sixty-two," Spike concluded.

"So Orlando gets through rousing the crowd and Mary makes the pitch, she was nineteen years old and she knew how to make the pitch! People were writing checks, can you imagine?!" Anna exclaimed. "I mean when I was nineteen years old, I could barely cross the street."

"You could tune cars," said Mary and Lucia.

Lucia continued, "So I say to Arnold, listen, Arnold, oh this was the smartest thing I ever did in my life, I said, take me home . . ." She panted hotly, the way she had for Arnold. " 'The house is empty,' I said, 'full of beds, huge comfortable beds, my sister is away at college and my folks are away in Tacoma, take me home and we'll have all the beds to ourselves.' "

"Did he believe you?" Spike asked.

"Why?" Mary laughed. "Wouldn't you have believed her?"

"I don't know, I never had this experience," Spike answered.

"So all the way home across the George Washington Bridge and up the Palisades Parkway, this cr-eep is grabbing my hand and pulling it over to him so I can feel how much he desires me because apparently he thinks that is a turn-on for innocent Armenian girls from Tenafly," Lucia said.

"Is it not?" asked Spike. Mary belted him gently in the arm. He laughed and caught her hand and held it.

"So now that my sister Mary has organized the meeting, brought in the speaker, made the pitch, and collected a fortune for the cause, she breaks out the stuffed grape leaves and the string cheese and the cakes and the coffee and *feeds* all these people," Anna said.

"And Arnold pulls up in front of the house and he sees all the cars and he knows he has been had, lied to, fooled, and used by this innocent Armenian girl," said Lucia.

"And Arnold goes crazy," said Mary.

"Vayrenee," said Lucia.

"Like a wild animal, he goes completely crazy," said Anna.

"So I don't stick around, right?" Lucia continued. "I run for the front door, screaming, Mar-eeee! Annnaaa! because my father is in Tacoma and my mother becomes catatonic in times of emergency."

"I'm on the stairs afraid to go down and mingle in my pink slippers," Anna recalled, "and would you believe Orlando himself comes with a plate and settles down right here and says, 'Okay, young lady, I'm ready to eat it if you're ready to tell me what it is.' But I have just heard from somewhere outside the frantic cry of my oldest sister."

" 'Help!' I'm screaming!" Lucia said.

"So down the stairs I fly," Anna said, "knocking this good food all over poor Orlando and through the living room comes big Mary, felling musicians right and left, and out the front door we go and we don't see a damn thing."

"Oh please, I did not fell musicians right and left," Mary offered.

"You felled me," said George Margosian, who had settled on the stairs with a plate of *kufte*. He fed a forkful into Lucia's mouth.

"We see nothing," said Anna. "We listen. We hear the sounds of a struggle, and Lucia going 'No no no' but we see nothing."

"I'm on my back in the rhododendron forest," said Lucia, "this eligible, highly recommended lawyer has his knee on my mouth and he is shredding my stockings and for the first time in the history of my long and varied dating career, I am about to be raped. So now I am frightened."

"Lucia grabs a rock and throws it through the living room window," Mary said, "and of course, all the musicians think, great, terrific, it's a race riot, the neighborhood is up in arms because Orlando has come to Tenafly, soon there will be burning crosses and Klansmen gathering, and they all leave by the back door, without their coats. But we don't know that, me and Anna. All we know is that Lucia is somewhere in the rhododendron forest going 'No No No!' so Anna runs into the rhododendrons and jumps on Arnold and starts to beat him up with her pink slippers."

"*Me* beat him up?!" Anna cried. "You pulled his belt off of his pants and whipped him so hard with it he was bleeding like St. Jerome!"

"You did that?" Spike said to his lovely wife. "You?"

"He was raping my sister," Mary answered.

"Poor Arnold goes reeling out of the rhododendrons, trying to pull up his pants," Lucia said, "and he runs smack into this ferocious terrorist with glittering eyes who threatens to cut off his balls with a six inch switchblade knife."

"What terrorist? What glittering eyes?" asked Spike.

"Me, it was me," said George.

"You, it was you?!"

"How did you get that knife, George?" asked Anna. "I always wanted to know."

"I got it from Orlando," George said. "He had come prepared for a race riot."

"George was the only musician at Mary's party who had not escaped out the back door," Lucia said, patting George's hairy hand. "Mom was standing at the top of the stairs in her dove gray crushed velour robe with the tatted lace shawl collar. She said: 'Why is it, Mary, that all your guests have left without their coats?' "

Spike threw his arms around the three sisters, laughing and hugging them, his salvation, his only family.

LATER THAT NIGHT, AT THEIR HOME IN ROCKLAND COUNTY, SPIKE and Mary made plans to redecorate their living room. They thought maybe they would paint the woodwork and add wallpaper, maybe, and bookcases to contain and organize their many paperbacks and photographs, make room for a kid to run and play. Maybe they would have other kids, they thought . . . . The police rang the doorbell. Behind them in the darkness of the road and the fields were several police cars with officers prepared for trouble. With them were two gentlemen from the FBI.

They said that in 1971, a U.S. Army installation in rural Pennsylvania had been broken into the dead of night. A security guard had been overpowered, tied up and blindfolded, and taken into the woods where he was not found until morning. All the draft records had been stolen. The building had been burned down. The truck which the perpetrators had used had been found a week later. It was a stolen truck. In 1975, before the statute of limitations ran out, an indictment was filed against the perpetrators, should they ever be found.

And surprise surprise, Mr. Russo, they had indeed been found. One of the people who had participated in that robbery—a certain Barbara Christian alias Barbara Crown—had surfaced and given herself up after years of hiding, and she had led the FBI to her cohorts in many crimes against America. Would Mr. Russo please come along quietly?

"Keep your courage," Mary whispered deep in Spike's ear. "A thing like this is just a test of will. Be deaf when they threaten you. Remember, you have money, lawyers, *family*, remember that. You don't have to tell them anything."

Spike kissed her. He kissed his sleeping baby. He kissed her again. He left quietly with the authorities.

The policemen put away their weapons, maybe a little disappointed.

Strong silent Mary called her relatives in order of toughness. First her brother-in-law, George. Then her father. Then her sister Anna. (By then she was finally weeping.)

The Karavajian family lawyers made an excellent defense but they were no match for the truth—Spike Russo (his real name; during the war he had lived under an alias) had indeed driven the truck which made off with the many files on the many young men registered with that military installation. He was charged with burglary, auto theft, kidnapping, destruction of government property, and arson. After a long trial, he drew an eight-year sentence. If he kept his nose clean, he would get out in three.

"But the war is over." Mrs. Karavajian wept. "The war is over."

"Wars never end," said Anna, her poor, lonely, middle-aged, spinster daughter Anna.

It was something she had heard before, in another life.

Chapter 3

FOR THREE YEARS, ANNA WORKED AT KARAVAJIAN PRESS IN ALL THE capacities she had detailed for her father at The Fish Place.

Then Tom Sarkissian gave up and retired to the Jersey Shore rather than continue fighting a losing battle for control of the company. It had become abundantly clear that Gabe would not sell out to Tom as long as Anna wanted the business, and Anna, little Anna with her chewed ponytail, poor Anna with her canceled wedding, Anna the bitch wanted the whole business.

When Tom departed, his old friends Jimmy and Vincent quit in solidarity and went to work for Vita Press. No tantrums this time, no stomping and pouting. This time, Tom made a more dramatic exit, standing by the reception desk and swearing (in English and Armenian) that some day he would have vengeance on those who had robbed him of his dream, his one and only chance to own something and enjoy boss power.

All work stopped. Sentimental folks wept. Superstitious folks trembled. Aram Hovad, the new foreman, stood paralyzed with shame and anxiety, for Tom had been his mentor at the plant, his teacher.

However, Francine Sarkissian, the receptionist, soon to be divorced from Tom's son and a great despiser of all Sarkissians, laughed and called Tom a self-important old fool (in English and Armenian and Arabic), breaking the spell of his threat and taking the curse out of it, so Aram could relax and order everybody back to work.

Gabe finally retired. Anna became president and chief executive officer of Karavajian Press, a job she loved, for which she had been inadvertently trained and groomed by her father. She had now held this position—without serious reversals of any sort—for three exhilarating years.

At thirty-seven, Anna had achieved her own name and place in the printing trades. She was recognizable at conventions and exhibitions as a moderately attractive woman who wore charcoal suits and low heels or sneakers, very little jewelry, and very little makeup. No one had ever seen Anna with her hair down. She kept it bound, a pepper and salt mass, with plain aluminum clips. Unlike the managers of larger firms, she socialized with her customers. She had no qualms about coming alone to a party; if she was seeing a particular man, she had no qualms about bringing him along. Her colleagues remembered a glassware salesman, very quiet; a plumber, very massive and, it was rumored, loaded; an Egyptian diplomat who told jokes no one had heard before, real fun guy; too bad it didn't last.

Mostly Anna was known as a workaholic who could be reached at her office at late hours and whose business was her life.

"The problem," said her brother-in-law George to Lucia when Anna once again phoned to say that company pressures prevented her from showing up for dinner, "is that Karavajian Press is too much for your little sister Anna, she just can't handle it and she's trying to make up for that by working herself to death."

Lucia slithered the perfect custard out of the oven, hypnotizing it with her green-gold snake's eyes: don't bubble, don't jiggle, don't fall, stay . . . stay . . . and slipped it under George's nose like the scalp of his worst enemy, perfect, just what he wanted and absolutely perfect.

He ate three large bites of the custard.

"Hmmm," he murmured. "Hot." He drank a glass of ice water. "It would be better if your little sister Anna would just admit defeat and sell out to Vita Press and go back to teaching math."

Lucia leaned across the table and touched George with her white soft manicured creamed and be-ringed hand. "Drop dead, Fatface," she said.

The debate about Anna's competence to run the business had been flying around her family like a lost ball of lightning ever since she had taken over as president, igniting dinner tables, burning beds, searing established relationships.

Lucia supported Anna but blindly, out of loyalty not respect.

Mrs. Karavajian had never forgiven her husband for letting Anna into the business and refused to discuss it any further.

Mary had her own troubles. It irritated her that Anna now talked incessantly of presses and film processors as though Mary really cared, when Mary didn't care at all. Spike had come out of prison two years before, in 1983, a man greatly changed. Clumsy in society, a stranger to his son, no longer competent as a breadwinner, he lapsed into silences which lasted for days at a time and he required much professional counseling. The impact of his misery was such that soon Johnny, their brooding six-year-old, needed counseling too, and Mary—who had always believed in shrinks—started going again herself. As it was the habit of the Karavajian sisters not to burden their old parents with troubles, Mary went to Anna for money. Talk of the business reminded her all too keenly of where she was getting her next mortgage payment and the wherewithal to cover her gigantic psychiatry bills. She didn't need that. She had her own troubles.

"How's this?" she said to Anna. "I promise I won't talk about what it's like to live with an ex-con and you promise you won't talk to me about your lousy customers!"

"Okay. I promise," Anna said.

"Tell me instead about your sex life."

"Well . . . let's see . . . since my charming Egyptian returned to Alexandria, I find that I do not miss sex very much. I mean I like it when I do it but then I forget to do it again for long periods of time. Last week I made love with a man whose last name I did not know. He took me to his apartment whose address I forget. I left at three in the morning. It was great. Maybe next month or the month after, I'll call him."

"Jesus, I'm sorry I asked," Mary said grimly.

"You should be."

"Don't you ever think about falling in love?"

"Not really," Anna answered. "I have this friend, her name is Sally Bangle, she's a set designer, she falls in love a lot . . ."

"You never told me you had a friend."

"She works at a theater in Queens. She's black and much younger than me and extremely beautiful, I mean knock out movie star beautiful, and she loves all her lovers. Since I've known her, she has fallen in love at least three times."

"How long have you had this friend?"

"About a year. The truth is, she's not just a friend, she's a . . . you know . . ." Anna bit her lip.

"What?"

"A, uh . . . well . . . you know . . ."

"What?!"

"I promised I wouldn't tell."

"What is she, goddammit?!" Mary yelled (thinking: *Amman*, it's happened, my kid sister is getting it on with girls).

"She's a customer," Anna said.

Although it was fun for Anna to kid Mary and a great victory to make her laugh these days, the fact remained that Anna still had no one to talk with about the business except her father. And he had proven untrustworthy. She had recently discovered (from Francine, knower of all scuttlebutt, carrier of tales) that every week he came into New York for a secret lunch with Aram Hovad, to check up on Anna and find out how she was doing.

Anna did not confront her father with his sneakiness (after all, it did run in the family). She told herself that checking up was Gabe's privilege and responsibility as boss *emeritus,* and harbored her resentment in the same way that she had harbored her ambition—secretly, even from herself.

Actually Aram Hovad was reporting to Gabe that Anna was doing pretty well.

She understood technology, Aram said, and realized that it had to be changed often, like underwear. She understood people and knew how to get work out of them, never let a birthday pass without a cake, never came back from a trip without some small present, although she still didn't fire the fuck-ups fast enough, Aram thought. If Anna had made any serious misjudgment, it was that she had expanded the business too quickly, so that now it was beyond its own capacities, requiring large infusions of capital to catch up. (Aram had in mind a certain Japanese press twenty-eight by forty-inch, four-color.)

For Anna, the business provided a new kind of cover—dark, dense, and complex as a jungle compared to her years as a teacher, which now seemed like years on an empty plain.

Her life had been small, family oriented, class centered; the same math year in and year out. In the quiet of those days, her loneliness screamed at all who met her, unmistakable and disfiguring as a scar. Her gray face broke her sisters' hearts.

But now that she was in business, her face was hidden. Her life burst with acquaintanceship, a variety riot, like a television soap opera introducing new characters and twists in the plot every single day. She rushed, she sold, she decided. The punches flew. She rolled. Meeting new people all the time, knowing no one well, chatting, flirting, she dedicated herself to speed and volume of production, she probed no idea deeply, spoke the truth of her heart to no one: she whirled in the dark among strangers.

Breathless, she thought: this is how the press feels, smeared with new ink every few hours . . .

Her sisters supposed they should be thankful that she was so busy.

She ate tuna fish from a can, standing up.

She had found her very own snug spot in history, between her father's past and her own future. Here in the booming, clacketing racket of the second floor plant, in dirty cramped quarters once thought spacious and airy, the machines crowded each other like strangers on a subway, young ones squooshing old ones, mechanical black cast iron nose to nose with electrical off-white vinyl, big gray Aram in his apron and work gloves shoulder to shoulder with svelte black Estelle in her cornrows and beads, and Anna was boss of it all.

She had already rented parts of the third floor for the computerized type compositor and the expanded art staff, now toiling in white soundproof quarters at high tables that hummed with inbuilt lights.

The big presses were breaking down from overwork. Anna would have to replace them soon. Mildred the Comptroller was breaking down from overwork. She required an assistant with a degree. The new machines required new staff to run them, and if Anna tried to cut a corner, employing someone less skilled and experienced for a relatively easy job, Heaven sent her a punishment. Like Krishna.

Krishna had been hired to operate the trimming machine.

But he trimmed everything crooked.

He was so sweet and cute and gallant that Anna told Aram to try him on the folding machine.

First he folded everything backwards. Then he folded everything inside out. When he finally got the hang of it, he folded everything crooked.

Three days ago, Anna had made the mistake of allowing Krishna to run the trimming machine once again (since Stan the Trimmer was out with the flu), and he had sliced off the tippy tops of four fingers on his right hand.

As it turned out, the fingers needed merely Band-aids until the skin grew back.

But the blood! The blood had dripped in a multitude of thin rivers all over the quarterly report of Bottom Oil, Karavajian's richest new customer! Anna had dressed like her sister Lucia for six dinners to get that account! She had dropped her price below reason! She had flirted with men who wore pinky rings! When she had been turned down by the guy on the line, she had used a friend of a friend of the family to invite her to a party where she knew she would meet the boss, and thus she went over the head of the guy on the line, building his dislike into the job like termites in a foundation, and despite all that, the job had come out beautiful, and now Krishna's blood had smeared and smudged hundreds of copies. Even worse, the plant had lost a full two hours because of the accident. Didn't every single person have to come watch Krishna bleed? Didn't every single person have to speculate upon the liability of the company, the role of the union, the extent of the insurance?

Krishna himself blamed the trimming machine.

Larry the Art Director blamed Krishna and threatened to cut off *all* his fingers at the palm if he ever screwed up again. Sweet, cute, gallant Krishna filed a complaint with the shop steward saying that Karavajian Press discriminated against Asians.

The shop steward was Francine Sarkissian. Francine came from Beirut. In addition to serving as receptionist for the plant, she was secretary to Anna the Boss, Larry the Art Director, and Aram the Foreman. Aram called her "a greedy *noreg*," an ungrateful newcomer who wanted instantly what earlier immigrants had worked for three lifetimes to get. He distrusted her rolling Arab purr and her seductive outfits. But even Aram admired the way Francine took care of Krishna.

"Listen to me, sweet boy," Francine said to Krishna. "I am an Ayz-ee-an. Nubar is also. Soy is and Choy is and so is Hamza, and Aram's father was an Ayz-ee-an and so is Anna's father, so you must do for yourself a favor, sweet boy, and take off the rest of the day to recover from your accident and also to withdraw your stupid complaint."

Finally everybody went back to work.

Then the big press broke down.

Big Mack blamed Estelle. "She wears too much jewelry!" he moaned. "It gets caught in the press and lodged in the gears, I live in fear she's gonna be strangled one day, I'm an overweight person, I can't take this kind of anxiety!"

Estelle blamed Big Mack. "You need a delicate touch with an old machine like this," she said. "He's got hands like watermelons and besides he leans on the motor so it can't breathe."

Mack took a break to calm his nerves. Anna opened the press lid and found a large brass bangle bracelet wrapped around the feeder gear. "I won't tell Mack about this if you will stop wearing so much jewelry on the job," she whispered to Estelle.

Estelle closed the hood and turned on the power. "We fixed it, Mack honey!" she called sweetly, grinning at Anna and flipping her beads and the errant bangle into her giant red handbag.

Then came good news. From the front desk Francine pressed the intercom button and said, "The Parks Department has just call and confirm order for ten thousand copies 'How to Build and Maintain An Ooo-rrr-bahn Roof Garden,' they send over specs by messenger along with purchase order today. Izaat not nice?"

All twenty-two employees smiled, thinking of overtime.

But then came bad news.

Aram Hovad rumbled out of his cluttered little office like a sea lion and shouted so loudly that everyone could hear him even over the Armageddon booming of the plant that they were going to be short stock for the Bite, Charper, and Pollaner job because they had received another totally fucked-up shipment from Tacoma Paper!

"Call that asshole Gottlieb in Tacoma, Francine," Aram roared, "and tell him for twenty-five years we been doing business with his father's company and never not once not once ever did we order 100 pound dark pink paper, what are they, lost their minds?! Tell Gottlieb if he don't replace this faggot stock by tomorrow noon, Hovad is gonna fly west and personal break his neck!"

Anna called Mo Gottlieb in Tacoma. (They had never met, but they had been talking on the phone as long as they could remember.) Like Anna, Mo had taken over the family business. However, Anna had assumed control in the midst of a piss-flood of bitterness and recrimination whereas Mo's way had been prepared and secured for him since boyhood.

It wasn't fair, she thought.

She was developing her company, expanding the client list, upgrading the equipment, while drippy little Mo was blowing away everything old Harry Gottlieb had worked to build.

Normally Karavajian kept ten or twelve thousand pounds of standard weight stock in standard colors on hand and called extra orders in to Tacoma if a big customer needed something special. Typical was the order for Mr. Cinzano of Mid-Manhattan Tech, who asked that his course catalog be printed on acid-free recycled paper. (Anna also used some for the newest macrobiotic menu of Bernice and Sarah's Nutrition Emporium; it seemed fitting.) However, the order had arrived late and wrong too, and had to be corrected, creating a time loss and a chain reaction of scheduling glitches down the line.

To Aram Hovad, bellowing that "fuckin' time is fuckin' money!" Mo explained that there was some mix-up on the loading dock. However, to Anna, he admitted that a rising rate of vandalism was to blame.

Mo sniffed. He blew his nose. His whiny voice caught and cracked. "It won't happen again, uh . . ."

"Anna," Anna said.

"Sorry, I always got you girls mixed up."

"I'm Anna," she said. "The one who is now president of the company, and responsible for its good name. Just like you, Mo."

"It won't happen again," Mo said.

But it did. It happened again and again. And today, once more. The delivery of heavy pink stock in skids that were supposed to contain enough satin finished ivory paper to print the annual report of Bite, Charper, and Pollaner proved to Anna that Mo Gottlieb was indeed a true asshole.

This time, he said he was being robbed, that his trucks were being hit on the highways and dummy stock substituted for the rightful paper within. Aram Hovad told this tale to Big Mack and Larry in the stairwell and they laughed like hell at drippy little Mo Gottlieb. Highway robbery! What a story! An eighteen wheeler equipped with alarms and carrying forty-two thousand pounds of paper is broken into and robbed while the driver has his dinner at a diner, do they expect us to *believe* this bullshit?! What are they, lost their minds?!

Anna straightened out the stock situation with Mo (hoping he wouldn't cry; he always sounded like he was going to cry any minute). Then she endeavored to calm and soothe her big foreman by buying him a midafternoon cup of coffee at the luncheonette downstairs.

She told him what she thought was good news.

She told him she had decided to purchase a certain very advanced Japanese press, twenty-eight by forty-inch, four-color.

He looked doubtful.

"You sure Mildred's gonna let you have the money?" he asked.

Oh, that was a serious mistake.

Anna's black brows knitted themselves together into one ominous ridge.

"Mildred counts the money," she said quietly. "She does not own it. Tell that to my dear father next time you have one of your pseudosecret lunches, and next time you want us to buy a new piece of equipment, lobby *me,* not him."

She paid the tab and left.

ALTHOUGH HE DID NOT LIKE TO ADMIT THIS, ARAM HOVAD HAD TO admit that Anna was just like her father.

She walked like her father, leaning forward with that prowling wolf gait, with all her feelings displayed on her large nose. She hunched her shoulders when she was tense, just like her father did.

Underestimating Anna had been Tom Sarkissian's undoing. Before Tom had even begun to realize what a dangerous woman Anna was, she had all their futures in her pocket like a wad of money. Aram's wife had warned him not to make the same mistake. So during the long drawn-out power struggle before the end, Aram had taken his wife's advice and Anna's side and now he was foreman of the plant.

"You betrayed me," Tom said. "I taught you everything you know, and you betrayed me."

"Don't pay any attention," said Aram's wife. "He tried to take the business out of the family and the family fought back, he's just a bitter old fart looking for someone to blame for his losses."

Aram believed his wife, he really did.

But he also suspected that there was an element of female solidarity in her position, and it made him uncomfortable. He wasn't used to it. Himself, he really didn't think it was quite right for an Armenian daughter to come from behind and behave like a man all of a sudden. And he couldn't help it, sometimes he slipped, and patronized Anna, and assumed that he and Mildred and Larry and all the employees of Karavajian Press still worked for her father.

She returned to the luncheonette.

"I'm sorry," she said. "I didn't mean to throw my weight around."

"I'm sorry too."

She gnawed her thumbnail, swallowing ink, and then washed it down with her new coffee.

"What are we gonna do about Tacoma Paper?"

"We gotta drop them," Aram answered. "This is the fourth time we got bad stock from them in the last year. Mo Gottlieb is not his father. The business grew too big and he can't handle it."

"You think it's true that he's being robbed?"

"No. But even if it's true, it's not our problem."

She shook her head and laughed unhappily. Aram knew she didn't want to abandon Gottlieb, that her need to honor Gabe's old connections sometimes tied her hands.

"Meet with some other suppliers," she said. "Get some other prices. But don't make any commitments, let's give Mo a chance to clean up his act . . ."

"Come on, Anna . . ."

"Give him a chance, okay?"

When Aram and Anna returned to the plant, they found that Larry the Art Director was screaming again because Mid-Manhattan Tech had revised the copy for its course catalog again, and Larry was going to have to adjust the design, *again!* and he wanted to know who he could kill about this!

Anna called Mr. Cinzano, the director of admissions at Mid-Manhattan Tech.

"How can we make your deadline if you change the copy when the catalog is about to go on press, sir?" she asked.

"You gotta make the deadline, you gotta, you gotta . . ." Cinzano said.

"But we can't, Mr. Cinzano, it is not humanly possible . . ."

"If you are late with this catalog, Mzzzz. Karavajian, I am gonna lose my job."

"Come now, sir, you are certainly overstating the case . . ."

"You women without families to support, you have no idea what it means to lose a good job, do you? Do you? *Do you,* Mzzzzz. Karavajian?!"

Anna hung up. In the quiet of her office, cut off from the thunder of the plant, she wondered why it was that so many people in contemporary ooo-rrr-bahn society seemed to be on the brink of nervous collapse. Larry, for example. Larry, a bald man in his thirties, married, loved, appreciated in his job, was sitting across the desk from her, running his razor sharp matte knife back and forth across his sideburn and cutting off tiny pieces of his remaining hair.

Anna rubbed her face hard, leaving black prints on her cheeks and chin. She became hypnotized by the sight of the little hairs raining down.

"Oh please don't do that," she said.

"Do what?"

INADVERTENTLY, REALLY QUITE BY CHANCE, ANNA DISCOVERED that part of her business was dying.

Anna's new accounts and spinoffs of new accounts were coming in so fast that she could not see the floor of the business for the lushness of its top growth. Working twelve hour days, pushing, selling, evenings, weekends, she was making the months go by at a dizzying pace, and her success demanded so much of her attention that she really never noticed a failure.

Then one day she came into the office extra early, to do some work on her files. The previous night she had spent in the arms of an especially nice man, the nicest man she had met in a long long time, and breaking her pattern of recent months, she had taken him home to her place. A wonderful lover, he had touched some well of passion in Anna which she had not been aware of before. ("One of life's major biological jokes," Mary quipped bitterly. "The older you get, the more you want, and they're too exhausted from their lives to give it to you. Watch yourself, kid. Soon you'll be groping stockboys.") Anna woke at dawn and was devastated to find her new lover gone. So she tried to heal herself by coming into the office extra early.

And there, while arranging her customer files in alphabetical order, she discovered that there was no "U."

The Union of Soviet Emigres had dropped off the client list.

Figuring the card was misplaced—Francine Sarkissian hated filing, and the neglected records slopped all over Anna's desk—Anna moved on to other concerns, and checked the status of the summer picnic menus for Bernice and Sarah's Nutrition Emporium.

No Bernice and Sarah.

No Mid-Manhattan Tech either.

Had Cinzano been so mad about his slightly delayed course catalog that he had dropped Karavajian after half a dozen years and thousands of pounds of acid-free recycled paper?

When she saw that the Armenian Archdiocese too was gone, her eyes began to feel heavy; the wakeful night caught up with her; she curled up on her old brown leather office sofa and fell asleep. Aram Hovad woke her.

"Bad news," he said. "Bite, Charper, and Pollaner just canceled their annual report. Now that Tacoma finally corrected the first screw-up and sent the right stock, what the fuck are we gonna do with all that satin finish ivory colored paper?"

Anna washed her face. She sat down with Mildred and Aram and the books. The books said that while Anna was dancing and whirling and selling, several of those little sentimental accounts which had raised three daughters, bought a big house in Tenafly, paid university tuitions, and supported dozens of employees and their families had just flown away.

One didn't notice because one felt so little loss. Aram Hovad was right when he said (as Sarkissian had in his time) that these were inconsequential customers, no longer profitable jobs; Karavajian Press was better off without them anyway. However, now that Bite, Charper, and Pollaner had defected, Anna and her managers became alarmed. They checked and found that all the accounts had closed out within the last six weeks.

Old friends off to the same reunion?

"The Nutrition Emporium was the first job I ever brought into this shop," Anna said sadly.

"Better talk to your father," Aram said.

"Do you have to bother him with this?" Mildred asked. "He's not well."

Anna took her hand. Mildred was such a sweet old thing, so loyal and loving. Rumors about her ranged from "She was never kissed; never had a single date," to "She had three husbands all of whom died from mysterious causes," to "She was just always in love with Gabe Karavajian, and working for him was her whole life."

Anna and her sisters and her mother, too, believed the last version.

"I have to talk to my father about this, Mildred, there's no choice."

In Anna's mind, the face of Tom Sarkissian flickered like a blinking warning light. She recalled that his last words to her had promised retribution.

Anna took the truck that evening and drove out to TENAFLY to see Gabe. She knew Mary would be there with her son (not Spike; he stayed away from family gatherings now) and Lucia and George would be there with their brilliant college girls, and that when she drew her father into the study for a private talk, her mother who hated such evenings to be interrupted by business would be diverted and mollified by her grandchildren. So it was a good night to go, she thought.

But it turned out to be the worst possible night.

For at precisely the same moment that Anna's truck rolled onto the George Washington Bridge, a Turkish diplomat was blown to bits by a car bomb in Paris. An organization calling itself the Secret Armenian Liberation Movement phoned the French media and took credit for the assassination, speaking of vengeance and justice interchangeably, as though they were the same honorable woman.

The news came to Tenafly by satellite, instantaneous, just as death had come to the Turk.

"Good, good," said George Margosian at the dinner table. "Good that somebody reminds the world."

His daughters, Lillian and Delia, saw how their grandfather bristled and darkened with hostility. They leaned on George. Cool it, Daddy, they said.

Sitting next to Gabe, Anna gripped his hand under the table and squeezed it. Cool it, Daddy, the squeeze said.

The political gulf between George Margosian and Gabe Karavajian stretched long and wide as the formal mahogany table itself, barring any negotiated understanding, even after all these years. George had grown quite famous in the world of serious music, his recording career now brilliantly launched, and he should have been a source of unmixed pride to his father-in-law. However, Gabe suspected him of supporting with hard dollars organizations too blood-stained to mention, while Spike Russo, the gentle pacifist, tried to recover from the ordeal of his imprisonment.

With Spike, an *odar,* and a man of action not words, it had been impossible to argue politics in a satisfying manner. But with George, a son of his people, Gabe felt free to fight so ferociously and to exchange such soul-shattering insults that Mrs. Karavajian would scream and cry and run into the kitchen and deliberately break dishes. For the sake of the women and the family peace, Gabe and George tried very hard not to sit down together at the table and discuss politics.

On this night, however, the news of the assassination in Paris took a seat among them, a surprise guest, and its presence triggered thoughts of the genocide in Turkey and soon each coffee cup represented an ancient home, each prone spoon the body of a martyred ancestor. The table itself became a battlefield.

Little John Russo seated himself at the table in the no man's land between uncle and grandfather, his black eyes piercing first one then the other. He sensed there would be a battle here. A troubled soul, from his first step toppled by the tides of incomprehensible politics, he waited for the first salvo, for an explanation of his plight.

"What does the SALM achieve with these murders?!" Gabe yelled. "They resurrect nothing. They restore nothing. They bring only *amot*, shame and dishonor to all the Armenians!"

"If you don't show the world you are a man, the world does not care when your children are slaughtered like animals!" George yelled.

"So. Now that our people behave like animals, I guess this shows the world we are men!"

George smashed his brawny fists on the table. The dishes levitated. Lucia pushed her mother and her daughters into the kitchen. Mary made no attempt to move her son.

"Weak-hearted liberal stupidity!" George yelled. "We lost everything because we were defended by people like you!"

Lucia sang out from the kitchen doorway that the trouble with the SALM was that they always killed nice Turks whom everybody liked. They should pick evil bastards, she said, drug pushers and Pope hunters, people whose murder the world could really get behind.

Mary had a more profound view.

"Violence never reminds the world of anything except all the violence which the world is still trying to forget," she said.

As usual Anna kept quiet.

She felt herself by nature an apolitical person, disinterested in the world's affairs. If pressed, she would say sure, she agreed with Mary, she was against violence. She certainly never expected to concur for one minute with her brother-in-law George. Therefore it shocked her, it knocked her out, that when picturing the entrails of the Turk exploding over the Seine, she experienced a surge of wild joy.

Was vengeance so very *wonderful?* she thought.

Did it feel so good that an old man like Tom Sarkissian, retired, comfortable, surrounded by grandchildren, would summon all his remaining strength and call in the favors of a lifetime to hijack Anna's least profitable accounts? Just for *vengeance?* Was that possible?

"Daddy, please," she said, "come in the study, I need to talk to you."

Her father slumped in his chair at the head of the table. He clicked his glass against his teeth. He paid no attention to Anna. Cursed with a self-critical inner vision which he had bequeathed only to her, he had the feeling that George might be right—maybe they *had* lost everything because of weak-hearted liberals like himself—and the idea of that was making him nauseous. (Or maybe that was just his heart again, preparing to attack.)

George reached across the table to touch him, but the table was too big, George couldn't quite reach.

"My father," said Gabe, "made little jokes in times of trouble, just like Lucia does. I remember when I was a kid, and the cousins were locked in the barn and burned up, even the old women, my father said, so, this is because we live among barbarians who don't appreciate music.

"He was joking. Crying and joking. And thirty years later, the nation which had *perfected* music did just the same thing, only more perfectly.

"And when these fools blow up innocent Turks, and our finest musicians support them, I say, so, this proves that our culture too has failed. We also, even we with everything we know, we have not advanced the world."

"Oh please, people don't live to advance the world," Anna said suddenly, surprising her sister Mary. "They just live in their little lives alone. Culture has nothing to do with it."

"You don't think maybe American culture had anything to do with Vietnam?" Mary asked. "You don't think maybe the culture of capitalism had any little thing to do with that?"

Anna thought for a moment.

"I think killers kill alone," she said, "even if they are in armies. And I think the guys Vartan used to take care of recovered alone. They didn't say to themselves: 'All this happened to me because of the greed of great corporations.' They said, 'Please dear God, help me learn to live without arms.' I think the kid who threw the bomb at the Turk got inspiration from the history of the Armenians but he will not get comfort from that.

We'll forget the crime. He's gonna have to live with it, all alone, just like Spike when he was in prison, all alone."

"A million flower children were in prison with Spike!" Mary cried. "All the marchers in all the demonstrations, all the people who tried to stop the war and humanize this country rotted in jail with my Spike!"

"I don't believe that," Anna said.

When she got home, Mary found Spike staring at the fire in the fireplace, and she tried to divert him from his preoccupations by describing this evening's unsettling encounter with the truth about her kid sister. Her little acolyte, Anna, the one for whom she had beaten up Arnold Burian in the rhododendrons, displaying far more courage than she actually possessed, was turning out exactly like their self-involved vain father: a business person, bereft of ideology, disengaged from history, antipolitical, invested solely in the personal life.

"People like Daddy and Anna will never understand people like us," she said to Spike.

"Just hold my hand, honey," he answered.

RECALLING HER OWN REACTIONS TO THE NEWS OF THE MURDER OF the Turkish diplomat in Paris, Anna now knew for sure that it was perfectly possible for Tom Sarkissian to plot and connive against her, seeking for a way to humiliate her and ruin her business even though it profited him not one penny, just for the satisfaction, the wild joy of vengeance.

She went to see Mr. Cinzano of Mid-Manhattan Tech.

"Why did you drop us?" she asked. "The catalog looked terrific."

"And so will next year's catalog," he said, with relish. "Only it will also be much cheaper."

"Who could give you a better price?"

"Why should I tell you, Mzzz. Karavajian? Why should I do anything to help you? Did you work maybe five minutes of overtime to help *me*, in *my* hour of need? Do you have any idea what shit I had to take from my dean when that catalog was late this year? Do you, Mzzz. Karavajian? Do you? DO YOU?!"

Anna tried her father's old friends at the Union of Soviet Emigres.

"Frankly, we were not getting the same grade of service from you after Mr. Karavajian retired," said the director. "You asked us to pay for editing. We never paid for editing before. And then Vita Press beat your price by 50 percent . . ."

"Did they bid on the same specifications?"

"What does that mean?"

"Same number of pages? Same number of half tones?"

"What does that mean?"

"Pictures, same number of pictures?"

"Precisely the same."

The little computer in Anna's head began to scan her mental spec sheet, looking for 50 percent.

"It doesn't make sense," she said.

"Few things do, my dear. Please give my regards to your father. Tell him I hope he's well. Tell him we miss him."

At four in the morning Anna rolled her head down on the straw rug in her loft, pricking her scalp, thrusting her behind in the air, stretching her legs and arms as hard and as far as she could, a human tent. But the blood that rushed to her head brought her no answers.

Vita Press was a much bigger firm than hers and had never really competed for such trivial business. It seemed unlikely that the management would now offer unreasonably low prices to entice accounts that would never amount to more than $10,000 in profit a year. She knew that Tom's old friends, the former head pressman and the former art director, were working at Vita, but how much influence could they have?

It made no sense.

"I'm missing something here," Anna said to herself, looking upside down through her legs toward the blasting stereo. "What am I missing?"

Anna burrowed into her office. She went over and over the bids she had presented to the small accounts, chewing her hair maniacally as she had done when she was a teenager. No one dared disturb her. Muttering, figuring, her shoulders hunched forward, she prowled through the plant like a wolf. She made everybody nervous.

The machine operators kept working, their heads lowered. The brochures flipped out of the folding machines, the untrimmed pages nested in the collator bins, the trimming machines cracked down, the presses poured forth layers of color. The business boomed like a great bomb cloud, growing higher and wider, higher and wider, and underneath, at the bottom, there was this obliterated epicenter where the bomb had dropped. Yes, she could have trimmed 10 percent, maybe 15. But 50 percent! It was impossible. Vita Press had to be taking substantial losses just to steal her least profitable customers, but *why?* So Tom Sarkissian could feel good?!

It didn't make sense. Some clear simple thing was escaping her.

"I'll tell you what it is," Aram Hovad offered the next day in the office. "What is escaping you is that it is now ten o'clock at night, our people are knocked out from overtime, we need to hire two new pressmen now, right away, tomorrow! Your big customers are screaming for attention. It's the big customers like Bottom Oil who pay your rent and my rent, forget the little fuckers!"

"The Armenian Archdiocese is not a little fucker!" Anna yelled.

The next day, Aram went over there and found the old priest, who was shocked to hear that the church had dropped Karavajian and talked with the business manager and immediately had the decision to use Vita Press reversed.

"Don't lecture me about cost!" he said to the young priest. "We never paid Gabe Karavajian what his work was worth in thirty years and we're not going to start dickering about cost now. I work with Karavajian. That's it."

Aram returned to the plant with layouts for three brochures that Anna would have to print for almost nothing and said: "Now are you happy?"

The next day, she moseyed into the Nutrition Emporium and bought some muffins from Bernice. (Sarah was hiding behind the counter, very busy juicing carrots.)

"I guess you're not doing a summer menu, eh?" said Anna. "I mean two nice sentimental women like you wouldn't drop the printer who staked you to your opening brochure without so much as a phone call of explanation."

Sarah began to cry.

"They offered it to us for half your price," Bernice said, not flinching. "What were we supposed to do? Say 'no'?"

"You were supposed to call me and tell me!" Anna yelled, pounding the counter, making the spicy muffins jump. "You were supposed to remember who helped you when you were flat on your ass!"

Sarah ran sobbing into the back room.

"Don't pay any attention to Sarah," Bernice said. "She thinks she's still in the suburbs with a nice overworked man to pay all her bills, she thinks she can afford a guilty conscience. You lost, Anna. Tough nuggies."

Anna bit her thumbnail thoughtfully. She saw that Bernice was acting; for all her stunning toughness, her hands shook when she wrapped the muffins. Where did she get her strength, Anna wondered? Perhaps, like a daughter of Samson, from her bushy hair. She herself had always shrunk from confrontations; had she not only recently chickened out of calling Tacoma Paper to say that she was discontinuing her account there, had she not asked Aram Hovad to call in her stead? At this strained moment in the Nutrition Emporium, she admired Bernice very much.

Sarah returned, sniffing.

"I feel so terrible about this, Anna . . ." she began.

"Oh please. Stop." She was finished with Sarah. "Tell me about the bid, Bernice," she said. "Was it the same quantity?"

"Yes."

"Same art, same layout?"

"Yes, yes."

"Same paper?"

"Nicer paper," Bernice answered. "Sort of off-white paper with a shiny finish, very classy and beautiful, not like that recycled shit you always gave us. We thought it would be very expensive, but it turned out to be much cheaper . . ."

Anna stared at Bernice. She did not speak. She picked up a carrot and chewed it up, the whole carrot.

"It's the paper," she said.

It was six o'clock on a Tuesday, a pleasant evening in late June. Anna cabbed over to The Fish Place and accosted Clemson Bite at the bar.

He had been her father's customer. She had met him in this very restaurant the day she decided to quit teaching and go to work in the printing business, it was for him and his lovely wife and his partners and their lovely wives that she had bought her loft and held her very first dinner party! She had flirted with him for *years!*

She asked him point blank if Vita Press had undersold her and if so by how much.

"Yes," he said. "By fifty-seven percent."

"Same specifications? Same paper?"

"The same," he said.

"It can't be the same paper," she said calmly. "I had to special order that paper and it didn't come in on time because the truck was robbed and the order had to be shipped all over again."

She leaned on the bar, suddenly very tired and relieved, and appalled.

"Can I buy you a drink, Anna?" asked Clemson Bite. "Or are you gonna leave now and blow up my car?"

ONLY GABE KARAVAJIAN HAD EVER ACTUALLY MET MO GOTTLIEB and that was a long long time ago, when Mo was in high school; Gabe recalled masses of pimples, that was all.

However, Anna had a very clear mental picture of Mo, pieced together like a police sketch from years of telephone observation. She knew he was short, that he had red rimmed watery green eyes and glasses and a dark full Jewish mouth (always open) and a big nose always running and bony knuckles like a certain geek she had dated in college. This was the man she saw when she heard Mo's voice, and she didn't like him one bit. So she was very glad when Aram Hovad came up with a list of other suppliers who could provide the same papers at comparable prices, hopefully with less hassle, and did the dirty work of closing the old account.

Gabe Karavajian and Harry Gottlieb, Mo's father, had done business with each other for twenty-five years or more. Anna's vague recollection of Harry rested on the one occasion he had come to New York with his wife. The Karavajians had brought them out to the house for dinner and then taken them to a musical in the city. Harry was the kind of guy who had to be prevented by his wife from tying his napkin around his neck at the table.

Once in a while, at conventions or exhibitions, Gabe and Harry met and bought each other drinks. When one of their children was graduated or married, they never neglected to send presents. Anna remembered that her father had sent her out to the bank to pick up a U.S. Savings Bond for the oldest Gottlieb boy, to honor his graduation from UCLA. And she thought she had also ordered a tree to be delivered to Mo Gottlieb on the occasion of the birth of his first child.

Anna protested to her father that it had become a little silly, after all these years, sending presents to people they did not know, in a city thousands of miles away.

"Listen, my beauty," Gabe said. "The older you get the more sentimental you feel about a guy who did business with you your whole life and never cheated you, a straight guy like Gottlieb, you'll see, Anna, in your time you will feel this way too . . ."

And in Tacoma, old Harry said more or less the same thing to Mo, as a check was made out and sent to the Armenian Martyrs Fund in memory of some guy who had been about to marry Gabe's youngest daughter.

Mo was said to be the less brilliant of the Gottlieb boys. He did not become a doctor like his brother but went into Harry's business. Then Harry got sick and died. In bars and union meeting halls Harry Gottlieb's old friends predicted that Mo wouldn't be able to handle Tacoma Paper. Too tough for the kid, they said, even though they knew it would probably have been too tough for them too. When they were young the great forests glutted the horizons, the pulp and the acid ran freely into the mighty lakes and nobody cared, nobody paid fines for poisoning the environment, nobody thought of recycling except in wartime, and paper was cheap, fine paper that drank the ink and held the image like a rock holds a fossil and made a good book last forever, that kind of paper was cheap to make and easy to sell. No more, no more, those times were gone, and Harry's old friends kind of knew they were lucky to be retired and not trying to make an honest living in times as tough as these.

The day came when new union leadership took over, "new pharaohs who did not remember Joseph," Mo complained to his accountant. It was demanded of Mo Gottlieb that he put three men on each of his big trucks instead of one. He refused. He raised salaries, added dental insurance. However, he would not increase the number of men on a truck.

The Tacoma Paper plant began to be plagued by pilferage and the cost of that soon merited its very own column on the accountant's books. The cost of money went up; the market for high grade paper shrank; so did profits. Mo's Board of Directors grew annoyed with him and insisted that he refinance with a new bank.

Then paper began to disappear from the trucks. One roll, or three skids, on this truck or that, from time to time. This embarrassed the company with its customers. Bearish foremen like Aram Hovad called from printing plants around the country and roared.

Mo asked his loyal employees on the loading dock to wear wires. They overheard nothing. He paid certain drivers extra to eat and sleep in the trucks, to never leave the trucks for one minute during a haul. However, those trucks were not robbed.

Customers abandoned Tacoma Paper.

Mo hired detectives. He installed television surveillance monitors. Some members of the Board urged him to consider a takeover offer now being proposed by a certain conglomerate.

Mo didn't want to sell.

The day came when he had no choice.

ANNA SPREAD OUT HER LEDGERS AND HER PRINTOUTS AND BIDS ON the straw rug and called Mo Gottlieb at his office.

At first, Mo did not want to take her call. As far as he was concerned, Karavajian was one of a hundred customers who had decided to drop Tacoma Paper during the last year. He figured the call was personal; maybe the old man had died; he didn't care; he had his own troubles. He told the accountant to get rid of her.

She told the accountant it was important. The accountant told her it would have to wait. She called the accountant an asshole and hung up.

Shaken with guilt (maybe the old man *had* died), Mo called Anna back. "I'm sorry, Lucia . . . oh, Anna, right? the little one, Anna, I'm sorry. Everyone around here is a little edgy . . ." Mo blew his nose. He had terrible allergies. Tacoma had never suited him. He should have been living in a dry climate with no pollen. Whenever he visited his children in Arad in the Israeli desert, his nose stopped running. Well, he would visit them again soon, maybe even settle down in their country, when this nightmare finally ended.

"When they steal the paper from you, off your trucks, what do they do with it?" Anna asked.

"They dump it. Sometimes they burn it. We hired private detectives. They found the ashes. If anyone had sold it, I swear to you, I would know, young lady. I got detectives all over. I broke my company with the detectives and the wiretaps and the TV cameras, destroyed my company trying to fight this thing. It's not the paper they're after. It's my name. If they ruin my good name, they get my company cheap."

Anna said she would call him back.

The figures told her Vita Press had been underselling her by 50–60 percent on all the little accounts. This was roughly the cost of the paper. If she had done that, she knew, she would have registered no profit at all. So it had to be that they didn't care about a profit, they were just trying to railroad the accounts, break the link, humiliate Karavajian.

There was no reason for the management of Vita Press to want to do that.

Something about her hoarse voice on the telephone, quiet as dust, deadly as dust, made the president of Vita Press walk out in the middle of his sunny Westchester barbeque and drive to New York. He met her at his plant. They checked his paper inventory. There were a dozen extra skids of satin finished ivory stock there, with Tacoma Paper markings, and no record that Vita Press had ever paid for them.

A terrified young salesman was summoned off the beach in Far Rockaway. The sun block was still visible on his nose when he arrived at Vita Press. He said one of his job folders from several months ago had contained a list of specific accounts to go get with prices he could quote. He begged his boss to believe he was very new then, still unfamiliar with the price structures of the company, just doing what it said on the sales call sheet, and he had no idea he was working with hot paper.

The salesman implicated Tom's friends. They were called away from a ballgame. They got so scared when they saw Anna Karavajian that they began to sweat in front of her, and they said yes, Tom Sarkissian dropped the paper at Vita Press but they did not know where or how he had acquired it, they begged their boss to believe that, they begged Anna to take it easy on Tom.

She called Mo Gottlieb again the next day. It was the Fourth of July. He asked her if he could tape what she said, and she agreed, just as the president of Vita Press had agreed to cooperate so that the innocence of his company would be established and his good name preserved in the printing trades. So Mo understood that she was for real.

One real, sentimental person among all the heartless bastards.

"Tom is a little man," she said, "very hard working all his life, and I wouldn't want to see him hurt. I thought maybe you and your lawyers could just scare him and make him say how he acquired your paper and one fact might lead to another and you would be able to use the information to help yourself. I mean I know what it is to take over your father's business. How everybody just waits for you to fail, and how scared you are that you won't be as good as your father. And we all heard the rumor that you were selling out . . ."

Mo Gottlieb put Anna on hold. He took off his horn rimmed glasses and blew his nose and reached across the desk to grasp the hand of his loyal accountant.

In the outer office beyond Mo's door, there sat a vice president of the Seattle branch of the Farmers' Bank, Harvard Business School 1978, smart young man, smart, and nice too. He was waiting to drive Mo out to a country club where they were to meet the CEO of a certain conglomerate and have lunch and talk about the deal they could close on Harry Gottlieb's whole life, his life's work.

Mo leaned out his office door.

"It looks like I'm not going to be able to make lunch," he said to the banker.

The young man laughed.

"You must be kidding."

"No."

"But you said . . . we went over the figures, Mr. Gottlieb . . . your financial position . . . *you came to us!* He's waiting for us! He's coming off the links this minute and he's ready to go!"

"Life is full of surprises."

Mo stood up very straight, looking down at the banker with cold slag-gray eyes. The banker had never realized how tall Gottlieb was, maybe because every time they had met before this, Mo was slumped in a chair like Abe Lincoln after the shooting, smashed, blasted, just about dead. But now that one receiver of the stolen goods had not dumped or burned Mo's paper, but had actually put it out there onto presses (for whatever reasons, because of anger or stupidity or some Armenian vendetta), now that he was going to force Anna Karavajian's petty little enemies to help him get names and tape and pictures of the blackmailing mobsters who had tried to destroy his company, and put them in jail with thieves and pushers so their names would be erased and their own children would want to forget them, now Mo Gottlieb looked every single bit of his six foot four inches, and he reminded the banker quite a lot of Ralph Nader.

ANNA NEEDED TO TALK. HER FATHER, HAVING HEARD FROM MANY men in the printing trades how coldly and ferociously Anna had tracked and cornered Tom Sarkissian, did not want to talk to her. It was too late, he said. The deed was done. He personally would have found another way, but she had chosen not to consult him, maybe there were reasons for that; he didn't want to hear them.

Her sisters had long ago lost interest in the business; they would not wish to be bothered with her problems. So Anna went over to her friend Sally Bangle's place with a couple of pastrami sandwiches and a bottle of wine.

Sally didn't mind. Her lover was at a rehearsal. Her boss, the rather manic actor-director Elliot Longet, was out at some affair raising money for their theater and would not pester her with urgent phone calls this evening. The frontal elevations for the set she was designing for *The Seagull* could wait. She had a spicy peach pie in the oven which she was sure Anna Karavajian would enjoy eating warm with vanilla ice cream. It wasn't every day that a woman as beautiful and powerless as Sally got to sit in judgment on someone else's life decisions, and she was flattered and she listened well.

"When I went to work at Karavajian Press," Anna said, "in exactly this season, six years ago in July, Tom Sarkissian acted friendly toward me, like an uncle. He felt sorry for me, I mean I was pretty pathetic in those days I think.

"Tom is taller than my father but not tall by American standards. He has gray bushy hair. He has brown spots all over his face. His mouth is little, always pursed, like he's chewing something in there that he doesn't want anybody else to taste, a secret piece of candy, something.

"He set me up in the old storage room, gave me a filing cabinet and a desk and a sign on the door that said 'Sales Department.' Really, he believed that Daddy was inventing a job for me, just to keep me off the streets until I could find a husband. I mean he never had a sales department in all the years, so why should we need one now? That's what Tom thought. But me, I knew we needed a sales department. And so did my father, really, although he didn't actually admit it.

"Tom was a gossip. Always pried and carried tales, that was his great weakness, my father once said, but my father forgot that I heard him say it, I mean I was fourteen at the time.

"So I made friends with the people who didn't like Tom—Mildred our comptroller, and Francine our receptionist, who was Tom's daughter-in-law then—and I made sure they told me anything he said about me, and if they didn't tell me, I would overhear, because by then I had learned to sneak around like my sister Mary. I could move in silence and sort of hang out in shadows . . .

"So I overheard Tom when he talked about me, to his friends the head pressman and the art director.

"Poor ratty looking old maid, he used to say . . . who can we get to take her out? Must be somebody around . . .

"I stayed away from the machinery. I tried hard not to look busy. I left doodles on my desk because I knew Tom checked my desk when I was out. And I went out a lot, making sales calls, I took somebody else to lunch every day. I brought in a lot of new customers. But I told Mildred about them, not Tom, because I didn't want him to know I was doing well, I wanted him to underestimate me as long as possible.

"My filing cabinet filled up. Mildred bought me two more. I guess Tom began to wonder about my files.

"Mildred told me that he came to her one day and asked: Why does Anna lock her files? And Mildred answered: Because she knew you would try to see what was in them, you old snoop. I tell you, Sally, she *cackled* when she told me that story, she just *loved* what was happening, maybe even more than I did.

"So then things began to get frankly bad between me and Tom. The head pressman complained a lot about me, said I wasn't watchful about schedules and demanded priority for my new customers, and he thought I was asking too much. So I made friends with his assistant, Big Mack, who wanted his job, and if I needed something extra, Big Mack gave me the overtime.

"The art director wouldn't pay attention to my accounts. I had nobody in the shop to use against him. So I just arranged with Mildred to subcontract with an outside art studio.

"Tom got very mad when he heard that, felt he had to take a stand. So we had this big fight. I mean he staged it, out in the open by the water cooler. He wanted everybody to hear when he put me in my place.

"But he didn't know who I was, you see. He thought of me as a luckless old maid like Mildred, and he figured to treat me like he had always treated her, with contempt and that awful false deference you get from the kids who hate you when you're teaching. What he had forgotten was that I was Gabe Karavajian's child and that I knew how to humiliate him in front of all those people. I knew exactly how to be his boss.

"I let him yell until he was tired out. I said obviously the needs of the expanding client list had thrown him into a panic. He was afraid he couldn't handle all the pressure. Well, so what if he couldn't handle the pressure? I said. I mean we would certainly understand, if Tom wanted to take it easy, maybe go home early a couple times a week, why not? Wasn't he entitled now that he was such a venerable old man? Don't you worry about a thing, darling, I told him, and I remember now, I patted him the way Mom and Lucia pat my father. How Daddy hates that, to be patted. Like dough, he says.

"I could just *feel* the people in the plant abandoning Tom. They lowered their heads and tried not to seem to be listening, but I felt them realizing that I was gonna be the winner . . .

"So after that Tom tried to fight dirty.

"We had a purchasing agent named Aram Hovad, one of Tom's protégés, and I saw that he was ambitious. I began relating to him, making sure he knew about my customers and their needs. We'd have coffee together on our break in the afternoon.

"Francine told me that Tom was telling people that I was trying to seduce Aram Hovad. I said, 'Tell Mildred,' because I knew how to manipulate the rumor pools in the plant, it was my plant, after all, and I knew Mildred would call my mother and my mother would tell my father and my father would have to have a meeting with me and Tom in his office.

"The truth is, we should have had that meeting long before then. But my father was too scared, about his honor and his good name, and his obligations . . .

"So I came to the meeting looking as much like a bag lady as I possibly could."

Sally Bangle had listened in silence to Anna's story all this time, but now she began to giggle. Soon she began to cackle, much like old Mildred.

"My father is sitting in his office. He is tired. He's in his seventies. He would have retired by now except that I came into the business. He would have sold out to Tom except for me. But he has never admitted that, he won't *admit* how much he loves me. I'm wearing my ten-year-old blue plaid lumberjack shirt and my white dungarees with the holes in the knees and my orthopedic looking foam soled hiking boots and I have not washed my hair in a week.

"Tom Sarkissian walks in with a three piece suit and a tie.

"Daddy says: Jealous people are slandering my Anna, Tom.

"And Tom says: I quit. You don't have to lay any more traps for me, he says, I'm quitting now.

"And my father says: Wait a minute, wait a minute, wait a minute, you got it all wrong, you just can't assume that every time a woman goes out for coffee with a man it's something about stealing him from his wife! My daughter is a worker! She's my daughter, look at her! She would never humiliate me by misbehaving with somebody in the plant . . .

"This is not about women, Tom says. This is between us. You made me a promise and every day Anna is here, you break the promise a little more.

"Well, my father feels for his heart. But this time Tom Sarkissian is not fooled.

"Tom says: Don't feel for your heart like you're gonna have another heart attack. You're not. I am the one with the broken heart, Gabriel.

"And he leaves forever, swearing vengeance.

"Everybody in the plant knows what is going to happen. Except my father. He stills treats it like an open question.

"He says: So, Anna, my beauty, what shall we do? We need a new foreman for the plant and a new boss.

"I said, I'll be the boss and Aram Hovad can be the foreman.

"He laughed.

"I said, don't laugh, Daddy, I have been waiting for this day for three years.

"He said: Don't say that to me, I didn't need to hear that, I didn't intend to disappoint Tom and dishonor myself for your sake, don't say that to me!

"So I put my arms around him like a good girl and I said, forget it, I didn't mean it, I'm sorry, I didn't mean it.

"My heart was *singing*, Sally! I wanted to jump up and down and pop champagne and tell him how I was gonna make state-of-the-art money at Karavajian Press! I wanted to tell him how I was planning to contribute large sums to charities that would say 'Karavajian' on them like monuments and that I was gonna dress for success like the women in the magazines and throw great dinner parties for our customers and I was gonna have the life that I wanted at last and he was gonna be more proud of me than he ever would have been of any fucking son!

"But I didn't say that. Because Daddy was so ashamed and miserable. He didn't want to know the truth about my happiness or admit that he had a share in my victory. I only said, I didn't mean it—I didn't mean it—forget I ever said it.

"After that, if there was a testimonial or a fund-raiser at the AGBU or one of the churches, they were always careful to seat the Karavajians and the Sarkissians at opposite ends of the room.

"And I knew Tom was out there, looking to hurt us, an enemy. I knew that. But I tell you, Sally, it didn't bother me. I could handle it. I mean, I almost *wanted* him to have his vengeance so he could rest easy and be satisfied and sort of tie off my remaining sense of guilt. I didn't want to fight him; I wanted to let the paper robbery pass like Aram told me to, Aram begged me to let it pass."

"Too bad there were complications."

"Too bad there was a victim."

Sally served the delicious peach pie. Anna had no appetite. She had come to a place beyond the reach of homey remedies, beyond busyness and energy, where it was not enough to be loved by your family or respected for your work or comforted by your friends. Despite herself she had gone out alone to meet her personal monsters. Now she knew she did not care that her father would have handled things differently. She knew how mad she was at her father.

Sally's lover came home from his rehearsal. Anna had to leave.

Sick with loneliness, she thought of calling the nice man who had abandoned her at dawn. Unfortunately, she did not know his number, did not in fact know his last name. For the first time in her new life that seemed to Anna to be a big mistake.

Chapter 4

DURING THE WEEKS AFTER HER VISIT TO SALLY BANGLE'S PLACE, an unfamiliar mood of exhaustion so flattened Anna that she now thought she must be quite ill. She had lost her appetite and had begun to love sleeping and did not dream and came to work bleary-eyed, astonishing the employees of Karavajian Press who had only just started feeling comfortable with her tense, aggressive energy.

Every time she tried to read copy, the letters bounced and smeared before her.

"My eyes are going," she said to Mary.

She suspected glaucoma. It turned out that she needed reading glasses. Mary laughed at her and told her she was becoming a class-A hypochondriac.

So when Anna felt lumps in her breasts and began to imagine malignancies and mastectomies, she did not call Mary but rather Lucia, who took her to a new gynecologist.

Anna told him that she felt bloated, as though her womb had suddenly tripled in size. She just knew that her ovaries had ceased producing estrogen: why else had her skin gone so dry? Why else did the August heat oppress her so? Why else was her mood so very black?

"You're fine," he said, discarding his plastic gloves.

The baseline mammogram screening proved negative. He said that the lumps she felt were really ribs, and he, too, laughed at her.

Anna stopped by at a vitamin store and bought one of every letter as well as a mineral supplement which came in tablets the size of almonds. She took all the bottles home and lined them up like the kids in *Oliver Twist* and took one serving from each. Expecting to feel invigorated, she began to clean her apartment for the first time in several weeks, and fell asleep in her hammock with the vacuum cleaner running.

Lucia's daughters, armed with college texts, decided it was psychological. They insisted that Lucia take Anna shopping.

Anna couldn't find anything she wanted to wear.

Lucia forced her to buy a pale blue summer weight suit with big shoulder pads and Anna forced herself to wear it. She purchased high heels. But she still felt nauseous a lot of the time, and there was a dull pain in her upper back. The first bite of a meal made her feel better but it was all downhill thereafter. She thought she had been poisoned.

Perhaps she had swallowed too much ink, she thought. Perhaps immersion in the cruddy waters of the Tacoma Paper scam had polluted her whole system; like the rivers of the Pacific Northwest, she was being killed off by the stinking effluents of the printing trades.

She went to an internist.

He ordered an upper GI series.

The barium made Anna throw up. She had to rest in a cold room on a stretcher that had surely this morning or last night or last week carried some terminal person to his final reward. The X-rays were rescheduled.

At the start of this hot, foggy day, the internist called with the results. Anna took the call in her office; the door tightly closed; the desk straightened; the worst expected.

"You've got an ulcer," the doctor said.

He recommended a diet of appalling blandness and asked if perhaps she had been coping with some extra additional stress during the past few years. Could she find a way to take the pressure off?

Go on a vacation, Lucia commanded (as they lunched at a dairy restaurant), a major escape, beyond seas, so the frantic highs and lows of this riotous career could not interrupt long naps on the beach, and if the plant burned down, or the New York City Government decided to use Karavajian for all its printing for-ever-more, Anna would find out *after* the fact, when she was rested and sporting a Bahamian straw hat.

Anna said, yes, sure, she would plan a vacation. But right now, today, immediately after this awful lunch, she had to prepare for a meeting with a certain Mrs. Sharon Gold at the Museum, where they were considering her bid on the Christmas gift catalog, a job so large, key to an account so potentially lucrative, that just thinking about it gave Anna a terrible pain in her stomach. And then she had to drive out to Queens to see the new set Sally had designed (she had to! she had *promised!*) and incidentally to show Elliot Longet the final proofs for the theater's season poster.

Lucia became very angry, declaring that Anna had absolutely no right to treat her ulcer so caddishly, and she stalked out of the restaurant.

Actually Anna did not believe she had an ulcer.

The real truth of her condition, she was sure, had been hidden from the radioactive eye of the X-ray machine by a chalky barium mist.

Actually, she thought she had cancer of the colon, like the President of the United States.

IN THE LADIES' ROOM AT KARAVAJIAN PRESS, ON THE MIRROR ABOVE the sink, there was a sign, hand-lettered by Estelle in the luscious fat cherry-red graffiti type style Anna recalled from her high school in the Bronx, which said:

> No food in the sink.
> No drink in the sink.
> And most important, don't forget,
> No ink in the sink!

Anna looked closely at herself. She was black and gray and smudged; just like the plant, she thought. She had taken on the coloration of this groaning old plant. In the bright white clean Museum, she would look like a visiting tombstone.

Grim but resolute, she washed her face. She rouged her cheeks and then wiped them almost completely clean with the heels of her hands. Across her wide eyelids, she streaked shadows and liners that were two or three, maybe five years old, for Anna applied these emollients so infrequently that they never wore out and remained with her until they disappeared in a change of pocketbooks.

She tried not to blink until the mascara dried.

Wincing with the pain, she brushed her soft wild hair with a steel wire brush and pinned it up from her neck with aluminun barrettes. Then she sprayed it with lacquer until it was neat and hard.

She took off her smudged white shirt, washed her armpits and her neck and her sweaty cleavage, threw on some talcum powder, and put on a clean blue shirt, darker than the suit. She put on her suit jacket. She kicked off her Tretorns and rubbed her feet. They were inlaid with calluses and corns. The minute they entered her high heels, she was miserable. She popped an antacid.

Of course her mascara had smeared. She wiped it off. She put on some lipstick. She looked at herself one last time and practiced smiling.

THE UNEXPECTED DELIGHTS OF THESE LATE-DAY ENCOUNTERS cheered Anna as she started out on the road to Flushing. She drove very slowly. Dusk had brought in a billowing mist from the ocean, and it was hard to see.

She planted the flower above the rearview mirror of the blue truck—a real flower, freshly cut—where had he been hiding it?! What an interesting man, this night watchman, lost in his smoke. He had false teeth. That was strange in a man not yet thirty . . . She wondered about him. She wondered if this was how she would live from now on, knowing many people slightly, guessing at their background dramas.

Sharon Gold who had impressed Anna with her white silk dress and her real gold bangles had been able to name every single person in a crowded room, and to rank them in the hierarchies of the art world, and to tell Anna much of their financial news. "He just bought . . . she owns . . . she just sold . . . he invests . . . ," indicating, never pointing, never ceasing to laugh and tell jokes and laugh again. How was it possible for a woman to *enjoy* her life so much? The joy of work, that Anna could understand; the joy of victory, being right, being righteous, she could understand all that. But the simple joys of just passing the time and chatting and gossiping and knowing clever things to amuse the company, that escaped her somehow. No wonder she felt sick. She was too heavy. She dwelled too heavily on the importance of things. She had to try and lose some of the weight in her brain that was placing such a great strain on her stomach.

Anna thought that perhaps she should now spend more time in the world of art. Perhaps the world of art insulated people against grief, gave them a higher purpose, and helped them forget the brutal realities.

Look at George, didn't he ride to heaven on that cello? Look at Sally, how she delighted in disco dancing and baking cakes and decorating windows and making love, look how much fun she had, and Elliot Longet too, how zanily he satirized his audiences and his theater and himself too, never draining his strength with imagining that while he practiced comedy, young men were being dragged out of their wives' beds and thrown into prisons and tortured, all their teeth pulled out, and sent into exile to sit illegally for all the foreseeable future in the dark . . .

The dark engulfed her. The hot black night closed in. She was lost.

Despite the fact that Anna had visited The Shelter on business several times, she could not now recall the way. Maybe she had made the wrong turn or missed one. No planes flew overhead to give her a sense of proximity to the airport, either by light or sound, and the stadium was invisible in the mist, so her major landmarks were gone.

She opened the window and hung out on her elbow, looking for small signs that might tell the way, but most of them were so overgrown with weeds that she could not read them. The heat of the day and the wet of the night married in a heavy vapor that melted her hair and wilted her flower. Her wipers could not clear the windshield. They squeaked unpleasantly on the glass. She saw no light, heard no human sound, saw nothing but the fog, heard nothing but the rumble of her motor. Having entered a landscape that reflected her state of mind, she found it blank as lead. Once not long ago, she had been quite sure, but now, tonight, she had no idea where she was going.

EARLIER THAT SAME DAY, ELLIOT "CAT" LONGET, PRONOUNCED Longhay in the French manner, called "Cat" because it was short for Catastrophe, had taken great pains to lock up his old theater securely. He had drawn down the clanking steel security screens and locked them from inside, then asked Sally Bangle to check them again.

One could never be too careful in Flushing. Even though Cat and Sally and Charles Borden III were now clearly unassailable in the squat, windowless building, Cat told the tech director he was worried that the dull night might suddenly flash danger; and he wished aloud that help were not so far away.

"Stay loose," said the tech director as he left the theater for the night. "You're fine; you're okay; you're fine."

The theater, renamed by Cat "The Shelter," hunched at the center of a neglected park, surrounded by weedy parking lots and rutted bike paths and forests now thick with untrimmed branches. A D-shaped structure with a three-quarter thrust stage jutting in from its straight side and doors on its belly side and precious little backstage space, the theater had some audio equipment, hi-fi but not stereo, and a light board so outmoded that young graduate technicians had often never used one like it before. The stage itself had come unhinged from the back wall as the building aged and shifted. Now a dangerous gap had appeared between wall and stage in which an actor or stagehand might catch a foot and fall and *for real* break a leg.

Given Cat Longet's reputation for technical disaster, that seemed a probability.

However, the theater's acoustics were fine, good enough even for musicals, and of the 299 seats, only about a dozen on the far left carried an obstructed view. The subscription audience was local, "loyal as peanut butter to jelly," Cat told his tech director, "and every bit as dull."

Originally Cat's theater had served as an exhibition hall, housing itinerant displays of foreign arts, especially during the sixties when international détente provided funding. However, as the world's rightward turnings grew more pronounced, such shows occurred less frequently and when they did, they needed larger quarters more amenable to security measures and the fancy wirings of the media.

So The Shelter was booted down to theater status, as antiquated armories sometimes are, and churches which have lost their charisma. The park itself, the whole park, in fact, had deteriorated. Rock bands and opera stars performed in Manhattan or in Jersey now; Brooklyn received priority among the Outer Boroughs. The local citizenry seemed not to mind; they basked in the delicious freedom of being neglected by bureaucrats, and their little stores under the elevated subway lines prospered. But at night, to Cat Longet and his company, the neglect made a critical difference. No cars cruised, no cops snooped, no gentle deer came a'munching as in the safer woodlands of Bucks County and Connecticut where Cat had often worked as an actor. No, this barely remembered sideyard of New York City snapped its twigs and crackled its dead autumn leaves scarily and hid junkies at night, desperate angry animals who would kill you for your watch.

Cat Longet had accepted the job of Producing Director at The Shelter as a fortieth birthday present to himself. No more! he cried, to motel rooms and cold pizza. Never again! he declaimed, to the stench of marginal success on his chic old clothes. Too long had he shunned marriage, owned nothing, no car, no condo, nothing, in the vain hope that the resulting empty spaces in his life would become hangouts for fame and fortune. For twenty years Cat had wrapped his lanky Bolgerish body around roles comic, tragicomic, seriocomic, darkly comic, and Rabelaisian. With his supple voice—many dialects mastered; many timbres available—he had captured just the right tone for a hundred different commercials. He had played every manner of extra in the movies and many incidental policemen, waiters, and resident physicians on television, spot by spot.

But no role *ran*. No future emerged.

At forty, Cat Longet had grown into a reliable singer-dancer-announcer-MC-voiceover-you-name-it-performer who could deliver the laughs in any medium. However, he had lost much of his frizzy, sandy colored hair. He had lost his mother and father and the ancestral home, he had no place to go back to and had collected all he was ever going to inherit (which certainly hadn't turned out to be much). His body had begun to show a little slack in the middle; his catchy wide grin ("the best thing you got going, Cat," an agent had said once) now needed dental repair, maybe even periodonture. His connections had either left the business or grown rich in California. They found it hard to remember Cat. ("They find it hard to remember their own children," he commented to his secretary.) For twenty years, he had worked steadily, and traveled everywhere, but he had gone exactly nowhere.

It was time to give up.

When the Flushing Municipal Theater offered thirty grand plus the use of a car plus a part-time secretary, Cat Longet accepted with alacrity and said thank you.

Two years had passed since then.

Cat's salary had been raised a bit, his skeletal staff had grown by two or three, his productions had received excellent reviews now and again in the *Times*. When a British company offered him a plum part (politico-comic American oilman doing dirty deals in Oman), Cat had demurred. ("Goodbye to all that," he said to some friends at Equity, waving his large expressive hand goodbye.) He rented a workable little house on Saultell off Corona. He cemented relationships with his theater's Board of Directors. He hired people who owed him and felt loyal to him personally—a custodian he had once alibied for in St. Louis; a technical director he had bailed out after a drug bust. At Joe Allen's, his old drinking buddies said it looked like Cat Longet had decided to dig in at The Shelter and play it safe, screw fame, screw fortune; above all, screw art.

Smart Cat, they said.

When there was no performance at The Shelter, Cat usually tried to close around six, in deliberate imitation of shopkeepers who observed decent civilian hours and went home for dinner. Tonight, however, he told his secretary he would be staying late for several reasons.

First of all, Sally Bangle wanted to hang around and do the detail painting on her set for *The Seagull*, the September production.

"You don't have to bother about me, sugar," she protested. "I'm fine on my own."

Cat insisted to Sally, in the presence of both the secretary and the technical director, that he could not possibly leave her alone in the theater at night, especially since he knew she would be crawling around on stage, rapt as Ariel on assignment, fiddling with the shady garden, *á la vieille Russie,* and would hear no intruder until it was way too late.

In addition, Sally had arranged for the visit of another single, unprotected lady, namely The Shelter's printer, Anna Karavajian. ("A nice woman," Cat told the Board member's wife. "Not dumpy but frumpy.") Anna would be delivering the final proofs of the season poster and Cat was frankly burning to see it. "Theater at The Shelter" it would say and be slathered up on walls all over the city. It would list the plays and their run dates and in one case—the Board's annual spring talent splurge, this year invested in an early Tom Stoppard comedy—their stars.

This poster had been unusually hard to finish. The director scheduled for the November production had been murdered by one of his *amours,* necessitating that Cat find someone else to direct *Corruption in the Palace of Justice,* which was not so easy, and took a long time, and made Cat very late with the poster copy. Despite the inconvenience to her company, Anna had been very nice and cooperative and deserved the courtesy of a warm reception for all her trouble, didn't Cat's secretary agree?

So as not to make waiting for Anna and chaperoning Sally his only reasons for staying at the theater, Cat had also scheduled a meeting there with one of the few playwrights he had ever liked, Charles Borden III.

Charles had come down from Vermont, where he taught college English, to make the final revisions on his play, *The Ice Cold Jungle,* a play about the war, not a funny play.

The safe, classic season at The Shelter usually made no room for original work of any kind. However, Cat had skillfully maneuvered *The Ice Cold Jungle* into "the blizzard slot" in February, when few people wanted to venture out to the theater anyway and (the Board of Directors could easily see) little would be lost financially from an investment in quality.

"Why do you care so much about this particular play, Cat?" asked the Board member's wife when she and Cat were alone.

He adjusted his earring and examined his improving gums in a small hand mirror. "Oh, I don't care," he said. He combed his short sandy beard. "Do I look like a person who cares? It's just that I might die suddenly, you see, and someone might write my obituary and I'd like it to be possible for the obituary to say that just once in his career, Cat Longet siphoned off a little extra for a good new writer, so that I do not exit the world in total and absolute ignominy."

This sticky night, Cat stood at the top of the center aisle, watching Sally Bangle and Charles Borden work. Gifted people, he thought. Why is it worth so little in the end to be gifted?

SALLY BANGLE CRAWLED ON HER KNEES ACROSS THE WIDE SET, PULL-
ing behind her a child's toy red wagon which was stacked with paint and
brushes, adhesives and thinners, scrapers and screwdrivers and scraps of
fabric patching. She wore a spattered purple turtleneck and gray overalls
that fairly engulfed her, making her all but invisible. Sally always wore
these shapeless clothes at The Shelter. They protected her, not just against
the paint and the paste, but against the lustful eyes of colleagues who loved
to ogle her small, voluptuous body, an excess of attention that often prevented her from getting her work done.

For similar reasons, she had wished to putter alone tonight on *The
Seagull* set: just not to be annoyed by the guys on the crew, just not to have
to deal with proving that despite her silky cheeks and proud breasts, she
knew more than they and could be their boss and order them around with
good reason. Just not to have to bother.

Sally was in a great mood tonight. She had a brilliant new lover who
really loved her and had given her for their one-week anniversary an orange transistor radio now nestled in the pocket of Sally's overalls. Its
delicate ear phones lay weightlessly on her ringlets and poured vitalizing
music into her head. She felt secure in knowing that she would have *four*
sets to design and build this season, for each production inevitably woke
some sleeping corner of her talent and she knew she was getting better,
that one day soon, she would be real good.

She had confided in her friend Anna that she was making history. "I am
the first person in my whole family," she said, "in all the sixteen generations my family been in this country, *the very first person* who ever got to
do what she loved to do for a living."

Although Sally was ten years younger than Anna and could have been
one of her students from the Bronx, she knew much more than Anna
because she was poor and black. Her experience with men, for example,
was gargantuan compared to Anna's. She spouted cynicisms which Anna
found illuminating, such as "Most American men didn't even know what a
clitoris *was* until after the fall of Saigon, sugarplum" and other homespun
wisdom like that.

For her part, Sally loved having a friend who, like her, worked at a
"man's" job and smelled from the chemicals of her trade. She sought
opportunities to visit Anna at Karavajian Press, for brainstorming sessions
about The Shelter's many posters and its all-important introductory season
brochure.

Sally noted that the men at the plant called Anna "Boss" and did not seem to be kidding. She marveled at how much easier it was for a woman to gain the respect of the men who worked for her when she was not beautiful!

Sally herself was beautiful as a black pearl. Had she not been determined to eat three squares a day, she might have done well at modeling. Her features were all soft, like those of Modigliani's subjects, and her eyes were very large, dark brown, almost black, the eyebrows slanting downward, making her seem ever on the verge of sadness and in need of help. She was the warm brown color of gazelles, and the literate men she met in the theater were always quoting the "Song of Songs" to describe her.

So then she had to go and look up "gazelle" to see what they were talking about.

Sally never went home to Louisville.

She told Anna, eating lunch on the steps of the Stock Exchange, that she didn't like her mother's new boyfriend. Also her younger sisters had written that the Food Stamps didn't stretch for all the mouths they had to feed, so Sally sent them money, and this made them think she had grown rich in New York, so now they hated her.

Anna sighed.

"I guess those who wish to be loved just have to learn to control their generosity," she commented, recalling the impact of her apples in the Bronx.

Cat Longet appreciated Sally Bangle because her work was solid and dependable. Her sets bore the clamber of fat actors playing rage, withstood angry exits with slamming doors and parades of stagehands shifting sofas. One day with a little luck and some better budgets, she would be good, she'd be terrific.

First, however, she had to get into the union. And for some reason, she could not.

Cat plugged for her, made inquiries, pulled strings, but to no avail.

"You think it's 'cause I'm black or 'cause I'm a woman or 'cause I quit school with no degree?" she asked angrily.

"It is because your sponsor and patron, namely me, is still insufficiently influential," he answered, more angrily yet.

Sally went over to Anna's house and stretched out on the straw rug, beating her pretty head on the floor and capturing straw in her ringlets like a farm girl.

"Ten years!" she hollered. "Ten years I been inching upward on the dicks of these damn fools, and not one of them has ever succeeded in really doing it for me! Now if the white boys keep me out of the union, how am I ever gonna do it for myself?!"

"Please. Calm down," Anna counseled. "Your problem is that you are an artist. Life is always very hard for artists because most people are assholes and don't appreciate beautiful things. Look at me, I'm your *friend* and it never even *occurs* to me to acquire anything beautiful."

Strangely enough, this self-deprecating observation restored Sally's good humor. Vowing to design so brilliantly at The Shelter that the union would come crawling, she returned to the library and poured through many books about Old Russia, British country houses, postwar Italy, and her personal least favorite, Vietnam.

Familiarity with The Shelter had not made its many physical problems less irritating to Sally. The more proficient she became, more devoutly she wished for a deeper stage which would fit back wall snugly; sight lines which did not require her to mask wings with dusty black velours; lights which did not wash out detail; a set dock which did not harbor dampness like a riverfront shack, warping all her door frames, imprinting all her upholstered pieces with mildew.

Her biggest gripe was the shop. Located in the basement below the lobby, it was windowless and lit with fluorescents which made it impossible to judge a color before it went on stage. Sawdust from the power tools collected on the floor, and though Sally and the tech director swept and vacuumed after the crew had swept and vacuumed, it was impossible to keep the damn place clean. Between the wood shavings and the chemicals, she was working in a firetrap. She imagined entombment; incineration; she identified with the South African diamond miners and did not cease bugging Cat with her fears.

"I'm gonna call the fire department," she said.

"Don't, please don't, please please. I have a plan."

"Apply for a grant."

"Grants take too long; besides they are only given to theaters which do work of surpassing artistic merit."

"So what's your plan, hotshot?"

"I have found an angel."

"Oh yeah? Well, I want a shop on the ground floor, behind the stage, with big windows and a loading entrance and a sprinkler system."

"When next the spring with golden daffodils comes blooming, you shall have the shop of your dreams."

He kissed her hand. Sally laughed.

"Save the shit for your angel, sugarplum."

Sally knew that Cat Longet was great with rich folks and might indeed one day be able to charm some dilettante and build her the shop of her dreams. But would she deserve it? What she had acquired in experience she still lacked in education. Because she did not know literature or history or languages, she made critical mistakes.

One theatergoer, overheard in the lobby at intermission, had laughed at her for using an Art Deco sofa in an Ibsen play. And in the single instance in which her name had been mentioned by a reviewer from Manhattan, he accused her of "grotesque misjudgment" in selecting a Chagall to hang in a Noel Coward drawing room.

Hell, she didn't even notice it was a Chagall! She just thought all those brightly colored people flying over Paris were especially suitable for a séance scene!

Cat comforted her with vodka and chocolates and said, "Ah Sally Sally Sally Sally, how will you ever achieve greatness if you refuse to realize that they are always wrong and you are always right?!"

A year later, the memory of the arch, nasty review still turned in Sally's heart like a melon scoop. Being good wasn't enough. You had to be right too. And to be right in the wide white world, you needed a degree.

Now look here at this damn *Seagull*, she thought (standing with Cat at the back of the house, just looking).

The birch forests were painted and in place, far beyond changing. But last night she had rummaged in an odd lot of books and glanced through another volume on Russia and discovered that the birch forests that were generally interspersed with tilting pines! So now, she was scooping her heart out because of the absence of those damn pines! Furthermore the stage furnishings she had selected turned out to be nowhere near ornate enough. A practiced eye would see immediately that they better suited Edison and Ford on one of their famous camping trips than a declining, bourgeois family in the twilight of the Czars.

What practiced eye?! cried Cat. Where?! Where?! Show me even one! Who in this godforsaken outback will know or care for the exact flora of a Russia forest or the perfect Frenchness of a Russian chair?!

"The *Voice* will come again and eat me and spit me out!" Sally wept.

"The *Voice* will not come," he said. "Nor the *Times.* Believe me. I promise you. I love the set. It's beautiful. You are beautiful." He hugged Sally, accidentally catching his black pearl in one of her earrings. For a minute, they were linked, laughing, nuzzling each other: kittens from the same litter. Sally wished to God she could love Cat, because she really did love him so much.

"Go back to work," he said. "Your good friend Anna will soon be here, and she will surely make you feel much better because, poor misguided oaf that she is, she thinks you are a great artist."

So Sally hung out on the stage floor, waiting for Anna to come and tell her she was good, painting *trompe l'oeil* moldings on the legs of the table, trying to correct the plainness, despising her ignorance, pissed at her mistakes, fearing all critics regardless of their rightness, wanting above all things—a penniless black girl from the Middle South with no Daddy— perfection.

CHARLES BORDEN III HAD SET UP SHOP IN THE THIRD ROW OF THE theater. He had laid a series of planks over the arms of the third row seats, to form a kind of endless table across the hall. Then he spread the pages of his second act out along this table, chin to crown like the segments of a totem pole, so that he could read the thing from top to bottom, "which is how it plays," Charles said, "top to bottom, not side over side, which is how it's bound."

Leaning on his polished oak cane, often pushing his glasses up on his nose, Charles limped along the length of the second act (humming, but not a tune), and when he was finished he would limp back to the top and start over.

Cat Longet could not understand how the American Army had ever managed to judge this lunatic fit for participation in an actual shooting war, but then again, maybe Charles had fooled the Army; playwrights *could* fool you. As a group they had quirks of unmatchable strangeness, which they often hid from the general public—seeming reasonable at the first read-through; normal on talk shows—and revealed only in the final heat of production. Cat had known writers who said they possessed magic pencils and who could not make revisions if these particular pencils were misplaced. He had known writers who could not produce one single word of dialogue unless they were too drunk to stand. He had known writers who needed to be alone on frozen beaches to write and writers who needed to be in bed with whores snoring to write, and if Charles Borden III could not detect the lapses in the continuity of his second act except by arranging its pages vertically on planks stretching the entire length of The Shelter's third row, then so be it: Cat quarreled not with harmless eccentricities.

Cat had originally received *The Ice Cold Jungle* by courier. A very extravagant way for any writer to submit his stuff, he thought, maybe this

guy is really a famous Hollywood screenwriter slumming under a pseudonym. ("Charles Borden III" certainly *sounded* like a pseudonym.)

These notions proved false. Charles had fooled Cat with the courier. But
by the time Cat realized that, he had read and rather liked Charles' play.

From the play itself, Cat expected Charles to be a wan professor with
bright eyes and patches on his corduroy elbows who would have spent
several summers scratching out this story of a surviving soldier surrounded by the bodies of his buddies, talking himself through the long
scary 'Nam night. Cat figured the professor would have been a reporter in
the war, or a male nurse; the play's point of view was more political than
personal, and it read a little smart and cold.

"Cold is fine," Cat wrote to Charles before they met. "Cold is terrific if
it comes out *chilling* on stage; it's only bad if it comes out *cold* on stage.
However, even if The Shelter does a great job on *The Ice Cold Jungle,* I
fear the play will only appeal to intellectuals. I'm up for that if you are.
There's nothing wrong with a *succès d'estime* when you're first starting
out. Come see me when you're in town."

Charles arrived on the winter semester break and turned out to be not at
all what Cat had expected.

He was a few years younger than Cat, except he was much older. He
had shrunk from six feet because of the severe injury to his right leg
sustained during the war, in which he had been not a reporter or a nurse,
but a front line officer. Now Charles Borden III possessed broadened
shoulders, the compensatory strength of the lame; he had to stoop and reel
to get around, and he leaned heavily on his strong cane.

Recently, he had begun to wear bifocals. His blond hair was going gray
and had already turned white over the ears. When Charles worked, when
he was *thinking,* he twisted and pulled at his hair so that as a result it
always looked wild and windswept. This was the only sign of unrest in
Charles, otherwise a monumentally calm person. His nose was long and
sharp, his mouth thin, his eyes very light blue. (The Board member's wife
said he reminded her of a WASP ancestor print.) But it was hard to see
Charles Borden's eyes because he had extremely thick shaggy yellow and
gray eyebrows that hung on the upper rim of his glasses like untrimmed
ivy on a Boston wall.

In the winter, when Cat and he met over their first beer, Charles did not
want to sit and talk about the play; he preferred to walk and talk. He said
he tried to keep moving as much as possible, a matter of circulation, also
personal preference. He took pills for pain, as few as possible. "They hook

you," he said in his abrupt New England way. "When you're hooked, you stop being a survivor."

Charles had returned to New York for two weeks this summer to work with Cat on the script. He stayed at a studio on the Upper West Side, lent to him by a vacationing friend. He always wore work shirts of an indeterminate blue gray color and khaki pants and the same loose floppy boots he had worn in the snow (Cat guessed because these caused the least discomfort to his wounded foot) and a leather belt, tooled with flowers and bearing the word FATHER across the kidneys. Charles Borden IV, his son, had created the (Cat thought monstrous) belt once long ago at a summer camp, and it was frayed with wear and age.

Charles told Cat that his two children, now young adults, lived with his ex-wife in Newton, Massachusetts. He was sending the boy through college and would soon have the girl's tuition to pay as well. Earning only adequate money at his teaching job, he needed more. He had begun to sell articles regularly, mostly about gardening in the Northeast. When a more famous author died in the middle of a book about tomatoes, Charles finished up the work and even made the deadline and became a client of the famous author's agent.

"Don't mind fixing things," he said. "But I'd make more money if I could learn to fix things for Hollywood."

So he had determined to upgrade his skills as a dialogue writer, and invested many months in the creation of *The Ice Cold Jungle.* Not to get some deathless lesson off his heart, he told Cat (although Cat didn't quite believe it; too much pain in the play; too much hate), but to learn—just to learn—scriptwriting.

His ambition was to be "discovered" in the theater so he could write for television and the movies.

Well, maybe not *write.* Cynical, chained to his debts, Charles Borden III no longer imagined himself an originator. No, his ambition was to *rewrite* for the movies.

He taught Henry James and Tennessee Williams.

He greatly admired Abe Burrows.

Thank God, thought Cat. A writer who dreams of success, not greatness.

Clear in his ambitions, Charles used Cat Longet as his teacher. He rested his chin on his fist and listened patiently to Cat's critiques, never responding or arguing.

To Cat, this was the miracle of the forthcoming theater season.

He could not remember ever having an associate like Charles or an experience like this in show business. In all his years as a performer, in production after production, power relations had weighed him down, lead in his shoes, power over, power under, power sharing, power owing. Cat estimated that fully half of his creative energy had been diverted from the work itself to the various power struggles surrounding and hounding and binding it. But he and Charles worked on *The Ice Cold Jungle* like two mechanics on a car, never glancing up to see who was in charge. "He's perfect for this moment in your history," the Board member's wife concluded. "A civilian. A pragmatist. When you need courage, he'll keep you cold."

Cat puffed on his pipe. He watched Charles limp along the stretched out script. He watched lovely Sally crawl across the stage. He counted the raggedy lights clustered in the theater's corners, thinking that they looked like crows on telephone poles in an old Hitchcock horror film.

He could not at this moment recall what it was that had drawn him into the theater to begin with. Had he really done it just to break his father's heart? Had he really done it just to escape from that awful town? Was it just wanting to hear people laugh, to make people *laugh?*

Cat opened a bottle of wine. Yes, that was it, that was all of it—wanting to make people laugh. How he had loved to hear the crack of laughter, cathartic as a sneeze or an orgasm! How strong he felt when he knew he could make people exist their lives on a wave of pleasure, even for one single instant! These two totally shitty decades of his had been lived entirely for the high of hearing people laugh.

And the high had not been worth the price.

No, it had not been worth the price at all.

I'm gonna be able to do what I have to do, he thought. I am not hooked on the laughter anymore. I am not hooked. Like Charles Borden says, that makes me a survivor.

He glanced at his watch, concerned because Anna Karavajian was rather late. Since he hated to be nervous, to pace and sweat like lesser men before a performance, he amused himself by imagining one.

"I HAVE AN IDEA," CALLED CAT TO HIS NEW FRIEND THE UN-SENTI-mental playwright. "I say we sign up the entire membership of the Drama-tists' Guild, dress them in khaki, send them off to Central America, and give them two years in hell. Some of them may return and be like you, Charles. I say this is the only way to save the American theater."

"Tell me something. What have you got against writers?" Charles asked. "Did a writer rob you? Rape you? Jilt your mother?"

"A writer named me Catastrophe," Cat answered. "So people call me Cat, short for Catastrophe, and my true name—Elliot—is unsung."

"You want me to call you Elliot? Will that improve your outlook?"

"Yes. But not my reputation, I fear."

Trying to forget Anna's lateness, distracting himself from worry, Cat told Charles the whole story.

It had started in Houston. Cat was playing the mad son of a farming family in a contemporary play about American bounty. It was an excellent role, surreal and funny, suitable for Cat's flappable limbs. In one of the more exciting scenes. Cat had to bring several bushels of carrots on stage and then take them all off, which he did, except he missed one. This single carrot rolled under his feet and sent him tripping and plunging into the set, a plywood and muslin approximation of a John Deere tractor.

The set collapsed.

The cowboy audience gasped.

Cat climbed out from under the wreckage, bleeding slightly from surface wounds, and continued talking about American bounty. The audience was so moved by Cat's inventiveness and endurance that at the curtain call, they threw their hats at the stage, stomping their boots with appreciation. His fellow players bought him drinks.

The set designer challenged him to a duel.

Then there was the incident in Portland, Maine. While playing an irritated detective, Cat got so carried away that he yanked the telephone off the wall shortly before it was supposed to ring and produce an important piece of exposition. The fast-thinking stage manager decided it would not be more believable if the exposition arrived by telegram. Thus, he ordered the doorbell rung. Cat thought the doorbell was the telephone with a strange new ring. He answered the telephone despite the fact that it had been torn off the wall, causing the audience to laugh and ruining the stage manager's great save-the-show brainstorm.

The pissed-off stage manager gossiped about Cat in many bars.

In a stock production of *Measure for Measure* in Connecticut, Cat played Angelo lusting after Isabella and leaped on her so rapaciously that her nun's habit tore open, revealing one of her breasts. This would have served the play perfectly except that the house had been sold out to three summer camps full of preteens who hooted and whistled, causing the actress who was playing Isabella to tell them to fuck off, which did *not* serve the play.

She blamed Cat and said bad things about him throughout the United States and Canada.

The most ironic of Cat's catastrophes occurred in New York City, off-Broadway, during the run of an original play by a woman who had since become very famous.

Cat was playing a robot.

This robot had been conjured out of flame and wires to assist the good guys in defeating their enemies. In the end, the robot attacked the bad guys as programmed and then attacked the good guys too, the moral being that revenge is a wagon which invariably rolls out of control.

One day at rehearsal Cat asked if anyone else in the company was having trouble with the fact that this play clearly ripped off a certain Yiddish classic.

No one else was having trouble.

The playwright, however, heard about Cat's remark and tried to have him fired. "Any actor who cannot tell the difference between a derivation and a rip-off is not smart enough to be in my play!" she screeched at her husband the producer.

He told her Cat was terrific and protected by a union contract and who were they going to get to replace him when the opening was two weeks away and why didn't she just relax and prepare herself for fame and fortune?

As the week of final dress rehearsals progressed, Cat's plastic robot suit began to fray and frazzle. The costume designer patched him together with silver-gray electrician's tape. On opening night, with all the critics out front, Cat plunged a bit too athletically into the final fray. His robot suit split open and the right half of his body popped out.

Not missing a beat, nor forgetting one line, he pulled the gaping suit closed from the inside and held it closed with his right hand for the rest of the play, killing and maiming both bad guys and good guys entirely with his left hand.

The playwright met him backstage after it was over.

"You fuck!" she screeched. "You ruined my play!"

"Correction," Cat said. "Your incompetent costume designer ruined H. Leivick's play!"

"I'm gonna kill you!" declared the playwright.

Her husband, who had seen her like this before, dragged her away before she could make good her promise.

Sure of the play's failure, the company sat around at the producer's house drinking and waiting for the *Times* to announce that all their work, their talents and hopes and dreams, amounted to a small hill of shit.

The *Times* raved.

"This darkly comic cautionary tale is enhanced by a brilliant touch—the peeling, disintegrating quality of the vengeful robot himself, who barely conceals that he is a mere man underneath his towering armor."

The playwright fell into Cat's arms, covered him with kisses and apologies.

"You're wonderful!"she bellowed. "I shall never cease being grateful for your inventiveness and endurance . . ."

Shit, thought Cat, kissing her back, shit, I hate this broad, I hate myself, I hate the *Times,* I hate this fucking business.

Despite his happy ending, Cat now found himself in serious trouble.

The chain of technical disasters had tightened around his good name, making him a suspect casting choice in many regional theaters. "Don't start with Elliot Longet," they said in the green room in New Haven, "unless you plan not to build a set."

However, a kindly director in Minneapolis overrode all fears and objections and insisted that no other available actor would make such a funny Agamemnon. So Cat was cast and west he went to meet his last frontier.

"It was in the bottom half of the long neo-Scandinavian winter," he said, pouring himself and Charles a glass of wine at The Shelter years later. "The play? A modern *Oresteia.* The style? Semi-funny. The author? That very same loony dilettante who had written the ripped-off ripped-robot play. She had been so buoyed by the wonderful reviews her first effort received that now she actually *believed* she was a writer. And, of course, she believed in me."

"Tell me more about this modern *Oresteia,*" Charles suggested.

"Clytemnestra said 'Up yours' a lot."

"I know this play."

"Orestes and Aegisthus tried to push each other in front of the A-train."

"People do this play all the time."

"In the stage directions it said that Agamemnon has a sour sea-stomach and farts constantly."

"This play has become a *classic!*"

"Correction!" hollered Cat Longet. *"It already was a classic,* don't you see?! That is the point!"

Cat leaped with bottle and glass aloft onto the back of a seat in the fifth row center and balanced there for a moment, swilling wine, and then set off across the sharp collarbones of the seats like a tightrope walker, steady, cold and steady, beat perfect.

"Imagine if you will this scene," he declaimed. "Agamemnon, the long-absent king, returns to his court, entering with a retinue of helmeted henchmen and dragging on his weary shoulders a long, very long, train of chain mail. His henchmen are wearing sandals, with thongs, knee high, wrap around, slithery leather thongs, got that?

"Now Agamemnon wants to kiss Queen Clytemnestra who has come to greet him. But to his chagrin, he finds he cannot move. Because one of his helmeted henchmen is standing on his train.

"So what does Agamemnon do? He tugs. He tugs again. He tugs harder. The henchman is not heeding the tugs because he has his own problems. His leather thongs have slithered down and tangled under his feet. Agamemnon's final tug sends him tumbling. His helmet rolls down the raked stage. Yet another unthonged henchman is upended by the rolling helmet. He loses control of his spear. The spear flies like an ICBM into the audience. It pierces the bulky knit of a lady in the mezzanine.

"Screams. Horror. Pandemonium.

"So what does Agamemnon do?

"He unhitches his train, runs off stage around through the wings and up to the mezzanine, and grabs the speared lady. 'Rise up, young woman!' he commands, 'and show the citizens of Minneapolis that you have not been killed!'

"She rises, holding the harmless prop spear aloft, holding Agamemnon's hand for moral support, and she bows, and the audience bursts into cheers. Joy. Relief. A Swede stampede has been averted. The audience collapses in gales of happy laughter."

"Bet you received a standing ovation," Charles said.

"Many," Cat answered, prancing over the rows, drinking and bowing. "Many many standing ovations. The chief of police came backstage to shake my hand. He offered me a job in crowd control. The cast poured champagne on my head. The kindly director kissed me and hugged me and one reviewer said I was such a brilliant comedian that the author should *knight* me for turning her play into an hilarious romp when it had started out to be semi-funny."

Cat stood poised astride the tenth and eleventh rows, a nimble colossus with an empty bottle balanced on his head.

"The playwright was waiting for me at my hotel," he said. "She too held an empty bottle. Also a razor sharp fencing foil swiped from the costume dock, not a harmless prop this time. She said: 'I am here to knight you, like it says in the papers. I dub you Catastrophe, Lord of Technical Disasters, the risen anti-Muse, destroyer of lines and scenes and lifelong dreams. Prepare to die, you fuck!' And with her hissing foil, she slashed at me, cutting off the sleeve of my favorite suede jacket and attempting to cut off my arm as well."

Cat tossed the bottle: Charles caught it.

"But that woman is famous. She gets prizes and honorary degrees. She's not just rich," Charles marveled, "she's *respected!*"

Cat Longet tore open his shirt, bared his chest. A horrible scarlet scar curved from his armpit to his neck, bitten with the teeth marks of a hundred stitches. He leaped from the seat back to the floor and made a muscle so Charles could see the scars writhe.

"Prominent writers came to court to defend her," Cat said. "Eloquently oh beautifully did they explain the umbilical relationship between an artist and her work and they made the judge see that her attack against me was not really attempted murder, oh no, it was much more like a loving mother's effort to protect her ridiculed and rejected child.

"Her husband the producer of the robot play—by then, he was her ex-husband—came and said she was crazy. My friend the kindly director, who would have directed *Corruption in the Palace of Justice* for us except that he was recently murdered, you see, he came and said yes, she was, really crazy.

"But the day belonged to those who had a way with words. She got six months of therapy and was soon released on the recognizance of her psychiatrist. I received some money to cover the cost of saving my arm.

"Today her works are called classics, and I am buried in The Shelter, and the only name I have in the theater is the name she gave me that night in Minneapolis: Cat, short for Catastrophe, Lord of Technical Disasters, the risen anti-Muse."

Out beyond the lobby there came a fierce rattling noise. "Sally!" someone was calling. "Elliot, Sally, are you in there?! Open up, for God's sake, it's scary out here! I've been lost in this damn park for an hour! Open up!"

"Wipe the spit out of your beard," Charles Borden III said softly. "Someone is at the door."

"Ah yes." Cat laughed. "Our printer. She is not in this fucking business. So she calls me Elliot."

To Anna, hot, exhausted, washed with fear, Sally Bangle's set for Anton Chekhov's sad play *The Seagull* looked like a magic garden. She loved it. Immediately she suspended all disbelief and accepted that in the mossy misty peacefulness of this clearing by a small forest, a chattering family might gather to watch the little theatrical productions of their troubled son, the one with the literary pretensions.

In the countryside evoked by Sally, no one could hear the pounding of revolutionary discontent in the hearts of the proletariat. A woodland garden, half wild, surrounded the lacquered cane table and chairs, and the table was set with a gold-embroidered maroon cloth and delicate china cups dotted by rosebuds. The comfortable chairs flowed with flowered shawls, their fringes sprawling. The little spoons were gold not silver. Each chair was anchored in spongy hills of soft moss, and brown-leaf begonias winked among the rocks. On an occasional table tilted under a low branch a balalaika leaned, so well tuned that any little breeze made it hum.

Some of the birch trees framed the garden and the troubled son's little makeshift stage. Hundreds of other birches slanted off in the distance, their branches a white tangle crisscrossing large clouds on the far horizon. Since the sun was just about to set on this garden, glints of bright orange light tipped in from the west, on each begonia leaf, on each faceted rock, even on the samovar, a great round brass masterpiece with ivory handled spigots. In the birch branches lanterns hung, tin Mohammedan lanterns with slanty eyes of golden glass, and inside each lantern an orange flame seemed ready to twinkle.

Anna moved slowly, magnetized, down the center aisle. It excited her to know that the closer she came to the set, the less fully she would feel the magic of the garden, the more clearly she would see its underpinning of technology and craft.

Sally crawled out from under the table. Oblivious to Charles and Cat, she had been painting orange streaks on the inside of the table legs and also, with an especially thin brush, orange glints on the westward facing fringes of the tablecloth. She was tired, glad to see Anna at last, and reached off the stage to take her hand and say hello.

Only a few minutes before, Anna would have sworn she had no more strength for anything today. But the mysteries of the set—which birches stood braced on the stage, which hung painted on drapes of invisible scrim; how the moss was really plastered nylon netting spattered with a million dots of gold and blue and many shades of green, how the glossy eyes of the lanterns were really slivers of amber gel—all these simple mysteries beckoned to her from the garden. When Sally invited her to see how it was done, she could not resist. She hitched her skirt to her hips and spiked herself up onto the stage, running her stocking, losing one shoe, recapturing her mist-damp hair with a hanging barrette, and this was how Charles Borden III first saw her.

Elliot was asking Charles what he thought of the poster.

Charles was peering from under his shaggy eyebrows at Anna Karavajian's behind, her neat blue skirt, her fancy lacy white slip and the strong anterior of her goldish legs.

"So what do you think, Charles?" Elliot was saying. "Too plain? Too straightforward?"

"Tend to prefer that," Charles said.

Elliot took one beat.

"Anna!" he yelled. "Come down, I want you to meet somebody!"

Charles Borden spit on his hands and smoothed his eyebrows. He gathered up his script. He checked his wallet to see if he had enough money for dinner. He took one pill. He knew Anna had noticed him, because when she came off the stage, she took care not to let her skirt ride up again.

"This is Charles Borden," Elliot was saying, "author of the third play in our season, which will now have an audience thanks to the wonderful job you did on this splendid poster."

Elliot then crossed up of Anna, squeezing her shoulders *en passant,* and exited stage right, so quickly and expertly that she felt downright manipulated and quite annoyed. Just because she liked being in Elliot's theater didn't mean she wanted to be in Elliot's show!

She looked through Charles' glasses into his ice blue eyes. She shook his hand, aware of the calluses on his palm. His hand was cool.

"It's nice to have a happy customer," she said.

"Hard to believe that *all* of your customers are not happy," Charles said. Immediately Anna found him less attractive. He was much too glib. "We were thinking of going out for dinner," he continued. "Will you join us?"

Anna had seen him take the pill. She had noticed the limp and the cane. She had noticed his strong shoulders and his teeth. But she was too tired, really, much too exhausted, much too dirty and grimy and sweaty with the various emotions of her workday to go out and have dinner now.

"Sure," she said.

Something began thudding up near the stage, a weight dropping rhythmically. Maybe it was Sally hammering. No, Sally was sitting at the edge of the garden, admiring the poster. Maybe it was Elliot. No, Elliot was stacking up the planks which lay across the third row.

The thudding sound grew louder.

"What is that?" Anna asked.

"That is the pounding of my heart," Charles Borden answered.

The thudding noise escalated into a dull booming, each boom stronger than the last. Sally stood up and looked around, bewildered. The package of proofs on the stage at her feet began to bounce; a teacup fell off the table and shattered. The little red wagon, anchored behind a rock, began to roll. Elliot vaulted over the seats and caught it just as it tipped off the stage, and jars of green and gold, blue and orange paint and paste flipped their contents onto his shirt and pants and beard.

Anna looked around wildly, thinking gas explosion, water main break, earthquake, impossible, there are no earthquakes in Flushing.

Charles was watching the back of the stage. His eyes had disappeared. "Up there," he whispered. "Behind the clouds. Behind the stage." His hand closed instinctively on Anna's upper arm.

The birch trees swayed. Boom. Boom. The fresnels clustered like crows on the light poles rattled; the mighty poles themselves began to sway. Boom. Boom. It rained plaster.

Sally Bangle leaped screaming off the stage as the braced plywood birches slowly toppled and the table collapsed and crashed and the heavy curtain on the upstage wall began to tear, thunder and dust billowing over the clouds, boom, *BOOM,* the fat samovar rolled bumping down the stage, careened off the rocks, bump, bump, bumpty bump, like a baby carriage Anna had once seen in a film about the revolution.

"Run," Charles Borden whispered.

Before she could think, Anna was running with Sally up the center aisle. A huge battering ram broke through the back wall of the theater, tearing the horizon to shreds. Elliot Longet stared at the gaping hole that followed, the battering ram enlarging it, boom, boom, smashing cinder blocks and the moorings of the stage so that the stage itself began to slide toward him, threatening to plow him under the seats.

Elliot ran as from a lava flow. Charles was limping toward the wings. Elliot raced to help him.

"No, stay back!" Charles yelled.

The stage left light pole crashed diagonally across The Shelter, falling between the two men, and the glass of its lights flew like shrapnel. Almost all the way up the aisle, one piece caught Sally in the ankle. She squealed with pain and fell crying into Anna's arms. Through the great hole in the upstage wall came four robbers wearing the grim masks of Darth Vader's helmeted henchmen.

One of them yelled, "Hold it! Everybody! Hold it right there!"

He had what appeared to be a terrorist gun, familiar as television. Trapped behind the light pole wreckage, Charles quietly grasped his cane.

The head robber pointed the gun at him. "Let go that thing," he said. Charles obeyed.

The robber ducked under the light pole, grabbed Charles' cane, and flung it across the theater. He took Charles' wallet and his watch.

Another robber leaped gracefully off the stage and bounded over to Elliot, and with a length of wire tied his hands behind his back. He got Elliot's watch and his gold chain. The two other robbers ran up the center aisle and shoved Sally and Anna into seats. Sally was sobbing. Anna wriggled out of her slip and tied it around Sally's bleeding leg.

One of the men guarding them took all the money the two women had. Another pulled Anna's silver earrings from her ears. Sally had too many earrings to even bother with.

"Those were my grandmother's . . ." Anna pleaded. "What can they be worth to you?"

"Don't negotiate!" yelled Charles. "Give them what they want. This guy has a real gun."

"You shut up!" the head robber shouted. He hit Charles once. The bifocals flew away. The robber stepped on them and put the gun to Charles' ear and held it there.

The robber who had tied up Elliot shoved him roughly through the tangled mass of wires and lights that traversed the aisle toward the front of the theater, toward the lobby and the box office. With Charles hostage under the gun, the two robbers guarding Sally and Anna now felt safe enough to leave them. They hauled ladders from the wings and began climbing over the ceiling and walls of the theater, unplugging the surviving lights, unplugging the sound equipment, systematically handing each item out through the hole where the disembodied arms of waiting accomplices received them. In a few minutes the robber who had taken Elliot loped down the center aisle with The Shelter's cash box and ran out the hole. The light and sound robbers took one last look around and followed him. The robber with the gun backed away from Charles, holding him in the sights of the weapon until the very last second, and then he turned and scooped up the brass samovar and disappeared through the hole.

Charles and Sally and Anna heard the robbers' truck pull away. The cold night wind whined through the theater, flapping the torn muslin branches and the shredded moss, making the unhurt balalaika hum. It was the only piece of Sally Bangle's set left in its place on stage.

In his box office, they found Cat Longet. He was sitting on the floor among thousands of scattered ticket stubs, among the wrenched pages of torn apart contracts and torn apart scripts, in a glossy mess of hundreds of actors' head shots piled up, trod upon, cast willy-nilly like old smiles in a mass grave.

Cat was covered with a mask of varicolored paint and plaster. The only remnants of his real face were the twin avenues cleared by his tears.

He was laughing.

"They got seven hundred and fifty-six dollars and eighty cents," he said.

THE COPS TOOK SALLY TO A HOSPITAL WHERE A SMALL SLIVER OF glass was removed from her leg and some friend of hers named Rex came to fetch her home.

Anna, Charles, and Elliot were held at the police station for a while. They huddled together. They tried not to be caught in the hullabaloo of picked-up whores and mugged dog walkers and exhausted lawyers jabbering on behalf of unrepentant clients, they tried to feel that *their* crime was special and unique.

"So who are you again?" asked a clerk-policeman who was losing track in the crowd.

"Longet," said Elliot. "Cat Longet."

"Oh, you're the guy whose theater was robbed with a truck-mounted battering ram, oh yeah, I remember . . ." and off walked the policeman with his checklist on his clipboard, satisfied.

After a time, a detective came and took them into his small office and questioned them with a tape running.

"My grandmother's earrings are silver," Anna said. "They have little blue stones . . ."

"They wrecked our set," Elliot said.

"From the Old Country . . ."

"They stole our lights, destroyed our stage, how shall we have a season now, I ask you, how?"

". . . so precious to me." Anna wept.

"What were they wearing?" asked the weary detective.

"Black shirts, all of them," Elliot said, "and Star Wars masks, soldiers of the Empire, Darth Vader's outfit . . ."

"Yes, right, how about in addition to that, Mr. Longet? What were they wearing in addition to that?"

Elliot thought for a moment.

"I was so scared, I guess I didn't notice, didn't notice . . . and I'm usually very good about details . . ."

"They wore brown work gloves and sneakers," Charles Borden said. He was twisting in the hard slat back chair, trying to place his weight on his good hip, and reaching with his bad heel for a resting spot on a shelf of the detective's bookcase. Where the robber had hit him, near his eye, he now had a large swollen purple bruise. Without his glasses to support them, his eyebrows collapsed, like shutters drawn, and he looked like he was summoning his facts medium-style from the deeps of a trance. "No, sorry. They wore cleats. Cleats, yes. Of course . . . They were already familiar with the theater. Must have been. They knew where the extension ladders were, they knew to bring along C-clamps to loosen the lights. The graceful one . . ."

"Which one was that?" asked the detective.

"The one guarding Elliot. Tied his hands with electrical wire. Reminded me of a dancer, didn't even bounce when he jumped off the stage, didn't even breathe hard when he ran . . ."

Anna stared at Charles with awe and admiration.

In the same robbery under the same gun, she had been blinded and he informed.

Elliot gave in to grief.

"He's right," he moaned. "He's right he's right he's right, my God, they must have been professionals . . ."

"The one guarding Elliot wore newish jeans, not faded, tight, and ironed, with a crease, never saw anybody iron his jeans who wasn't in show business, and he also wore pale blue athletic socks."

"Do you *know* how many actors I have not cast?!" groaned Elliot.

"The one guarding me wore baggy brown corduroys."

"Can you even *imagine* how many light men I have fired?"

"He wasn't as tall as the one guarding Elliot," Charles said.

"If I tried to make you a list of those who might conceivably feel vengeful toward Cat Longet or his Board of Directors or the three other directors we would have had working for us this season, why it would reach from here to Malibu and back a dozen times . . ."

"Would you please be quiet for a minute, Mr. Longet," said the detective.

The tape recorded a thoughtful silence.

"More?" asked the detective.

"I think the two men guarding me and Sally were frightened," Anna said. "Maybe it was their first time . . ."

"Why do you think that?"

"Just a feeling. They reminded me of the kids in my math classes the day before the night when their parents were coming in for teacher conferences. Very scared, springy in the way they walked, and breathing through their mouths a lot."

The detective smiled and shook his head. He did not take the woman seriously. Despite her background as a schoolteacher in the Bronx, she seemed a stranger to trouble, and her intuitions about the robbers struck him as warped by motherly inexactitude. The crazy painted guy who ran the theater was clearly hysterical and to the detective incomprehensible. But the veteran with the John L. Lewis eyebrows and the steady nerves, he was the best witness to pass through the precinct all week.

"You know what I thought at first?" Elliot remarked. "At first I must say I actually thought it was the revolution come to root out Chekhov's silly liberals in their garden . . ."

"What's he talking about?" the detective asked Charles.

A policewoman stuck her head in the door and said some people had come for Mr. Longet. It was the Board member and his wife.

"Sally got hurt, that was the most frightening thing," Cat told them on the way home, "and Anna's earrings apparently meant a great deal to her. But the star of the evening was Charles; he immediately realized it was an inside job and he remembered everything. I tell you, they'd better burn all their clothes, that gang of thieves, or the police will know them by the pressing of their pants and the blue of their socks." He relaxed and grinned in the big car. "When Charles Borden III got through, the list of suspects included every disgruntled actor and technician who ever crossed the wide and rambling paths of Cat Longet."

ANNA DROVE CHARLES TO THE UPPER WEST SIDE APARTMENT WHERE he was staying. She led the coral dawn into New York. The first glints of light reached through the back window of her truck and turned the rearview mirror pink and intermittently blind. Anna did not much notice the dawn; to her, it was just an optical annoyance. But to Charles it brought a particular clarity of vision and a synoptic understanding of events, just as it did to the surviving soldier in his play. At dawn Charles Borden knew the answers. It was his best time.

"Why shouldn't they steal?" he asked, sitting next to Anna in the passenger seat of her truck. "Stealing is a way of life in this country. Public officials do it routinely. Nobody is even surprised. The people realize that the big corporations are stealing from them. So they steal from the big corporations every chance they get. They grab lumber from construction sites. They pretend their kids are young enough to get into the movies for half price. Think of it, think of how much stealing you have seen, just you, say, in the past year . . . think of it . . ."

Anna did not want to think of it and wished Charles would find another subject to discuss.

His voice pleased her, though, soothed her, and sent out a familiar signal. She heard this pounding, pounding down between her legs, resounding on the inner walls of her body, and she laughed and shook her head, thinking, Jesus Christ, here we go again, Mary's right, you think it's all over, thirty-seven years old, middle age is on its way, dwindling estrogen, dry skin, but it isn't over, it's stronger than ever, and the mere sound, the pitch and cadence of some voice with the right signal and boom boom, she was ready to burst open like the back wall of The Shelter.

Unobstructed by even one single other vehicle, she lowered her truck onto the access road at the Midtown Tunnel to Manhattan.

How strong, she wondered, is the belt called FATHER?

"In the English Department where I work," Charles continued, "there's a supply cabinet. Full of paper. Pencils. Printer ribbons. Enough to run the whole department for a month. But at the end of every week, it's all gone. Pilferage, the dean calls it. Nobody turns anybody in because everybody does it."

Anna laughed.

"Oh please, everybody does *not* do it," she said. "Some do, some don't. I mean I think it's just a matter of self-control." Keeping her hands tightly locked around the steering wheel, turning her knuckles pale, doing fifty even sixty in the dark tunnel.

Charles shifted beside her. He was trying to straighten his leg, holding his thigh with both hands to get it placed right and exhaling from his throat a dim rumble of pain.

Anna realized with horror that the passenger seat must be adjusted forward as far as it could go, for both Nubar and Lewis were little men. Beset with guilty feelings, she reached over and released Charles' seat. It slid back suddenly on grinding gears. She could not see him very well in the tunnel but she knew, she could *feel* from the way his body relaxed, that he must be more comfortable now.

He turned to look at her. His hand on the dashboard was very hard, the nails short but not bitten and not polished; no rings. The meadow of pale hair on his forearm caught her eye.

Emerging into the light, she felt ashamed of her Draculette Red fingernails. Charles stared at her and she began to lose control. She had been thinking about inviting him back to her loft, but that was in the dark, in the tunnel, and now that he had the sun mounted on his shoulder like a rocket launcher, and he could stare at her and she couldn't look at him because she had to look at the road, she was afraid he would see her too clearly and find her not desirable. And the minute she had that thought, she grew nervous and felt compelled to say something.

"Until my father got sick," she said, "he ran our business for thirty years and he never stole from anyone ever."

"You must have a very small business," Charles responded.

Anna hit the brakes and turned away from the road, glaring at him fiercely and ready to be very angry.

He was laughing.

She remembered how he looked after the robber hit him, like a white wall, blank and flat, no eyes, no teeth, no lips. Now that he was laughing and he wore no glasses, his nice teeth stuck out and all the many wrinkles around his eyes sparkled and crinkled like spiky blades of grass.

"Elliot says your play is good," she said, "a play about the war."

"Took me fifteen years to recover from it, write a play about it, and find a theater willing to put it on. So the theater has this night been robbed of all its equipment." Charles laughed, but then again his laugh was very limited, more like a clearing of the throat than a release of the emotions. "My luck," he said. "No one will ever make a dime on my play."

"Is that important to an artist?"

"What?"

"The money? I mean is the money important to an artist?"

"You think I'm an artist?"

"Aren't you?"

"You think artists should be better than other people?"

"Yes, I guess I did . . . I do . . . uh . . ."

With the back of one finger Charles touched her cheek.

"Well, you are in luck," he said quietly. "Artists *are* better than other people. Writers are better than other men. They're more generous. More sensitive. They require less food. Less football on Sunday afternoons. They are much better lovers, writers are, much better . . ."

She unloosened the last of her hair, letting the breeze from her window blow it toward him like a banner. He caught one wild curl, then let go.

"I meet writers sometimes," he said, "gee, they make so much money. They come to school to lecture us, advertising writers, television writers. I sit up there in Vermont with the stupid kids who buy their papers and cheat on their exams, and I dream, like a little kid, I dream of writing a prime-time smash hit television series, don't care how bad it is, don't care what a disgrace, don't care if history never remembers one illiterate line . . . that is what my dreams are made on, Anna. Now does that sound like the dream of an artist?"

"Well, people love television," she said. "I mean they really like television much better than reading anyway these days. Myself I don't watch television. It's not that I don't like it, I mean every time I watch it, I like it, but then I neglect to watch it again for long periods of time . . ."

He said nothing. He was leaning back staring at her very intently, as though he were about to shoot her out of the sky.

She sped across town to the West Side and headed north and she knew she was in control again, she could smell the heat of his breath in the truck. She parked across from the building where he was staying.

"Will you come back to New York?" she asked.

"Yes."

"Could we see each other then?"

"If there is not another man."

Charles reached down and plucked the wilted flower from the floor of the truck.

"Oh, that was a gift from a grateful employee," Anna said.

"Grateful for what?"

"For his job!" She stared at him, amazed at his cynicism. "Are you crazy? Why would I want to see you if I had another man?"

Charles squinted at her, amazed at her naïveté. "Is that a serious question?"

"Oh go on," Anna said, totally disgusted. "Go on, go . . ."

She reached across him and opened the door. He kissed her. He wrapped her hair around his hands and kissed her once more.

The game of who was and was not in control ended for Anna. She did not care that the Upper West Side was awakening around her and might be offended by the erotic shuddering of her truck. All she could think of was how much she desired Charles Borden.

Luckily Charles had the wit to lock the doors and to haul himself and Anna over the gears between the two front seats and into the windowless rear of the truck. He pulled her down onto him. She buried her face against his shoulder blade. He gripped her tightly. She came before he did.

Drenched and weeping, thinking, "What have I become?! *Who* have I become?!" she drove away quickly, while Charles Borden limped and listed

into the building where he was staying, hoping not to meet anyone who
would see that he was having to hold his pants up because the extraordinary Anna Karavajian had broken their zipper and snapped in two the belt
called FATHER.

SHAME SEIZED HER. SHE THREW THE FLOWER DX HAD GIVEN HER
into the street, where it would be run over. The hot morning breeze
threaded itself through the empty holes in her ears.

She dropped the truck at the plant. Nubar and Lewis were just coming
to work. They said good morning. She backed away, terrified that they
might get close enough to smell her—because she was sure she stank like a
junkie whore—and went home and poured herself two glasses of vodka.
She threw her clothes at the air conditioner. Then, sleeping, she met up
with her fear.

She dreamed of the purple welt rising, the scarlet stain spreading, the
bright paints dripping. In her dream she tried to stop the multicolored
tides of fear from rushing out of her body by plugging herself on the barrel
of the black gun. Maybe it went off; anyway the fear poured out of her and
she woke up all wet, drenched, drenched again just from dreaming, and
even more ashamed than she had been before she went to sleep.

In the shower, she got angry. She prayed that some eccentric prop like
the samovar would give the robbers away and they would all be caught
and locked in leg irons. If justice could not be done, she wanted vengeance,
she wanted her earrings back and her great-grandfather's dairy farm and
the Bite, Charper, and Pollaner account and a bomb to blow the bastards
all to hell.

Recalling what her father had said about terrorism (". . . we also, even
we with everything we know . . ."), she segued into self-hatred.

It made her sick that she was a sympathizer with violent acts, that she
could rouse strong men from their summer afternoons and make them
tremble, that probably even already today she was reputed to be the terror
of the printing trades, oh she could not bear the idea that she was capable
of tearing the pants off a guy she hardly knew.

In the mirror, she saw bruises on her behind where Charles Borden had
urgently held her only hours before. Her knees were scraped from rubbing
on the hard floor of the truck. These small injuries came as a surprise to
Anna. She had not felt them happening.

She tried to eat an apple and considered going to work.

But then she threw up in her bathroom.

She called in sick.

Francine phoned Lucia, saying, "Something is not right with Anna." Lucia phoned Mary. Mary took the day off from work and came roaring into New York in her ramshackle, muffler-less station wagon. Lucia was waiting for her on Broadway, in front of ASCAP. Wearing an ecru linen cape.

They found their sister Anna in her bathrobe, barefoot, pacing up and down the pale, paneled loft. She wore sunglasses. She cracked her knuckles. She was thin as a twig.

"They had guns," she said. "Real guns."

Mary sat on the bed, holding Anna's hand.

Lucia took off her cape. She took off her matching ecru linen dress, hanging it carefully in the front hall closet. She took off her shiny tan alligator pumps. She removed her earrings and her gold watch and several gold chains and tucked them into her tan alligator pocketbook. Stripped now to her bra and slip, she filled a bucket with hot soapy water and got down on her hands and knees to scrub the floor, and then she mopped the paneling and then she vacuumed the straw rug and wiped clean the glass topped steel belted radial table.

She unhooked the hammock and put it down to soak in the kitchen sink. She cleaned the kitchen. She cleaned the bathroom with disinfectant. She collapsed in the gray metal chair and snagged her stockings.

"Why is it you have nothing in this entire loft which does not cut and scratch?" she called to Anna.

Anna was crying. Her final reaction, much delayed.

"They took my earrings," she said to Mary. "Our grandmother's earrings."

"Speaking of our grandmother, they could have raped you and killed you, ever think of that?"

"Why did this have to happen to me?!"

"Will you stop! It was a robbery! It didn't happen to you, you happened to be there and you came through unscathed, lucky you. There's a certain selfishness in the way you see things, did you ever notice that?" Mary asked. "Either it's got to be *because* of you or it's got to be *aimed* at you!"

Anna sniffed. Her nose had turned purplish. Her hair splattered the pillows like an oil spill.

"You're right," she said. "It's good that you came. You always make me see things more clearly. I wish I could do something for you. I mean I know what a bad time you've been having, how lonely and frightened you must be trying to help Spike get well and being both parents to Little John . . . Do you need extra money?"

Mary laughed and hugged her. "Ah *seerelee kuyreegus,*" she said, "what a good kid you are!" She kissed Anna and brushed her hair back from her face. "Sure I need money. I always do. Sad to say. I guess I always will."

Lucia came and sat down on the bed.

"Didn't you realize that you have forks and knives under the living room sofa?" she asked. "I mean didn't you miss them?"

Anna held their hands.

Like pillars on either side, they supported her.

She thought that they were the strong ones and she was the weak sister.

"You never notice anything," Charles Borden would say to her. "Not about yourself. Not about the people around you. Beats me how you managed to drive a car all these years without running over anybody."

She would laugh.

He would stroke her shoulders.

"You're a dangerous woman," he would say.

Chapter 5

CHARLES FIGURED SHE HAD USED HIM, THAT SHE WAS A TOUGH NEW York businesswoman who had most likely made it with a hundred other guys in the back of her truck. So he didn't call her.

But he couldn't forget her.

The tomatoes in his Vermont garden had ripened while he was gone. Their smooth flesh felt like her flesh in his hands. Bending to pick the long yellow beans, he was brushed by a cloud of dill and reminded of her hair.

He went to visit his mother in New Bedford. His tall son, Charles IV, joined them. They sat on the porch at dusk, three blond people drinking gin, content to say almost nothing. In that quiet, he almost forgot her. Then they went to dinner at the home of neighbors and while the able-bodied men played football, Charles tended the barbecue; and the sight of the soft ash burning in the black bowl made him shudder and chuckle and mull his unabating desire.

Well, so, he would not be able to forget her just yet.

His son went to the movies with some friends. His mother fell asleep in front of the late news, her needlework cascading off her lap. He called New York information and got Anna's number.

Then he figured if she was at home, she would not be alone. So he did not call her.

With Charles IV, he sailed to a lonesome place where he could swim and not be seen. The clean salted water of his youth and home cleared his brain. Of course he was not one of hundreds, an everyday event; impossible; impossible that she could fake that freshness of passion. Hadn't she demonstrated her innocence over and over? In the dark she had sensed his pain and released the seat to let his leg stretch. In the theater she had bound up the wound of her friend. With the enthusiasm of a little kid, she had leaped up on the stage to see the set. No, she was a considerate woman and, like this ocean, buoyant and deep. Not to be forgotten.

He went to New York one more time before the start of school, to see his agent and pick up some new work. He dined with Elliot and asked about her.

"My few meetings with Anna Karavajian have centered on bungled deadlines and burgled stage lights," Elliot said. "Thus I hardly know her. My overall impression, however, is that she is quite dull."

Charles smiled.

He called Anna at her home. Her machine told him to leave his message at her office. He called her at her office. A woman who sounded like a terrorist said she had taken a vacation, far away, beyond seas.

Probably with some broker, he thought. My luck.

Back in Vermont, he wrote an article for a homes-and-gardens magazine about the underground war between the worms and the onions. And while he was sitting at the typewriter—one last try before he really did forget her —he wrote her a letter.

"Listen," he wrote. "It didn't mean nothing to me. I'd like to see you again. Call me if you're interested."

This without salutation or farewell he scribbled on a piece of yellow legal-sized paper and forcefully, with characteristic determination, turned his mind to the new school term.

ANNA RETURNED FROM THE CARIBBEAN RESTED AND VERY DARK AND incidentally very rich, for she had enjoyed a run of luck at the gaming tables. Flanked by wildly excited men who kissed her hands every time she picked up the dice, who cried, "Numbers! Numbers!" as she tossed them willy-nilly across the long chipstrewn green field, she captured the night and the hearts of her fellow vacationers. She was welcome at everyone's table thereafter; in the bar, everyone wanted to buy her a drink.

Yet she found no new lovers.

Various things she did combined to discourage all comers.

First, she was unvaryingly friendly, said hello at breakfast, offered people lifts to town in the car she had rented. Especially friendly to no one. Unvaryingly friendly.

Secondly, she showed great interest in children. She could always be asked to keep an eye on them while their mother went to answer the phone or buy Cokes. She was observed to spend one entire day at the beach building sand castles with them.

Thirdly, she was willing to talk at length to married women.

But worst of all, she swam too well. She swam slowly in ten or twenty rippleless laps at a stretch, and after she was through swimming well, she slept soundly in the sun, for hours, her blackened hands dangling off the chaise.

Clearly, she was tired beyond waking. The one time she appeared in the casino and won all the money, she resisted several offers to go dancing afterward, she could not be induced to drink to excess.

Not until the night before she left did she spend any time alone in the company of any man. They got into a bitter political argument about Central America. Anna had never done this before in her life. The man knew more than she did about his subject and reduced her to knee-jerkishness, making her feel stupid and inept. Now that he had put her in her place, he felt that she would respect his superiority and gladly sleep with him. This proved an awkward misjudgment. She left him alone on the starlit balcony and let some other woman sleep with him.

In New York, she found good news and bad news.

Spike had taken a job with a landscape company, sweaty work, often very hard, but steady. Mary still called him several times a day, just to check, but he seemed less depressed and she somewhat less pressured as a result. Anna's senior driver Nubar had been taken to the hospital in the middle of the workday, complaining of chest pains, scaring the shit out of everybody. He would be okay but he would never be the same. Sighing over the passage of good times, she agreed that Aram should hire an additional driver.

The Parks Department, pleased with its urban roof garden brochure, had placed several new orders, equally (in the opinion of Francine) wasteful of the taxpayers' money. No accidents had occurred at the plant; no blood; no major breakdowns. All in all, Anna felt that Aram Hovad had done an excellent job of running Karavajian Press in her absence. Surely this was good news—but Anna reacted without joy, stung by the knowledge of her own replaceability.

Her mail told her that the Bite, Charper, and Pollaner account had returned to Karavajian; not so Manhattan Tech and the Union of Soviet Emigres. As for Bernice and Sarah, they were dissolving their partnership, because Sarah was getting married to a wealthy widower from Armonk and wanted to be a nonworking wife.

Only one letter in the tall stack was marked "Personal" and had not been opened by Francine.

Anna read it again and again. She put it aside and did two days' work. When she had grown accustomed to being called Boss again and was not feeling quite so expendable anymore, she read it again. And in the golden days of autumn, she called Charles Borden.

She left a message for him at the English Department.

It came to him on a little pink slip.

When he saw her name, he rubbed his eyebrows fiercely, astonished at his good fortune.

He brushed his teeth before he called her back.

THE SMALL STONE HOUSE WHICH CHARLES BORDEN RENTED IN VINtage, Vermont, had lasted for about one hundred years. When Anna arrived there, on a Thursday night for a three-day weekend in late September, it was falling apart. The wide plank flooring sagged and billowed perceptibly, and the rugged roof beams had been so weakened by the gnawing of carpenter ants that the tenant before Charles had been forced to augment them with steel beams nowhere near as picturesque. All the door frames had warped, so all the doors had been shaved to fit, giving the interior a bent and buckled look which matched Charles himself. When Anna hung up her clothes, they slid down the cockeyed closet pole and bunched up in the corner.

A Cambodian screen partitioned the one large room into a sleeping half (two wood slat beds made up neatly with navy wool blankets) and a working half (metal office desk; orthopedic support chair; gray sofa topped oddly with a May-colored afghan Charles said his mother had made for him; and one thousand books).

With the help of two of his Modern Drama students, Charles had built extensive brick-and-board bookcases, anchored into the stone walls by metal mountain climbing spikes. Anna took note that they were arranged alphabetically by author. She could find only four which she herself had read, and those only in courses taken long ago.

Heat came from a large black pot-bellied stove. Music came from a ghetto blaster, a gift from his colleagues on his fortieth birthday. Charles also owned an IBM office electric typewriter, but he said he tended to work these days on the word processor available to him at the college. At the foot of his bed, he kept the television. Virtually the entire roof of the house was disfigured by its huge aerial. In a dark corner, he kept the weights he worked out with and a wheelchair, folded.

Charles said that the tiny refrigerator and two burner electric stove in the kitchen served him fine, for he liked his potatoes boiled, his fish fried, and his cereal cold, and he never gave parties.

"Best not to trouble this old place with too much company," he said.

He had converted the old root cellar into his storage closet. Here he kept his many manuscripts, his tax records, his vacuum cleaner and mop. Soon, he said, there would be sacks of wintering vegetables from the garden and canned goods to tide him over the days of impassable snow.

Anna had been with Charles for an hour. He had not stopped telling her about the house during that time. Finally she turned to him with bright eyes and kissed him, and he led her to one of the thin beds and they made love. "Now," she said, "tell me about your house."

Charles' house had a beautiful heavy oak door with a red stained glass window in it and a big iron knocker he had installed, a seafaring rope ring from the foundry in New Bedford, originally used for mooring fishing boats. Deep-set flagstones led down from the house to a stone footbridge. In wintertime the stream was frozen solid. In the spring, it would gush with waters from the mountains that rose beyond the broad grass meadows abutting Charles' back yard.

In the morning, he showed Anna how he edged this yard with dwarf fruit trees and, outside their shadows, planted his garden. The garden had begun quite literally as a source of food. For fifteen dollars, he said proudly, he could plant enough vegetables to feed himself and any visitors who might come all summer and for another fifteen he could maintain the trees and make them bear bounteously. He stewed the peaches and froze them; his tomato sauce warmed the cheap pasta throughout the long winter.

In the last several years, he had further augmented the profits from the garden plot by writing short pieces about such homey events as the best angle at which to stake Big Boy tomatoes and the least disgusting way to massacre slugs. When greater whimsy was wanted by a certain magazine, he wrote a pretty piece about the benefits of weeding within earshot of soft music. He recommended Debussy and Anne Murray. "Makes the roots limp," he wrote.

Anna asked Charles if he ever grew flowers.

He said no.

Few of his colleagues in Vintage knew that he moonlighted as a horticulturist, for he did not discuss his articles nor did he show off his neat, weedless plot. He tied his T-shirt around his head in the heat and hoed alone, feeling that his children's lives were planted here, and that the sweat which dripped on the bean patch was quite simply owed to them.

Charles Borden gardened for precisely the same reason that he wrote about gardening: to pay his debts.

He tried to keep that attitude in the theater as well, to the joy of Cat Longet. "But it's hard," he admitted to Anna as he handed the crisp apples down to her in the small orchard. "Hard to stay cool in the theater." Hard not to care, not to feel fucked over by fate once more that The Shelter had been gutted and robbed. Much as he disliked to admit it, Charles had been looking forward to the production of his play. Its sudden loss left an ache, he said, "like when I was a little kid."

Twenty cottages just like Charles' faced each other on the south end of the main street in Vintage. Most of them were covered top to bottom, all sides, with ivy. (With the permission of the landlord, Charles had torn his ivy off, saying it raised the roof and barred the windows.) The cottages stood apart from the commercial center of town, shabby relics of days when the great textile mill still worked. The mill owner had built them for his employees and then charged for rent and coal. When his daughter closed the mill, she left the houses to those living there at the time, small recompense, she felt, for generations of brown lung and penury. Charles sometimes spent the better part of a winter evening trying to figure out how a dwelling which could now barely contain one single man had once sheltered a family of ten.

In time, the town fathers thought that the houses should be torn down. But then a dying robber baron decided to bribe his angry gods by building a small liberal arts college in Vintage, and he bought all the land including the twenty cottages, and historians came, sociologists and political scientists, students of painting and music, and they said no, don't tear anything down, this is history, this must be preserved.

This?! These rancid boards swarming with field mice, these old stones that raggedy children peed against in winter, *this* must be preserved?!

Emma Goldman spoke here, said the historians.

The town fathers laughed and drank their bitter coffee and chewed their pipes. Sure, they said, Emma Goldman spoke here, she screamed bloody murder here. The streams on either side of Main Street were clogged with the bodies of those she exhorted to rebellion. Big deal. The rebellion was crushed.

However, since no public money was involved, since the bequest that saved the cottages also saved the meadows from shopping centers and the mountains from mining, the town fathers had no choice but to agree. They watched with mixed emotions as Vintage College renovated and rehumanized the tainted site.

The old mill had burned down long ago, a clear case of unprosecuted arson; all that remained were a stained concrete floor, now pierced by scrub maples, and chunks of charred walls, where tough little sparrows nested. Right on these ruins the college built its chapel—a plain white church, Presbyterian. The town fathers considered this the stupidest idea yet. However, the school's first president insisted that ashes had to be kept in order to be risen from.

This thoughtful man gave Vintage College a good name with poets and philosophers. (He had no use for science. He said it was destroying the world; someone else could teach it.) And into the twenty little cottages, he moved unmarried members of the college community like Charles, and their music and their books.

ON FRIDAY AFTERNOON, CHARLES LEFT THE COTTAGE TO ATTEND TO academic business and Anna was free to wander among the huge ochre and orange maples and low stone buildings of the lovely campus. To be at the college this weekend seemed to her a much more mysterious and exotic sojourn than her recent visit to the emerald islands.

Here she had this odd new lover, ascetic as a monk, determined to live impoverished, girded with an iron self-sufficiency, and still dedicated to such hot emotional pursuits as literature and fatherhood and the satisfaction of her (apparently limitless, she thought wryly) sexual needs. The gorgeous fall foliage, the quiet and freshness of a campus where no cars were allowed, belied the ferocious history of the place. And Charles himself had hidden his wounds from her, careful not to let her see him naked, wearing socks to bed.

So now Anna too found that she was complying with the mood of concealment, of something kept back and secret. She forced herself not to contrast these well-dressed kids with their spiky hair and magazine clothes with her own math students in the Bronx, not because she did not want to remember her school (she would never forget it!) but because she did not want to remember her loneliness in those days. She had told Charles about her business. But she had told him nothing of her past.

She settled in the back row of his classroom as the kids came streaming in. She heard Hennessy and Taylor, two massive jocks in front of her, refer to Charles as "Old Iceberg." She discovered by furtive listening that it was pretty hard to get a B in his classes and impossible to get an A. On term papers, one sophomore girl advised a freshman girl, he was very strict about structure, less so about writing style and relentless about content.

"I heard he's a druggie," said the younger girl.

"Well, he pops pills at the water fountain in the hall in front of everybody, so it can't be anything too serious," said the sophomore. "Anyway, who cares? People around here live on junk, they smoke it, they swallow it, they sniff it, how else are we supposed to get through the fucking winter?"

The freshman shuddered.

"How'd Old Iceberg hurt his leg?"

"In the war," said the sophomore.

"Which war?" asked the freshman.

The sound of his cane was heard in the corridor. The kids in the class got quiet. (Jesus, Anna thought, they're *frightened* of him, they're frightened of this thoughtful, unhappy man! How does he do that?)

"So what'd you think of *Daisy Miller?*" he asked the class.

Nobody offered an opinion.

"Come on, group, wake up, did you read the book?"

Well, yes, they said.

"So did you like it? Did it make you cry?"

Hell no, they said.

"No tears for poor Daisy, eh? Guess you thought she got what she deserved, kibbitzing the night away at the Colosseum with Giovanelli . . ."

Who?

"Aw shit . . ." Charles murmured.

The girls fixed their makeup. The boys doodled and cleaned their nails with penknives. Hennessy slept soundly.

"Was it her innocence?" he asked. "Is that what turned you off?"

A short swarthy girl in the back row said, "I didn't believe it."

"You didn't believe in her innocence?"

"You gotta admit, it's hard to believe."

That was when Charles saw Anna. She smiled and waved her fingers secretively.

"Does nobody believe in her innocence?" Charles asked.

"It's that nobody believes in anybody's innocence, Professor Borden," said Taylor, and all the kids laughed, Anna with them.

"Daisy was such a tease," the swarthy girl continued. "She led Winterset on . . ."

"Winterbourne," Charles said.

"Him too."

The class laughed. Not Anna this time. She crossed her legs and put on her glasses and stared at the back of the smartass girl with direct and unmistakable loathing.

"What about the message Daisy sent Winterbourne from her deathbed?"

"It was a lie."

A black girl named Cassidy muttered, "No way."

"Well, it could have been a lie," said the swarthy girl. "Maybe she was capable of lying through her teeth even on her deathbed, saying she wasn't engaged to the Italian, just to appease her mother and make Winterset feel creepy."

"Winterbourne," Anna hissed. But the swarthy girl didn't hear her.

"Probably she thought she wasn't gonna die. Nobody does who's that young and strong. She figured she'd get well and that's why she took steps to keep up the pretense of her innocence. I don't believe anymore that those girls in that time were innocent. I think they screwed around just like we do, but they kept it a secret, because men were so much more powerful then and could dump you if they felt you had betrayed them and then you would starve. Keeping it a secret was fashionable then, like those fancy flounces and bows Daisy wore on her dresses."

Charles checked her name on his class list.

"Miss Suarez . . ."

"Call me Donna."

"I'll call you Miss Suarez and you'll call me Professor Borden. Tell me something, why do you think it is your right to doubt the conclusions of the author? He's not a newscaster. He's not leaving it up to you to decide. He's telling a story. It's *his* story. And he says Daisy is innocent."

"No, the Italian said Daisy was innocent."

"Giovanelli. Why would the author have him lie?"

"To protect Daisy's reputation. It was the fashion then, like I said, to lie."

A very dirty boy with pimples, slouched like a sack of garbage in the front row, murmured: "You're full of shit, Suarez. Daisy was a nice girl. Dumb but nice. Just because all you women are whores today doesn't mean it was always so."

Anna got up a little to see him, her eyes wide with alarm. An extremely good-looking girl sitting right behind the dirty boy slammed her three-ring binder down very hard on his head. The crucifixes in her ear swung and flashed. He said "Owwww" and collapsed on the floor at Charles' feet, making the class laugh.

Knowing that Charles now had a problem she herself would have been unable to handle, Anna hunched over and bit her bottom lip.

"Get up, Ignatoff," Charles said.

Ignatoff didn't move.

Charles prodded him in the ribs with his strong cane.

Ignatoff didn't move.

Charles planted the cane firmly on Ignatoff's chest so that he *couldn't* move, and leaned on it.

Anna grinned and applauded without making any sound.

"Miss Suarez, that is an idiotic analysis of *Daisy Miller,*" Charles said dryly. "I do not teach novels which are meant to be interpreted or doubted in this class. You kids are too dumb for that and much too lazy. I teach novels whose wisdom is tried and true, undeniable, beyond argument, got that? Don't be cute with Henry James. He does not respond well to it. I do not respond well to it. Learn first, then you can show me how smart you are."

Some of the kids in the class who had been hiding in shadows sat up and revealed themselves.

"I cried," said the black girl named Cassidy. "Just to think of her dying so young, 'raw protuberance among the April daisies,' that image knocked me out . . . it must be awful to die so young, for no real reason."

Charles smiled. They sure could get to you, the doltish kids, they could stumble over your truth where it lay sleeping and wake it up in a split second: the night, the blood, the bay the river the war the fire-filled night.

"It was because of the Europeans," said the jock named Taylor. (The jock named Hennessy was still sleeping.) "They had all this class consciousness, they couldn't believe she could go out with a plain guy like what's his name and still be a high-class girl. I felt sorry for what's his name."

"Giovanelli, dammit," Charles snapped. "If you can't master Giovanelli, what's gonna happen to you when you get to Ranevskaya?"

Who? they asked.

On the floor, pinned, Ignatoff squirmed. "What about Winterbourne?!" he cried. "Doesn't anybody feel bad for old Winterbourne, lonely as shit in a strange country, living on guilt for the rest of his life? He might have had a *chance* with Daisy Miller."

The girl with the crucifix earrings—Miss Halloway—looked down at him and said: "A chance for what?"

"Love!" yelled Ignatoff. "Romance, family, comfort, peace, happiness!"

"Oh poo. Winterbourne didn't want that," she said. "He wanted a roll in the hay and he was just pissed when he thought Giovanelli was getting it instead of him."

Ignatoff writhed under Charles' cane. "You got a problem, you know, Halloway?" he complained. "You're a real underestimator of men."

"That's my great strength, Ignatoff," she said, and all the girls laughed, Suarez and Cassidy, all the girls.

Anna listened, her face resting on her hands, learning more than all of them.

"Write me five hundred good words about what happened to Winterbourne after Daisy died," Charles said.

Now? they asked.

"Now," he said. He moved his cane. Ignatoff got up, clutching his ribs where the cane had pinned him. "Not you, Ignatoff."

"But I *know* what happened to Winterbourne after Daisy died!" Ignatoff protested.

"That's why you don't have to write the paper," Charles said.

"Well, what do I do then?"

"Go back to your dorm and bathe," said Charles.

CHARLES TOOK ANNA TO DINNER AT THE HOME OF A FRENCH PROFESsor. She wanted to bring wine or flowers. Charles insisted on bringing a large bag of russet potatoes from his garden. Anna thought that was really stretching frugality to the point of absurdity. However, the hostess seemed delighted.

Mutually exclusionary terrors made the evening awkward. Charles' colleagues could not remember when they had last met a real live honest-to-God executive from New York. Anna was overwhelmed by the erudition of the company and, when the conversation turned to politics, kept her mouth firmly shut.

Saturday morning, while he was sleeping, she made her way to the market and bought good things to eat. He watched television. She cooked. (And Anna *never* cooked.) He graded papers. She harvested fruit.

In the college bookstore, he introduced her to Cassidy and her boyfriend, the newly sanitized Ignatoff, and without asking Charles first, she invited them for brunch on Sunday before the football game.

He took her to see the chapel in the shell of the old mill. In one of the hymnals, she found a cellophane packet full of cocaine. With half a dozen kids gaping at her, she sprinkled it (to Charles' delight) like salt into an abandoned birds' nest.

She admitted by candlelight in an Italian restaurant that she had never read *Daisy Miller.*

The Vintage team won by a touchdown—Taylor's—in the last four minutes of the game.

It was really a wonderful weekend, Anna told her sisters. She expected that it would prove the beginning of her first real love affair in a long long time.

However, only a few days later, Charles Borden III, alone again, gearing up for the long winter in his cold house, decided that like the kids in his novel class, he believed in no one's innocence, and he went back to thinking that Anna Karavajian was fucking broker after broker in the back of her old blue truck.

ON THURSDAY, LUCIA CALLED HER AT WORK, YELLING: "FIND A TELEvision! Cat's on!"

"What are you saying to me? I'm working. I'm busy."

"Cat Cat ELLIOT LONGET, he's on the tube now this minute, find one!"

"Ah *seerelee kuyreegus,* please," Anna groaned, "I don't watch soaps, I don't watch sitcoms, Elliot is always on those things, I'm working."

"It's 6:30 at night, idiot! There are no soaps or sitcoms on at 6:30! He's on one of those entertainment wrap-up things and he's making a plea for money . . . and . . . well, that's it, you missed it, forget I ever mentioned it, goodbye."

Anna looked at her watch. She sighed. She had not exactly lost track of the time, rather she had semiconsciously misplaced it. For the last week, she had been semiconsciously working later and later, because it pained her more and more to go home and find no blinking light on her machine, no message from Charles.

She called Lucia back. Simultaneously Sally called on the other line. So they both told her.

"You shoulda seen him, sugar!" Sally laughed. "This was one of his great moments!"

"He looks terrible," Lucia said. "Tell the truth, has he got cancer?"

"He put on his *Marat/Sade* makeup, I swear to you, he had fucking *sawdust* in his beard!"

"He pleaded for public support. 'Save The Shelter!' he said."

" 'Help us resurrect our fallen temple of art!' he said. *No shit!* That is exactly what he said!"

"My heart broke just to hear the story, and I already *know* the story." Lucia sighed.

"You think this is gonna work, Anna? You think our smart Cat is really gonna rouse the angels and *rebuild* the old rattrap?"

"George and I were thinking maybe we'd have a fund-raiser for The Shelter, what do you think, Anna?"

Anna chuckled and went home. On her machine there was a message from Charles.

"Elliot says he's going on television and launching a public relations campaign to save The Shelter and wants me to come to New York next weekend and write speeches and propaganda for him. Is this true or is this just Elliot? Call me and let me know. But if you're already seeing somebody else, don't call me."

Anna did not call Charles that night. She thought it might be wiser not to go on with a man so obsessive in his suspicions. The next day, Elliot Longet came to her office with a breathless young press agent who had been retained to help launch the "Save The Shelter" Foundation, which had already begun receiving checks and offers of help from people like Lucia. They wanted Anna to print invitations, promotional mailings, press kits. The press agent pressed Anna's hand and looked deep into her eyes and said, "Can I count on you to give this top priority, sweetheart?"

Anna called Charles.

"Everything you heard from Elliot is true," she said. "And I am not seeing anyone else, where do you get these notions? I mean what is your *problem?!* I sleep with you, I cook for you, I audit your classes, I harvest your fruit, I cook for your *students.* Jesus, what more do you want, Charles?! Come to New York."

Elliot called Charles and begged and pleaded.

"I need you, Charles. We're going to have two and three fund-raisers a day, Anna's brother-in-law is even giving one."

"What's he like, Anna's brother-in-law?"

"He's like *George Margosian,* that's what he's like!"

Charles called Anna and left a message on her machine. "You never told me your brother-in-law was George Margosian," he said.

Elliot sent him a wire. It came to the English Department office, making the secretary there think that Charles' mother had died. Trembling, she handed him the telegram. It said: "Desperately need your master touch on speeches for inarticulate angels. Cat."

Charles called Elliot. "Not unless I get paid," he said.

"Will it be sufficient pay that The Shelter should reopen in May with your play as its maiden production? Publicity. Notoriety. Press press press. 'A great new play in a magnificent new theater!' says the promotional release. Think of it."

Charles said, "I'll come. Call Anna and tell her."

"You're coming!" Anna exclaimed on the phone minutes later. "Elliot's press agent got him mentioned on Page Six twice this week. She also got somebody to write an article about him in the *Village Voice*. It's called 'The Great Stage Robbery.' "

"Wish I could think of things like that," Charles said to the English Department secretary.

He got a colleague to cover his Friday class, took the late-night bus to New York, and, feeling pretzelized, went straight to Anna's office. She was standing between two roaring presses, arguing with some big guy in Armenian, and no less than half a dozen people were listening, waiting for the outcome of the dispute. Anna had the last word. She was wearing a charcoal gray suit and sneakers, her hair was pulled back, her face was smudged. She gave him the key to her apartment but did not kiss him, barely smiled at him, he assumed because so many people were looking at them.

"Don't call Elliot right away," she said. "Get some rest first, you look knocked out. Don't drag yourself to Queens. Make him come to you."

"Somehow I didn't realize that you had such a big business," Charles said.

"Does that bother you?"

"Maybe."

"Oh stop. I'm so glad to see you."

"Yes," he said, and with one finger, touched her arm. She blushed. He laughed. He left.

"Now here's the story," Elliot said, stretching his long legs out on Anna's wicker sofa. "A certain Queens Congressman has agreed to be chairman of the 'Save The Shelter' Foundation in order to improve his image, tarnished by clear and obvious connections to organized crime. He has never been to The Shelter. He has never been to a play. He's a sweetheart, an angel. His friends often like to give away green cash. He needs a basic pitch which he can commit to memory and deliver with different opening jokes to audiences throughout our city. Any words over three syllables, please capitalize the syllable to be accentuated, e.g. AcCENtuated. Be moving, effective, and very fast."

"I need a typewriter," Charles said.

Elliot's press agent went out into the street and returned twenty minutes later with a typewriter.

Charles wrote a moving and effective speech for the inarticulate sweetheart of a Congressman. He read it to Elliot. Elliot said it was too hard for the Congressman to say. Charles rewrote it.

He read it to Anna when she came home. She thought it was wonderful; she could not believe that Charles had written this great thing twice already in the space of a single workday.

Charles could not believe that she had been to meetings at the Museum and on Wall Street, a luncheon at the World Trade Center and an exhibition at the Coliseum, that she had sold two new accounts, fought with the bindery which had overcharged her 3.8 cents per copy, and fired her comptroller's new assistant all in the space of a single workday.

She undid her hair and took a shower. Elliot called and said he wanted to return with his press agent and have another meeting.

"Sorry, pal," said Charles. "The workday is over," as Anna walked wet and naked into his arms.

HE LIKED HER CLEAN TAN AND WHITE LOFT AND HER ELABORATE stereo and the half-built model of a whaling ship on her steel belted radial coffee table; reminded him of home (the ship, not the table). He liked the big bowl of apples in her refrigerator. He left her sleeping and walked her dog, Daniel. He didn't like her neighborhood. He liked her dog. When he came back, she was making coffee. He loved her navy blue bathrobe.

"Okay," he said. "Who's building the ship?"

"What?"

"The model ship, the whaler."

She laughed. "Oh sit down, will you? I hooked up the stereo. I invented the table. I'm building the ship. You're really something."

She sat far away at the other end of the table where he couldn't reach her.

"When are you going to let me see your leg?" she asked.

"Stepped on a mine," he said. "Don't want you freaking out."

"Has that happened to you? Women freaking out?"

"Were you ever married?" he asked.

"No."

"Why not?"

"He was killed in a car accident two days before the wedding."

"How old were you?"

"Twenty-two. Will you tell me about your children?"

"Not now," he said.

She came over and sat on his lap. She kissed him. Eventually she got him into the shower and, giggling, groomed his eyebrows with her toothbrush. She fell asleep again in the late afternoon with her head on his belly and her breasts nestled around his penis and her soft hair floating out over his bad leg, lightly, lightly on the old scars.

They went to Lucia's fund-raiser which she had organized speedily by calling all the rich people she knew, demanding $2,500 minimum and offering in return *haute cuisine* pot luck and a place in performing arts heaven. Elliot arrived with Sally who wore a purple sequinned caftan, and a pink and purple feather curved around her hair, and opalescent rings on every single one of her fingers. Anna had been hoping she would bring her new lover, but no such luck, she was keeping him a secret. Symphony types, record company executives, music business lawyers, all sat fascinated as the Congressman made his speech. None of these people had ever seen Elliot Longet act or direct, but they all believed in his prodigious talent.

Thousands and thousands of dollars were collected. To honor the occasion and the generosity of the guests, a great contralto sang, and Lucia's youngest daughter accompanied her. Charles rubbed his eyebrows like a man trying to wake up from what must be a beautiful dream.

"The earth has moved!" George said to his beaming wife. "She came to our house with a music lover!"

Anna asked Charles please to let her give him the money so he could fly back to Vermont and not suffer on the bus. He wouldn't take it. "Enough that you give me such good times," he said, kissing her strong hands. As soon as he arrived back in his stone house, he called her. She was home, waiting for his call. Two days later, he called her again. Anna recognized as background music from Charles' tape machine the voice of the great contralto.

"Elliot's gonna do it," she said. "Sally says he's gonna do it. The way things are going, I wouldn't be surprised if you guys really are back in business by May."

To Charles, it was astounding.

The Ice Cold Jungle, that "interesting original" which had started out under the pall of intellectual charity, had seemed a lost cause for February, what with The Shelter so badly damaged in August, and Charles had long ago kissed his production goodbye. However, Elliot had somehow (really miraculously, Charles thought) convinced someone on the Board of Directors that with public support at an all-time high, the theater deserved a loan in advance of the insurance payments. "They've hired an architect!" Anna said. (Well, that was fast, Charles thought.) "He's done plans, I mean Sally has *seen* them, she's going to have everything she wanted!"

Charles' friend the French professor came to him with an article from the *New York Times,* which described how luxurious the new Shelter would be, noting the description of the set dock (moisture-tight, fireproof) and the new shop (airy, sunlit, sprinkler systems) and the new theater itself (red carpets, navy tweed seats, rebuilt wings, state of the art lights).

How can this be? Charles wondered. How can Elliot Longet have created the *cause célèbre* of the forthcoming theater season just because that crappy old barn was relieved of its antiquated equipment plus $756.80?! Can any press agent be that good? How much insurance had The Shelter been carrying anyway? What Board member would be moved to make so generous a loan?

Charles laughed his flat, raspy laugh in the office of the English Department.

"What's so funny?" asked the secretary.

"Friend of mine is beating the system," he said.

AS THE WINTER CAME IN, SHE LEARNED THE TRUTH ABOUT HIM. IT was as she had expected. Charles had once been rich. He had once been secure as the old dollar.

Charles Borden I, the grandfather, sold real estate and insurance in New Bedford and passed on quite a large company to the father, Charles II. In his turn, Charles III expected to study business. He learned how to balance the books at an early age.

For amusement, he became something of a local jock hero. One year, he won all the short races for his age group in Massachusetts. During the summers, he worked for Charles II and sailed a small skiff with his buddies on the choppy harbor.

They drank a lot. Their parents drank a lot. If the statue of Herman Melville supporting pigeons by the sea ever fired the imagination of Charles III, he certainly had not known it when he was young. When he was young, he thought nothing. He drank, he went sailing, he spoke without feeling to his parents and they to him, and he thought nothing, at least that was how it seemed to him by hindsight.

The summer after his freshman year in college, Charles went partying with his friends at a local clam bar. A pretty girl there engrossed him, so he did not go out speedboating with the crowd.

The two fast boats, each carrying eight drunk kids, collided in the moonlight and nobody survived.

His cousins died. All his friends. Their arms and legs and heads bobbed in the water and the fire and the oil like cooking shrimp, and the endless agony of their funerals eviscerated the town: the seamen's chapel bell tolling, *"All lost, all lost."*

The sea air was poisoned for Charles forever after. He went back inland to school and allowed his English teachers to distract him.

In the best of times, his father, Charles II, offered little comfort. He read fiction but never discussed it. His mother knitted, or maybe it was crocheting or embroidery that she did, and polished her silver spoons. The only person on earth who seemed to understand how Charles suffered in the wake of the harbor crash was the young girl he had met that night, who he felt had kept him from dying. He went to see her and, unhappy and careless, got her pregnant. So of course they married. He had no choice but to quit school at twenty and go home now and work for his father. All he could see out the office window was the great Atlantic.

The year Charles IV was born, Charles Borden II made some bad decisions and began to go broke.

His son, he found, was no help to him. At night when the father wanted to talk about the disasters threatening their established business, he would find Charles III sitting at the living room table, writing stories in longhand on yellow legal pads.

The daughter-in-law, Midge, said this was a new thing. It was driving her crazy. They never went out, she said. They never hired a babysitter and went out, even for a lousy movie.

"You are losing your wife," said the father.

"I want to go back to school, Dad."

"We're in trouble."

"I want to change my life."

"I need your advice."

"My advice is that we should go broke and start over."

"You bastard. Heartless bastard."

Midge decided to solve all their problems by getting pregnant again. She said she wanted to have her kids quickly, *now*, so she could live. Charles sold a short story and brought the check home to her for Christmas. It really wasn't very much; it hardly helped at all. His father looked up from the account books and said nothing. His mother looked up from her nee-dlepoint and said, "Good for you, dear."

Charles sold another story and another. He began to write a novel about growing up in New Bedford and, on the basis of the first hundred pages and an outline of the rest, was paid some small money by a publisher. Although Charles accounted these as considerable literary victories for a young man with barely two years of college, his wife and his father re-mained unimpressed, consoling each other for what they considered Charles' madness, his unwillingness to take nine-to-five work and do a man's job of supporting the children he had fathered. When and if he showed up at the office, it was only to insist with renewed vigor that the family business could not be saved, that it *should* not be saved since its continued existence just kept everyone poor and made everyone sad.

One day he made a deal with his mother.

He asked her to take care of Charles IV and little Valerie so that Midge could go back to work and he could go back to school and get a degree in American Literature. His mother said, "Well, all right, dear, if you think that's best."

Midge did not think it was best.

As far as she was concerned, she had borne the worst that her life was supposed to bring when she had borne two children. From here on, every-thing was supposed to get better. Being a salesgirl again was not what she called "better." She wanted to go out and have a good time. So with her young husband, Charles III, enrolled at the university, using up every extra penny for books and tuition, using up every evening finishing his damn novel, she started going out and having a good time with other men. She made sure Charles found her in their arms. This forced him to see at last that he would have to give her a divorce and support his cute little kids from afar.

In 1967, three years before Anna Karavajian was to have been married, Charles Borden III joined the Army, offering several years of his life in exchange for a promise of continuing education under the GI Bill. Since he was trained in bookkeeping, he figured he would sit out the war at a desk. But he was mistaken.

"My luck," he whispered to his mother in the VA hospital outside of Boston.

She seemed strangely younger since his father's death, sitting by the bed, smoothing the white sheets with her white hands, never looking directly at his wounds. She did not complain. She had the family home, free and clear, although most of the antiques and all the silver had been sold. Rent from an occasional boarder augmented her Social Security. She had two healthy grandchildren who had not forgotten her. She had Charles' novel, praised by a few critics and dedicated to her.

She felt that her son's plan might work out in the end. He would get his doctorate. He would become a professor of American Literature. He would sell many articles, and perhaps write some more good fiction of his own as well, and his name would be respected, as his grandfather's name had been respected in the early days of New Bedford, when times were better and ships full of hopeful young men set out to sea.

All the anguish and bitter recriminations of her family's past life she set aside, like a stained cloth she would not have on her table. She fixed her pale blue eyes on the nice things, the pleasant things; the good manners which she taught her grandchildren, the warm handmade afghans she patted onto their sleeping bodies on nights a bit too cool. Between herself and the agony of her wounded boy she erected a white wall, white as her slender hands, and she held it there until his medication took effect and he stopped crying.

All this will pass, she said to him as he slept.

And it did.

Good days will come, she said.

And they had.

ANNA HAD MADE A TERRIBLE MISTAKE WHEN SHE CONTRACTED TO DO the mailing for the Museum catalog. Her mailer simply could not handle such a huge job. Three zip codes fell out of the computer like autumn leaves and drifted away, irretrievable.

Her instinct was to cover somehow, to find the missing zip codes and correct the mistake before Sharon Gold could hear of it. For two days, she sat in the mailer's airless bunker, rolling dense lists up the black screens. Her brain danced with little green numbers. Her eyes felt like lead balls. Then she ran out of time. She had to go to the Museum and tell Sharon.

Sharon turned white as her clothes. "How could you permit such incompetence?" she snapped. (Weeks before she had been kissing the air beneath Anna's ears and taking her to lunch because the catalog was going to turn out *soooo* beautiful!) It was a humiliating moment. No comfort could be drawn from the fact that this was the error of a subcontractor. Anna was responsible. Sharon replaced the mailing list. For some reason known only to those anonymous assholes who had devised the programs, not only the three missing zip codes but four others as well came up on the replacement list. Thousands of New Yorkers received *two* Museum catalogs, and Anna took the worst financial beating of her business career.

Under these circumstances, she could not meet Charles in Vermont as planned.

Her father, all packed for Florida, delayed his trip to try and make her feel better.

He had once printed ten thousand brochures *three* times, he said, because the blue came out wrong on the first run and the back page smeared on the second run. He had once sent the proofs of a precious family history to Jerusalem where a certain typesetter had special Armenian lettering unavailable anyplace else, and the proofs had been stopped in customs and by the time they were released the typesetter had *died* and his sons had sold his business and moved to Paris! Someday Anna would tell her own children these stories to cheer them when they screwed up, Gabe said, kissing her and finally leaving the plant to get in the taxi which was waiting to take him to the airport.

The idea that her father still thought she would have children made Anna cry and go home and drink vodka. Late at night, Charles knocked softly on her door.

"You sounded so miserable," he said. "Figured I'd better come."

SO HE RUBBED HER FEET AND TOLD HER ABOUT HIS CHILDREN.

Charles was seeing his children more frequently these days: Charles IV, a freshman at Northeastern, skinny, thoughtful, studying nothing in particular, winning races now and then; and Valerie, much more of a hotshot at eighteen, eager to graduate high school and be off to the glittering boulevards.

She found it hard to understand why Charles could not get her a glamorous sinecure at one of those fancy homes-and-gardens magazines which published his articles.

Charles tried to make her see that he had been supporting two households for many years, that he had saved every dime he could so she and her brother might go to college, and he *wanted* her to go to college. Though she kissed him and hugged him and said, "Pl-easssse, Daddy," he would not let her off the hook.

It startled Charles to see on Valerie's face the passage of anger—not disappointment, but the bitter, dangerous look of the self-pitying shortchanged.

"Don't be angry," he told his little girl. "Don't allow yourself that lapse

of self-control. Anger makes a woman resistible. Your mother got so angry
that I left her. Your grandmother never gets angry. That has enabled her
to survive with dignity."

"What did she say?" Anna asked.

"She said: 'I don't want to survive! I want to go out and have a good
time! Just give me the money! It's my money!' "

"What did you say?"

"I said no."

"What did she say?"

" 'You bastard,' she said. 'Heartless bastard.' "

"Amman . . ."

Anna hugged him. In her heart of hearts, she kind of sympathized with
Valerie, chained to the priorities of a man who had not raised her. However, she did not argue with Charles. He had come to be with her and
comfort her in a bad time, something only her family had ever done for her
before, and she was on his side.

She could not at this moment imagine any situation in which she would
not be on his side.

Charles said that when the kids were young, Midge had made it very
hard for him to see them.

He would arrive for his visitation weekends to find little Valerie crying,
saying Mommy was upstairs crying: she didn't want to leave Mommy. If
Charles would just give them the support check and maybe a little extra
and then go away, that would be best.

One weekend, he had come to take Charles IV to a Red Sox game and,
in the middle of the sixth inning, found that the pale-haired boy had no
idea who he was, thought he was just another of Mommy's boyfriends.
They all took him to Red Sox games.

Soon enough, however, Midge began to want to invest more heavily in
her social life and felt tied down by her children. She began calling
Charles, asking him to take the kids. He always said yes, he was free;
nobody was inviting him for madcap weekends on the Cape at that time.
There were hours at the end of the day when he just could not walk
anymore. When his son, then twelve, came to visit, he found Charles in the
depths of the wheelchair. So now he finally had a way of distinguishing his
father from other men.

In time, the iron-fisted animosity between Midge and Charles began to
unclench. They got tired of it. Life's little adventures brought along other
people who treated them worse than they had treated each other. The

financial responsibility of the kids necessitated that they have lunches in Boston, like business partners.

Midge married a man whom she had seduced and stolen away from his former wife. Plagued by obligations to his old family, this man promised to feed and shelter but in no other way support Midge's children. All the rest —the bicycles, the winter coats, two weeks at a summer camp for Charles IV during which he made the ill-fated FATHER belt, a trip to Paris with her high school French class for Valerie—came as always from Charles.

Last year, he told Anna, a younger woman had seduced Midge's husband and stolen him away. Now Midge was on her own again, pushing forty and strapped for money again, since she had saved nothing in all the years, she had spent every last nickel on going out and having a good time. Undaunted, she lifted her face and worked out her body. She dressed like an actress. She hunted for one more husband, a really rich one this time, someone old who would die quickly and leave her loaded.

Although Charles' literary ambitions had always maddened Midge, she now concluded that therein lay her salvation. She urged him to get rich at writing. Try television, she said in a Boston diner. Stop writing about string beans. Make up a funny sitcom. If you're so nuts about gardening, make the central character a gardener . . . come on, Charlie, think of something funny about a gardener!

"Well, are you gonna?" Anna asked him.

"What?"

"Think of something funny about a gardener!"

"When you think of something funny about a gardener," he said, "you tell me."

"I never think of anything funny," Anna admitted.

This made Charles laugh. He wrapped Anna's feet in hot towels, and hugged them against his chest, getting his shirt wet.

"Midge asked if the kids could spend Christmas with me at my mother's house so she can take a vacation in Florida with this new man she's seeing," he said. "Hope it's serious. My son says it isn't. Just another reef encounter, Dad, he says. But I hope."

"What does Midge look like?" Anna asked.

"She's got long pink fingernails and gold streaked hair. She dresses like your secretary Francine, lots of cleavage. Always did. She was always a pig." Anna gasped and took her feet away. "And there you have the main reason I keep my daughter, Valerie, chained to my priorities. So she'll be an educated woman and have some way to feed herself besides fucking."

THEY WENT OUT FOR A WALK.

Halloween had just come and gone but the antic spirit of that holiday hovered still in the crisp air, the store windows still carried black and orange remnants of goblin trimmings. A stationery store displayed witches' hats spilling Scotch tape and magic markers; all the sweaters in a sweater store were hung on fiendishly grinning black cats. To Anna it seemed that even the most ordinary endeavors in her city were lit with cleverness and unabating wit; she felt thrilled to live here; as only those who are no longer lonely love to live in New York.

She and Charles walked on through the shadow plays of the silver moon. They came to a store that sold witchcraft paraphernalia and magic spells.

Satan himself leaned over the sign at the doorway, beckoning with a crooked talon. He wore one earring. Best thing about him was his grin. Anna giggled and tugged on Charles' sleeve. So okay. How could he resist her? He opened the door. It creaked. They stepped inside. The floor went "UNHHH." A salesman approached. He had a crewcut like a marine. His face was powdered white and his lips were painted black. He wore Calvins.

"Is there any little thing I can help you with, folks?" he asked. "We got potions, we got talismans, we got black masses all written out in English . . ."

"Just browsing," Charles said.

Anna screamed.

She had stumbled on the shrunken heads.

Charles peered carefully into a stinky bin.

"Dried rats," said the salesman. "Wonderful in stews."

Anna went, "Yuch! Yich! Ich!" to a glass cage full of spiders and hurried away down the Aisle of Blood.

It was available by the vial, the pint, the half gallon, in easy-pour cardboard containers, the same kind used for milk. "Give me one of your boots," Anna whispered. "I think I'm going to lose it." She grinned. She had Dracula teeth. She bit Charles on his neck.

"I do hope you intend to pay for those teeth, madam," the salesman mentioned.

Charles reeled up the Aisle of Bones, right into a rack of skeletons. They rattled horribly. Sally Bangle appeared, gripping an ochre femur.

"Oh hi," Sally said. She sighed with resignation. Despite the spiritliness of her fuscia fur, she looked downhearted. "I guess we all had to meet up sometime somehow. This is my friend Rex."

A chubby young man parted the bones like Wyatt Earp entering a saloon and stood at Sally's side. He glared at Charles menacingly, winked at Anna, snatched the femur from Sally and, wielding it like a swagger stick, goose stepped and waltzed through the store, singing, ". . . *in stiller nacht,* dum deedle dum . . ." Sally giggled and ran off after him.

There was definitely something strange about Rex.

Anna peered. Anna puzzled. "Is it . . . is it . . . ?"

"You got it," Charles confirmed. "He's a woman."

Anna clutched a skeleton. It provided no support.

"How could I have not noticed something like that about Sally?"

Rex summoned the salesman.

"How much for dis occult songbook?" she demanded, pointing with the bone.

He said $37.50.

"Pay the fool, Sally," Rex commanded.

"But I haven't got any money, honey," said Sally.

"I almost strangle you for dat."

Rex stopped suddenly, and held a vial to the light.

"That's cat's blood," said the salesman.

"I don't vant to know whose, you imbecile!" screamed Rex. "I vant to know how much!"

"Before she was doing Dr. Mengele," Sally whispered. "Now she's doing Mel Brooks doing Dr. Mengele."

"A dollar eighty," said the salesman, wiping sweat off his face powder.

"Make dat a dollar fifty und vee do business!"

He agreed. "Anything to get rid of her," he murmured surreptitiously to Anna and Charles. "She gives me the creeps."

"What're you gonna do with the blood, Rex?" Anna asked.

Rex winked. "Bewilder the police," she said.

Through the moonlit streets they toodled, following Rex like the rats of Hamelin. She decided to do Chaplin. She helped herself to Charles' cane, tipping her bowler hat and waggling her eyebrows to amuse the passersby. Anna skipped alongside, laughing.

Charles leaned on Sally. The moonlight made her face glow. Where she pressed his arm, a sweetness pierced his coat and warmed his blood.

"Beats me why a woman with your powers should be wasting her time with a male impersonator," Charles said.

Sally stiffened. Her large eyes flashed angrily. "And I myself was wondering why a man with your education would be wasting his time trying to remind people 'bout the damn war," she answered.

"Sorry."

"I admire Rex," Sally said. "She's got talent."

Charles stopped a moment to rest.

"What's her last name?" he asked.

"Pumpkin."

"What's her real name?"

"Rochelle Frumkin. But what she calls herself is who she is to me, sugar."

"Tell her to give me back my cane."

Not only did Rex return the cane, she took Charles' arm away from Sally. She had decided to do Joan Rivers. She leaned into his face and interviewed him as they walked. Her breath smelled of liquor.

"So tell me, Major . . ."

"Lieutenant."

"Tell me, Lieutenant, all the women out there in that audience are dying to know, what's it like to kill people? I mean . . . can we talk here? Did you ever get off on it? Let's have the truth. Don't we all want to know this?" she asked a couple of passing strangers. ("Sure," they said. "Right on, you got it.") "Do your victims clutch at you when they're dying? Do they make rattling sounds? Do they go AGHHH?!"

Rex fell suddenly to the pavement, gagging and retching, jerking spasmodically. Innocent bystanders thought she was having a heart attack.

Sally and Anna pulled her up, laughing, apologizing to the crowd which had gathered. "She's doing the late Oskar Werner," Sally said.

Anna ran back to be with Charles, who had fallen behind.

"Come on, let's buy them some dinner, Charles, she's so crazy, I mean I never met anybody like her before in my whole life, she's so funny, the things she can think of . . . come on . . ."

"I haven't got enough money," he said.

"I'll pay," Anna said.

"Prefer you don't."

She quickly slipped a wad of cash into his pocket, not letting him protest further. He noticed, although she did not, that she had stepped in a few drops of freshly spilled blood.

At the restaurant, Rex ordered a steak and devoured it with the appetite of the famished.

"I work at a gym," she said in her normal voice. "Hose the sweat off the sauna. Spar with the jocks. See my scars?"

She peeled off her eyebrows, pointing to the pink skin underneath where she had shaved off her own eyebrows completely. Then she made the eyebrows into a goatee and got ketchup on it. Anna and Sally laughed; so did the people at the next table.

"To my Daddy, the girdle king of Cleveland," Rex declared. "I am the hideous sapphic offspring he prefers to disown and forget. In Daddy's memory, I wrote a song about when he took me sightseeing in Egypt. Wanna hear it?"

Charles said, "Not really."

"Ignore him," Anna said. "Sing."

Rex stood up. She played a few introductory bars on the glassware and she sang:

> *A camel took me for a ride*
> *He paid me well to ride him.*
> *And he was slow and gray and gold*
> *With a gaudy rope to guide him.*
> *I thought we'd thunder*
> *'Cross the sand*
> *And I would sleep beside him*
> *But I was too young*
> *And he was too old*
> *And they never quite untied him.*
>
> *What a blunder, little man,*
> *Not to thunder*
> *When you can.*

"Who were you doing that time?" Charles asked.

"Oum Kalthoum!" Rex proclaimed. "I try to be all things to all moments, but to Sally, I am unique, to her I am a goddess, a river, right, schnookie? In Sally's honor, I am writing a novel called *French Kisses*. It concerns a nefarious enemy plot to undermine confidence in the city of Cleveland and thereby drive a deadly wedge into the American heartland. The only one who can prevent this disaster is voluptuous Desdimona, the top French operative in the Midwest."

Anna shook with silent laughter. Under the table, she grabbed Charles' knee. He pushed her hand away and took some pills. She turned to look at him, taken aback by his sudden ill temper. However, he didn't seem to be mad. He seemed to be fascinated.

"Desdimona's cover is Salon Sixty-Nine where she works as a blow dryer. Each week, the fiends try another dirty trick. They incite race riots. *They set fire to the river,* can you imagine?! They kidnap the City Council and replace them with look-alike thieves and pushers from the Vladivostok city jail. They try *everything* to make the Americans look stupid and venal, but Desdimona knows this is all a calumnious lie!

"She puts out the fire. She single-handedly stops the riots. She reinstates the *real* honest upright City Council.

"The enemy wedgers attempt to fry Desdimona with an electrolysis needle. They put henna in her ratatouille. But she always survives to save the day.

"Every time the grateful citizens of Cleveland want to throw her a parade, she lowers her azure eyes and says 'Don't sank me. Sank France!' "

Rex then ate Sally's baked potato.

"It would make a great TV series," she said with her mouth full, "but it's too dirty."

Charles took off his glasses and smiled. Even Sally who had privately called him "ice on a stick" began to see what her friend Anna found so attractive about him: the crow's feet, the generous teeth.

"How does your father feel about your work?" he asked Rex.

"I told you," she said. "He has disowned and forgotten me. He doesn't know about my work and he doesn't care," she said. "Right now he's into dying."

"Sorry," Charles said softly.

A bewildered young policeman appeared.

"Uh . . . excuse me . . . uh," he said nervously, "Is . . . uh . . . is anybody here bleeding?"

At first Anna and Charles and Sally just gaped at him, not comprehending. Then they saw the trail of blood leading to their table. The vial which Rex had started dripping at the witchcraft store was finally empty.

Rex winked.

Anna could not stop laughing.

UPON HIS RETURN TO VERMONT, CHARLES LOADED THE STOVE WITH wood and then settled at his desk to work on an idea for a television show. He had finally thought of something funny about a gardener. The Congressman's speech, some rewrite for his play, these things he could do quickly. But the sitcom was a slow birth, and painful. Charles would write one sentence, then watch television, then write another two sentences.

He worked and worked around the clock, stopping only to go out and walk—three miles, every day, no matter what the weather—to keep his bad leg alive, and to teach his classes. He fell asleep in his clothes and worked some more until he was finished with the first draft.

At dawn, drinking wine, excited by his own energy, absolutely clear in all his intentions, he thought it would probably be the wisest thing to call Anna right now (the bitch, stuffing her fat wad in his pocket) and tell her (without letting her speak) that they were finished, that he was up to here with her dilettante sister and her ready-made family business and her Levantine money and most of all her sick dyke friends, and then hang up fast (without ever letting her speak).

He did not call her. Instead, he got himself another woman.

She invited him for dinner. Pictures of her dead husband peered at Charles from small tables in her house. Sure, she wanted him to spend the night.

Swift as vengeance, he took off his pants and watched her eager face wither. He got dressed and walked home in the bitter cold, enjoying a great lucidity concerning the limitations of the jerks around him.

He pulled out the thin little story idea and rewrote it so that jerks would like it. He made it as funny as he could, but he did not laugh. He polished it until it was slick.

Anna called. She said she wanted to see him this weekend. Could they meet halfway, in Boston maybe?

"I'm working," Charles said.

"Come on, don't be a grind, get on a plane."

"Can't afford to get on a plane."

"Since very soon you will be a famous playwright with lots of money who can easily pay me back, I'll pay," she said cheerfully.

"Well," he said, "if you're ready to pay, there must be plenty of local guys who are up for it. Call them."

Tears sprang into Anna's eyes in New York. He could hear them pop. She slapped herself in the face. Charles winced and hung up.

So. That was that. Someday he'd have women as far away as London and Malibu and he'd fly out to see them any weekend he wanted, first class, without a second thought.

The phone rang.

"You're an asshole!" she screamed. "You make me feel degraded like a whore, no wonder your students ridicule you and your daughter hates your guts, you are a joyless psychotic creep, go fuck yourself!"

He rewrote the sitcom idea one more time. He took it down and down and down, below beneath contempt, took it down to such lows that prehistoric stone fish, blind and deaf and armored against the cold in the deepest canyons of the ocean, would find it funny, and this idea made him laugh out loud in his icy house for the first time since he had begun writing the comedy. Then he put it aside again, figuring after he graded his Modern Drama papers and read what the jerks had to say about Edward Albee, he'd be inspired to find a way to take it even lower.

His students felt the lash of his sarcasm. They noted that his eyes and lips had disappeared. Watch out for Old Iceberg, they advised each other. He's cracking. Must be trying to kick his habit.

By the end of another week, the finished rendering of the sitcom idea was on his agent's desk in New York.

It snowed and snowed in Vintage. A lot of the kids and the professors too didn't make it to class. Too much trapped indoors, the college community began to drink very seriously. Puddles of puke sullied the immaculate drifts.

Ignatoff came around to help Charles dig out. Touched by this gesture, he thought of Anna, the way she had crouched in the shower to peer closely at his leg and feel it, matching it against the good one, imagining the flesh whole again and how he must have looked running races as a kid, asking if anyone had thought to search for his toes in the jungle, wondering if she would have the presence of mind to retrieve a severed limb or digit from the site of an accident and rush it to the hospital with the victim.

He called her. Francine wouldn't put him through. He left messages on her machine at home. "Listen," he said. "I'm sorry. It's that I'm ashamed of my poverty, it makes me vicious. Please don't be mad."

When the phone rang, he hoped it would be her, but it was his agent. Funny stuff, Charles, he said. Funnnn-eeee. He was sending it to another agent he knew in L.A.

One night the cold broke and a thaw came and then it froze again. The next morning, every branch of every tree, every tiny shoot and leaf and blade, every pebble in the road was coated with ice that sparkled rainbows on the snow, making the young girls merry as bells again.

So she called him.

CHARLES ORDERED TICKETS TO *MADAM BUTTERFLY* (A SPECIAL PER-formance, with great voices) and he paid for them by credit card, even though that was the most expensive way: he usually *never* bought tickets that way. He flew down to New York with the ski vacationers.

At La Guardia he took a shave and a haircut. The barber smeared some gook on his eyebrows. He had his old boots shined. He figured he looked as good as he was going to look.

Anna had agreed to meet him by the fountain at Lincoln Center at 7:30, a half hour before curtain. He had three hours to make it from the airport to the Met, under ordinary circumstances a forty-five-minute trip. But the year's worst blizzard had locked up New York the day before. Its residues —mountains of plowed sooty snow closing off whole lanes, knee deep pools of crusted ice water at corner crossings—had confounded rush hour ground traffic and pushed the natural ill temper of the city in winter beyond containment.

The citizens glowered, growling, gray-faced. At the airport, Charles saw two women come to blows over a taxi. A nice man tried to separate them with gentle mockery. They turned on him like guns.

Heeding the advice of a cab driver who said the suburban highways belting the airport were notched with horrible accidents (crashes not of poor judgment, but bad will, creating endless delays), Charles took a bus and then a subway to Manhattan.

The bus was packed. No one gave him a seat. Charles parried the lurches and bumps with his good side as much as possible.

The subway steps were slippery. Charles descended with great care. He hugged the right wall. He kept his cane as close to his body as he could. But the teenagers leaped down the steps like Inca couriers racing, and of course one of them caught the toe of his sneaker on Charles' cane and fell four or five feet to the ironclad landing below, hurting himself.

"Why'd you trip me, mother fucker?!" the boy screamed.

"Didn't mean to," Charles said, pulling him to his feet with one hand and thus letting the kid know what a powerful right he probably had. The kid got the message.

"Fucking gimp," he snarled and bounded away.

The train was stuffed with bad smelling people and their coats and *Posts*. An old, dirty train, it had been signed to death, like a story with too many authors, and no longer knew what it was. Was it a public vehicle with an obligation to carry passengers to their temporal destination? Was it a canvas for painters trying to paint themselves out of the subway?

Perhaps because of its identity crisis, this train stopped, in a tunnel, beneath tunnels, and then the lights went out, signifying to all on board that the train brain had ceased functioning.

Oh shit, the people whispered; shit. Somebody's gonna go crazy in here;

somebody's gonna freak out and start shooting; Holy Mother, please, don't let it be the guy next to me. Don't let it be me.

They waited in the dark, their noses freezing. They tried not to step on each other's toes or read too much meaning into the sound of anyone's breathing. Every single one of them was afraid of every single one of them.

Charles knew that in a panic he would be trampled. He needed room. How could he get them to give him just a little more room?

He shifted, grunting, and coughed once. Instantly, all those near him moved further away. Where did they find the space? he thought. How could they manage to make themselves even smaller than the fiendish subway had required them to be for starters?

Finally the train got going again, although the lights never returned, and a voice on the loudspeaker told them they would all have to deboard at the next platform because there was a fire on the tracks.

Charles coughed. The people around him retreated even further. What do they think I have? he wondered. Probably some new disease they just began to fear last week; probably AIDS. Imagine, to understand such a disease, they have to understand the death of cells, the difference between a virus and a bacteria, the suspension of immunity, think how brilliant and sophisticated they have had to become to be afraid of me.

Charles coughed again.

He didn't need to cough this time; he just wanted to see if he could really scare the shit out of these jerks.

Instantly he found at least three feet clear all around him, a moat of isolation and happy quarantine, and he could lean solo on the subway pole and stretch out his leg and stretch out his cane and the New Yorkers kept their distance.

On the stairs heading up to the street, he coughed repeatedly, letting spit collect on his lips, closing his throat partway so he'd turn good and purple, and they pranced gingerly around him thinking, "Oh God, *saliva!*" and nobody tripped, nobody fell and called him "mother fucker," because nobody wanted to come anywhere near the gimp with AIDS.

At Forty-second Street he surfaced to find that night had arrived. Charles had been traveling for two hours since his plane landed. He had not been able to sit down once during that time.

His wounded leg, which didn't like to be cold and wear wet socks, had begun to hurt on a metaphoric scale. He could not safely take another pill just yet. Dragging himself out the Port Authority doors, hoping to find a cab, he embarked on one of the tall stories he had invented to express the pain, the way women express milk from their breasts when they have too much for their new babies.

Charles mentally recast his body as a white shmoo, that soft bulbous creature invented by Al Capp as an incarnation of manna. He decided his body was a shmoo, pierced in the right leg area by a big black cigar. The cigar was smoldering. It was burning a big hole in the shmoo. But the shmoo had great resources and could become exactly what the situation called for in an instant—ham to the hungry, umbrella to the wet—and so now the shmoo became an Italian ice. Ice. Every muscle in Charles' lower body tightened and bunched and froze. The smoldering black cigar standing in for his blasted leg was now engulfed by Italian ice. Of course it fizzed out harmlessly.

The victorious shmoo tried to hail a taxi. No luck.

The buses were too crowded even to consider.

It looked like Charles was going to have to walk to the Met.

Putting his brain in neutral, casting his memory far and wide to catch a thought transporting, he retrieved the frizzy-haired physical therapist who had smacked him in the face when he inquired about amputation.

Just to be out of pain, Charles moaned, not to be seven-tenths a junkie forever.

"Forever is no more!" the tough little guy answered. "Forget forever; he got plugged in the jungle, who gives a shit? In fifteen years they'll fit you with silicone calf muscles and bionic toes. In twenty years they'll implant a little bullet in your brain that will make pain obsolete. In friggin' *minutes* the world advances, Borden. Keep your leg. I guarantee you'll live to have days when you can't even recall the war."

Thinking ice over burning, will over pill, Charles limped and listed uptown on the hard-trampled englaciated sweep of snow and gravel that led to Lincoln Center. The muscles in his buttocks and lower back, which he had mentally frozen in order to stifle the smoldering cigar now ached for warmth, blood, oxygen. Massage! they cried, whirlpool!

Charles imagined that he was ice on the Bering Straits and then summoned herds of reindeer from Siberia to go thundering across to Alaska, making the blood flow but keeping the nerves cold. He was beginning to go a little crazy, he knew. Play psychological games with your body long enough and *win* enough and you may not be able to come back, you may have pushed through beyond flesh, as the chaplain had said, like Jesus and Akiva and the Indian mystics and Saint Jerome.

The New Yorkers trudged alongside, passing him, jostling him, unaware that they disturbed the migrations of reindeer with their rudeness. They did battle with their coats and boots, like soldiers on a forced march. He couldn't make it if he continued to think of them as enemies. Somehow he had to absorb them into his biorhythmic fantasies, and recast them as allies.

Okay then. So we are *all* soldiers. Me and them together, we are urban guerrillas assailing a palace of light called the Metropolitan Opera, and we can take this place, even though we're a ragtag army half-frozen, because the defenders are fat and lax; they hardly know there's a revolution going on; they're only interested in tuning up; they will not so much as glance away from their music stands until we have captured their chandeliers and ravished sweet Cho Cho San in her flowery bower.

Okay, Charles thought. This is the assault on *Butterfly*. I am but one of thousands. We have made it to Fiftieth Street. Only thirteen blocks to go!

A strangely familiar melody awakened him to reality. It was a van with Vermont plates, crawling uptown playing chain tunes with its tires on Broadway. The driver hung out his window, lost and confused. Angry New Yorkers ground their horns at him. A long-haired woman in the passenger seat harassed him with a map. On the windshield, this poor jerk already had a ticket, on account of his musical tire chains, forbidden in the city.

Charles slogged through slush puddles and tapped the driver's window with his cane.

"Can I help you?" he said. "I'm from Vermont myself, I teach Literature at Vintage."

"Oh praise God!" cried the driver. He had a great bushy beard. "We're summoned to join our brethren in Brooklyn for a spiritual retreat, but we have become lost."

"Brooklyn? Well, okay. Best way to get to Brooklyn is to go straight up Eighth to Sixty-third Street; I'll ride with you and show you if you like."

"Only if you're going that way, brother, we don't wish to inconvenience you."

Charles laughed. So did the reindeer.

The servants of God slid their van doors open and welcomed Charles, their faces fresh and faithful. They offered him some of their French fries. When they got to Lincoln Center and let Charles out, he told them to go west and then south. They blessed him for his kindness.

They marveled at the Met.

They thought it was beautiful.

They thought it was a church.

The assault on the Met that frozen night involved thousands of particular persons, defying type, picked it would seem by fate, not culture, for enslavement to their life's passion, romantic opera. This condition struck at random, without regard for family history, seizing one brother and not the other, a wife but not her husband, often manifesting itself suddenly, late in life.

The traffic helicopter which puttered overhead looked down at the opera lovers and marveled at their dogged forward thrust, how they clambered over snow mountains, forded icy rivers, apparently unmindful of how much frozen muck sluiced into their boots, already humming in anticipation of the humming chorus that would soon bring dawn to Nagasaki. The closer this peculiar population came to the peeking Chagalls, the more they seemed transformed by their messages of hope and love and beauty, and they reached out their hands to help and steady each other, to help even total strangers who limped and stumbled and coughed and might have God only knows what sort of hideous illness.

"Now just hold my arm, young man," said the little old lady to Charles. She wore a brown mink coat and black rubbers and a red and blue crocheted cap with a pom-pom. Charles tried to smile at her. He was facing a set of six towering steps. "Hold my arm and we'll do it slowly together," she said.

Okay, so they started up the steps. But he had to stop, he just couldn't make it, his supply of mental tricks had been exhausted. A banker's teenage son saw Charles' distress and with the help of an exchange student from Kenya hauled Charles over the steps. A dentist in furs swept up the little old lady who leaned back in her arms like Scarlett O'Hara, laughing romantically and kicking her feet. Charles' case was immediately taken up by a very fat Honda dealer and a sportswear buyer from Saks, who guided him toward the fountain, patiently waiting as he found new footing for his cane before every step.

Anna saw him.

She came running toward him recklessly and fell on her ass.

A television executive picked her up gallantly; a bus driver brushed the slush off her coat; they handed her to Charles. Anna did not say anything. She felt embarrassed at having fallen on her ass. Charles had to look under her tumbling hair to see her laughing.

Well okay, so he hugged her to him, and she rubbed the lower part of his back—some instinct of hers; she didn't even think about it—and they settled into their seats.

Charles held Anna's hand. He twisted her hand in both of his, gently, like a handkerchief, and when Pinkerton and Butterfly sang of their love, he held her hand against his belly. She slipped a few of her fingers inside his shirt, between two buttons. The music pulled him from high to high, triggering an emotional release Anna had seen before in her sister Mary and her brother-in-law George, but never honestly felt herself. Charles' mouth opened slightly. She knew he was approaching ecstasy, stretched up and up by the escalating sadness of the music, and would be helpless before the first act ended. He sobbed a little; his eyes poured forth tears and so did the eyes of many thousands; but these were not really tears . . . *"Un bel di vedremo . . ."* sang Butterfly; we shall come together; we shall love each other somehow, find happiness together; maybe even peace . . . these were not tears that made Charles Borden's face and all the other faces in the Met so fresh and young and wet as new babies' faces. No, Charles was not weeping. He was melting. He had finally traveled beyond his pain.

Hail, Puccini.

ON THE LAST DAY OF THE YEAR, THEY PLANNED TO DRIVE UP TO SEE Spike and Mary and help them in their long-delayed project to paper the living room and install a wall of bookshelves to hold the various stereo components and high piles of paperbacks which had been lying around on the floor of the farmhouse all these years, catching rug fuzz and silverfish.

Charles knew that this, his first meeting with the Russos, was a big deal in Anna's mind. That unnerved him. He determined to tell her that he didn't want to go. However, one evening he returned to the loft with a pizza and overheard Anna talking with Mary on the phone. If he had been a more honorable man, he might have made some sound, to warn her of his presence, but he could not resist, he was dying to know what she said to her favorite sister about him, so he remained silent in the doorway, scarcely breathing, hugging the pizza box to muffle its telltale rattle.

"No, I don't know whether he's talented," Anna was saying. "He doesn't ask me to read the things he writes . . . Yes, you're quite right, I think it definitely is a sign that he doesn't trust me . . . No, I did not tell Charles about Spike. If they become friends, Spike can tell him.

"I'm not hiding anything like it was a dirty secret, dammit! It's just that I don't think he has to know everything about my family. We're not getting married, we're just having an affair . . . don't tell me I'm trying to sound sophisticated. I *am* sophisticated! I'm almost thirty-eight years old and you still treat me like a kid with furry pink slippers . . .

"Are you all right? I mean is he talking more? Is he getting along okay at work? Do you need any money? Don't worry, I'll bring some . . .

"No, for the last time, I will not tell Charles about Spike . . ."

So now of course Charles had to go ahead with the excursion to the Russos' house, for he had become wild with curiosity.

They dressed in their oldest clothes. They collected all the brushes and hammers and bolts Anna had around the loft and packed them into her tool box. They bought wine and were just about to set out when Sally Bangle called, sounding wretched.

"Rex is working," Sally said. "She's got a box of Ritz Crackers and a box of prunes and she's eating them one after another and working. We were supposed to go out dancing tonight, but Rex has got this idea for a new novel now that she's done with *French Kisses* and I can see it's no use, she's just gonna be working for the whole rest of the day and night and when she's tired, she'll fall asleep right there on the floor. You guys got any plans for New Year's Eve?"

Anna put her on hold.

"Maybe I should say no . . ."

"Say yes," Charles said. "She'll help us with the living room."

"But I wanted . . ."

"Whatever the big secret is with your brother-in-law Spike, Sally's presence won't affect the telling one way or another."

"There's no big secret," Anna protested.

"Don't like it how you keep things from me," Charles said.

Anna frowned. She knew she was a pretty good liar and a great secret keeper. It impressed her that Charles had sensed a deception. (It did not occur to her that he had listened in on her conversation.)

"Spike did three years in Lewisburg for destroying U.S. Government property during the war," she said. "He was against the war; he burned his draft card; he burned the flag; he stole draft records and burned them in a big bonfire in the night . . ."

Charles took the phone. "Come with us, Sally," he said. "Looks like we're going to need you."

So they set out in Anna's truck, with Anna driving, the soft yellow muffler Charles had given her for Christmas coiled around and around her neck, battening down her hair, wrapping her ears and much of her mouth. Sally sat next to her. Besides her tool box, she had brought several packages. "Just stuff," she said. These were stacked on her narrow lap, burying her. She refused to shift them into the back for fear that their contents would break on the bumpy ride. She wore a bright pink hat and matching gloves and a pink and purple jacket with dozens of little zippers. The back and sleeves of the jacket had been embroidered by Rex with patches from all over the world, from skiing in the Alps and scuba diving in Eilat and climbing the Eiffel Tower and backpacking down the slopes of the Grand Canyon. Sally swore that whenever she wore the jacket, she had a good time, that the colors and the patches brought cheer and frivolity.

Behind them, Charles Borden stretched out on the back seat. He watched the fast food spots and the drop-in car radio stores and the ascetic low computer factories flip by over the toes of his boots. The junk on the highway seemed to go on forever; charmless; garish; the culture of debris, Charles thought; his country had seemed to him for some time now mostly wreckage with bright spots of wealth. He tried not to look. He raked his eyebrows down over his new glasses like a final curtain.

"What's Rex working on now?" Anna asked.

"Another 'deathless satyricon,' " Sally answered. "That's what she calls it, don't you love that? She always puts down her work. She does Groucho. She says if she's good at it, how great can it be? I tell her, sugar, comedy is not chopped liver! She doesn't listen. Her new novel is called *The Financial News with Hope and Peachy.*"

Anna giggled.

"Turn on the radio," Charles said.

"It's about a woman who goes into business and all her relatives expect her to fail. But she's got a demon called Hope who does the books and destroys the competition. Don't you love it?"

"Yes," Anna said.

"Turn on the radio," Charles demanded.

"Trouble is, the competition has a demon too. They've got a special demon called Peachy who hangs out in their wrist watches and clings to the inside of the armpits of their short-sleeved white on white shirts . . ."

Anna laughed softly. "Tell me who is stronger," she said, "their demon or hers?"

"Theirs is much stronger."

"Why? Why does that always have to be?"

"Because she is possessed by her demon always," Sally answered. "And they slip theirs on and off like wrist watches and shirts. That's all I've read so far."

Anna glanced into the rearview mirror to catch a glimpse of her lover as she said to Sally: "Lucky you that you get to read what Rex is writing, that she asks for your opinion even though you are a mere techie with no literary background . . ."

Charles reached up and pulled on her muffler, threatening to choke her if she did not shut up and turn on the radio.

Anna turned to her favorite music.

"Audiogarbage!" he protested as the beat bore down.

But the women began to sing along with it, they sang the backup and the solo, they sang the bass and the sax, they pulled out of the traffic into the north and sang themselves into a beautiful forest, gray trees whistling by, stands of pine and leafless maples with fuzzy birds' nests in their highest branches. Anna did Turner. Sally did Springsteen. They sang Charles to sleep. He woke up in the Russo driveway among onion fields whitened by a light snow.

Spike Russo looked to Charles like a nineteenth-century millworker, the kind who had posed stiffly for pictures which still hung in the library at Vintage. He had gone almost completely bald, and all the hair of his head seemed now to have transferred into his mustache, which was bushy. He wore whitish dungarees, the color of that day's sky, and a gray work shirt. He poured Charles some coffee. They sat in the kitchen.

They sat on opposite ends of the battered drop-leaf table, long ago painted blue, on chairs that did not match. They rested on their elbows, on their beat-up hands. Spike kicked another chair closer to Charles so he could prop his leg on it. Johnny sat between them, his black eyes piercing first one man then the other, seeking for whether there would be war at this table or peace.

Mary showed Sally and Anna the work to be done in the living room. Her plan was to rid the room of its stained ochre walls and gray woodwork by putting up new paper that looked like mattress ticking, thin blue stripes on white, and then installing light pine bookcases. She had already scraped and painted white the moldings and windowsills herself. She said she did that at night, after their son went to bed, during the long hours when Spike sat and stared at the fire in the fireplace, not talking to her.

"He stares at Little John the same way he stares at the fire," she said. "The poor kid gets hypnotized by his staring. Drops down to sleep in his tracks like a narcoleptic." Tears glittered on Mary's black lashes. She had taken to wearing her long black hair in a flat coil at the back of her neck. A bone clasp held it in place. She had stopped wearing earrings. Nothing moved around her face. Even her bracelets lay quiet. "He's like forgotten how to make love. I mean he's been out three years, but he still can't remember. He wakes me up and does it suddenly, just drops off snoring afterward. Imagine that . . . my Spike . . . my Spike who used to do it so good."

Anna hugged her, saying have patience, the shrink is right, wait, wait.

To keep themselves going, the Karavajian sisters played tapes of their brother-in-law George zinging riotous music on the oud, and they bounced to the beat of the *dumbeg,* swinging their hips and hooting. Exotic birds, Charles thought, observing them from the kitchen door. Their razor blades grew thick and dull with paste. Sally consulted her tool box and found the dozens of extra blades she always kept there, advising that a blade was good for one trim, maybe two, and then you had to throw it away. Deftly she slung her tape measure over the walls and the paper; pencils protruded from her hair and ears. She ordered Mary and Anna around, and they followed her directions tirelessly. She loved that; at last a crew which did not grope her ass or challenge her authority. She loved George Margosian's music and gyrated like a rock star on her ladder.

In the kitchen, Spike Russo prepared lunch for his son. The lunch was home-ground peanut butter on home-baked whole grain bread with a side of alfalfa sprouts and carrot sticks. Johnny picked. He chewed very slowly with those few teeth which had not fallen out. He did not look happy.

Pressing his finger to his mouth for silence, tiptoeing to the kitchen door, closing it firmly, stationing Charles against it as a guard, Spike reached out the window for a certain flowerpot and revealed that he had hidden there a forbidden box of Twinkies. The flowerpot then fell off its ledge and broke. Spike shook his head ruefully; another stashpot smashed. He threw the Twinkie box to Charles. Johnny jumped up to catch it but missed. Charles threw it back to Spike. Johnny missed again. The sight of him laughing, with peanut butter and whole grains oozing through the hole where his front teeth used to be, was so disgusting that Spike finally let him catch the Twinkies. He devoured three. He allowed his father and Charles to have one each. Mary beat on the kitchen door. She said she needed to wash the paste off her hands. Johnny stashed the empty Twinkie box in the refrigerator. No, that was a terrible idea, Spike said. Anxiously he scanned the kitchen for a new hiding place. Charles stuffed the Twinkie box in his boot. Mary was allowed into the kitchen. She squinted suspiciously at Charles and Spike and Johnny, who were now putting on their coats to go outside and play.

Meanwhile Mary, Sally, and Anna had finished the wallpaper and begun to build the bookcases. Sally revised Mary's plans somewhat, recommending that they build the wall-wide unit in three sections. Smart Mary, detecting an expert, did not argue. Sally cut the pine with a circular saw, spraying sawdust on Anna's paste-encrusted eyebrows. Anna drilled the holes for the angle braces. Mary screwed in the bolts. Her hair was beginning to fall out of its bone clasp.

Mary and Anna raised the first bookcase section up to the wall and Sally bolted it there with steel braces, beating the wall with the back of her hand gently until she found the uprights that would support them. Anna began cutting the pine for the next section.

Spike and Charles and Johnny played with a foam rubber football, under a special set of rules by which only Johnny could be tackled. The snow was falling more thickly now. Soon the roads would be impassable. They decided to go to the store while they still could. They bought milk and shrimp and clams and haddock and canned chicken soup, they bought bags of potatoes and onions and crunchy bitter salad greens and parsley and a box of chewy gumdrops in Christmas colors, much reduced in price. Little John wanted all the red ones. But so did Spike and Charles. So they divided the red ones and gave Johnny the green ones and the white ones. He strung these on a length of thin wire Spike happened to have in the glove compartment, and hung them around his neck. This shopping trip took the men a long time because they had to make so many decisions and also because the roads going home were slick with unplowed snow and very dangerous. Johnny took a little snooze on Charles' shoulder. Spike drove intently. He and Charles ate all the white gumdrops off the necklace.

When they got home, the second bookcase unit was just being hauled up and bolted into place against its companion, a snug fit. One unit left.

Charles brought in some firewood from outside. He crouched at the fireplace with his bad leg outstretched, like a Russian dancer, waving the little flames upward.

Spike and his son sat in front of the fire and stared at it.

Charles made dinner.

Anna smashed her finger with a hammer. Charles ran the cold water over it. She rubbed her face against his sleeve, that was a very sweet thing she did. She was covered with sawdust and paste, and she stank from sweating.

"Why is it I have been feeling so scared lately?" she asked. "I mean scared of people I met years ago who didn't scare me at all when I met them. A girl junkie who hit me. An angry father at school who cursed me out. That robber in The Shelter who took my earrings. Why am I so scared?"

"Something to lose," he said. He kissed her mouth.

She helped Sally and Mary raise the third bookcase unit into place

Sally stood at the far end of the new room and admired their work.

"My mother," she said, "is real beautiful and she's always got a man. But all they give her is pretty clothes and pretty girls. The one man she was all ready to love forever bought it in the jungle. Nothing lasts for her since him. But this bookcase is gonna last for two maybe three generations, you watch. Let's have a drink."

She opened one of her packages. Vodka. She and Mary and Anna had a glass together. Then they broke out the polyurethane and painted the bookcase.

In the kitchen, Charles began to heat up in the vapors of a thick fisherman's stew. The smell of paint and fish reminded him of home. He put the big chocolate cake Sally had brought and the wine he and Anna had brought on ice. He hummed.

Anna began to vacuum the new living room while Mary packed up the day's garbage, the stiffened remains of wallpaper, the blunted blades, and the pounds of filthy rags. Johnny helped Sally collect the scraps of pine and threw them into the fireplace. They burned quickly.

Spike joined Charles in the kitchen and helped him make the salad.

"The worst thing," Spike said, "was that so many guys I met inside couldn't remember the war, or the war against it. One boy who was in for attempted bank robbery—he asked me why if I was going to steal, why had I stolen papers and records, why had I not stolen something of value?"

Charles checked on the stew. It was simmering fine. He took a couple of pills. He leaned on the refrigerator and put his bad leg up on one of the kitchen chairs.

"I met a guy there," Spike continued, "his name was Orlando. He got into a shootout with the police once long ago and he is serving years and years, he's about our age: well-educated; black. I asked him if he remembered ever having been at a fund-raising party in Tenafly, New Jersey, at a big house, where there were these good liberals who raised money for his cause . . . I tried to remind him . . . three sisters, I said . . . three fine-looking sisters with spicy food and a lot of conscience . . . but he didn't remember.

"You gave your knife to a musician there, I said.

"But he didn't remember at all.

"Don't tell Anna because she'll tell Mary."

Inside, in the living room, the women swept the drop cloths off the furniture and folded them up and put them away. They moved the furniture back into place. The bookcases were already drying and dulling down. The new wallpaper looked like it had been there forever, and the light white and blue room took on the shine of the incoming sunset. Mary hugged Anna and Sally.

Charles sent the boy to announce that dinner was ready.

Anna changed the music to *Aida*.

Sally opened her last and bulkiest package. It was the well-tuned balalaika which alone had survived the attack on The Shelter. Johnny strummed and picked; very soon he was picking out the melodies of songs.

They washed up and ate together and welcomed the New Year.

Chapter 6

AS THE PRODUCTION OF HIS PLAY APPROACHED, THE DEPARTMENT chairman and the dean allowed Charles to arrange his classes and exam schedule to accommodate casting and rehearsals in New York. It seemed to them an excellent investment. Their school could only benefit from the presence of a respected dramatist on the English faculty, no matter how little he actually taught.

So he stayed with Anna, parked his weights and some of his clothes in her loft, and began despite his reticence and hers to pervade her life.

Anna did not mind having Charles around. However, she did not altogether like the impression his presence was giving people. For example, her employees treated her with more love and less respect if Charles was looking on. She asked him to stay away from the plant. That left him feeling insulted. Hadn't he let Anna come to his English class? Karavajian Press is not a class, she answered, it is a business—and insulted him even more. To put her in her place, he breezed into the plant one afternoon when she was working late on a Wall Street account, and he took Aram Hovad out for a beer.

Charles' desire was to find out about the other men in Anna's life.

Aram told him all about her father.

FOR REASONS INCOMPREHENSIBLE TO ANNA, CHARLES BEGAN HAVING terrible trouble with Elliot Longet: big fights, in her living room, on her phone, in the middle of her nights, centering in large part on the issue of casting.

Casting the play obsessed Charles. He knew little about acting, less about actors, and therefore found himself helplessly dependent upon Elliot Longet's judgment. This made him angry. It made Elliot cocky. It strained their friendship.

It maddened Charles that the casting process gave him and Elliot so much power over men who might well have more talent than they did. The power embarrassed Charles. He felt degraded by its artificiality. To sit in a half-dark theater and judge (clearly desperate) people, to be treated by them with such elaborate false respect, oh that had to taste sickly sweet to any man familiar with one-tenth of his own sins. Certainly it tasted that way to Charles. But not to Elliot.

Watching Elliot strut down toward the stage, beckon with one crooked finger the actors to kneel down and listen closely to his advice, watching him make an actor do it over again and interrupt and dare to look bored, Charles felt nauseous. No behavioral abomination, no excess of affectation seemed beyond Elliot Longet at casting.

He dressed all in black, with knee high black leather boots and a great brass watch dangling on a chain around his neck (it chimed unnervingly on the half hour), and sometimes a long white silk scarf with black fringes and the mysterious monogram "HC."

Hume Cronyn? conjectured the actors. Hoagie Carmichael? *Harold Clurman?!*

Like Rasputin displaying his gifts from the Czarina, Elliot struck awe and terror into the hearts of guests to the palace, and indeed The New Shelter was becoming exactly that, a palace of light and sound and plush scarlet carpet.

Charles felt that Elliot strode around it with an unbecoming regality: was it possible that one successful publicity campaign could have so eroded his sense of the ridiculous? With a harsh slap of his hands, he summoned the assistant stage manager and sent her out for coffee and a certain particular kind of Danish, calling her "Sweetheart." If the light crew made noise in the fly space, he slammed down his script and screamed: "Are we to be constantly interrupted by inconsiderate clods?!" When an auditioning actress went into a quake, too nervous even to get her lines out, Elliot flew up to the stage and patted and stroked her, not to extract a better reading from the mildly talented girl, but to make sure she would tell the really good actors who were waiting to read that they must disregard all signs to the contrary, because *au fond* Elliot Longet had a really soft heart.

Once Elliot arrived late for casting. The actors were all studying their scripts in the green room. Elliot gave each of them a piece of hard candy. They sucked gratefully. Charles had to leave the room, gorge rising.

PRIVATELY ELLIOT TOLD THE BEST ACTORS WHO AUDITIONED THAT Charles Borden was a manic-depressive, a drug-dependent *poilu* who had to be treated with the utmost respect and kindness but never under any circumstances asked a direct question about his play lest he freak out and do himself or the inquiring actor some violence. Only Elliot knew how to handle Charles, Elliot said. Because Elliot was accustomed to the craziness of writers, Elliot said.

To Charles he explained that all actors were innocent, indeed, dumb, indeed they *made* themselves innocent and dumb deliberately, the better to absorb the role at hand, and that they had to be treated with utmost affection and kindness but never under any circumstances given any direct information by Charles about his play lest they become disoriented as orphans who are no longer sure which big guy is their Daddy.

Charles could not believe the actors were that stupid.

However, they seemed perfectly willing to believe he was that crazy.

Not one of them ever spoke to him beyond hello.

THE MAJOR SUBSTANTIVE ISSUE BETWEEN CHARLES AND ELLIOT CON-cerned the casting of *The Ice Cold Jungle's* main character. Charles wanted to cast a little Italian guy with a big nose who made light men cry with his readings and fidgeted, groping for the words and producing real sweat. Elliot wanted to cast a tall, graceful black guy whose voice reached the farthest corners of The Shelter even when he was feeling sad.

This fellow—he called himself Emerson Hall—reminded Charles of someone he had known . . . maybe seen . . . maybe bumped into on the subway.

"I cannot tolerate Charles a moment longer!" Elliot protested to the Board member's wife. "He keeps saying Emerson reminds him of some-one!"

"Be calm," she said. "Stay cool. The theater is gorgeous. The equipment is state of the art. The Parks Department has agreed to relandscape. You're on the verge of a new life. Just be calm."

"Charles Borden is a detail freak!" Elliot cried. "He is capable of fixat-ing on the pressure of a handshake, the vibration of a football! I shall be undone by this terrible tension! I must get Charles out of casting!"

"Sorry, baby," said the Board member's wife. "You can't lock the writer out of casting until you're in the movies."

Charles rocked in Anna's hammock, thoughtful as a walk on the beach in winter.

"I don't like Emerson Hall," he said to her (she was gluing the last mast onto the whaler). "But Elliot was on his side and pushing for him even before he came through the door."

"Maybe Elliot knows him from some other show."

"They don't admit to that, either of them."

"Maybe Elliot just thinks he's great."

"The little Italian guy is great, Anna. I may be new at this but I'm not an idiot."

"All right, all right, so maybe Elliot really does know him and owes him a favor."

"And my play is the payoff."

"Oh stop, Charles, please . . ."

"Don't think I like that."

Anna climbed into the hammock and began to tickle him.

"You got glue all over my sweater," he said.

She sat up astride him and sighed and sighed.

"Okay. How's this?" she said. "My sister Mary always puts things in cosmic perspective. She says: you're worried about being robbed? Be glad you're not dead. So let's say you are me and I am my sister Mary. Last August you thought your play would never be produced, that you would never break out of gardening articles and teaching *Daisy Miller,* and now your name is in the theatrical trade papers and you're bitching and moaning because your director wants to cast the second-best actor. My sister Mary would say that makes you a self-centered ungrateful asshole." She kissed the glue on his sweater. "You should thank God for Elliot Longet. He's a genius. He turned a disaster into a grand opening. I mean I know he poses and lies and fakes and he's power-mad but he makes things happen. You've got your show, Sally's got her shop, I've got you, in a manner of speaking, from time to time . . . And what was lost? A tin samovar painted brass, a bunch of lousy old lights . . . Sure I'd like to have my earrings back, but all in all, if Elliot had planned that robbery himself, it couldn't have worked out better for everyone concerned."

Charles grew very still.

He stopped fingering the buttons on her shirt. His eyes turned white.

"It's final callbacks tomorrow," he said. "I want you to come."

"But I don't know anything about . . ."

"Don't care what you know. You look at Emerson Hall tomorrow and tell me what you *feel*."

THE FIRST THING THAT HAPPENED TO ANNA WHEN SHE ARRIVED AT the theater the following day was that Elliot Longet tried to throw her out. Assuming his most severe and forbidding face, he seized her by the elbow and steered her toward the front doors whence she had come.

"I don't want you at casting," he said.

"Charles does."

"He exceeded his authority when he invited you, my darling girl. Now get out of my theater before this escalates into a fight you will live to regret."

Some eerie shadow came up over Anna Karavajian. Her eyebrows united. Her voice dropped an octave. ("I thought she was going to turn into a man before my eyes," he marveled later to the Board member's wife.) Gently she took Elliot's great brass watch in her hand and scooped her hand round and round the chain until it had tightened around his neck.

"I really hate being threatened, Elliot," she said.

She released the watch.

She thought Elliot was going to hit her.

Instead he burst into tears and exited stage left, tearing at his beard.

Anna sat down in the theater. She was very nervous. Sally leaned over her shoulder and whispered, "Take it easy, sugarplum. *They're* auditioning, not you."

As it turned out, she thought all the actors were brilliant. The Asian girls who were trying out for the one woman's role, the dumpy old men who were trying out for the part of the colonel, she told Charles they were like a bunch of flowers, each beautiful in a particular style: how could one choose?

The little Italian guy trying out for the lead gave one of his great readings. Anna loved the way he moved his eyes one way and his hands another and his torso yet another way, like the war was inside himself, like the center wasn't holding anymore and he had lost his sense of which way to turn.

"He's terrific," Anna said, and Charles seemed pleased.

But then Emerson Hall came and knocked her out.

"Oh Charles," she whispered, "he's so strong and commanding, he like writes himself across the stage, you can't see anything else but him, I mean the whole stage just disappears. Elliot's right, honey. This is Elliot's business. He knows. Do what Elliot says."

"Tell me something. Does Emerson Hall remind you of anybody?" Charles asked. "Do you feel like you've seen him before?"

"Yes," she answered. "He reminds me of a great big basketball player I once had in my math class. His name was Arthur; he could run like a deer and carry two hysterical girls down the hall like they were sacks of groceries and he was ticklish. This Emerson Hall makes me love him the way I loved Arthur . . . I'm sorry, Charles, but I think he's fabulous."

Charles walked away from her.

"Way to go, Mother Courage," Sally whispered.

Anna knew from the way Charles leaned on his cane, almost parallel to the floor, that he was furious. With her? For not supporting his choice? With Elliot? For being right? With his own play, for being so adaptable to so many actors, black and white, handsome and ugly, tall and short, fidgety and graceful, a wide range: too wide?

"EVERYTHING THAT LITTLE GUY HAS GOT, YOU SAW TODAY ON THIS stage," Elliot declaimed, "there is nothing more, nothing more, trust me. But Emerson Hall is a *star*. He has resources you and I cannot yet imagine. He will give us a great performance, he will make the material resound."

"He's ten feet tall and built like Mr. T!" Charles said. "Who will *believe* he is afraid of the dark?"

"Everyone," Elliot declared.

"How, how?" Charles asked, not facing Elliot, facing the stage.

Elliot perched on the seat backs like a black panther, fearless and all-powerful.

"Because I will make it happen and he will make it happen, that's how."

"Thought I made it happen," Charles said dangerously.

"Only initially, Chuckie boy. You want to play the game, you've got to learn to pass the ball."

"And are you gonna catch it, Cat? Or is a light pole gonna fall on you?"

Sally twirled her curls and stopped breathing. Up among the lights, the technical director hung suspended.

"Will you guys cut it out?" Anna yelled. "You want to fight, *fight*, don't pick at each other like a couple of chickens." She shook her head in disgust and left.

"Who said that?!" Elliot screamed. "Who dares to mock me in my own theater?!" Fury unbalanced him and he tumbled among the seats head first, his long legs sticking up and his vermilion socks bobbing.

He called Anna later and left a message on her machine. "Don't ever come back to The Shelter, darling girl, you have a big mouth."

Charles did not defend her.

"But I was right," she said miserably.

Big deal, he told her. She had a big mouth, and she would have to learn to keep it shut.

Even though she didn't want him to, he made love to her. He hurt her arms. He did not care that afterwards, in the dark, she sat wakeful, pissed off, unsatisfied. Elliot called at two in the morning. The Board member's wife dialed for him, shoving the phone into Elliot's hand when Anna answered.

"Disregard my previous message," he said. "Let me speak to Charles. Please."

Anna woke Charles with the gentleness of a boot camp sergeant.

He went out to meet Elliot at some bar. When he returned it was dawn, his best time, and everything was clear. He sat on the edge of the bed, watching Anna sleep, watching the light on her back softly creeping.

"Put up with me," he whispered. "I lost my kids, I lost my men, I lost my health. It's hard for me to lose now. I hate losing. I take it badly even when it's for my own good." Her eyes flickered open. She started to turn over on her back, reaching for him. "No, don't touch me," he said. He pulled the sheets off her and crouched over her and kissed her back and her behind and her legs; he brought her to the edge of fainting, but he never let her touch him.

ON MONDAY SALLY BROUGHT KARAVAJIAN PRESS A FLASHY PAINTING in a Rousseau-like jungle, all red and green succulent leaves, and Larry, Anna's art director, fitted it for a poster with white letters saying *The Ice Cold Jungle* by Charles Borden III, directed by Elliot Longet, starring Emerson Hall.

Elliot took Anna out for lunch, "to make up for my unspeakable behavior," he said, "and to win back your affection, without which I have been bereft." Anna giggled. She let him kiss her hands. He had a surprise for her. In the dust behind the theater, he said, some landscaper from the Parks Department had found her earrings, the ones that had belonged to her grandmother, silver, with little blue stones.

Anna wept with joy to have them back again.

AT THE OPENING OF CHARLES' PLAY, ELLIOT LONGET MINGLED AMONG
the critics and the Board members in the gala, sellout house. No longer
obligated to look destitute or inspire terror, he now gave full throttle to his
natural ebullience and good nature. He wore white boots and white para-
chute silk pants and a tan suede cowboy jacket with fringes over a "Save
The Shelter" T-shirt, baby blue. He was so happy, he didn't even look thin.
Sailing through the sellout crowd like an agile yacht, he picked up one
beautiful woman after another and escorted them and their satins and
diamonds on guided tours of The Shelter's fabulous new men's room. He
spotted the talk show host who had made him famous and made sure not
less a personage than the dazzling Sally Bangle chatted with this man and
his wife and his wife's satins and diamonds. With the talented young press
agent always at his elbow whispering, Cat was absolutely sure of where to
go and whom to meet and whom to honor.

He cozied up to the television crews and asked them to pay special
attention to the tiny red maples ringing the theater ("a special favorite of
our most generous Board member's most generous and lovely wife," he
announced, forcing her and her proud husband to take a bow). He thanked
the Mayor and the City Council and the State Arts Council and had all the
angels of the "Save The Shelter" Foundation (including Lucia and George
and the newly sanitized Congressman) presented with gigantic bouquets of
white roses in the teeming lobby before the show, while the press shoved
lesser lights away and took pictures.

"I do believe our Cat has turned into biscuits and gravy overnight,"
Sally said to Charles, squeezing his hand.

He had never seen her looking so beautiful. She had dressed herself in
silver sequins, she wore them even on her fingernails.

"Is Rex here with you?" Charles asked nervously.

"No, I threw her out," Sally said.

Anna gasped. "What happened?"

"She lost her job at the gym and decided to write *The Financial News
with Hope and Peachy* full time while I played breadwinner. I said, so long,
sugar, get somebody else to fill your plate."

"What happened to *French Kisses?*" Charles asked.

"She got bored with it. Didn't even get it typed. Last time I looked, it
was stuffed in a shoe box next to the garlic. She'll probably misplace it. I
love her in my way. I do, really, you know, Anna, but it's just too hard,
she's a fruitcake, she talks right out loud to her characters. I woke up

once, three in the morning, Rex was in the kitchen yelling, 'Whose orifice do you think you're in anyway?! Go bite your own toenails!' "

Charles Borden began to laugh.

He recognized the critics from the *New York Times* and the *Village Voice* and *New York Magazine* and he began to giggle uncontrollably.

"It's fear," Anna said to Sally Bangle.

Charles inched toward the front door.

An agent from California introduced him to a glamorous woman, very tall, familiar from magazines, who told Charles she was looking for a movie, did he have a movie?

The agent from New York introduced him to a television producer who was interested in his sitcom proposal.

He passed Ignatoff and Cassidy, who had hitched down with his friend the French professor. Like Charles himself, these Vintage fans were seriously underdressed for the occasion, but at least Ignatoff did not smell.

He stopped by the water fountain to take a pain pill. Gabe Karavajian was there taking a nitroglycerine.

"Is this a good business for a grown man to be in?" Gabe asked him.

"No," Charles said.

His own son, Charles IV, all trussed up in a three piece suit, hugged a spot on the wall, fidgeting. Charles looked into his eyes. For the first time in their lives, they kissed each other.

"Go hold Anna's hand," Charles said. "She's very nervous."

He made it through the teeming lobby outside into the cool night. Spike and George, Mary and Lucia and Mrs. Karavajian milled around there. Across the moats of darkness, they reached out to him and shook his hand and wished him luck.

And then he lost them, lost them all, they meant nothing to him that night compared to his anxiety. He couldn't breathe. He couldn't watch the show. He walked through the parking lot, among the twinkling white lights on the little red maples, thinking his own lines:

"God, get me through this night, out of this pit . . ." he thought.

He sat on a fender praying.

Emerson Hall sat in Sally Bangle's green and red jungle, trying to become a star.

"You know what I'm gonna do, brother?" he yelled. "I'm gonna go home and get myself on the tube, I'm gonna tell it straight. You are no longer innocent, Americans, I know, you overcharge, you lie and cheat, file false returns, fuck liberty and justice, you don't believe in anything but the breaks."

"Give me a break," Charles said to the moon.

"The Europeans got nothing on us, right? Right?!" Emerson said, threatening the audience with his fire-filled eyes. "Henry James is dead and gone; welcome, I say welcome to the Old Country!"

Spike Russo wept.

Charles threw up in the bushes.

AS ELLIOT LONGET HAD UNDERSTOOD ("FINALLY!" HE LAUGHED to Emerson Hall, "after a lifetime of misplaced emphasis!"), *The Ice Cold Jungle* owed its success least of all to the quality of the play (it was no better than many bombs; Charles knew that too), but mainly to the historical half-life inherent in audience perceptions; in short, to the times.

"Guilt matures," the Board member's wife had said when she first read the script, "like a U.S. Savings Bond. Let's cash in."

Deciding to ignore the regular subscribers in his audience ("They wish to be obliterated by their entertainments," Elliot declaimed, "not pierced by them"), he aimed *The Ice Cold Jungle* squarely at critics and agents and polemic-hungry intellectuals and history professors who would urge their classes to attend—in short, to the opinion makers. He judged that no white actor would touch these deep thinkers as effortlessly as Emerson Hall did, and he was right, their hearts bled on cue, all through May and June, bled fame and fortune.

Emerson Hall was featured in a hot black magazine. He got television auditions. He lent his unforgettable voice to a series of radio commercials for a beer, which then sponsored the Yankee games all summer, and he made more money than his family had ever dreamed of. Like a god, like a river, Emerson moved them out of Brooklyn forever.

The directors of a great convention center in the nation's capital began paying court to Elliot. They needed a producer of ceremonies, awards, dinners, retrospectives, testimonials, festivals. They had reviewed his credentials carefully: saved The Shelter from bankruptcy; pictured with cognicenti literati glitterati on the social pages; voted by *Women's Wear Daily* one of the twenty best dressed men in New York. So much for Cat, short for Catastrophe, Lord of Technical Disasters, the risen anti-Muse. In only a scant three years Elliot Longet had so brightly outclassed his old reputation that no one remembered it.

The convention center offered him three times what he was earning to come to Washington and work for them. He chose a successor to run The Shelter and spent the rest of the summer buying new clothes.

The Ice Cold Jungle did not get Sally Bangle into the union or win her even one good review. That made her feel sad. Her new lover comforted her.

He had come to New York on business and some admirer of Emerson's had brought him to the play. While they were drinking wine from paper cups in the green room, he had fallen for Sally. He described her to his law partners as a glitzy little Bohemian from the New York theater, who could knock you out with her rap on lumber. And yet she possessed a Southern freshness. When she was sad, as she was now, she reminded him of a weeping cherry hanging its sweet flowers down.

"Hey now, baby," he soothed, "nobody can build a whole jungle on a shoestring budget and expect to show the world how talented she really is. You need money to shine, girl."

"It's that I don't know enough," she said unhappily. "I don't know literature, I haven't read history, and everything I do I'm just guessing at and I need to go back to school."

"Whatever you want," he murmured, stroking her smooth arms. He took her to Jamaica for a wonderful vacation. She returned very black.

For Charles Borden III the good reviews of his play brought a woman from the *New York Times'* interviewing. She reminded him of Midge, her fingernails were that long. Her intensity made him so tense that his glasses fogged up. "Gee, that was hard," he whispered to Anna when she finally left.

She printed one or two of the things he said. However, it was the fact that his picture appeared in the paper—his *picture!*—which made Anna's colleagues and family think she was living with a celebrated man. At one of Lucia's dinner parties, George Margosian introduced Charles with pride and unconcealed relief.

Sharon Gold of the Museum, who no longer even *remembered* her anger with Anna, called to say she was throwing "a fabulous bash" at her chic apartment, wouldn't Anna bring Charles along?

Sharon kept Charles on her arm all night.

When he came by the plant to pick up Anna, all work stopped so everybody could shake his hand. Aram Hovad bought him a beer. Francine Sarkissian and Estelle and Shirley presented him with the "Saroyan" award for writing a play near Armenians. Francine asked him outright if he was going to marry Anna or if they were just screwing around.

His New York agent and the California agent worked closely together. They quoted the reviews of Charles' play, which said "clear, well-wrought, solidly constructed, challenging." They called him a "hot young writer" as he approached his forty-second birthday. By that process of oddly connected pressures and dumb luck which had launched so many careers, Charles' merry little sitcom proposal was sold to a television production company which sold it to a network which paid well for the right to develop it.

He phoned Anna from Vermont to tell her the good news.

"What's it called, so I can tell people?" she asked.

"*Crazy Daisies,*" he said. "Takes place in a greenhouse. Little John will find it hilarious."

"Please! Stop! Can't you ever enjoy anything?!" She laughed. "I'm so proud of you!"

"Have to grade final exams," he said. "Looks like I'm gonna have to give Ignatoff an A."

OF COURSE IT WAS MORE PRACTICAL FOR CHARLES TO GO ON LIVING in New York during the summer vacation, now that he was being offered so much work and needed to have lunch with people and huddle with them in their offices. Since his name had come to mean a little something, his gardening articles for the coming year brought better rates of pay than ever before.

He began talking to a film producer, who had seen and liked his play, about rewriting a certain movie script which even after three writers was still in big trouble.

Anna came home one night, hot and knocked out from a profitable day at work, and found that he had made some dinner, that there were two plates on the table and two wineglasses. It looked very nice. It tasted very good. It was just tuna fish salad, but it tasted wonderful.

In time, the rigid habits of Anna's loneliness, so well cultivated, began to grow seedy from lack of attention, much like Charles' garden in Vermont. She had been accustomed to shopping for food on Thursdays, a large order, which kept her kitchen stocked for a full week. Now she snooped through chic grocerias and bought fancy salads in plastic tubs, enough for one meal only. She tried to cross a street and, distracted by a fruit stand, ended up buying a dozen gourmet plums during gridlock.

Charles seemed to acquire books and tapes and papers in great numbers, very quickly, and these piled up around Anna's bed. The Vintage house was prepared and organized to hold them, but here in New York, she had no containerized space; he couldn't even unpack the cartons of manuscripts he had brought down with him and he had to dig through them like a squirrel if he needed anything.

Anna decided she would build cabinets, and maybe a special "tapecase" in which the audio cassettes could be stored upright, like books. This project engrossed her during evenings while Charles read or wrote, stretched out in the hammock, inpenetrable as a dense sea fog, humming, but not a tune.

Every morning without fail, Charles would work with his weights until the pale hair in his armpits was curled and wet and black, and sweat rolled down from behind his ears onto his neck and shoulders. Clearly Charles' rigid habits of loneliness were not quite so optional as hers. She monitored her reactions to them with the sensitivity of a seismograph. Was she ever put out? Did she ever feel oppressed? Did she need to be talked to more? (For Charles could roll out silence like the great ocean itself.) Did she need to feel more adored? (For Charles was not a great demonstrator of affections.) Did she miss the touch and feel and smell of other men?

More interested in herself than she had been in years, Anna embarked upon those long introspective reveries and campaigns for self-improvement peculiar to very young women.

Her image, for example, what could she do about her image? Charles Borden said she was a sweet, easy woman, that she relaxed him with her tranquillity and her slowness to anger. However, one night when she was working late at the plant, she had found a little note from Aram Hovad to Big Mack, crumpled and discarded on the floor.

"Big M," it said. "Little Missy very pissy, cover up your balls. A."

This bit of accidentally gleaned insight into what grown men said about her caused Anna to rush into her office and stamp her feet. Why was she being so misjudged? Why did she have a reputation for fearsomeness when she wanted to be known as a pussycat?! Why was she simultaneously so many different women?

"The major event in your life," Charles said to her, "was your father's heart attack. Took his strength away from you and at the same time paved the way for you to take over his business. So you're sad and glad at the same time, and that's your problem."

"Oh please," she said. "My problem is that my lover died."

"If I died tomorrow," he said, "you'd replace me day after tomorrow." Anna gasped. Instinctively, she made the sign of the cross in front of his mouth. "Your problem is that the lover-who-was-exactly-like-your-father died, that *particular* lover. You are obsessed with your father."

"No, darling," whispered Anna. *"You* are obsessed with my father."

Regarding his own multifaceted public image (Anna loved him; Emerson Hall thought he was manic-depressive; his daughter, Valerie, thought it might be best for her if he died), Charles insisted that if only Charles II had remained prosperous—like all the Bordens since the Revolution—then he, Charles III, would have had enough money to stay in school and still support his family and would never have gone off to war and ended up a penurious gimp and *everybody* would have liked him.

Anna picked a different starting point and came up to a happier conclusion.

"If all those kids had not blown up in the harbor, without you," she said, "then you would never have asked yourself 'Why do I alone remain?' and you would never have become an introverted person and a writer like Melville and nobody would have thought much about you at all."

Charles burst out laughing, tore off his glasses, threw down his book, lifting her into the hammock with only the strength of his arms, and hugged her and kissed her. "Oh, my Anna," he chortled, "if only you had read Melville, you would know I am not a writer like Melville."

She brought him joy, she could see that, distracted him from his nagging sense of bad luck and his deep, deep suspicion, oh yes, she knew that with her bare hands she had from time to time melted the frozen soul of Charles Borden III.

The trouble was, Puccini could do that also. Anna had seen it happen; and she feared that her impact on Charles might one day prove insubstantial and fleeting as a mood created by a melody.

For the first time in her life, she began to identify with her sister Lucia, the decorated plaything, the grateful servant, purveyor of pillows and florals and billowing curtains. This upset Anna. She had her pride, after all. So when Charles went off to Connecticut one weekend, to discuss how to rewrite the ailing movie script with its producer and now its director too, she resolutely turned in the opposite direction and curled up on the wicker sofa and began to read *The Turn of the Screw* by Henry James.

Feeling scratched and splintered, she rolled onto the straw rug. Feeling itchy, she switched to the hammock. The straw blinds clicked rhythmically against the window glass in the breeze from the air conditioner, irritating Anna no end. The tile floor looked medicinal and wan. What the hell? she thought. Styles change. And the very next day, she went out and bought new sheets for her bed. They were blue with tiny white flowers. She bought new wine and new wineglasses with pink stems and pale chintz pillows for the sofa and a voluptuous long-haired rug to replace the straw, which she left on the street for those less fortunate than she to haul away.

She filled her loft with pink and white lilies. The smell of them engulfed Charles when he returned, and he burrowed into her like a wasp.

He told her he had the movie job. It was another war story. "Guess I've been typed," he said, "but what the hell?" The problems were structural. The director wanted him to go out to L.A. for a few days.

With delicious pride, Anna told her family this wonderful news. Gabe Karavajian called Charles personally—an unprecedented gesture—to congratulate him. Even he with his limited understanding of the contemporary world, even he knew that rewriting for Hollywood was a better business for a grown man to be in than teaching Poe and Hawthorne.

George Margosian called too—to commiserate. He could not imagine anything more irksome than having to rewrite someone else's work for no credit.

ANNA AND CHARLES PLANNED A VACATION FOR AUGUST, RIGHT after his return from L.A. They would go to New Bedford to see his mother. Charles IV, and even the remote, possibly hostile Valerie, would join them there. Then they would go off to the Cape alone. Charles had rented a house. It was all arranged.

Anna needed clothes for her vacation. Soon after Charles left, for the first time in a very long while, she went on a prolonged and lavish shopping spree. Her bathing suits were three or four years old. She thought they looked fine because she had not worn them too much, but Lucia's daughters declared them shapeless and out of date, not something a rising Hollywood mogul would like his lover to be caught dead in on the fashionable beaches of Cape Cod. So when Lucia and Anna went to modernize Anna's stock of beachwear, the girls came along, just so that no real horrors were perpetuated.

Under the clear skies of summer, the midtown streets chimed with the performances of magicians and singers, reggae bands and unique carolers who speeded the shoppers on their way and gladdened Anna's heart. Catching sight of Lillian and Delia in their scarlet shirts, a young man without eyebrows held out his hat and sang:

> Let's hear it for the glittering girls
> As they go out to play
> They scale the city
> Paint it red
> But still it's gray.

Instantly his four girlfriends chimed in and made the tune a madrigal, all harmony and counterpoint, as though the words were just tags on the melody and meant absolutely nothing. Lucia and her daughters didn't hear the words. They continued to cut on through the crowds, not letting Anna pause for a second look at the strange singer, although she wanted to. She felt she had met that young man before. She felt a weird chill on her back, like the young governess at Bly detecting a wisp of peril in the perfect blooming day.

In a great midtown department store, Lillian and Delia insisted she try on a black bathing suit with gold diagonal stripes on it.

But when Anna tried it and saw how it looked on her body, she became hysterical. "Lucia!" she screamed. "Come in here right away!"

Lucia dashed through the maze of dressing rooms, ducking into half a dozen—sorry, sorry, oh my God, sorry—until she found Anna, collapsed on the floor among the mirrors, laughing so hard that her eyes streamed tears and the fillings in her backmost teeth could be clearly seen.

The bathing suit she had tried was cut rather gently on the top; Anna's moderate-sized chest stayed moderately well hidden. However, in the back, the bathing suit was cut so low that the division of her buttocks showed deep and dark as the Continental Divide, and at the hips it was cut so high and toward the crotch so narrowly that had Anna not been wearing underpants, her pubic hair would have billowed out on either side like a large black cloud.

"That's the style!" Lucia protested.

"It is the style for women to go to Cape Cod looking like apes?!"

"Will you stop?! Don't you read the magazines?! Don't you *ever* shop?! Don't you realize that you're supposed to buy some gook and take it off?"

"But I'm an adult!"

"You leave a little patch."

"Did you do that, leave a little patch?"

"Of course not, I don't go to the beach at all since my legs turned to shit. But the girls do it."

"*Your* girls?!"

Lucia rushed out of the dressing room and grabbed Lillian and Delia by their armpits.

"Come show your Aunt Anna your little patches."

"MOM!"

"Get in there and show her before I break your neck!"

In the end, Anna bought the black bathing suit and another one as well, blue, different on the top, but not different on the bottom (they were none of them different on the bottom that year) and several other frocks and smocks and pants to wear to the beach so that she would not shame Charles, who was after all (her nieces told her at every cash register) spending the better part of a week in a city where the most beautiful women in the world paraded around naked all day and all night and especially loved to reduce hot new writers to *luleh kebab* with their long blond legs and gigantic tan tits! Anna had to compete! cried the Margosian sisters, flinging diaphanous nightgowns at her head.

Anna and Lucia chased the girls down Fifth Avenue, beating at them with their pocketbooks, and the glittering girls giggled and tripped and gripped the arms of their Aunt Anna and kissed her and carried all her many packages.

THE NIGHT BEFORE CHARLES WAS DUE TO RETURN FROM LOS ANGE-les, Anna stood in front of her bathroom mirror, looking at the bottom half of her body. She knew what she had to do to appear on the beaches this summer, but she was not at all sure that she *should* do it. Mrs. Karavajian had brought an aesthetic from the Old Country that valued hairlessness, and she had urged her daughters to keep themselves smooth all over, shaved legs, clean armpits, not one dark hair remaining above the mouth. But there were limits, mystical maybe or maybe political. Mary had told her that the Moslems liked to cut the folds and lips off the insides of women's bodies when they were young and then sew them up and shave them clean, so they were tight inside and passionless forever and hairless outside as virginal little girls. So it did not seem to Anna Karavajian a decent Christian thing to do, this shaving the hair of her body down to a little patch, it seemed to imitate the values of more barbaric times. But she was going to do it, goddammit, because it was the style.

So first she turned on Tina Turner to calm her nerves.

Then she smeared on handfuls of baby oil. Then she applied some of the stuff her nieces had urged her to buy which smelled like fabric softener combined with new ink and press cleaner. She put a little on the tip of her finger. She smeared it on one small corner of hair. She waited eight minutes like it said on the bottle . . . talk about private dancing, she thought, talk about being an object and a slave . . . and then she wiped the little corner. But the hair didn't come out. She applied the stuff again. She waited 10 minutes. It said on the bottle not to wait any longer than 15 minutes. She wiped. The hair didn't come out.

Anna really felt that she was going to cry.

She sagged onto the toilet seat and read the directions again.

It said that people with very coarse or tough to remove hair should wet themselves down first and then put the stuff on, so Anna tried that. But her hair would not come out.

She called Lucia.

"It's not a good time," Lucia said and hung up. (Either she was cooking or fighting with George.)

Anna went back to her potions.

She smeared the depilatory on in big glops. This time her hair came out, but also her skin came off, and she really did begin to cry.

Lucia called her back.

"I can't believe you are crying about your pubic hair! What have you become, an adolescent?! If you can't get the gook to work, go to a specialist and have yourself waxed!"

"Ich! How could you suggest such a thing to me?! I am your sister!"

"Please! You are driving me crazy! Pretend you're having a baby and shave it off!"

"Won't that create unsightly stubble?" Anna asked.

Lucia hung up.

Anna began to shave.

The hair was too long to shave. So first she had to cut it with a scissor as short as she could, and *then* she shaved it. She felt sick. She felt sicker than she had when her mother took her for electrolysis, because she had *agreed* that the hair above her lip was ugly, but she did not agree about this, she liked her pubic hair, it was a regular with her, a nest, it had been in the same place for twenty-five years!

The phone rang.

It was Charles.

"They still don't like the prison camp scene," he said grimly. "Gotta rewrite, be a week late, maybe even two."

Anna stood dripping oil and cream and water, dripping little soapy clods of hair in lather. The mess ran down her legs and carried her with it to the bottom of her endurance. She felt dizzy; she felt drowned.

"Anna," he said. "Honey? Are you there? Gee, don't be so silent. I'll get home eventually . . . Anna . . . ?"

"Yes," she said. "I understand. Just that I was longing for you . . . so counting on having you back . . ."

They could hardly go on talking and soon hung up. Anna dried herself off. She put on her pants and went looking for Daniel.

"Take me for a walk, Daniel," she called. "I need some exercise. I'm washed up as an odalisque."

The old dog lay stretched out on Anna's new blue sheets.

At first she thought he was sleeping.

ACTUALLY IT WASN'T THE WORST THING IN THE WORLD, TO HAVE Charles far away right now, she told her sister Lucia. She had no time to take a vacation anyway. She was doing too well.

Roughly coincident with the opening of Charles' play, and only a year after the attack of the paper thieves, Karavajian Press had begun to grow (in the spirit of the times) from the top up, its richest clients becoming richer and richer.

Sharon Gold's office at the Museum constantly ordered exhibition brochures and mailing pieces, with such extravagances as die cut cover designs and gold pages (although Anna never got a mailing contract from them again).

A large soap company bought Bottom Oil, kept one of its directors, and sent the other two job hunting. As each of the fired executives found a new place for himself—one at a brokerage firm, one at a slick business magazine—he sent his underlings back to good old Karavajian.

The brokerage firm required fat quarterly reports in four colors.

The business magazine went on line, 240 pages a month.

In cautious increments of one and two, Anna added ten new employees. She rented the rest of the third floor. She leased two more delivery trucks. She fired the incompetent Krishna. She appointed Francine as her own personal secretary, authorizing Aram and Larry to hire someone else and share.

Finally, she summoned the courage to approach Mildred the old comptroller and admit that she had been forced to hire a computer company to take over Karavajian's billing and record keeping.

To Anna's astonishment, Mildred cackled and declared she was thrilled to have all the little pieces of paper out of her hands at last, and she said sure, she'd "supervise" the new accounting operation, maybe she'd also take some time and go to the track if it was okay with Anna, and Anna kissed her and hugged her gratefully.

"You fooled 'em all, didn't you, Little Missy?" old Mildred said. "They thought you'd fall on your ass, those sexist pigs from the Old Country, but you fooled 'em all."

Upon hearing the touching story of Mildred the Loyal, Sharon Gold burst out laughing. It had been absolutely years, she said, since she'd heard anyone use the feminist vernacular; why didn't they prepare an alcove in the Museum where they could put Mildred on display?

Anna thought Sharon Gold was an asshole.

Skinny as a sick person, all dressed in white at all times, Sharon told Anna that she had a hunk who came to her home at 5:00 A.M. to exercise her and a masseuse who came at twilight to iron out the kinks and with all that she still spent at least an hour every other day at the gym, dunking in the whirlpool and picking up on the financial news.

Sharon knew everything that was happening on both coastlines. She spun out names and events and wove them into a tapestry of anecdotes and connections and predictions which, she swore to Anna, constituted the essential fabric of their lives. She was not trying to amuse Anna when she said things like "It's not what you know, it's who you know" and "It's not how well you feel, it's how well you look."

Her habit was to eat in restaurants where she could charge her meal to the Museum. She would order chicken, eat perhaps one quarter of it, and ask the waiter to wrap it up so she could take it home, where she would reheat it at the end of the day (after the masseuse left) and have it for dinner.

"It's not what you eat," she said. "It's whether you pay."

(Anna thought she had once heard her sister Lucia say, perhaps in a McDonalds or a Burger King when the Margosian girls were little, "It's not what you eat, it's whether you cook." In Sharon Gold's version was writ the New Age.)

Anna expected Mary to laugh along with these tales of Sharon.

"Please," Mary said, "let's not forget one little thing, shall we? This woman you profess to despise is making you rich. Pilfered chicken notwithstanding, Sharon Gold is helping Anna Karavajian become a hotshot of the printing trades whom old, misguided feminists like Mildred speak of with boundless pride. Don't knock it, kiddo."

Sharon endeavored to become much friendlier with Anna after the success of *The Ice Cold Jungle* and the appearance of Charles Borden's face in the *Times*. However, after Karavajian Press took on The Movie Company account, Sharon became positively chummy.

The Movie Company—TMC, Inc.—was an investment group, funded by mysterious insurance firms and British agribusiness. Anna had met its New York executive at one of Elliot's "Save The Shelter" fund-raisers. A nice quiet gentleman from Northern Ireland, wearing gray on gray tweeds, he modestly told Anna that TMC, Inc. would be distributing fifteen films this year and producing seven of them and was in fact looking for a New York print shop to provide local support—brochures, posters, magazine inserts, whatever—was Anna interested? Yes yes yes, Anna said. She did not mind being paid by a Finnish bank, nor did she let it concern her that all of the movies associated with The Movie Company were sickeningly gory and pornographic (except for one or two which were brilliant hallmarks of cinematic achievement).

"The shit pays for the art," mused the gray on gray gentleman from Northern Ireland.

Sharon Gold was dying to meet him.

AT THE START OF THE SECOND WEEK CHARLES WAS IN LOS ANGELES, Sharon Gold arranged for Anna to have lunch with Richard Garfield of the Farmers' Bank. Garfield was Sharon's new boss. He had stolen her from the Museum by offering her wonderful money.

Not only did Sharon authorize a lot of work for Karavajian before she left, but she now could deliver the huge Farmers' Bank account as well. It was all set. Anna had only to lunch today with Garfield, and be nice to him, "maybe flirt with him a little," Sharon said, "and for God's sakes, when he talks money, don't play like a girl."

Anna did her best. She wore the red dress she had bought for the opening of Charles' play. At eleven-thirty, she went out and got her hair done and her nails manicured, then stopped back at the plant to let Estelle, Shirley, and Francine approve her. (An empty ritual by now, but still fun.)

She was all ready to go when Charles called. He sounded groggy, only half-awakened out there in green L.A.

"Dream of you all night, can't get it down in the morning, like a little kid . . ."

"Oh please please don't talk to me that way in the middle of a business day, I'm just going to have lunch with a banker."

"Watch your ass."

Richard Garfield of the Farmers' Bank met Anna at a lovely new East Side restaurant he had chosen. Anna had never heard of it. They sprang up, colorful as annuals, these places, and then disappeared, new ones every season. What happened to the people who wanted to eat lunch in the same place for twenty-five years? she wondered. The nesters, the regulars, where could they find shelter in these swiftly moving times?

Whoever had designed this place had done so with a craft and an intention similar to Sally Bangle's in *The Seagull* set, simulating light where there was none, painting the table linens in a pointilist shimmer of apricot and gold and ivory, choosing lattice backed chairs that let light flow through them and brass accessories to let light bounce off them and creating false walls of windows facing gardens drenched in floods of sunlight. So successful was the change of mood wrought by this design that Anna had to struggle to remind herself that today was a cloudy day and that it would soon be pouring rain outside. Like the oases of fake sun in one of her favorite science fiction stories by Ray Bradbury, this restaurant locked out the stress and shouting of the city and restored the soul of the working woman.

Anna felt bad that her dress was red.

She would have preferred to match the colors of the restaurant.

She wondered if this was the reason that Sharon Gold always wore white, so as never to clash, never to seem out of place or abrasive no matter what the setting.

The nicest thing about Richard Garfield of the Farmers' Bank was that he did not present a grand persona. He was just a plain man. He just wiped his glasses. He just smoothed his thinning hair. He smiled at Anna in a friendly sort of way but his teeth weren't dazzling and he didn't sport a tan or a perfect body like Charles' California agent. He wore a white shirt with some sort of white design on it and a gray suit or maybe it was brown, Anna would not be able to remember. She would not be able to recognize him at a small dinner party only a year later; that was how unprepossessing he was, how unlike Elliot Longet and Sharon Gold.

Sharon herself would have explained: "When you got it, you don't have to flaunt it." In fact, this was precisely what Richard Garfield said to himself about Anna Karavajian, and so he liked her immediately; he was immediately impressed with her; he figured her for a very successful woman.

"Sharon Gold told me you deliver what you promise, that's what she said and if that's true, we're gonna be good friends," he said, "drink up, drink up"—filling her wineglass—"is there a Mr. Karavajian back at your plant to tell you what to do?"

"No," Anna said.

"Peachy," said Garfield.

Something buzzed. Anna looked around, puzzled, then realized it was Garfield's watch.

"This watch," said Garfield, leaning close, "not only tells me the time and date and temperature everywhere, it buzzes off when the dollar exchange rate alters anywhere and, it can call up the going price for every single currency at any given hour of any given day in any given capital of the Western and, for that matter, the Eastern world."

Anna laughed, charmed; she wanted to see the watch more closely and parted the wineglasses to peer at it.

"Let me fill you in on a little something I've learned, pretty lady," Garfield continued, filling his glass and her glass too. "They're all the same, all the worlds. The Soviets and the blacks are the same as the British upper classes, and recently I've had to deal with a lot of bright young women like yourself, and they're all the same, too, everybody wants a piece of the pie, and I have learned in my travels that the pie is big, real big, pretty lady, big enough for everybody who takes the trouble to dig in."

Anna sincerely hoped that was true.

"Now I've got your bids in my office, also those layouts you sent over, it all looks fine to me. I have got one little problem, however . . ."

Oh Jesus, he's going to tell me my price is too high, Anna thought.

". . . your price is too low," said Richard Garfield.

"There's no room in there for anything except your costs and your profit. I would say"—Garfield calculated quickly by the little digital buttons on his demon watch—"I would say you could make your price eighteen or maybe even nineteen percent higher and still beat all the competition . . . and then you just arrange an ordinary rebate, and if you do that, then I assure you, Anna . . . may I call you Anna? . . . I assure you that you will have the account as long as Sharon Gold and I are at the Farmers' Bank."

Anna put her wineglass down very slowly. The wine inside made little waves because her hand was shaking. Richard Garfield felt real bad to have unsettled her so.

"Oh my dear, I am so sorry," he said, taking her hand, "you look like you have seen a ghost, did I scare you? Did you think I was gonna tell you that your price was too high? Ha! Well, don't you worry about a thing, pretty lady, you put your man Hovad in touch with my girl Sharon and they'll work it out and everything is gonna be just peachy." Anna smiled. She did not withdraw her hand. She knew Richard Garfield would be relieved to see her smile, that he was a gallant and worldly gentleman who would not for anything upset a pretty lady.

"Now, tell me about this consortium that's doing so well in the dirty movie business," he said. "I hear they print with Karavajian. I hear they do their banking in Finland. Doesn't seem fair, does it, to bank with the Finns when you're making your money in the USA?" His watch buzzed off. "There goes the old dollar. Mutating again," philosophized Richard Garfield.

Trying to appear calm, not to let her astonishment and, yes, her excitement show, Anna told him everything she knew about TMC, The Movie Company. Apparently it was more than he knew; he felt grateful for her assistance. He held her arm as they walked out into the pouring rain. He offered to give her a lift back to the plant in the limousine he had waiting. However, Anna did not accept his offer. She did not want him to see the old sooty building squashed under the West Side Highway, because he might conclude that her company was less successful than she had made him believe.

It dawned on Anna that if the Farmers' Bank account fell into place and the Museum account kept expanding and TMC decided to go ahead with its public stock offering, in which Anna could invest for an insider's price, she might be able to consider moving her operation to a nice clean building in the suburbs, with grass and azaleas.

Her father had never been able to consider that.

She realized that as of today, she could be more successful than her father.

The rain pounded on her umbrella; her just-coiffed hair began to wilt; but Anna didn't care, she strode through the streets in her high heels swiftly, a steel-footed New York woman, her gold-glass sunglasses sparkling with drops and her lipstick perfect. Young girls in doorways looked at her and thought, ah, that's who I want to be, that's whose life I want.

She traversed the curbs mindlessly, the fastest woman in New York, and she broke the light barrier.

The atoms of color in a pointilist world reversed themselves. Anna joined the white stars in a black void; a galaxy. Some special-effects guy Vartan played football with had given Anna and all her generation of moviegoers his starfield for a vision, and they used it, as she did now, in all moments of excitement, essential protein of the imagination, metaphor for everything, from escape to success.

In her galaxy, Anna was a spacecraft whooshing in from the foreground. She passed stars shining. On each one a moment of her life was pictured, bent a little and blurred, like a reflection on a brass doorknob.

She saw herself as a little girl with her hair in bunches, riding high on the rolling skids of paper while Nubar and Louis pushed her (young men then) and she laughed and screamed.

She saw her father playing backgammon with Tom Sarkissian on an overturned crate in the stock room, everlasting game, with cigars, and there she was in her dungarees, resting her face on her father's knee, watching the game, learning.

She saw Tom bending over the big press, showing Big Mack and Aram Hovad how this particular machine operated. It was new then, and last week she had sold it. On another star she saw herself sitting with Mildred stuffing bills into envelopes and sealing them with the help of a little sponge that never left its wet dish. She heard the clatter of Mildred's adding machine. She heard the greeting of the old priest (dead now) when she and her father walked into the cathedral. She heard the choir sing, saw the soldier in the pew sleeping. Poor guy, she thought. Cute guy.

A Con Ed truck turned her corner and splashed her with yards of filthy water. She whimpered with anger and slowed down; the galaxy disappeared. Anna's red dress hung like a dead bandage. She growled.

Down the street behind her came a pack of dogs, all lunging and barking and salivating horribly.

The young man who was holding their leashes was wearing roller skates and they were pulling him along the street at a breakneck pace, but he was not restraining them, no, he waved a Mets banner over their heads and sang out, "Go go go, my mad doggies! *Allez allez yallah yallah!*"

"Watch where you're going, asshole!" Anna screamed.

The boy pirouetted on his skates and bowed to Anna with a familiar flourish.

"Just trying to make an honest living, schnookie," Rex called.

Anna gazed after her as the mad dogs pulled her beyond retrieval.

ALL ANNA DID WHEN SHE RETURNED TO THE PLANT WAS GO TO THE bathroom, that was all, a routine encounter with the "No ink in the sink" sign, with her own familiar face (now a little paled by anxiety). All she wanted was to wash up and change into dry clothes and sensible shoes. But in the sink Estelle had left her big red pocketbook. Anna had to move it to wash her hands.

She could not move it.

Too heavy.

"Stealing is a way of life in this country . . ." came Charles' dry, ironic voice remembered.

Impossible, Estelle could not be stealing anything, what could she be stealing?! Pens?! Pencils?! Yellow legal pads?! In her mind's eye, Anna saw the supply cabinet at the English Department office in Vintage College emptying out like a flower shedding petals in time lapse photography, the stacked boxes of paper clips and reams of paper flying away. She knew she had not been listening hard enough to Charles Borden when he told her that story. She had been longing to put her hands inside his shirt, she had ignored many things he said in the heat and press of her desire. However, now that he had been gone for ten days and she couldn't have him, she had begun to remember everything he had ever said.

"Nobody turns anybody in because everybody does it . . ."

Maybe Estelle was doing it too! How had Richard Garfield, that sleeze, that lowlife, even come to know Aram Hovad's name?! Maybe Aram was doing it . . .

Anna hauled the red pocketbook out of the sink and lowered it to the floor, wrenching her back. Karavajian Press clearly possessed nothing of any *value* that a press operator might steal in her big red pocketbook. Except that Estelle could possibly be stealing things that were worth nothing, just to harass and trouble the company. Had not Mo Gottlieb of Tacoma Paper told Anna that crooks on the highway were stealing his paper in worthless little bits, hoping to ruin the good name of his company with old customers like Anna? Had not Mo turned out to be right and not paranoid? Maybe the same thing that had happened to Tacoma Paper was happening to her!

Impossible, Anna thought, impossible, Karavajian Press was having its best year ever. Weren't the rich new accounts growing richer all the time? If disloyal truckers were robbing Tacoma Paper, if Sharon Gold was on the take, if the kids in Charles' English class hired others to write their papers, if some vice president nobody remembered took bribes in the White House, that was *them* and had nothing to do with Anna's plant or her people!

Estelle flushed the toilet and came out of the john.

"I had to . . . uh . . . move your pocketbook . . . so heavy . . ."

"Twice I got mugged," Estelle said. She crouched down on the floor. She took three bricks out of the pocketbook and lined them up so that they leaned against each other, like dominos. "Never again," she said.

ANNA ASKED HER FATHER TO HAVE LUNCH WITH HER LATER THAT same week at the apricot restaurant where she had met Richard Garfield. He did not feel comfortable there, but she had known that would be the case. The headwaiter remembered Anna: oh yes, of course, he smiled, the quiet lady with the abrasive clothing, guest of Mr. Garfield, won't you sit here by the east garden . . . and on and on, showing a degree of respect rarely heaped on Anna, and never before in her father's presence.

Gabe Karavajian had shriveled. Dark pockets of sagging skin underscored his eyes. His dapper little mustache seemed too large for his face now, and his hands trembled. With a weary sufferance he listened as the *maître d'* recited all the scrumptious specials of the day. Then he ordered broiled fish without salt or butter.

"I'm thinking of putting Mary on the payroll," Anna said.

"Why? Does she need money?"

"I've been giving her money for years!" Anna exclaimed. "How do you think she's paid for the shrinks?!"

Gabe looked hurt.

"Does Spike know?"

"I think he pretends not to know."

"But if you send a check in the mail, he won't be able to pretend anymore."

"Oh please, it's so much more convenient this way! I mean sometimes I'm so busy I forget to bring cash for Mary and then she has to suffer the embarrassment of reminding me. She hates that and so do I. Let's just make it simple."

"If you put her on the books, you will create trouble between Mary and Spike," her father said. "Even pacifists are funny about money."

Anna laughed and shifted out of her chair across the table from him into the chair next to him.

"Should I invest in The Movie Company? They're going public."

"I don't like them," said her father. "Once I was at the plant and on the big press I saw a poster for one of their movies, it was a naked woman lying on her back tied to a table and above her chest this big meat cleaver was hanging and all around there were these slabs of meat on hooks like in a packing house. It was called *The Butcher's Block.*"

"At Karavajian Press, we call it *S and M Rocky.*"

"I never printed anything I was ashamed of, Anna."

She did not flinch.

"How do you feel about kickbacks?" she asked. She shifted out of the chair next to him into the chair opposite from him so that he would have to look her in the eye. "What do I do when a potentially huge customer wants a big kickback?"

"I don't know anymore," he said. "It's different now."

"Come on, Daddy . . ."

"I did business with people who knew me," he said. "Armenians who valued my good name and theirs. They asked me for low prices but they never asked me to put anything in their pockets . . . and when we expanded and began to work with outsiders, and they *did* ask me, again and again, I still felt afraid, the *amot,* the shame, that men in the printing trades should meet in the steam room and say to each other 'Gabe Karavajian paid off my production man . . .' "

Anna laughed. "And I'm afraid they'll sit around in the whirlpool at the gym and say 'Anna Karavajian plays like a girl.' "

"Don't start paying thieves. If you start, you can never stop."

"Mo Gottlieb didn't play ball and they almost ruined him, Daddy."

"Now now, you must not compare yourself to Mo Gottlieb, he's a man, it was much more serious for him, he couldn't get out. But you can get out any time you like . . . if maybe you want to get married and move to another city . . ."

"Stop."

"We can always sell the company."

"Daddy!"

Gabe shifted out of his chair into the chair next to her.

"Aram Hovad says you are in love with Charles Borden. *'Verahn gu khentenah,'* he says, 'she's crazy about him'; since Borden has gone to California you come to work at six in the morning and you stay past ten, Aram says . . . Is that true?"

"Yes."

"Does he propose marriage to you?"

"No."

Gabe sighed and sighed. "Oh Anna, *seerdus,* my beauty, make him marry you, a woman must not be alone. These pressures of the business, they are unhealthy for you, unnatural. It makes me feel sick to think of you making deals, handing out payoffs. Go back to your original destiny. You should be doing charity work, saving orphans, you are a sentimental person . . . look how sentimental you are being about this illegal night watchman . . ."

"DX is a gifted man!"

"But you must see that his presence in the plant endangers all our people."

Anna got up and walked once around the table, to prevent herself from becoming overtly angry. Then she sat down opposite her father.

"Don't call them 'our people' like they're helpless peasants from the Old Country, Daddy, any one of them could have blown the whistle on DX long ago."

"And how long ago did you file those papers? Years: right? Years! You will never be able to make that man legal."

"He's a magician, a comedian, he made fun of the government! They put him in prison! They nearly *killed* him there! They pulled out all his teeth!"

"My company should not be hiding people who are wanted by the law where they used to live!" Gabe insisted.

"Please, Daddy! When Talaat Pasha was the law in the Old Country, everybody you *knew* was wanted!"

The old man groped in his pockets for a nitroglycerine.

"I'm going home," he said. "I don't like this restaurant. When you invited me here to lunch, I expected to hear news of your forthcoming wedding, I did not expect to talk business. When I want to talk business I will have lunch with Aram Hovad."

He walked out.

He knew he had hurt his beloved daughter, that he had left her gasping and weeping in a restaurant where it was important for her to maintain her dignity and the respect of people. Without a doubt, he had put her in her place.

The minute he arrived home in Tenafly, he called her to apologize.

Her secretary, addressing him with awful false deference, said Anna was in a meeting and would have to get back to him.

LUCIA TOLD ANNA THAT SHE SHOULD NOT FEEL TOO BAD THAT Charles was dallying with some bimbo in Hollywood (for that was what she and Mary believed; nothing Anna could say in Charles' defense would change their minds; not for one minute did they buy the idea that it took more than two weeks in another town to rewrite a prison camp scene). It was not so wonderful to be nailed to one man anyway, Lucia said; better to have lovers, for they did not take a woman's strength and all her youth and then throw her away in her middle age.

At forty-six, Lucia Margosian had grown not fat but thickened, like a sauce. Once the *femme fatale* of the Armenian Student Union, she had danced at so many parties and broken so many hearts as a young woman that when she finally married George, she felt exhausted from dating, more than ready to retire and serve the twin causes of motherhood and serious music.

Now it appeared she had served too well.

With her witty conversation and little dinner parties famous for their desserts, she had advanced her husband's career inexorably, leaving

George himself free to rehearse and compose and record and teach his master classes and concertize the world over. Lucia dressed him, she fed him, she patrolled the long silences he required. And so he became famous in his field, a brilliant musician capable of securing stipends for violinists who wanted to study in Vienna and ensemble jobs for flutists who wanted to perform at Tanglewood. He had, in short, a certain amount of power, the ultimate aphrodisiac according to a former secretary of state who clearly spoke from personal experience. And ambitious young women in the world of serious music played for him and sang for him and made love to him on sofas.

Lucia blamed herself entirely.

She told Anna that to live with an artist was ultimately demeaning, a service job at best. She described for Anna the murderous rages that would come over an artist upon reading bad reviews of his work; the long nights when he would prowl the living room, weeping because his fountains of inspiration had dried up; the bitter arguments with colleagues over the sharpness of a D chord on one of eight tracks, which no one in the listening audience would have detected in a million years; and the ego, Lucia said, the insatiable ego, which required homage from octaves of women.

"I am not in the least upset," said Lucia, drying her eyes. "But you are much meaner and tougher than I am, Anna, and you would not be able to stand my life for five minutes."

George himself did not pay much attention to the girls who hauled him into their pretty embraces. Since he would never think of getting a musician a job unless that musician was qualified, their efforts were mostly wasted. There was just no payoff with George. What he loved was his cello and his oud and his angry Tashnag politics, and his wife, he loved her above everything in the world, from the minute he had seen her weeping in the rhododendron forest, desperately pulling her torn dress down over her knees, he had loved Lucia Karavajian.

What he had forgotten, however, was her honor, and how precious that was to her sisters.

Spike Russo dared to defend George.

"Come on, baby," he said. "Lighten up; George is just fooling around." Mary poured hot coffee on his lap.

Anna dared to be more creative.

She arranged for Elliot Longet to call Lucia at her home, in the morning when George would be there practicing. George answered. Elliot stammered, babbled inanities, then hung up guiltily. "This absurd exercise in infantile sisterhood," as Elliot called it, could not possibly work, he declared, because a man of George Margosian's prodigious talents could not be so easily aroused to jealousy; it was much too base an emotion to entrap a genius.

The third time Elliot called, George threatened to have him killed.

"You know I would do anything for you, my darling girl," Elliot said to Anna, "but they do expect me to arrive in Washington in one piece, so as of today, the show is over. Bye bye."

ON A SATURDAY NIGHT IN THE HEAT OF AUGUST THE FAMILY GATHered at the Karavajian house in Tenafly for one of their periodic dinners. George and Lucia had been fighting. Mary and Spike were not getting along too well either. What had started out as a funny little plot to make George suffer had escalated its effects beyond Anna's wildest dreams, and now she regretted having concocted it, she hated the tension in the house.

Her mother was furious with her.

Anna had fulfilled Mrs. Karavajian's most heartfelt predictions. She had lost her innocence, her sweetness, and now dressed like a successful woman—some pale lilac outfit with pants and a flowing kimono top, much more radical than anything Mary had ever worn—and kept her fingernails short and polished white. She had somehow acquired a large, complicated watch, very masculine. It chimed professionally. She drank vodka openly in her father's house. When she thought her mother was not looking, she scratched herself in the crotch area like a football player.

Everyone in the family had heard the stories emanating from the Pacific Northwest, about the dangerous litigation now commencing against certain Teamsters, everyone in the printing trades knew how Anna had involved Vita Press, and how Mo Gottlieb's lawyers had forced Tom Sarkissian to give evidence. These reports gravely distressed Gabe Karavajian; he lost sleep over them. To think that his little girl had come so close to making such serious enemies . . . to think of it . . .

"I told you," his wife said. "I told you she was smarter and tougher than you, and that if you gave her the business, she would turn it into a little empire, I told you that, but you didn't listen, you thought she would play with it like a child with a toy. You have never understood Anna."

Clearly the older girls, on whom Mrs. Karavajian had always counted to moderate Anna's eccentricities, had lost all their influence over her.

Mary depended on her for money. Lucia depended on her for moral support during this crisis with George. Her nieces looked up to her; she was their role model, and in her disappointment with marriage and family, Lucia now *encouraged* them to feel that way.

Like her older daughters, Mrs. Karavajian assumed that Charles (being a writer and therefore presumably just like George) had met an actress or some other beautiful woman in Los Angeles, and this had turned his head, and now he was finished with Anna, they would not see him in their midst again.

Mrs. Karavajian felt sorry about that.

She had liked Charles and enjoyed his play. The son with the braces and the pimples and the three piece suit had made a nice impression on her. She would have been disturbed that Charles was an *odar,* except that Anna was so old now, her mother felt compelled to look with favor on any honest man who courted her. Too bad, she thought. Too bad.

It was all over.

Gabe was sick and old; Spike was wounded and taciturn; George was a wild man, useless for anything except the beautification of the airwaves; and Anna, her little Anna, had become the leader of the family.

She beckoned Anna into the kitchen and closed the door.

"Your sister Lucia has gone crazy," she said. "You must speak to her and tell her to go back to George."

"Lucia has not left George."

"As good as. Just as good as. When he comes home late from a concert, there is nothing for him to eat, he has to go out to restaurants."

"Who told you that? Did George complain about it to you?"

"No! Worse! Lucia bragged about it to me!"

"Mom, please stop. I can't take this now. I have had a horrible week. Charles didn't come back on time. My dear old dog died."

"Talk to Lucia. Promise me."

"I promise."

Her mother took her by the hand.

"I am very proud of you, the way you handled that terrible thing with Tom Sarkissian without bothering your father or involving him. You did right. You acted with strength and honor. You are my strongest daughter."

CHARLES ARRIVED THEN.

He came to the front door and made sure that Anna was there, and then he paid the taxi and entered the house. He looked a little tired from the long plane ride, but still much better dressed than anyone remembered him, and tan, and very fit. His hair was combed and his eyebrows were plastered down in an orderly fashion. He had begun to grow a beard. Although it was coming in gray, it made him look young. He wore beautiful new boots.

For Mrs. Karavajian, Charles had brought a large box of Italian chocolates, and a bottle of very good scotch for Gabe, UCLA sweatshirts for the Margosian girls and for Johnny too. And earrings for Anna, gold, the most expensive present Charles Borden had ever bought for anyone.

Johnny gave him a big hug hello.

Lillian and Delia stashed his suitcase.

Gabe shook his hand at first and then made a decision to embrace him like a man.

Charles was home.

His name had not been mentioned all evening except in Mary's soft curses ("the son-of-a-bitch, to fuck over my kid sister, if I ever see him again I will chew off his other leg"). But now he was home, instantly exonerated of all suspected wrongdoing, and the family opened for him like a safe harbor.

Lucia and Mary sat Charles down on the sofa. They put a pillow on the coffee table so he could stretch out his leg in comfort. They bracketed him snugly, like earmuffs, telling him family secrets, crisscrossing him with their soft arms as they talked him through the snapshots in the old albums. Anna as a little girl on a tricycle; with her class at the Armenian after-school school; dripping at the edge of a pool, holding a little trophy; in high school with the prize-winning birdhouse she had built; as a brides-maid at Lucia's wedding (yellow and white); in college crowded on a bed with her friends making funny faces; as a bridesmaid at Mary's wedding (come as you are); as a bride-to-be with a frizzy-haired guy holding her tightly—his thick blunt fingers gripping her shoulder and the watch on his wrist turned inward, the way a physical therapist would turn it.

Charles peered more closely at this picture.

"Is that Vartan?"

"He was very short," Mary said.

"Gee, I knew him," Charles murmured.

"What?!" Lucia gasped.

"I just wrote to him."

"Charles! He's been dead for sixteen years!"

"Name was Garba, right? Never knew his first name. We called him Garba the Strong. I knew him in Boston. He took care of me. He belted me with that hand there, the one on Anna's shoulder, convinced me not to cut off my leg. And this week I went to see a doctor in L.A., does cosmetic surgery, big Hollywood doctor, and he said he could give me a new calf muscle and a new knee and rebuild my ankle and most of my foot. I made an appointment for the surgery and I wrote to Garba, care of the VA hospital in Boston, hoping maybe they would forward it—guy like that must get lots of letters from guys like me—to tell him that what he said had come true and to thank him. So. Seems I have more to thank Garba for than I ever dreamed."

Anna's sisters thought it was a good omen. They wiped their eyes and put away the pictures. Charles settled back in comfort. Mrs. Karavajian brought him some food. Anna rubbed his cramped and tired shoulders— wonderful instincts, that woman. He liked the way she looked in her silky lilac clothes; liked the way she looked in her new gold earrings. He didn't like her watch. Maybe next time, he would buy her a new watch.

He figured that in due course, he would buy her everything the old man ever wanted her to have, and then some.

Eventually the dishes were done, George stopped giving Johnny a lesson on the oud, the family quieted. And Gabe Karavajian told this story . . . all had heard it, of course . . . but he told it again on this particular night in honor of Charles Borden.

We're still alive, he told. We escaped the fate prepared for us and we are still alive in New Jersey. Listen . . .

"When I was thirteen," Mr. Karavajian said, "my family tried to send me out of the Old Country through Smyrna. A beautiful city, now they call it Izmir. I went with my teacher. We were a group of ten boys. Our families had booked us passage on a French ship, anchored in the harbor, and our teacher held the passports and all the papers.

"But the Turks recaptured the city. Our teacher went to the French mission for help, but he was run down by the horses, shot . . . and we were alone . . . and we had to run. We ran toward the harbor. We lost each other.

"Oh I prayed . . . like in your play, in the end of our play, Charles . . . I prayed to God, get me through the night, out of this . . . what was it? . . . this 'pit'; yes. They set fire to the beautiful buildings and the gardens. All the people of the city were running away, but there was no place to go. Only the harbor where the ships were anchored.

"I ran into a house which was not on fire. In front of me . . . right where you are sitting, my children . . . there was an old man, dead, his blood was already dry, and black. I took some candlesticks from the house and ran back into the street. When a Turkish soldier stopped me, I gave him the candlesticks and he let me pass.

"Everywhere the soldiers had taken what they wanted; the brass coffee pots, even the earrings out of the ears of the women . . . the poor women . . . oh, the young girls . . ."

Karavajian clicked his glass against his teeth, shaking his head; the strangeness of the world . . . and fate . . . and war . . . the strangeness . . .

"So I got to the harbor," he said. "Behind me the city of Smyrna was burning. I never saw such a big fire, I thought this fire must be seen as far away as Europe and America, no one could miss such a big fire, now isn't that funny, children? Eh? Well . . . I was just a kid, *eench keedayee?* I knew nothing, how could I know the world would care nothing for the children of the Armenians? . . . So I jumped in the water, splashing around, looking for the French ship. They will have my name, I thought. They will know my ticket was paid for because in their country, they are not barbarians, they keep records of such things. I called up to the sailor: *'Je suis chrétien pour l'amour de Dieu! . . .'* And he looked around him to make sure no one would see. And he threw me a rope."

The old man laughed.

"And he was not French, was he, Anna, *seerdus*, my beauty?"

"No, Daddy."

"He was American. It was an American ship. He hid me . . ."

"In his bunk," Anna said. "In a duffle bag at the end of his bunk below deck."

"He disobeyed orders to hide me," her father said, "and so this is why I leave my good sense at home and I let my sentimental little girl keep her night watchman, the one with no papers, the one from Salvador."

Anna glanced at Charles in the half-dark. She could not see what he was thinking.

"I wrote to that sailor who saved me for fifty years until he died," said Karavajian. "I sent him pictures of my little girls. And whenever I grow impatient with my little girls and dislike the way they defy me and talk back to me and settle down with this *odar* and that *odar,* I say to myself, well, God be praised, at least they were not born in the Old Country."

MOSTLY WHAT HE WANTED TO DO WAS HOLD HER.

He took her to visit his mother and children, but only briefly, because he had to return to Los Angeles very soon and much of the vacation he and Anna had planned was already gone and he wanted to be alone with her in the few days they had left, he wanted to hold her.

It made her feel sad that his daughter, Valerie, had greeted her coldly. "She's a greedy kid," Charles said. "She wants everything I have. She's afraid you will take it away from her. Don't worry about it. My boy loves you, and so does my mother, and so do I."

He kissed her so she would not say anything else. He really didn't want to talk.

He took her to silent, sheltered, shady places, where the surf could not be heard and no wind set the sand grass rustling, and he held her in his arms for hours.

He built himself a wide castle of sand to lean on and an embankment to support his outstretched leg. She lay back across his lap, resting her head on his good knee. He smoothed her hair back from her brow, over and over and over. He stroked her shoulders, he stroked the sun darkened flesh of her upper arms; with the back of his hand, he stroked her neck and breasts, just slowly and gently, in the morning and the twilight, all the day.

Sometimes she sat straddling him, nestling her face against the hollows in his chest. He pulled the blanket around her and covered her so that no one passing could see what he had and envy him and ruin his joy. He immersed his face in her hair and then opened his eyes, like a little kid trying to see underwater; but he couldn't see; and he didn't mind; her soft hair flowed into his mouth and his nostrils and he breathed it like a fish, his element. He said poems about oceans into her hair and her ears.

Like a fluttering bird, she played around him, brushing her nipples against his back and teasing his neck with her eyelashes. She wriggled down and burrowed her face into his belly button. She held his testicles in a friendly way, like they were his hands. He poured sand on her breasts and watched it slide down, he poured some more and she wiggled it off, giggling, and then he poured some more and blew it away.

After a few days his taut shoulders relaxed and drooped; his neck un-clenched.

Her steel feet became pliable again. She moved her toes. She danced in the sand, an exotic bird by a northern sea. She alighted in his arms and, with her sea-green eyes lifted, she listened to everything he had to say.

" 'So unlikely an adventure,' " he murmured, " 'to stumble into such a well of sympathy . . .' "

What he was quoting from, she did not know, but she knew he spoke of her. She thought of him as she thought of herself, a stupefied survivor climbing away from a tangle of wreckage and broken bodies and dying screams. She knew that he often lost his mind in the street, as she did, and arrived from one place to another only on the strength of some fantasy. If he did not describe for her the scenes of carnage he had forgotten or tried to forget, well, she didn't care; she had heard quite enough stories from men who had been intimate with barbarism.

So she lifted her hips high off the blanket, and she held Charles with her strong legs so tightly that he imagined nothing bad could ever happen to him again.

No sooner had Charles left again than Anna threw all caution the way of the straw rug and converted the second bedroom in her loft into a study for her lover. She found a place which specialized in the construction of comfortable chairs for handicapped people and bought one for him. Much like its counterpart in Vintage, it had an additional advantage, it came with a foot-stool, on which he could prop his leg, for the time being, until the leg was fixed. She called his friend the French professor and asked him to check which sort of computer with which sort of software Charles used at the college and then she bought him a compatible machine, knowing how pleased he would be to be able to carry not great manuscripts but neat little discs back and forth from Vermont.

The computer store was in the heart of the diamond district, on a street teeming with business people and trucks being unloaded by black boys and Orthodox Jewish boys all sweating together in the August heat. Black coated Hassidim babbled in Yiddish while the accoutrements of a Japanese microchip culture were stacked up around them. Anna stopped to buy a souvlaki. It seemed to her that all the history of human endeavor had coalesced here and that she stood centered in the warm eye of the metropolitan world. She smiled at strange men freely, not fearing anything. And once again, to ruin her contentment, she heard the singer. The same singer who had serenaded Lillian and Delia, the same plastic demon who had raced the dogs past Anna in the rain.

It was Rex, and she had changed herself again.

She looked like a girl.

She had long striped black and orange hair. She had eyebrows. Around her eyes, she had painted circles of black. She wore a white habit like a medieval monk, with a brown sash at the waist and a hood hanging down in back. And she was alone. No reggae drums, no swinging girl groupies to back her up. She held a set of silver chimes which played ringing notes but no melody. When she stroked them, the street looked up briefly from its hot, busy day and then continued on about its business.

Resolving not to be bamboozled once more by these eerie masquerades

—after all, Rex was not a demon, she was a real woman—Anna spoke to her directly.

"Rex," she said. "Do you remember me?"

"No," Rex said. "I forgot you and your beautiful black friend, I forgot you all." Chime. Ring.

"Where are the dogs?"

"They're dead," Rex said. "They ate each other." Chime.

No one else seemed to see Rex as she prepared to sing her song. Anna felt alone with her, felt the sting of her resentment, felt helpless to explain what Rex most assuredly must believe, that Anna had somehow contrived to steal Sally back from her, redepositing her into the world of men and their needs, their machines and their ambitions.

"It was your fault," Anna said. "You drove Sally away. You were too hard to live with, too selfish and self-involved. She's an artist too, she needs taking care of just like you, and now she's found a man who is helping her and loving her and sending her back to school . . . Come on, Rex, lighten up. You're too clever to be as crazy as you try to make everyone believe."

Anna made this defense as much to comfort herself as to convince Rex, because truly, Rex did scare her now, she had amused her once but today especially, she filled Anna with a not-so-vague sense of dread and foreboding. Why did she materialize like Miss Jessel in *The Turn of the Screw,* "terrible, miserable woman," invariably at times of joy and excitement at the thrill of a new purchase, a lucrative deal? Whose soul was she after? Like winks of the mind, a series of potential tragedies occurred to Anna: her father might have another heart attack; Spike might hang himself; the girls . . . oh Jesus, the glittering Margosian girls . . . wasn't the song Rex sang to them a mean, gray song? Was it a curse? Was something going to happen to Lucia's beautiful girls?!

Rex mounted a strong crate and chimed. Thinking she was about to announce the return of Jesus, the Jews rushed past her as though she were bad luck. They did not listen to her song.

> *I write my anthems with a pen,*
> *That's shaped like somebody's dick.*
> *It's strong and dark and hits the mark*
> *But it comes a bit too quick.*

Call the cops and tell them to get that freak away from my store, said the old man to his manager.

It knocks me out and so I doze
But when I wake again
My strength is back
And I attack
With my magic phallic pen.

The business people stopped and gaped and the truck drivers hooted and
Anna stood riveted to her spot on the street. The police came by, not
rushing. There's a crazy woman out front of my store singing dirty filthy
songs, the old man told them.

And this is how a loveless girl . . .

sang Rex.

Gets to screw the whole damn world.

The gentle policeman sent her away.
Anna laughed at herself. What an idiot she was, to be frightened of an
unfortunate wretch who had to parade her bitterness in public to make a
living. She felt sorry not to have given Rex some money . . . but then
again, why should you throw money at someone who was selling a song
about something so base and cheap as vengeance?
Watching Rex disappear, Anna understood for the first time, really understood, why it was that her father felt that George was gravely mistaken
in his support of the terrorists. It was no charity to add to the anger of the
mad world. No, it was just more madness.
Her father was right about things. In the end of days, her father's way
was best.
She hailed a cab and went back to the plant, and called Richard Garfield
at the Farmers' Bank.
She told him that she had carefully considered his proposals and that
they did not suit her way of doing business. She asked him to convey her
regards to Sharon Gold.
She would not have dared to try and explain to Lucia or Mary or Sally
or even to her incisive, beloved Charles the series of events and intercon-
nected impressions and memories that led her to this dangerous decision,
because she was sure she would not have been able to tell it in any clear
way, and they would have laughed at her, worse, she might have laughed
at herself. So she never told them, didn't tell her father either or Aram

Hovad or Mildred, people whose very lives depended on the wisdom of her decisions and who could have felt she had acted rashly, that ultimately she had played exactly like a girl.

But the relief she felt at the moment she hung up the phone—Garfield was still on, trying to understand if he had heard her right—the relief was physical, "like the burst of a thunderstorm to a day of suffocation," she thought, recalling the image from *The Turn of the Screw*.

It was the first time that she had ever in her entire life thought in literature.

She was proud of herself. She felt a great love for Charles Borden, who had introduced her to this new and wonderful set of tools.

THE STUDY WOULD BE HIS COMING HOME PRESENT. ON FIRST LOOK, Lucia shrieked and burst into gales of mock tears. "I never thought I'd live to see the day when you would buy a braided rug!" she cried, kissing Anna Croix de Guerreishly on each side of her face.

"Oh stop . . ." Anna laughed.

Actually, she had spared no expense to outfit the room very quickly so that it would accommodate all Charles' many quirks and works, recalling how precious her father's study had always been to him, and wanting Charles' success to be crowned with the same comfort. Although Mary did not approve—she leaned on the door frame and looked around and said it was downright sicko to give your lover a present that your father would have liked better—Anna didn't care. Charles deserved everything. He had suffered enough and he deserved every little thing that money could buy.

His own phone with its own number and its own answering machine so that he wouldn't have to wait through messages from Aram and her mother before finding out what his agent wanted to say. His own tape deck with its own headset so he wouldn't have to fight her rock for his opera. His own bookcase, intricately scaled to hold not just the cassettes but the large manuscripts which had never been unpacked from their cartons. A long sofa he could stretch out on, long enough for Charles IV to sleep on, selected primarily because its pale blue tweed (she would not admit this, even to Lucia) matched his eyes.

With her sisters chattering and bantering and eating potato chips elsewhere in the loft, Anna began to fill the bookcase with Charles' treasures. She placed the beautiful model whaling ship on a central shelf and, around it, arranged some pictures, taken in Cape Cod, which she had framed. Charles IV and Valerie laughing, even Valerie, and Mrs. Borden among her marigolds, wearing a large straw hat and an antique brooch. Charles himself and Anna by the blue water, all sunburned.

She began to leaf through the manuscripts—so much, so many—all the pages of prose her lover had written which she had never read.

She was touched by the emergence of his first novel, the one he had lost his children to write. It was huge and dog-eared, scribbled with blue editing. The stories he had published as a boy-husband were sandwiched into an old folder; the magazines from which they had been torn were long since defunct, and Anna thought of having them laminated because they were beginning to crumble. The newer works she arranged in a neat pile. All the gardening articles had been Xeroxed recently, because his agent felt they might soon be anthologized into a summer-weight book. She found the funny little sitcom idea which he had sold, his first Hollywood sale, which was now being developed by other writers. If they ever got it on and it ever ran, Charles would make a fortune by percentage, but of course, one couldn't think about that or even dream of it because it was so remote a possibility and so wildly titillating. But here it was in her hand, the summation of Charles' most cynical ambitions—*Crazy Daisies*. Smiling to herself, she recalled him sitting in her old blue truck, telling her with self-deprecating honesty that he dreamed of writing a prime-time, smash-hit television series, don't care if history never remembers one illiterate line . . . and how charmed she had been by him, by his teeth and the wrinkles at the corners of his eyes . . . and his honesty.

Anna began to read the slender manuscript.

She could see from the crossings out that the title had been originally *Garden Plots*, for the show was set in a plant nursery in Detroit and the approach—to Anna's delight and surprise—was satirical, kind of like one of her personal favorites from days gone by, *Batman*.

She could see from the correspondence attached to the manuscript that a certain man in Burbank didn't like *Garden Plots* as a title, he thought it sounded grim, so Charles had suggested alternatives: *The Greenhouse Effect* (too nuclear, wrote some marketer, in the margin) changed to *The Adventures of Esmerelda* changed to *Green Thumbs* changed to *Crazy Daisies*, which was not Charles' title but the contribution of a stranger and which they loved in Burbank.

Her glance caught the phrases and bits of text.

"Voluptuous Esmerelda, the spy, the top French operative in the Midwest . . . nefarious enemy plot to undermine confidence in the city of Detroit which our heroine calls Des Troits . . . Esmerelda's cover is Crazy Daisies, a plant nursery where she works as a fertilizer . . . Every week, the fiends try another dirty trick . . . bugs in the birches . . . laughing gas in the Miracle-gro . . . plants in the plants . . . drive a deadly wedge into the American heartland . . . inciting race riots by turning all the black lawns yellow . . . kidnap the City Council and hold them hostage in a boxwood maze . . . azure eyes . . . everything to make the Americans look stupid and venal . . . Agent Orange in her ratatouille . . . azure eyes, lowers her azure eyes . . ."

"Jesus Christ," whispered Anna Karavajian in the new study.

" 'Don't sank me,' says Esmerelda the Spy . . ."

Anna began to cry.

" 'Sank France!' "

Anna cried and cried.

Chapter 7

IT TOOK ALL THEIR STRENGTH TO KEEP HER FROM DAMAGING THE computer.

It took all their patience to get her to stop carrying on and tell the story clearly. Once they understood, they laughed and told her to go to bed.

She would not sleep and she would not shut up, flailing at them with every detail of every event which could have led Charles to do what she clearly believed was an evil, terrible thing.

They laughed at her but they could not get her to laugh at herself.

It grew so late, finally, that they called home and, explaining nothing, giving no details, told Spike and George that they were spending the night at their little sister Anna's house.

"So Charles adapted some nutsy broad's idea without getting her permission first, well, wow, gee whiz, I'm shocked, horrified, unhinged entirely." Mary laughed, and so did Lucia.

For hours and hours, they kidded Anna, did imitations of her red-rimmed eyes and miserable sniffling. Lucia ordered in Chinese and tried to feed her with chopsticks; she refused to eat.

Mary with her long fingers poked around for those tender spots of self-doubt which had always made her love Anna so much. She poked and poked but found only strange new patches of frost, and finally, frustrated and disgusted, she gave up the search.

"I know what your problem is, kiddo," she said, her mouth turning up in a small smile of Class A condescension. "You are looking for a reason to end your love affair with Charles, any reason, because you're scared to death of long term commitments to people. You made a room in your house that said 'Charles Borden III' on it and you panicked. This is a pattern with you, or hadn't you noticed that? It's why you didn't stay teaching, it's why you didn't marry Harry, and now the printing business has even further shortened your attention span, you've developed the emotional rhythm of the folding machine, you're addicted to turnover."

"Maybe that is true," Anna acknowledged. "I also can't bear the idea of sharing my life with a thief."

Lucia struck her finger in her mouth and mock-vomited into her vodka.

"You're missing something," Anna continued. "I mean, some little thing isn't getting through to you. Let me explain it again so you won't think I'm crazy."

"I don't think you're crazy," said her sister Mary. "I think you are a self-righteous, disloyal shit."

The three sisters were in the gay bar down the block from Anna's building, the one that was paneled like a mountain den. They had settled there after their disastrous Chinese dinner because Anna thought the bar a friendlier place under the circumstances, territory more neutral than the beautiful new study, where her boundless need for Charles was displayed in every expensive detail, where his romantic opera tapes could play to her (Lucia had tried that) and his lead weights could reproach her, twisting her heart, disturbing her certitude.

They had already put away two rounds of drinks (each astonishing the other with her capacity . . . when did she learn to drink that way? they thought; I know when I learned but when did *she* learn?). They were very tired. The sensitive men who ran the place tried to stay discreetly out of ear shot, and at one and two and three in the morning when the regular customers came in, that was quite possible, but now dawn was approaching and that hushed time before closing, and the strange women were still there, and it was impossible to be deaf to their argument, impossible not to think about those diaphanous ethical questions which divided them and to wonder where you would have stood, if it were you . . .

Within the high walls of a walnut booth, the three sisters hunkered down and huddled their heads together, Anna on one side of the table, Mary and Lucia on the other.

Mary stuck to the inside wall, clicking the salt and pepper shakers together in one of her dishpan hands like a castanet. By contrast, Lucia—laughing ironically, stroking Anna's sleeve from time to time, mugging even—tried to keep things light.

She *swore* to Anna that the swiping of ideas, on its surface a matter of great dishonor, was actually just an expectable glitch on the flickering screens of the media, especially since it had now been proven that the number of plots was finite (what had she heard? twelve basics, fifty variations, some formula like that . . . much like the formula for the number of melodic lines in any given scale). Since the piracy of ideas and stories and songs and all things beautiful could not be stopped, Lucia explained, the system just went ahead and rewarded it and then nudged the perpetrator into sharing the profits with the originator *after* the fact, through the process of suit and settlement.

"The musicians tell you 'Oh I didn't realize,' " Lucia said, "or 'I thought it just came into my mind' or 'Look,' they explain, 'one person gets an idea, it stands to reason that thirty-seven other people will get the same idea at the same time, that's the impact of a culture on creative minds' and you can't deny there's some truth to that, Anna, or there's this one, I heard this recently at a charitable affair—(Lucia now summoned a quite passable Northumberland brogue)—'But one listens to so much music, my dear George! How in the world can one be expected to keep track of what one might recall from this piece or that piece or some other? If they feel I've adapted a few of their tunes, and I may have inadvertently, by all means, tell them to call me, let's discuss it, by all means!' "

"Did they discuss it?" Anna asked.

"Sure they did, darling," Lucia answered. "They discussed it all the way to the bank."

Mary screamed softly. She unbuckled her hair and shook it out. She tried to slide over Lucia and escape from the booth, but Lucia stalled her with a body block and pushed her back into place by twisting the neck of her sweater.

"Tell the truth," Mary hissed at Anna. "Is it because he's a cripple? Now that you've finally stopped looking like a bag lady, you think maybe you can do better?"

"Why is she being so vicious to me?" Anna asked Lucia. "Is it because I give her money every month, off the books so she doesn't have to pay taxes and her husband can pretend not to know about it?"

"It's because his play didn't win the Pulitzer Prize!" Mary cried. "Or maybe it's because Daddy doesn't like his thin straight *odar* nose!"

"She's gonna make me hit her," Anna said to Lucia.

"No, she isn't, darling," Lucia said, patting both of her glowering sisters simultaneously. "She's just trying to show you that you're making a fool of yourself. Now. Try to understand this. If the television show never gets on, as most do not, then this crazy woman . . . what's her name? Rex, right . . . Rex will never know the difference."

"I will know," Anna said. "I know! What am I supposed to do, *not* know?!"

"Please. Stop. Listen. If this crazy Rex does not know that her idiotic little idea has been adapted and put up for sale, then she does not know she cannot go right ahead and sell the original herself. So maybe she will. And maybe it will sell . . ."

"As what? An X-rated comedy video for sick kids?" Mary asked.

". . . and then she'll make some money," Lucia continued, "and be resoundingly middle-class, like Charles."

Mary laughed, rubbing her face briskly. She ordered coffee, "not decaf," she said, "high test."

"It doesn't make any difference if the idea is idiotic!" Anna cried. "It doesn't make any difference if the author is crazy! She's the author!"

"Imagine the worst-case scenario," said Lucia calmly. "The show turns out to be a go. She sees it on television. She recognizes it as her baby."

"How is she going to do that if there is no resemblance to the original?" Mary asked. "I mean if Charles managed to disguise the thing so that only our squeaky clean Anna in the whole wide world would recognize it, how's it gonna be recognizable after six other writers and then actors and the producers and their lawyers and accountants and phalanxes of studio executives get through with it?!"

"I am trying to make a point!" Lucia insisted. "Would you shut up for five minutes and *please* let me make my point?!"

Mary sighed. She pushed past Lucia and moseyed over to the owner who was wiping up the bar and asked him if he had anything at all to eat.

"Now," said Lucia. "Listen. Say that by the remotest of chances, this crazy woman Rex recognizes her idiotic work on television. What can she do? She can sue Charles. Since as you say her father is the girdle king of Cleveland, that should be no problem for her. And then Charles will have to retain a lawyer and amend the credit lines on the show and give her some money, which she probably would never have made if Charles had not cleaned up her dirty story and sold it to television.

"So. Either way Rex comes up a winner. I would venture to say it was her lucky day the day she ran into Charles Borden."

Lucia tossed down the rest of her vodka, patted her mouth, fished in her pocketbook for a lipstick and a compact, fixed her mouth, and then ordered a cup of coffee.

"I've got it!" Mary exclaimed, sitting down at the table again with a plate of yesterday's tuna salad and some toasted English muffins. "It's because he asked you to marry him. He has, hasn't he?"

Anna nodded. Yes, on the cool dunes, in the shade of the tall grass, yes, he had.

"So that's it." Mary sneered triumphantly, poking Lucia with her elbow. "He asked her to marry him and commute back and forth with him between Vintage and New York and give up Karavajian Press, which everyone knows she acquired by the highest moral and ethical standards."

Anna wanted to scream and cry, "Unfair! Foul! Low blow, you spiteful bitch!" But she had no strength just then.

All Lucia's good nature finally failed her.

"How could you not tell me?" she asked. "How could you not tell me that he asked you to marry him when you knew that meant so much to me?"

Anna sighed wearily and tried to decide which of her two sisters she despised more at this moment. Somehow, over the years, they had developed an elaborate misapprehension of who she was, and so they had fallen out of touch with her . . . but even as she thought that, Anna realized it was not really true, they had not fallen out of touch or become less than her loving sisters, they had simply taken on the philosophical colorations necessary to live each one with her separate man.

They had been married and she had not been married.

They had their commitments.

She still had her own good name.

"If you had ever been in business," she said, "you would know that no one steals in ignorance."

Lucia groaned and rolled her eyes towards heaven.

Mary slammed her glass down on the table. "Oh please! Stop! Are you gonna try and make us believe you have been in *business* all these years?! You have been in a protected workshop, kiddo, like a handicapped person, you have been backed up and supported and pampered by the men who really run the company who let you *think* you run it because they want to make it up to you that once in your life you had a terrible tragedy! That business was promised to Tom Sarkissian like a fucking bride! It was promised to him from the time we were little girls, and you used your Daddy's great, maybe even slightly unnatural, love for you to make him dump his obligations to Tom, everyone knew that, it was the shame of the family! Daddy made you the rich one! He made you the independent one! But not once in your whole life did he ever make you face the truth, which is that every wonderful thing you have was stolen somehow, so please, please, please let's not hear any more bullcrap about who is ignorant and who is a thief!"

Anna got up slowly and left the bar.

"Jesus Christ, you're a killer," Lucia said to Mary. "I thought you'd had too much psychiatry but now I think maybe you haven't had enough."

Anna came back. She pulled Lucia out of the booth and tossed her onto the floor like a shovelful of snow. She slapped Mary three maybe four times and poured the coffee on her and then from her pants and the various pockets of her coat she pulled all her loose change and a couple of dollar bills and she threw the money at Mary. She tore the new gold earrings out of her ears and threw them at Mary. All this happened in perfect silence, without tears, and it was over quickly, although it lasted a long time.

ANNA WALKED IN THE DIRECTION OF UPTOWN, HER HANDS SHOVED deep into the pockets of her old dungarees. Shaking her head from side to side and muttering and reeking of drink, she was taken for a young vagrant by the other vagrants in that neighborhood and not bothered. Her ulcer bit. She had begun to feel sick with fear.

She was afraid that if she confronted Charles with her true feelings, he would throw her out of his life.

A hard man at his worst, he had never bent from his opposition to casting Emerson Hall (even after the play's success, he maintained that the little Italian guy could have done better) nor had he ever released the unhappy Valerie from his plans for her education. He had failed the voluble, swarthy Suarez despite her creativity and failed Hennessy the sleeping jock despite the resulting fury of the football coach at Vintage. When it came to money, he was pathological. His very life hinged on the getting of it; his debts made him sleepless; it had taken him many months to learn to accept her generosity without punishing her for it and he had not been comfortable with her father until he was able to stride into the Tenafly house laden with gifts like Santa Claus. Alas, the theft of Rex's idea had proven lucrative. It had wiped out many debts. Anna figured she would not be able to convince him that he was in any way unjustified in doing exactly what he had done.

And then she would have to leave him.

And then she would miss him so much that she would have to go back to him.

She would go ahead and marry him, and then she would be more committed to him than to her honor. And they would live together always with the expectation of a just reward spreading like rancid butter on their daily bread.

"How could you not tell me?" Lucia had wept, cut to the heart. "How could you not tell me that he asked you to marry him when you knew that meant so much to me?"

"Because I didn't say yes and I didn't say no, I said, let's live together and see, because sometimes he has been so cruel and full of hate, because I don't know whether I can put up with all the shit left over from the damn war . . ."

"Ah you're such a wimp," Mary said. "You're such a coward."

Okay, Anna thought, so Mary might be right again: maybe she was a coward.

And it was cowardice plain and straight which now drove her to conceive of a way to make Charles do what she wanted without a confrontation. If only she could find the manuscript, some *shard* of the original manuscript of *French Kisses* . . .

She walked sixty blocks, and arrived in the morning at the home of Sally Bangle.

Sally's protector had ensconced her in a pretty apartment overlooking the East River. It had a doorman who checked out Anna with formidable suspicion and would not let her move past the front desk until she was accepted from on high.

"What's the matter with you?" Sally asked.

"It's Charles. It's about Charles."

"Come on in. But first, take off your shoes," Sally said, for her carpet was white and fluffy as a meringue. Anna sank down on the low pillows by a low table. She did not notice the beauty of the place, that the walls were draped with Moorish cottons and in plush oases everywhere, large caravan pillows were clustered and all the tables cluttered with bowls of candy and candied fruits. She looked terrible to her friend: wrinkled, shrunken, an owl after a downpour. Even the cleverly concealed lights, filtered by filigreed screens, nested in nooks behind vases, most of them gelled a flattering pink, could not improve the look of Anna this morning.

"Remember after we met you and Rex in the witchcraft store, we went to a restaurant and Rex told us the story of her novel, it was called *French Kisses* . . ."

"I never saw her again, Anna."

"*French Kisses,* dedicated to you."

"I forgot her, you hear?"

"Charles originally called it *Garden Plots.* Now it's *Crazy Daisies,* a thrill-filled comedy for the whole family. He has sold it to television under his name with a few changes. Detroit instead of Cleveland. Esmerelda instead of whatever her name was originally. In his version, the City Council is held for ransom in a boxwood maze. There's Agent Orange in the ratatouille. Plants in the plants." Sally began to laugh. "Like I said, it's a scream."

Sally rolled among the pillows, giggling wildly, "No shit! Somebody went out and actually made a soup from those old bones!"

"Stop laughing, Sally, please oh please . . ." Anna had cried half the night and still she seemed about to cry again. "Have you got the book? If you've got the book, then I'll take it to him like I don't know anything and I'll say, look what I found at Sally's house, *French Kisses* by that crazy girl Rex, remember her? And he'll realize that the book exists, and that he has to abort this damn rip-off and he'll never know that I knew or cared, and everything will be fine, everything will be peachy . . ."

"There is no book, sugar," Sally said gently.

"You said it was in a shoe box next to the garlic!"

"Either she took it with her when she left or I left it behind when I moved up here."

Sally made some coffee and placed before Anna a fat cherry pie she had made the night before, cutting a thick wedge and serving it on a pink crystal plate. Anna couldn't touch it.

"Oh you poor honey," Sally said, "you really have suffered about this, haven't you? There is no need, sugar. Rex Pumpkin is a rich girl, real rich, she spent her whole life being waited on by maids while she wrote songs and stories and books, dozens of them, they are nothing to her, she just writes them and throws them down and then she writes some other thing. They pop out of her like cherries from the pie, and if Charles took himself a little piece, what the hell, sugar, she's not gonna miss it."

"That's the deadly wedge," Anna said. "That piece of the pie. She could turn it against him."

"She's drunk half the time."

"She'll attack him with her magic phallic pen."

"She never published anything, never copyrighted anything, she's not serious."

"Her father is rich and powerful."

"Oh her father is dead, sugar. Long gone. She read his obituary in the newspaper right before we broke up."

Anna rocked with disappointment, hugging her knees. She had stored a vision of the old gold camel-faced businessman in her imagination, a standing threat, the first line of defense. She had assumed Charles had forgotten him and how mean and vengeful he might be. Now she thought that Charles too might have read his obituary.

"We've got to find the novel," she whispered. "We've got to find it, Sally, please . . ."

Sally hunted through the fading set designs she had stashed in treasure chests, pulled out the rolled up tissuey elevations, the memos from Elliot Longet and copies of contracts they had made and snapshots of the hot-blooded brawny crews. She and Anna looked for even one chapter, one page of *French Kisses*.

They found battered old scripts and annotated set descriptions stapled to sketches. They found *The Seagull*.

" 'A platform roughly put together for private theatricals . . .' " Sally read. " 'Bushes . . . A few chairs . . . A little table . . . The sun has just set . . .' "

They found an original manuscript of *The Ice Cold Jungle*. " 'The scene is a jungle,' " Anna read, " 'very dark and so dense that it can mask the decomposition of men.' "

So they sat in silence.

Having gone through every piece of paper in Sally's files and chests and dressers, they could do no more. Here in this contemporary reflection of the women's quarters at the Sublime Porte, there was no trace of *French Kisses*.

"You didn't say one word about my apartment," Sally said.

"Oh I'm sorry . . ."

Sally took her hand and leaned close to her. "Anybody ever tell you that you are real bad at noticing things?"

"Yes." Anna sighed. "I'm sorry. Your place is beautiful."

Sally laughed. Rats in the stew.

"Don't you ever feel guilty?" Anna asked. "I mean taking this man away from his wife . . ."

"No," Sally answered. "But ask me again when I've got my degree and I'm in the union."

So the plain truth of the money itself finally came home to Anna.

Privileged people had to know their place, after all.

If only for this reason, she never considered guilt-tripping Sally on behalf of so cavalier and worthless a lover as Rex, who had left Sally lonesome, begging for company on New Year's Eve. She did not share with her friend what she now realized to be the true meaning of her series of darkly comic encounters with Rex—which was that the brilliant and eccentric, spoiled and rich Rochelle Frumkin wasn't rich anymore. No mansion back in Cleveland to go home to. No maids to wait on her anymore. She had, by her own testimony, been disowned and forgotten. And if she raced mad dogs through Wall Street in a summer storm and invented songs on the sidewalk like a bag lady, that was because she could think of no other way to make a living.

LUCIA CALLED FRANCINE IN THE AFTERNOON.

Francine said that Anna had called and told them she would be out of town for a few days on a selling trip, they didn't know precisely when she would be back.

Mary called Sally in the evening.

Sally said Anna was long gone.

Lucia called Charles in Los Angeles. She asked if he had spoken to Anna. He said no.

"Expect her," Lucia said.

She hung up in that manner peculiar to the Karavajian sisters, who never ended their phone calls with an ordinary goodbye.

Charles wondered why Anna should be coming to see him when she knew that he would be flying home to her in just a few days, his work in this large sunny city all finished for the time being. However, it gladdened him to think that she would soon be in his arms and he would be able to tell her all his good news and big plans for the coming year. New courses in the fall. A possible new script to rewrite in the evenings. Surgery at Christmastime. The spring semester off to recuperate. A new body by summer. By next summer, a new life.

He went to the market and bought apples and plums.

Anna reasoned that with the old camel dead and *French Kisses* disappeared, she would have to call Charles a thief to his face and argue her own case against his behavior.

She didn't want to do that. She was afraid.

So now, she tried to change her mind.

She had discovered that with every hour's delay, she felt less strongly about the issue itself; she had less will, *more* fear, so much fear that she had begun to doubt her own sincerity. Maybe she didn't care as much as she had originally thought she cared. Maybe if she set up her so-called passion for honor and her sense of shame like a target in a shooting gallery and just kept letting people she respected bombard her arguments with patient explanations and wounding ridicule, the whole calamity might be talked to death, and she might be able to forget it completely and never have to confront Charles about it at all.

So she went to Washington to see the man most likely to make a final mockery of her deepest feelings.

Elliot greeted her blearily; it was 7:00 A.M. on a rainy morning.

He felt bad that his mauve apartment was so disheveled and quickly closed the door to his bedroom, from which someone he barely knew had departed around dawn.

Anna looked mean and old to him, and altogether too neat. She had her hair in a bun. He found himself frightened by her, the way she paced up and down his living room like a stiff-necked crow. He felt she might peck him to death.

He put up a pot of coffee and leaned across the kitchen counter and caught her hand and grinned. (The best thing you got going, Cat; use it; use it for all it's worth.)

"Come now, my darling girl, what means this sudden appearance? Are you in trouble? What do you hear from Chuckie boy?" Elliot pulled his gold satin prize-fighting robe closely around him. "I had a letter from him some weeks ago, he sounded in great spirits, invited me to come and stay with him and pay a visit to this magic doctor he's found who can eradicate the worst of scars . . ."

"There's been a robbery," she said.

"Oh really?"

"It involves Charles."

"And who exactly was robbed, my dear? Was anybody actually hurt? Who was the victim?"

"That's who I'm afraid of, Elliot. The victim."

Was there an accusatory arch to her black brow? Did she purse her mouth primly, look down her long long nose? How dare she?! thought Elliot Longet.

He lost his temper and made the single greatest blunder of his long, clumsy career.

"You have some nerve marching in here like this and acting the moralist with me!" he declaimed. "No one profited from that robbery as much as you! You were a lonely old maid, a miserable ink blot with nothing to do at night but deliver posters, and I brought Charles into your life, and Sally, friends and beauty and excitement, even celebrity! Believe me, if Emerson Hall had not been paid off with the leading role, Charles Borden's play would never have merited so much as a *listing* in the *New York Times!* Every step of that robbery was blocked and planned, for months. The performances, the staging, the timing, all all all a work of genius, I say, GENIUS! I wrote the script with my own intuition, so well that you and Charles and Sally played your parts perfectly *without ever having to act!* And now, look! The Shelter is a tech theater showplace! Charles Borden, the least comfortable of men, is luxuriating in a hot tub by the fair Pacific! Impoverished Sally Bangle is the queen of black Yuppiedom, and Emerson and I are finally enjoying some of the rewards that men with our level of talent deserve! So a robber baron insurance company was parted from some of its ill-gotten profit, so what?! This was a victimless crime that altered every life it touched for the better, including yours!"

Anna squinted at Elliot . . . and then she began to laugh, she could not stop laughing, and Elliot realized that she had never known the truth until now, that he had gone and blown the premise of his finest production, ruined it as surely as if he had answered the phone in response to the doorbell; a technical disaster, a catastrophe.

The perking coffee bubbled up and exploded, spraying the kitchen. The risen anti-Muse tried to restrain it and severely burned the palm of his hand.

"Were there *other* people in the gang of robbers whom I might know?" Anna asked. "I mean besides Emerson."

"Oh no," Elliot said, "just a bunch of hungry techies, and one Vietnam veteran, a professional, to carry the gun."

He smeared some butter on his burned palm, but then he dropped the butter on the floor and slipped on it, crashing into the dishwasher and bruising his shin. The dishwasher popped open and spilled (what else?) steak knives.

"Thank you for returning my grandmother's earrings," Anna said. She was still giggling a little; aftershocks.

"Oh you have Charles to thank for that," Elliot answered. "He recognized Emerson, you know . . . had you known that? No, I guess not . . . he recognized Emerson by his *gait,* the man has an uncanny eye for detail, notices everything . . . and he threatened to turn us in if the earrings were not recovered. Well, you can imagine, Anna, I was so eager for his cooperation at that point, I would have ransacked every pawnshop in New York to get your damn earrings back. But it turned out Emerson still had them. They were unsalable, you see . . . worthless . . . same as the samovar. Emerson wanted to keep it on his dining room sideboard, like a trophy, but I said it was too precise a relic and so we filled it with debris from the back wall of The Shelter and drowned it in the river."

Of course, Elliot stepped on a knife and the sole of his foot began to bleed (nothing too serious).

"Does Charles have any talent?"

"Do you realize, Anna, that if you do not leave right away, I am going to die in a household accident?"

"Does he?"

"He's a brilliant mechanic, he will do very well rewriting other people's scripts."

"Does he need to steal to make a living?"

"Everyone does," Elliot said.

"But a gifted person . . ."

"That kind most of all."

"You sure fooled me, Cat," Anna said. "I thought you were just a big talker." She walked out of the apartment.

Elliot took one step and slipped on the buttery floor and fell on his behind. He felt a very sharp pain in his rear end. Must have busted something back there, he thought. When he sat down, his butt hurt, so he stayed standing to give it a rest. He tried to figure out what Anna could do to him, if she would go to the police . . . but why should she do that?

He called the Board member's wife to warn her, then Emerson, then Charles. The pain in his behind had become excruciating. He realized that Anna Karavajian had, in effect, broken his ass. So, for virtually the entire length of his flight to the Bahamas, he stood in one of the vibrating little lavatories, claiming (through the door to the concerned stewardess) a sour stomach.

MARY RUSSO CALLED CHARLES. SHE WAS CRYING.

"What do you mean, she isn't there?! She's got to be there by now! I know she doesn't want to talk to me, Charles, I know I said terrible things to her, but she said terrible things to me too, she's hurt me too all these years . . .

"I think maybe I just lost control, sitting in that new study with all those state-of-the-art comforts . . . and then I kept tripping over your goddamned weights, it was like tripping over the war again . . . and I just all of a sudden didn't know what we had fought for or why my Spike went to prison, I felt like an MIA who got shot down in the war and nobody remembered me . . ."

He interrupted her. He said he couldn't understand her, she had to try and control herself, he didn't know what she was talking about.

"Please make her talk to me, Charles."

"I swear to you she's not here, Mary."

"She takes these personal things so seriously. We told her compared to the bankers on Wall Street you were a fucking saint! But she was ready to leave you, Charles . . ."

"Let me talk to Spike," he said, hoping to elicit a better picture but Mary hung up, and when Charles called back, there was no answer at her house.

He had been expecting Anna for two days.

Whenever he went out, he left a note on the door for her so that she could get the key from his neighbor's housekeeper. He had filled his pantry and his refrigerator with all the things she liked to eat. At night he waited for her, willing her to show up at any moment; and when he closed his eyes, he did so lightly, sharp and alerted; he had not slept that way since the war.

He could not understand why she should be mad at him.

Elliot's phone call made that even less clear.

"All I know is that she's gunning for you like Medea did for Jason," Elliot said. "Please call me if she comes, leave a message on my machine and I'll call you back from Nassau. Remember that we were partners in art, at least partners in craft, Charles . . ."

From this, Charles concluded that Anna had finally uncovered the truth about The Shelter robbery. Gee, she was slow . . .

"You have nothing to fear from me, Cat," he promised.

"I know that, my friend . . . but Anna . . . who is she anyway? Can she be controlled?"

CHARLES CALLED LUCIA IN NEW YORK.

George Margosian answered the phone.

"What's going on? Where the hell is Anna?"

"They don't know," George whispered. "They haven't told the old folks yet, but the fact is, they haven't got a clue. Lucia said Anna had a terrible fight with Mary about something you did and that she was on her way to L.A. to kill you."

"Why are you whispering?"

"I don't want Lucia to hear. She would really leave me if she knew I had told you this. But whatever you did, Anna's getting back at you."

"What did I do?"

"*Do you think I give a damn what you did?!* Listen to me. Yesterday

Francine, Anna's secretary, *noreg* bitch, an impossible woman, calls my lovely wife, she says big flowers have come to the plant for Anna. Lucia figures it's you apologizing for what you did."

"WHAT DID I DO!?"

"Francine reads the card to Lucia. It's from someone named Gottlieb. He's coming to town. Wants to take Anna to dinner. He signs the card 'Gratefully.' Next day Francine calls again. She says this Gottlieb stopped by the plant to see Anna. He's got more flowers and he's wearing an eight hundred dollar suit, he treats Aram Hovad like a war buddy, buys him drinks, buys Larry and Mildred drinks, and he's eight feet tall."

George Margosian leaned very close to the phone, pressed his lips to Charles' ear.

"You've got to watch them, Charles, I say this to you like a brother, you don't need any more pain. The older they get, the more they want, and if you work a little too hard, maybe neglect them, fool around a little, they humiliate you and tear your heart out. Think before you go ahead with this marriage, Charles. It's not going to be a simple thing to be tied to one of the Karavajian sisters."

Charles took his bike for a ride through the pleasant, quiet neighborhood, admiring the bougainvillea and wondering why it had no smell, crushing the fat leaves of succulent evergreens in his hand and wondering why they produced no sap. When the sun set over the Pacific, it was huge and orange but he had come to distrust much of what he saw here and no longer believed it was the real sun. He went back to work, wrestling the eighth draft of the last scene of the war story into a nice straight line that ran from the hot tub on the back patio through the living room all the way to the front door.

So she had betrayed him. Well. So.

Determined to present a smooth and unconcerned exterior, he went out to get his hair cut and his beard trimmed. And when the hot air of the blow dryer hit his ears, it came to him . . . was it possible? Yes, with Anna, it was possible . . . it came to him what had made his sweet easy woman so angry.

ANNA CHECKED INTO A HOTEL CALLED LES ETOILES. THEY GAVE HER a room fit for Esmerelda the Spy.

It had two double beds and a color television with many cable options, including hard core, and a bathroom literally wrapped in cellophane that said "Sanitized," strips of it lying across the toilet seat, across the tub, the bidet, and the shower door, like ribbon around the bottles of liquor her clients gave her for Christmas. The phone had "call waiting," except that no call waited: no one knew Anna was in Los Angeles.

She stepped out on the balcony facing the Hollywood Hills. Since she had been considering for several days her sister Lucia's jocular analysis of the realities in show business, and Elliot Longet's horrible benediction ("gifted people most of all, most of all, my darling girl") weighed so heavily on her heart, she immediately imagined the California gold rush and all the grizzled miners who must still be up there in those hills, in ghost form, seeking their lost fortunes, knocking on the doors of mogul homes in the night, and calling spookily (because they were miners) "Mine mine mine." Clearly she was an asshole to fret about plagiarism, the common cold of thefts, mere coughs and sneezes; ghost complaints: nothing.

She felt relieved. As she had hoped, her discussions had weakened her resolve.

She had not gone directly to the airport from Elliot's, but had taken another half-day to visit the black marble Vietnam memorial and find the name of Sally's father. Immersing herself in Mary's philosophy, she considered the notion that every single ideal and ethic ever taught to American children might really have been plugged in that jungle, that there was no shred of hope for personal morality when political morality had long ago made its last stand, and that she was waging a phantom battle for rhetorical ends.

She almost convinced herself to miss the plane. Even though she had come to California in the end (sleepless again on the calm flight), she felt that if she gave herself another day, she might still be able to turn back.

So she did not call Charles to say that she had arrived.

She gave herself another day.

He sat on his patio on the usual sunny morning, grazing his bad heel over the roiling waters of the hot tub, evaluating his situation and his options.

Mentally he swam past all the steps in between to the bottom line, and concluded that she would leave him.

Sure, she might show up one of these minutes. She might yell at him for ripping off that bitch comedian who did schtick about the dying and the killing and spilled blood in the street and made them all walk in it. But when Anna came right out and said she was leaving him, all that would be her *excuse,* not her reason.

Her reason would be some rich guy who was eight feet tall. Her real reason would be another man.

Charles felt no particular astonishment at this turn of events. It was not the first time for him, after all.

The other men eyed her in the restaurant at breakfast. She had washed and put on the one dress she had brought with her and tried with limited means to look as pretty as possible, because she wanted to be noticed, needing to reassure herself that she could still attract a stranger and that no decision she made today would be made from the vantage of her last chance.

Are you alone? they asked. Do you mind if I join you? I couldn't help noticing that you read the newspaper while you were eating, that's a sure sign of a lonely traveler, just off the overnight plane from New York; mind if I sit down?

Maybe she would like to meet them after they got through with their meetings in Long Beach and Santa Monica, they suggested. For a drink, for a meal. Just not to be alone after a hard day of selling in a strange city.

Anna turned down these amiable propositions. Nevertheless, she felt pleased to be able to conclude that if Les Etoiles held a prom tomorrow, she would not be the only girl without a date. She stacked up the meaningless accretions of masculine attention until they achieved a certain height, and then she climbed up on them to an improved bargaining position.

To make herself tough and gird herself for what might come, she sang all the hard-hearted woman songs of her teenage years.

Had she not gotten along without him perfectly well before she met him? Well, she would get along without him now. If he called her a self-righteous disloyal shit and sent her packing, she would in fact get along *better* than before, because she was so much younger and cuter now than when she had first met him.

As her damn sister Mary had pointed out.

As she had so recently been reminded by Elliot Longet.

Charles imagined him hanging out under the languid propellers of a rotating ceiling fan, like Alec Guinness after the Lavender Hill heist, wearing tropical whites, sipping mint daiquiris. He would have seduced or befriended every single attractive person, male or female, in the Bahamas, and would surely be regaling them with tales of Queens, waiting patiently for the long arm of the law to reach out and waft him away.

Poor Cat would wait in vain, Charles thought. He would stew and tremble in the Caribbean until his fancy new job was gone and all his old associates had given up discussing his sudden disappearance, a mock exile from an unremarked crime, for Anna would never tell about the robbery at The Shelter.

She had no interest in Elliot Longet's soul.

That distinction belonged entirely to Charles Borden.

Gee, she was a dangerous woman, Charles thought. To make strong men flee.

And frankly having begun to fear her arrival, he got dressed and went to Beverly Hills for a meeting with his agent, leaving no note for her on his door.

Anna went shopping.

In a store window, she saw a dress she thought was nice. She inquired within. The price was three thousand dollars.

The agent said the new script to be fixed was not a war story but a very gory murder story, and even though by Charles' standards it was total shit, TMC was producing it and they knew how to make considerable fortunes out of total shit. Because of their training in agribusiness, the wised up agent quipped. Charles ought to say yes, advised his agent, and he did, and they went to lunch.

Anna bought a white dress in another store, and shoes, and a pocketbook. Then she decided too many people here wore white and so she bought a black suit and other shoes and another pocketbook. Then she had her hair done, and all the gray blacked out.

She was famished from shopping.

She went to a restaurant and ate a triple decker club sandwich and then an enormous ice cream sundae. Halfway through it, she realized that every woman in the place was staring at her.

His agent ate tuna fish turned out of its can onto an otherwise bare plate.

People are starving in Los Angeles, Anna thought.

NOT FOR ONE MINUTE DID CHARLES BORDEN BELIEVE THAT HE HAD committed an immoral act.

A man who had been forgiven for leading other people's children into death by being blown into a million bits would be hard pressed to castigate himself for borrowing an idea in a city surrounded by the ghosts of robbed miners chanting "Mine mine mine."

Given the industry standard, he figured his personal behavior could suffer scrutiny by Mother Theresa.

He had never in all the years abandoned the support of his kids, nor had he neglected a sentimental debt to his first wife, despite her treachery. He paid for the maintenance of his father's grave and wrote to his beloved mother on Monday evening of every single week, enclosing larger and larger checks.

Yet he had met women here who denied the existence of children they had borne when they were young, only not to be dated at a certain age, and he had met men here who could not find time to eat with kids living under the same roof with them, much less heart space to mourn their suicides.

Encountering an icy current in the warm city that chilled even his cold sea blood, Charles pitched the angle of his conscience against it and sailed the prevailing winds, just as he had done at The Shelter, comprehending the folksy grandeur of Elliot's caper, and as he had learned to do in Saigon, meeting men who had the cool to loot the confusion and the danger and survive, well-connected and ultimately quite rich.

Oh yes, in the context of the times, Charles felt himself a regular boy scout.

He knew he had nothing to fear from the self-called Rex. If the television show, now mutated beyond recognition, ever got on television and she saw it and discerned a relationship, she could come and seek a settlement from the cadres of writers like himself who had done precisely the same thing in their day, and had the same thing done to them over and over and over. They all knew the system. He figured, bottom line, they would make some sort of middling fair judgment in Rex's favor.

So he was cool. He was fine. He had nothing to be frightened of. So why was he frightened?

He was frightened like a little kid.

My mommy is mad at me, he felt, because I did something bad, and she's not gonna believe me when I tell her I didn't do it or didn't mean to do it, and she's gonna give me a licking with the back of her silver hairbrush.

God help me, he thought. I'm afraid of Anna Karavajian because she, with her black tans and inky fingernails and screaming Armenian arguments, reminds me of my white-haired old mother, who has never raised her voice in her entire life.

How was this possible?! Did this mean that he lusted after his mother as much as he lusted after Anna? Did this mean that he respected Anna as much as he respected his mother?

He rubbed his eyebrows and made them wild, tore at his hair and his beard and, itching with anger and self-disgust, read through the gory story.

Anna hated her new hairdo so much that she took a swim in the hotel pool and ruined it. Her days and nights inverted, still unable to sleep, she watched a pornographic movie in her hotel room with the shades drawn.

Needing comfort from the ignominy of fear—for he had hoped never to feel afraid again after the war and it pissed him off no end that some woman's naïveté should have returned him to that dark place—Charles went out and courted a lovely actress who wanted to be in a TMC movie.

He brought her home. He tried to make love to her and proved impotent . . . and Anna wasn't even turned on by the movie: it bored her stiff; it put her to sleep.

The actress woke Charles at sunset, his worst time. She was kissing him goodbye with a touching tenderness, as though she really cared for him, really gave a damn whether he got it up or not and sympathized with whatever was ailing him and would be available any time again soon, whenever he wanted her: gee, they could dissemble, these bitches, they could carry you to hell with their lies.

To Anna, Rex came in a dream.

She was wearing a black mink coat, floor length, like a legend (okay, a goddess, okay), and it surprised Anna in her dream to see how clear her face was, how well-remembered that eyebrowless face. At Rex's ears and throat, diamonds glittered, and on her toes she wore rings, like the women of the Old Country, she wore rings with diamonds and bells in them. Every time she moved, even when she only smiled, there was a jingling, as of caravan bells. She grinned. She started to open her mink coat, not like a lover, not like a flasher, like a terrorist, and her body inside was all wires and plastique and ticking like a bomb.

Charles eased himself into the hot tub on the deck in his back yard and closed his eyes and slept, as he had slept once or twice before, immersed to his armpits in black waters. He saw himself whole again, stumbling with two good legs upon his giggling, somnolent men, and tearing the hash pipe away from them, flinging it toward the horizon toward the black fields and then commanding them to follow him toward the river, figuring it would be safer than the fields, and so they did; with the old songs still on their lips they came staggering after their smart, cold drug-free officer. The bomb went off. It woke Anna but did not scare her. The tender young boys exploded in great sprays of gore, their heads and arms cascading into the river and bobbing there, like lobsters cooking, plop plop bubble . . .

The endless agony attacked him and he opened his eyes.

He looked for his toes.

He groped the slippery tiles for his pills.

It was evening. His very worst time.

She had turned down bankers. She had sustained terrible losses. She would not be afraid to give him up for the sake of her honor.

He did not know how he could live without her.

As the pills and the beating water did their work, the sweat of comfort and the sweat of terror commingled in his gray beard.

She came in her old dress. Her face was calm for she had slept well and knew her own mind at last.

She had examined every circumstance and taken into consideration the ever-bending, geodesic pattern of context and history crisscrossing every circumstance. If this latest war was not reason enough, she had considered, imagine it in combination with the wars before that, and the wars before that, in combination with the legacy of slavery and holocaust and genocide and the interminable madness created by addiction. Was she not a liberal like her father and her sister Mary? Did she not seek for reasons? Could she not find background and justification for every single heist and swipe and kickback and were not all the reasons pretty good actually? Tom was disappointed; Emerson was black; Sharon Gold was a girl; Elliot was a genius; life wasn't fair; the Turks needed a scapegoat after the humiliations of the Great War; the union needed jobs for more truckers after the last recession; the vice presidency of the Farmers' Bank didn't pay enough; the vice presidency of the United States didn't pay enough; the times were bad; the bitch made jokes about the killing and the dying and the war (it was her insensitivity; it was her fault) and her idea was just lying there (it was her fault) on the table in the restaurant, ready to be snatched like magic out of thin air.

"If somebody don't eat that last piece of cake, it's gonna be thrown away!" joked Sally Bangle on New Year's Eve. "Now that sure would be a terrible waste and shame, wouldn't it, sister?"

I cannot keep the soul of the whole world, Anna said.

What do you want? he asked.

I can't keep myself from dishonor, there's too much already, I drink it, I swim in it most of the time, it has no taste or smell.

I'll do anything you want, he said.

But this time the dishonor has your smell and your taste. How can I ignore that when I love you so much?

I'll give her the money if that's what you want, he said. Restore her name, call her the author, give her the money.

That's what I want, Anna said.

Okay okay, he said. Just don't leave me.

He reached for her hands because he was shaking and feeling kind of cold, and he needed her help to get out of the water.

IN FRESNO, VARTAN'S MOTHER PICKED THE LITTLE AMERICAN FLAGS off his grave—they had worn out and faded since Memorial Day—and sat down on the folding chair she had brought, preparing to read him the newest letter.

She always read Vartan all the letters that came from the sons of her countrywomen. When she got older she would extract from her daughter a promise to continue reading the letters to Vartan after she was gone, so they would both rest easy.

"This newest letter is from a man who sent it to you first in Boston," she said to her dear boy. "A wonderful thing has happened to him. He has been saved."